DON'T MAKE AN ENEMY OF GOD

MITCHELL

ISBN 979-8-9941909-3-7 (softcover)
ISBN 979-8-9941909-4-4 (hardback)
ISBN 979-8-9941909-5-1 (ebook)

www.jmitchellbooks.com

This book is a work of fiction. Names, characters, places, and incidents are the product of the author's imagination or are used fictitiously. Any resemblance to actual locales, events, or persons, living or dead, is purely coincidental.

Printed in the United States of America.

Mitchell Books

DON'T MAKE AN ENEMY OF GOD

MITCHELL

CHAPTER 1

DOOM

Tamaco showed mercy not normally associated with his station. He refrained from beheading the groveling messenger at his feet, but only because the man's destiny was not yet fulfilled. Nonetheless, he had the man lashed on the spot for having the audacity, the gall, and above all, the stupidity to deliver bad news to him of all people, the Lord High Priest. Without further consideration, he sent him away with a penalty of death should he return without the Seer. Tamaco's bane.

Severely chastised, but still breathing, the courier sulked towards the edge of the pyramid where an armed soldier joined him, and together they descended the stone steps. Tamaco's sages had a nasty habit of mysteriously vanishing once informed their presence was demanded by his Highness. With the stakes so high, it was not going to happen this time. The golden blade sleeping in its pig leather sheath was possibly the reason for his confidence. He felt his belt to make sure it was still there. He was not a soothsayer, yet he had a strong feeling it might be employed before the day was through.

Evening came and the setting Sun cast long dark foreboding shadows that gaily cavorted out of all proportion to Tamaco's movements. Under the cover of this twilight, when light and goodwill give way to night and unholy deeds, the messenger and his charge returned.

"So mathematician, what is this I hear? Your envoy tells me you can only foretell a thousand years. After that, the future is un-calculable. Is this true?"

"It, it is your worship. I cannot... it's as if it doesn't exist. I will not say what this means, I cannot decipher it. Perhaps it…"

The cringing man stopped in midsentence as Tamaco raised his hand demanding silence. He needed to reflect on this grave news, but at least he was happy to receive a coherent answer from the quivering man.

"Tonight, I believe I am blessed." thought Tamaco thanking the Gods for this moment of clarity. They were willing to grant his request, as in years past when the Gods had bestowed their bountiful favors. A rule free of rebellion and good fortune, but this news was not good. Should peasants hear, a revolt would end his reign, and he did so love the throne and the rewards.

He took out his ceremonial dagger, approached his minions, and plunged it deep into the heart of the guard. The soothsayer and messenger were next. Now all the witnesses were silenced because of his quick thinking. Tamaco reasoned that the Gods had imparted on him not only lucidity, but also wisdom.

"Accept these sacrifices O Gods that bequest me my kingdom." he cried aloud after carving out their hearts and raising them to the sky.

If only it were that easy for modern day clergy. Mightbe.

~~~

A thousand years later in a world that was no longer flat, a milling mass of worshipers watched Pope Gregory turn and leave the balcony slowly and solemnly. It was a well-rehearsed, graceful exit perfected in a manner befitting his eminence, passed down by his predecessors' centuries earlier and Pope Gregory wasn't one to change it.

He had bigger issues.

Like every day of his brief reign, this day was filled with dread and the feeling of impending doom. His serious demeanor suggested reverence and veneration to his followers, to his lofty position of Pope, and they thanked God at the wisdom of his election. Pope Gregory prayed to God for something too, answers.

With nimble and dexterous hands that lied about his age, the pontiff closed the French windows silently behind him. The churning masses in St. Peter's square seemed a million miles away as he steadied himself against the elegantly mulled glass doors.

He had experienced a growing sense of foreboding for several days. Its weight was taking its toll on this middle-aged man. He eventually lifted his bowed head and liberated a kind but tired smile not wanting to appear rude. He had lost the ability to produce a genuine one a week earlier, when he was just a lowly cardinal. It was not a coincidence that his two closest aides, the American Cardinal, Paul and the Polish Cardinal, Krowski, had also lost this simple gift.

It wasn't the fact that they had rigged the election of Cardinal Gregory to vault him to the highest Christian office, nor was it the murder they committed with their bare hands that had stolen their smiles. It was the 'why'.

CHAPTER 2

ONLY EXPLANATION

He had lost it. There was no other explanation. For a fleeting moment the thought that the Devil was wrong overcame him causing a hot sweat. He stopped this dangerous belief and worriedly looked around to see if it had been overheard. He was still breathing so he reasoned that the Devil had not. He spewed a breath of relief. Here was a man who had looked fully into the face of death and survived. But it was only a temporary reprieve because unfortunately for Rank his problem persisted, and there was no praying for a miracle, not here, not in Hell.

His damnation, hundreds of years ago, hadn't surprised Rank. His life had been unscrupulous and ruthless; a life of thieving, lying, rape and incidental murder. Death came abruptly as he'd been caught stealing from a blacksmith, a trade well-versed with hammers and their punishing application. The suddenness of his death prevented him from asking for redemption and he had a suspicion that he hadn't endeared himself to God.

"Stealing from 'church' probably didn't put me in hitch good books." he thought.

For every sin he took responsibility for, there were a hundred he denied. There was hardly any good or noble deed ever done in his living life, or in the life he now endured. So when he was received by the Devil with open arms, he could not think of the reason for his warm welcome.

His elevated rank in Hell was due to a heinous act he had perpetrated many years earlier in a travelling circus, where he raped a young and innocent midget girl called Boleyn. His crime caused the victim to become so distressed that in her vulnerable state, she had accepted a deal from the Devil. This more than pleased him. In consoling her, The Devil cast a spell that converted her into an instrument of hatred and malice. She became the Red Witch Boleyn, the most powerful witch the World had ever seen.

When he was on Earth, which he called 'Topside', Frank the Lip was the rapist's name. He was jeeringly branded the title in a cruel childhood because of his twisted cleft-plate and resulting lisp. Frank's life on Earth was so miserable the prospect of Hell didn't scare him, (that soon changed once he was there.) On Earth, he had been nothing; but at least in Hell he had been awarded a rank as high as any man could receive. They were demons of-course, and their word was law; if broken one risked great peril.

"Theresth' no women in Hell", lisped Rank to his subordinates with conviction, "because they be the Demons." Unknown to Rank this guess happened to be true.

When ill-fated women came to Hell, they faced ongoing rape from men which would enrich the life of the males. To avoid this, the Devil transfigured them into the ruling demons. Gigantic, grotesque and disfigured humanoid shells, they towered over the tallest man. They answered to the Devil and should there be any open dissent or rebellion, a meeting with him in his private quarters resulted. A most undesirable appointment as in his regal presence, demons reverted to their former female selves. In fear of the Devil they were constantly vigilant. Sadistically quashing any hint of riot or revolution with savage beatings and lashings, dispensed from their weapon of choice, the cat o'nine tails.

Rank knew not to make even incidental eye contact with the bitter and vengeful monsters. He had learned the hard way that a sudden lick from a whip could swiftly follow.

Rank had a title that afforded a few privileges and some slack. Most particularly was an officially sanctioned crew, as opposed to gangs that hell-mates congregated in and which the demons spent all their time breaking up.

Hell-mates vied for a position on an authorized crew, and this was something Rank had benefited from. A newcomer named Ego judged the lay of the land and saw that power led to privileges. He

5

realized Rank had been bestowed a modicum of authority (he could never have earned it) and that he was one to befriend.

Rank tried not to notice his subtle tributes or be flattered by his clever ideas that he claimed Rank had thought of. Rank responded with beatings not unlike the demons. Yet the man persisted in his obsequious ways, and Rank's will quickly weakened as Ego's compliments couldn't help but go to his head.

"It's pretty nice to have someone suck up to you." he found himself thinking.

However, Ego was still going to have to pay dearly if he was going to sway Rank enough and make a lasting impression. An opportunity occurred on his second day. A demon caught Rank slacking off work, something he did more than occasionally. Ego intervened to protect his superior and in response, received an unrestrained brutal lashing from a vengeful whip. Again, three days later, more lashings.

Rank was floored. No one had withstood punishment even close to this. Therefore, he promoted the man in the blood drenched white shirt to be his sergeant, Number 2IC. This was a stroke of genius.

He didn't have to wait long before the Devil sent an envoy to visit Rank and relieved him and Ego of their current position. They were surprised and ecstatic to be promoted and assigned an extraordinary task. They were to oversee the arrival of a special delivery in Hell Level I, at the Landing Dock.

"The Landing Dock! That's nothing compared to this." whispered Rank to himself.

"What a breath, what luck, oh my Devil." he exclaimed.

A doomed soul arrived by boat on a motionless black river called the Styx. So impenetrable was the mist hanging over the Styx that the boats appeared as if from nowhere. Using a long pole to push off the bottom, the ferrymen would render their sad cargo to the Landing Dock. Every male soul arrived this way. The condemned man was unceremoniously unloaded and being officially in Hell, became a Hell-mate.

The foreboding port resembled the large cavernous places cavers dreamed of finding. Only, here, the darkness of the glistening jet-black granite walls was menacing and ominous. Modern floodlights on tall tripods illuminated the landing area making it look like an underground 'U Boat' dockyard. The sight of the monstrous demons striding maliciously up and down its length shook even the most hardened of men.

"Remember Ego." said Rank, "Hell Level I. The Landing Dock. I can't believe it.

It'sth… comfortable there… it'sth lush and warm, OMD, Hell Level I."

Although Rank dreamed like a lottery winner, he was on a roll. Ego had saved him from three evil beatings and now, after promoting him, his new sergeant had snagged their additional promotions and a doddle of an assignment.

They were going to be wardens of a single soul, a man called Phil.

In a few days and after taking a couple of gambles, Ego was promoted twice. He was now the subordinate warden over the soul of a man he hated and was more than pleased.

Additionally the Devil granted Rank a second crewmember for the task, a man called Vin, recruited from Hell's Level II. Like Ego, he'd only been in Hell a few days. Like Ego, Vin, whose name had been Gavin when he was Topside, hated Phil from the moment they met.

After Rank assigned Vin to be Ego's assistant, Ego sent Vin on a mission that ensured he would take a beating from a demon. Ego wasn't in Hell for nothing. He would make damn sure that Vin would be his subordinate.

Ego ensured Vin got the right message when he said, "Ask that demon where we could get some freshwater." knowing full well that he'd receive a lick of a whip for his impertinence and stupidity.

He believed that although Vin had only been in Hell a little longer, that he was so stupid he wouldn't know if there was freshwater down here or not. Thanks to his natural leadership skills, he also knew that in time Rank's crew would soon belong to him.

Another skill Ego honed was sizing people up. He thought Vin and Rank were well matched in slowness, but reckoned Vin's laziness was way beyond all norms. He was right.

Knowing this pleased Ego immensely believing he could manipulate him easily. As if to confirm, Ego he watched Vin return from an encounter with a demon, groaning in pain and bemoaning his lot.

"This was great." thought the gleeful Ego, and he and Rank laughed nastily without exerting any effort to hide it. Vin's role as whipping boy was sealed.

Later that day after sending Vin to look for freshwater again, Ego gave Rank a smug smile, which Rank easily returned. It also came with the question,

"Why do'th you hate Phil so much?" Ego vented his hate-filled feelings about him constantly without explanation.

"You know 'im before, while Topside yesth?" he persisted, "And why doesth the Devil needs us to preside over Phil?"

Ego was about to say, "Good question", but he caught himself and stopped, not wanting Rank to think that it was. Instead he told Rank some of his story omitting much of the inconvenient truth, (the corruption, the bribes, the murders). Nonetheless, he did tell Rank that he was probably more familiar than anyone else in Hell with the doomed soul, and that if it wasn't for Phil he wouldn't be here. Nothing was further from the truth.

While Rank and Ego stood on the Landing Dock like best of friends, Rank asked Ego his name Topside.

"Angelo Diablo."

Now, almost a day after Phil was supposed to have arrived, he had not appeared. Ego couldn't believe it. He had watched attentively for his arrival while Rank and Vin leisurely moseyed up and down the Landing Dock as if on vacation. It was hard for Ego to get Rank focused on the task as he was enjoying bullying Vin at every opportunity.

"That's my job." thought the envious Ego.

The problem was that they seemed to have lost Phil. Although Rank was in charge, Ego knew the reason for their choice as Phil's wardens was his prior association.

He knew that the Devil would punish both him and Rank equally if something happened. Consequently, his mind had back peddled frantically. He had taken three crippling beatings from the demons just to impress Rank and get a promotion, now he profoundly regretted it. If he hadn't sought authority then he wouldn't be facing the anticipated dire consequences.

"The Devil would probably lash into Vin too," he thought, "no one would be spared, although Vin would most likely get off the lightest."

Ego put all those thoughts out of his mind for the time being and focused. First, he needed to shape up the deteriorating Rank. This proved to be difficult, as Rank was ranting and worse still drawing the demons' attention. Barely containing his temper, Ego grabbed him and shook him firmly in a secluded dark corner.

Ego whispered a threatening grimace into Rank's ear,

"Get a grip Rank, you're making the demons look at us. We have to think of something. You've been here the longest, where the fuck has Phil gone?"

Rank appeared to regain control, but in reality, he was beating himself up for his stupidity in choosing Ego as his 2IC. Being a bigger man than he only reinforced his regret, he couldn't tell him to "Getth Lostth."

"I dunno."replied Rank,"tisn't meth fault that Phil's not'ere,its 'im." and deep down although he wouldn't admit it, Ego resentfully agreed.

Ego's loathing of Phil deepened and Vin cursed him vilely. Although Ego had only seen Gavin's dead body on Earth, he couldn't help but notice the depth of Vin's hatred. Yet it seemed strange as Vin's reasons were scant and yet that he wholeheartedly believed Phil was the cause of his tenure.

"At least I have a good reason." Ego thought to himself.

However, nothing changed the fact they had lost Phil and they were going to have to tell the Devil eventually.

They all remembered those thrilling words, "Rank... Phil will be arriving in Hell within the next few seconds. Standby."

Rank waited dutifully.

Ego waited planning his revenge. Vin waited like a seven-year-old.

"I hate him. I will confront him face to face, man to man. (Only if big old Ego is close by mind.)"

Seconds drift by slowly in Hell, so Rank was not concerned that time seemed stagnant.

"It was probably the Devil being impatient, thinking it would take seconds rather than minutes." he muttered to himself.

Rank assumed the Devil could be impatient. Ego knew it.

After a quarter of an hour, signs of nervousness started to show on the faces of the three. When minutes turned into hours, they became panic-stricken. When a day passed, they almost broke down. Ego held the team together with his strong mental and physical presence.

They asked a thousand times "Where the hell is he?"

They wondered if somehow, they had missed Phil's arrival. Or had he escaped? Possibly a demon had taken him down into Hell without telling them, but no one was going to ask!

Ego looked around and about the pier for what seemed the hundredth time. An impeccably groomed jet-black goat stood behind them, its stench not unlike the demons. It was harnessed to a magnificent carriage like one used for a state funeral. Perched on top was a beautiful jet-black lyrebird that screeched loudly as if attempting to betray them.

"Stupid bird." thought Vin as he wasted time cursing the animal.

"Was its beauty the distraction that averted their eyes at the critical time Phil arrived?" wondered Ego. "Did it cause them to miss him? Was that how it happened, how they missed Phil, or had he just not arrived yet? You know what; the Devil really, really wants this guy. Look at these animals - magnificent. Wow, the lyrebird has an onyx-like sheen. And why's Phil getting a royal funeral, the first in a very long time."

"Why? What's so special about Phil besides everyone hating him, looks like that even includes the Devil. Anyway, we'd better not screw up but that's exactly what we're doing."

"Hey, hang on, has anyone checked the casket?"

Ego furtively walked round to the back of the coach, checked over his shoulder to make sure that Rank and Vin weren't watching; then he quietly pried open the stunning black lacquered coffin lid and peered in.

"Fuck. Empty."

It was a crushing blow. He wanted to be the hero who found Phil and got them out of a jam. So he prayed that Rank or Vin didn't see him.

"Fuck it."

He gently lowered the lid and savored the beautiful 'whosso' noise it made as the lid fit perfectly. Then he surreptitiously made his way back to the front of the carriage hoping that he hadn't been missed. The last thing he wanted was to have an idea that was wrong, and be seen as wrong.

Meanwhile, panic stricken Rank ran up and down the planked promenade shouting at demons to get out of the way. It won him several lashes from their whips which he hardly noticed.

Time became strangely fast for Hell and another day came and went. With dread they realized they were in the biggest trouble ever. They didn't know it, but they weren't the only ones having a bad day; the Devil was too.

~~~

It was obvious Phil belonged in Heaven, but the Devil had his reasons - so against all that was right and good, he undertook a Shanghai to imprison him in Hell.

Normally a delicate and complicated operation, the Devil struggled with a nasty wrinkle in the forbidden act. Phil's body was dead, so his soul would leave his body and rise towards Heaven. Although Phil's body was oficially deceased, it appeared to be alive.

The confounding setback caused him to be more than fearful that Phil's soul would escape, he redoubled his focus. It took the Devil a week of dark, ancient magic to accomplish the task. Maintaining secrecy and the apparent slippery nature of Phil's soul made the extraction more than a challenge. It was hard to locate, and required the Devil to customize spells designed only for Phil. Meddling with dusty old powerful but brittle spells was painfully slow and irritating.

"Damn it," hushed the Devil, "he's pissing me off so much that now he really deserves condemnation." If the Devil really didn't need Phil in his jail, he would have given up and let Phil ascend.

"But that would mean *SHE* would have him and *she* wants him as badly as I do. *She* has the same questions, concerns, fears. So I have no choice."

The Devil toiled and searched for Phil's soul and he believed that he was closing in. He alerted Rank and his crew to expect Phil anytime.

Unfortunately, the Devil's call was premature. Several times he thought he'd apprehended him only to seethe with anger at the lack of confirmation from below.

After scores of attempts he was finally successful.

CHAPTER 3

NOT EVERYTHING WORKS OUT

The sheets were cheap but clean in the well-used bed where Brodie slept. His arm throbbed due to an intravenous needle, constant reminders that he was in a hospital bed.

Upon waking, a sigh of frustration escaped, instantly followed by regret. He peered across the hospital room and was excited to see that the bombshell who shared his room was asleep and hadn't heard his weak weary groan. "Lucky."

She was the first person he saw when he came into the room post-op. Though he was obese, recovering from a heart attack and in his early forties, he wanted her to think he was a dude who still had the goods.

Despite his exhaustion he planned to fake a cough, wake the woman and apologize. The perfect excuse to start a conversation. A sudden micro-nap thwarted the idea. When he recovered however, he felt refreshed and then reopened his eyelids with anticipation then disappointment.

A woman's shape filled his view of the opposite bed, but it was not Kelly. Awake, he eyed an older lady in front of him who was putting his chart back.

"She wasn't dressed as a nurse."

He stared at her, not thinking that it was rude as she stared back. "Still got it, you dog."

He mustered a weak smile. She returned it kindly.

Then she asked an unexpected question, the last thing he could anticipate.

"You believe in God above, yes?"

"Sure." attempting not to sound feeble, "You know, and it's not that I don…"

A smooth and generous voice stopped him in his tracks as she started reciting something.

They were the last rites, his.

Her hand made the sign of something approaching but not exactly like a cross.

He tried to speak but didn't have the energy to interrupt her monolog.

He wanted to ask, "What the hell is going on?"

A strange feeling hit his chest like the beat of a bass drum. He'd taken his last breath.

CHAPTER 4

TROUBLE DOWN AT THE DOCK

Seeking a scapegoat, Ego blamed Rank for dawdling along the Landing Dock. Then he blasted Vin too, before cursing Phil for being Phil. In a flicker of hope, Ego wondered if Phil made good his escape when a new arrival, in a futile attempt to avoid Hell, had jumped into the river.

"Maybe, yes, that must have been it."The incident caught their eye just at the moment that Phil's boat entered."Hey wait a minute, in fact, maybe that was Phil and we just didn't recognize the dripping wet idiot."

"Vin, go down to Level II and check to see if that person who jumped in was Phil." commanded Ego as he repressed a shout of victory.

"It wasn't" replied Vin flatly.

"DO IT!" threatened Ego glaring into Vin's frightened face. "OK, ok." retorted Vin trying not to look too scared.

Vin ran down into Hell Level II, a wasteland, and looked around. He knew the escapee wasn't Phil so he'd used the opportunity as his means to get away from those "Two assholes."

Vin, or Gavin Topside, always sought a break rather than exert himself. At home, here in Level II he'd noticed a slight breeze just cool enough to cause a shiver when he was in the open. Trying to seek some shelter, he stumbled onto a secret nook right next to the river. It was out of sight of the Demons too.

"Awesome."

"Vin is taking hours; he must have found Phil and is getting a demon to help." said the hopeful pair.

He'd actually settled in for a cozy nap. He returned hours later to the waiting Rank and Ego. Their optimism turned to anger when Vin returned alone.

Lying was a quality of Vin's that embodied his nature; thus he easily parried their questions. On Earth, he lied to the Yellow Witch Ruebella, convincing her that she should blame Phil not him. Rank and Ego were just another two suckers. In Vin's mind, he didn't even think he was even lying it was so natural.

Deceiving Ego, however, was an achievement as his instincts were sharply honed; he was a born detector of non-truths. Ego accepted Vin's tales of endeavor and disappointment believing he could sniff out a liar.

Ego considered recalling all souls that had disembarked in the last twenty-four hours, hoping that a bureaucratic mix up had occurred: one that revolved around the erroneous ushering of Phil into Hell under a wrong name.

Ego felt that he was the only one coming up with anything, but at the same time he would have dissed anyone else's ideas. If he wasn't a stakeholder in finding Phil, he would have smirked and watched Rank and Vin panic and fret. But his ass was on the line too, so he had to participate, contribute, lead.

With Vin's disappointing news they realized they had little choice other than to man up.

Ego took control. "Ok. Ok. We've lost Phil, what are we going to do? If we're all at fault, or no one is at fault, it won't make a difference as the Devil won't care. So let's figure this out."

Despite their differences, they united under the shadow of a common enemy and considered their options. Rank had a terrible inkling that the Devil, no matter how busy he was, would be coming down to check up on them if he didn't hear from him soon.

After a heated debate, they became hushed as they knew and had to admit that they had lost Phil. That left them silent because they all knew what was to come next. They were going to have to tell the Devil.

"What choice doesn't have Ego?" cried Rank, his speech was worsening under the pressure. "Come'on, what else can we do? Phils ain't here. We can't find 'im. The Devil it bounds to come down here soon and find us out. Were lost 'im. I don't like it neither, but we got no choice."

"It's true Ego." chimed Vin submitting to Ego's leadership.

"OK, OK." said Ego, taking command again, "We tell him the next time he calls, G... help us. But sure as Hell, it ain't gonna be me 'cus look what he did to me Topside." Ego pointed to his face, a façade of hundreds of tiny scars and melted peeling skin.

Rank and Vin stared in disbelief that Ego as Angelo D. met the Devil on Earth and was a victim of his wrath. They cringed at the thought of the pain he'd suffered, understanding his fear for the first time.

There wasn't a need for Rank and Vin to speak. No one wanted to be the messenger.

A deafening silence followed for what seemed like an eternity. All three stood opposite each other like statues until Rank offered the solution.

"We can draw straws."

Ego with the quickest mind realized there was no other way and at least he could be sure that no one, other than himself, cheated.

"Good idea Rank." said Ego as he quickly approached the waiting funeral landau and selected three straws from the goat's feeding bag. Turning his back, Ego broke three straws into three equal lengths, and then he took one and made it shorter. He turned around and faced Vin and Rank.

"Choose."

The place went quiet as Rank and Vin stared at the tops of the three beige pieces of thin cane. Eyes darted from one person to another. The choices these two would make would seal Ego's fate, cannily he forced the shortest straw forward towards the pair.

It was time. Vin chose first. Ego knew it wasn't the shortest straw. So now Rank would be choosing for both of them. With almost imperceptible body language, Ego engineered the shorter cane in Rank's direction.

"Fuck!" ran through Ego's mind like a church bell. "That dumb Rank's too stupid to have picked the right one. I should have been obvious and pushed it straight at him.

"Fuck it."

Without waiting and thus not giving Ego another chance to cheat, Vin revealed his straw and Rank followed. Just as Ego was about to show his hand, they were rudely interrupted by the Devil who summoned the warden.

"RANK." echoed the Devil.

Desperately Rank looked at Ego's eyes then his hands.

Ego knew that the Devil would consult Rank, so he opened his hand to show Rank that he had the shortest straw and that it didn't matter.

"Me Lordship." said Rank. He answered the Devil's command and tried not to fall to his knees in fear.

In a deep burbling voice the Devil demanded, "Well, Rank? I'm waiting."

Rank began,"We'ss, er, we'ss got er…"

Like a voice out of nowhere, "Phil is in our custody your highness."

Rank and Ego were dumbfounded.

They had no doubt that Vin had just doomed them.

CHAPTER 5

MORTALS ARE THE WHIM'S CHANCE

The ancient entity sulked in the dark. Several weeks earlier she had an encounter with a stranger. During his misadventure, she had over indulged and mistakenly spewed too many negative numbers at the man. Sometimes, a negative times a negative becomes a positive. At that precise moment, two experiments occurred elsewhere in the World. The foundational nature and combined confluence of these acts endowed upon the man something beyond her imagination. And she no less, suffered its adverse rebound.

Just a day passed before the man disappeared from her awareness. It was at the same moment the Devil possessed his body and stripped him of all his illicit entanglement.

When she thought of this man, she found she'd lost her abilities. She couldn't see him.

Who could have known? Imagined? Foretold?

Not even her, the mightiest of all had dreamed of such an outcome.

That unfortunate moment haunted her.

Furthermore, she experienced an unusual feeling that something was wrong. Diving deep down into her numbers she saw a pattern. She detected a repetition of numbers that shouldn't have existed.

Then she pondered when she lost sight of the stranger, was that the same time she felt this twinge? She was *Pi*, the ruler of chance. She knew a fluke as great as this signaled something important.

Her easy life of instigator, agitator and spoiler had abruptly ended. The many unpredictable incidents, happenings and actions that had occurred outside the scope of both God and her now required attention. She would have to get her hands dirty.

Her challenge was to affect the outcome without detection. "Be's careful, and keep to standard deviations."

"I's sick, yes I's am's. Hopes no one knows. Protects myself." "Could be terminals."

"NEVERs say the word, luckys."

"The Devil thinks he has him... and all of it wrongs."

"He's thinks I's doesn't know, but I's doess. I's know everything about hims."

"Hah's, only I's know it'ss."

"I's will, however, kill hims. Becauses I's know, when no else does, Phil is alives."

"Phils is alive, somewhere, 'cus I'm sick and it's he whose sickening me."

Murder would ensue.

CHAPTER 6

ALMOST, BUT NOT DEAD

It was a dark, cool place, yet he was warm and cozy. It was home. He was in his body, one that extended beyond its physical flesh. He was in a harbor, a safe haven, in the shelter of his Shoes. He gazed up seeing dancing sunlight as if from the bottom of an ocean.

Phil was hurting badly.The Devil had shattered his reflecting silver-mirrored eyes and then slowly stripped him of his Entanglements. His Shoes had saved him and hidden him from the vicious attacks,because they were as one with Phil. He reacted instinctively and in perfect harmony with their thoughts. Now, a week later, he dared to think rather than hide, and weird thoughts entered his head.

"Whatever I did, could it have been all three of us acting as a single unified entity?"

He seemed to be alive and safe. He heard and obeyed The RhomSong Diamond and this saved his life.

Unknown to the eternal mortals, God, the Devil and *Pi*, a fifth life force was born, an addition to the existing energies of mind, body, soul and entanglement.

This fifth dimension was forged at a single moment when entanglement, magic and science intersected in an impossible convergence. The moment created the union of Phil and his Shoes.

Phil and his Shoes were it; they were RhomSong.

The Devil, God and *Pi* could not see or feel it. It was an oasis in the fabric of the Universe, a five-dimensional rhombus of life unknown.

In ClearStream's ruined church, the Devil savagely obliterated Phil's entanglement in his third attack, transported himself into his battered body, and covertly inhabited it.

21

To onlookers, the battle between Phil and the Devil continued. Cleverly, the Devil furnished this charade pretending that Phil was alive, but in reality, he was in full possession of his body.

Certainly Phil's soul was destined for Heaven, and this would deny the Devil the chance to get the answers he so desperately needed.

How did he acquire entanglement?

How did he survive the Devil's escape on the stage in Salem? Most importantly, how did he produce the negative square reflection? He wasn't the only one asking the same things.

So the Devil plotted to intercept Phil's soul, capture it and imprison him in Hell.

Under normal circumstances, for an ordinary mortal, this would not be easy. However, any attempt to steal such a significant soul such as Phil's, and to do it secretly, would require real stealth.

Nevertheless, even with these mitigating pretexts, capturing Phil's soul was proving harder than expected. So hard in fact that he couldn't suppress a niggling feeling that he was missing something. There was nothing but incongruences when the Devil thought about this man.

"Phil should have died from the pain alone during my escape from The John Abbott Shoe. Somehow, he survived. Unscathed nonetheless. Astonishing. Then, when he should have lived, he died. Exasperating. Even now, his soul has vacated the heart and chakras' for over a day. So he's dead. Yet his body doesn't know it. Devil Damn It. That's seemsto be typical of this man."

The Devil searched and swore some more, "So his soul must be trapped in his body somewhere, that's why it's still 'alive'. That damn Phil. I'll get him, I'll damn his soul. That's what I DO."

The Devil rifled through his body. He knew that God had not secured Phil's soul but it was only a matter of time, so in desperation, he resulted to drastic measures.

Dark Magic.

He didn't know that Phil and his Shoes were now a single entity and the Phil he sought was no more. Phil was lost to him the moment he mercilessly robbed him of his Entanglements in the ClearStream Chapel. How could he know that his actions were the forge that completed Phil's transformation?

Phil was the only man to ever acquire entanglement, now, its absence, unpredictably, facilitated the free flowing of his RhomSong. Unencumbered by the fourth life force, it now ran smoothly and frictionless through Phil's being.

Phil was a changed man and no one knew it, mortal or otherwise.

Employing ancient curses, The Devil continued his search having no idea that Phil had taken refuge in the Shoes. How could the Devil know Phil's soul had retreated into this abstract plane the instant he heard the diamond? It was impossible for the Devil to conceive that such a thing was possible.

From his sanctuary, Phil watched the Devil smash into his empty consciousness like an angry bull. He tore through his mind and body and left no cell un-ravaged, but Phil's soul remained missing. He fearfully watched as the Devil ripped and gorged on his empty consciousness, spitting it out in terrifying rage.

Swallowing his pain, he remained absolutely still and just hid. He did nothing, he was null. He was tired and hurting so badly that all he wanted to do was fall asleep. He didn't dare. To avert his eyes from the turmoil above might reveal his location. Instead, Phil watched.

He saw the Devil launch into a series of frightening incantations. He wielded deep and dark magic dredged from the depths of his Black Entanglement. To no avail.

Then, after inquiring his minions below one last time, he got the reward he'd strove so hard to obtain. After five days of intensive effort, Phil's soul was now a prisoner in Hell.

Triumph.

The Devil had ground it out and captured the elusive spirit.

His gofers Rank, Vin and Ego solemnly declared that Phil's soul was secure in the funeral carriage. The Devil sighed with relief and cursed God for her mercy. *She* was never far from his thoughts. Stealing Phil was as much to do with her as it was him. He knew that God wanted Phil too, because the same questions plagued them both.

CHAPTER 7

KEEP TRYING

The Devil feared God's intrusions and that the slightest mistake would deliver Phil to her. This time, unlike the seventeenth century, the Devil wasn't going to be outmaneuvered by an agent of God or an interloper like John Abbott. Nor was he going to be as cocky. To this end and being careful not to be traced, he scoured the World seeking individuals with deviant behavior.

"A terrorist attack in New York. That should do it." smiled the Devil. All air traffic in the States was suspended.

"Perfect. That should keep her busy."

Paranoid ideas controlled his thinking; however, he was now certain that God was suficiently distracted, that he could continue to conjure and cast shadowy spells in Phil's body with impunity.

It was all worth it, "RHAAW", the Devil bellowed.

He felt empowered and elated because Phil was his, God be damned. After five days of worry and intensive slog, the statement from down below was the confirmation he needed.

Then he killed Kelly, only not to death, but like her love, to a coma. "Phil is dead, but his body lives. Kelly is dead, but her body too lives.
They're not the living dead, not Zombies, no, they're the dead living."

For the first time since his escape from the John Abbott Shoe, the Devil relaxed. He owned Phil, the strangest manifestation of entanglement in history. He replayed and gloated over this victory.

"I was the silent ghoul, invisible, deft, a genius. My spells were indiscernible. Yes." said the Devil, "I found and stole Phil's soul, and left him in a coma. Fuck you God, there is nothing you can do. Phil's soul is mine. And Kelly, I'll deal with her later. Or, or, take Kelly now - God, see if I care."

Luckily, for hell-mates, the river was easy to ignore due to its location along the edge of Hell, like a ring-road around a city. They were more concerned with surviving the wind-swept arid landscape and seeking shelter from the marauding demons.

Breaking the silence that had consumed the trio, Rank let Ego and Vin know that because of their mission, they were receiving special protection and passage. Even as Vin acknowledged this, hoping to find another secret nook he continued his study of the crumpled ruins between the road and the river. He made mental notes of locations for further exploration, including a spot near the impending last gate of Green-Hell.

The Styx passed under five brick arches built into the cliff wall. Next to them was a pair of huge wooden doors that separated Level IV from V.

A Yellow-Eyed Demon, larger than the last and the tallest yet, commanded the doors to open. Once the entourage had hastily marched through, the same Gate-Demon ordered the towering doors to close.

"Hope coming back up will be just as easy as going down." thought Vin.

The buttery colored sky that greeted them in this uncharted level seemed angry in comparison to the previous 'tranquil' green skies of fire. Ego wondered if the fiery skies of Yellow-Hell were enraged for their trespass. He surmised that it was always like this and that the flames were more intense and cooler.

Hell-mates learned with surprise that Hell's fires burn cold. Hell is a cold place, without God's love, what else could it be?

The Styx River descended with them as it continued to run parallel to the road. Although it was a shadow of its former width from the Landing Dock, it had gained in malice. With every descending level, it became narrower, darker and eviler.

Ego presumed, as they entered the red Seventh Level, Red-Hell, that the reason for this was that the torments had become more brutal and torturous. For all the dread of Hell, until the band reached this red echelon, for many, life on Earth was far worse. However, on Earth, the gift of death was the escape, whereas here in Hell there was none.

Upsetting for Ego, the skies roiling fire in Level VIII was a dull pewter hue. He'd assumed that the colors of Hell matched the colors of the three witches.

"I wonder if there's another witch." he muttered to himself. "Must be worse than the Red one if there is, as this is a lower level, if that's how it works?"

The Eighth Level was a barren and desolate gray landscape. Solitary distant screams occasionally broke the silence, or were they just echoes in their heads warning of a descending madness? The Styx had dwindled to a creek winding downward towards the final destination.

Their gaze followed it all the way to a lonely small black door in the distance.They knew their destiny lay behind that gate. Suddenly, they all wished to remain in Gray-Hell knowing that their fate, unknown, laid waiting for them there.

As if notified of their approach, the Gate-Demon stood waiting patiently with an evil grin on her lips. She was without doubt the largest monster in Hell, three times taller than Ego. Dire images of torture at the Devil's hand swam in their heads, but they forged ahead unable to avoid their fate whatever it may be.

They approached the entrance to the bottom of the Universe.

Here all hope ceased, other than their own, which was fading fast. Vin's initial indifference to their predicament had vanished and his lie was finally weighing on him - well the possibility of its exposure, not the act of doing it. He was quite comfortable with that, but along with the others, he wondered:

"Did the Devil know that they were attempting todeceive him? Was their punishment waiting there, behind that door? Would it be eternity for them in Hell's final bastion? Would they be doomed forever and suffer all the torments that are implicit with it?"

Without any options other than to keep on moving, they swallowed hard and did just that.

The door was a massive and impenetrable nine yards high and nine feet wide made from timber with no earthly origin. Thick metal edges and square studs secured brass bands that crisscrossed the length and breadth of the imposing structure. The door itself was set back into a gleaming black recess, reeking of doom and foreboding.

The Gate-Demon beckoned the door with her index finger and it swung obediently although unwillingly open, as if it dearly wished to keep its secrets. If the group could let the door have its wish, they would have, but dutifully, they crossed the threshold and descended into the nadir of Hell.

Before them was a horrifying sight. A sunken lake of molten lava formed the bottom of a giant cavern. Jutting out of its center was a rocky outpost, and on its plateau, stood a jet-black cubic building.

The three instinctively shielded their faces with their arms, before they realized that the flames that licked and danced above the boiling lava radiated no heat.

As the door closed behind them,the reins that attached the goat to the carriage clattered to the ground, and the animal trotted off to one side of the door before turning to stone. The lyrebird, flying like a fat turkey reached a pedestal on the opposite side and it too transformed.

The two sentinels guarded the only way out, Ego believed, ready to spring to life should someone try to escape."Now we're down to one lyrebird, in Vin." he mused.

Emanating from a tunnel at their side, the Styx stewed out of a single brick archway and fell over a forty-foot precipice into the waiting cauldron below.They stared at the river's fall and ignored that the Styx's would *turn* on them because, even now, no one could tell which way the river was going. The bubbling and boiling stream wound its way towards the black monolith in the distance, and its black steam wafted upwards and around a high wooden causeway.

The way ahead was over a pier, a rickety path that was supported by tall, slim, charred stilts that thrust their way out of the traversing river. Several old, stunted and charred piles stuck out through the lava, remnants of older, burned-out and derelict causeways that once gave passage to the island.

More like crude than water, the Styx battled against the constant onslaught of lava. Hissing fluid and molten rock and flames presented a truly evil scene.

Steadying himself against their new adversary, Ego grabbed hold of the harness and motioned the other two to do the same. Vin relinquished the rider's seat, and only now did the other two realize his cunning. Had it been anywhere else, they would have acted on their resentment, but as it was, they had a job to do.

The carriage lumbered slowly forwards over the loose planks. Every now and then it became stuck in the occasional larger gaps between the floorboards, and required controlled heaves from all of them to get it moving.

They tried their best to evade the odd cloud of steam touching them, and held their breath when it was unavoidable. Not a moment too soon, they descended the last rickety planks to the safety of the wide rectangular plateau.

Their last sight of the island's cliffs was of the incredibly resilient River Styx. A single narrow thread of it rose out of the steam at its foot in the lava moat and vertically straight up to the plateau from which it fell. Still the river's direction defied detection, and there was no mistaking that the 'water' was the most evil ever.

When they gained landfall, and as always Ego was the first to take note, the river flowed through the narrow gaps between six-foot square ceramic pavers. The river's predictable source, (or mouth,) was at the door of the enormous solitary onyx cube.

The building towered above them, black and beautiful, but full of mystery. Rank, Ego and Vin were awe-struck with the edifice, but it also hardened them to their task.

Ego lowered the harness gently to the ground, unable to hide a respect for the monument before him. Being mindful not to tread on the floor's cracks, he ventured over to the prison cell and its strange, disquieting, open door.

It was a forearm in thickness. It told of cryptic mystery and banishment. Both the monolith and door were made from an unknown metal that shone with a quiet, cultured deportment. And something was clear - the door was impenetrable.

Ego took a wild guess, because that was the way he was, that it was solid mercury. He didn't know that he was right and that it was the Devil's favorite element.

While Vin and Rank looked on, Ego inquisitively wandered inside the cell. An altar made from a single massive diamond dominated the center of the room and balanced impossibly on its culet in an unholy, unstable equilibrium. The flawless jewel flashed all the colors of Hell: green, yellow, red, gray and black. Its cuts were coldly clean and precise, and its facets ground to maximize the reflection of light, generating a firestorm from within its depths.

Typical of his insecurity, Ego experienced a pang of jealousy. "The Devil hates this man, values this man more than anyone,

ever. Who was Phil? What makes him so important? What was wrong with his eyes?" Ego, a man who didn't need another reason to hate Phil had found one.

"Better get on with things. I must admit though," thought Ego after he paused a moment to compose himself, "not so bad considering the wretched souls in Level Seven of Hell, Level Nine appears to be relatively benign."That was until he felt a shard of cold fear that stabbed at his very heart, and at that moment he realized.

The black cube was not just a jail; it was the blackest hole in the Universe.

The coldest place, absent of God's love, embrace and warmth. A place she knows not, a place lost to her.

It was a place that a prisoner would exchange the diamond for the company of a centipede.

Suppressing raw panic, he dashed out of the cell panting and most unlike him sought the other's comfort.

"OM..." whispered the exhausted Ego. "OM..."

The others said nothing - lest they dared to enter themselves.

The awkward silence that followed was broken by Vin who examined the cell door in detail and made a discovery. "Look."

At eyelevel, the door boasted an oval the size of a turkey dish, with an elongated opal as its lens centered in the middle. This was a spyhole put in place to provide the jailer a means to gloat at his prisoner's plight. One other decoration was a rectangular nameplate inscribed with a single word, *Phil.*

The team was kick started into action. Together they inspected the door and its massive complex hinges that allowed for the door to slide and swing. They tested the doors range and marveled at its balance, as it was smooth and easy to move despite its immense weight. They took one last look at the lock before they got on with their last act of deception. They knew what had to be done.

Without a word, they followed Ego's idea. They pulled the carriage round and backed it up as close to the door as possible, leaving only enough elbow room to maneuver Phil's coffin into the stark room. Should anyone have watched, there was less chance to see that it was empty. As they drew closer to concluding their terrible ruse, their movements became more anxious.

The Devil could materialize any second and smash them to smithereens, but even as they thought about it, a tiny flicker of hope lit in their racing hearts. Taking big breaths they heaved the coffin into the vacant room.

The carriage and the half open door obstructed a direct line of sight. The three braced themselves against the coldness of the place, and spent a minute pretending that Phil was being processed.

35

When they believed they'd stayed long enough to feign his imprisonment, they took one last run over the amazing jewel to experience the cold, crisp feeling. Then they got ready to leave. They controlled the urge to rush due to the bitter chill and revealed the unoccupied coffin to Level IX. This time they made their actions overt, leaving the lid off the coffin so that anyone who watched would see it was bare.

Then, in a mad dash, they bolted out. With teeth clattering, they went about warming up by rubbing their hands together, but fueled by the growing glimmer of hope, they were soon hot with anticipation.

Was it possible that they could get away with it after all?

They were all so close now; all they had to do was shut the door. They were about to place their hands on the door when Vin let out a cry.

"Oh No, if the Devil were to look though the peephole, he'd see that Phil's - "

"In his cell" interrupted Ego just in time, but not quick enough to stop Rank from swearing.

"Shite, yer rite, what do we do Ego?" panicked Rank.

Ego suddenly jumped up in excitement, grabbed hold of Rank's leg and took some dirt from the bottom of his always dirty shoes, and wiped it on the inside of the peephole's porthole.

"Perfect." he said when he checked it.

The others checked too - and couldn't see inside whatsoever. "Great idea, Ego, yer really smart yer know." said Rank, "Why don't yer put some dirt on thisth end?"

"Thanks Rank, because the Devil could just wipe it off." said Ego, who was thinking, "And you're really stupid."

In what he deemed to be another inspired thought, Ego removed the key from the keyhole and checked if it went all the way through - it didn't.

Motioning the others to help, they swung the door into its position parallel to the jail's wall. With their hands on the two handles, they closed it by pushing forward. The door's fit was so precise that it was the most satisfying of jobs.

As the door slid into its jam, it took longer and longer to shut as the air had to escape. With time, it fit perfectly and snuggly like a piece of flawless engineering, which is exactly what it was.

The key was solid and with it resting in the palm of his hand, he rocked it up and down weighing it.

Ego, the real leader of the group, inserted the key back into the key hole. The feel of the key in the lockbox was one of sex. A perfect fit.

"Turn the key clockwise, one complete turn, no more, no less." Ego turned the key.

The action was smooth, even and snug.

The key's fob was a non-symmetrical design, so Ego was able to easily see that he'd only turned the key that once. He heeded the Devil's instructions exactly, wary of unknown but probably painful consequences of not doing so.

"One complete clockwise turn." he declared proudly.

A clockwork ticking noise started causing them to look at each other with some disquiet, before they grasped that the mechanism to lock the door had started. Then the clicking drew louder and slower, until, and they all held their breath, the very last click, the last tumbler lurched over and the door was locked.

Then Ego did an amazing thing. He removed the key, looked at it intensely for one last time, and then without warning *threw it into the lake of molten lava.*

An Earth shattering, bone crushingly clap of thunder crashed down upon them. The diminutive flames that licked from the lava burst to life and roared, tall, loud and with vengeance. The clap rumbled and echoed throughout the cavern, but finally it became quiet enough to hear their yells.

"EGO!" yelled Vin. "What the hell 'ave you done?"

Ego returned a shout with defiance. "The Devil can't see the inside because I've, I mean, we've covered over the peephole, and he can't get inside because he doesn't have the key. And if he asks us, we can say we did what we thought he wanted us to do.'*Lock him up and throw away the key.'*

The door was locked - forever."

He almost laughed. Revenge, in any small measure against the Devil was satisfying. Vin smiled since this was something he appreciated, a lie in action not words. It was beautiful. As for Rank, with time it percolated into his slow brain. Then it dawned on him as the penny dropped. Suddenly, for the first time since they'd lost Phil, it looked possible that they could get away with this.

It was better than getting away with murder. Rank was ecstatic. Vin was beaming. Ego was smugness in persona; he'd earned it. No one could stop grinning.

Vin did a mock throw of the key and suddenly they were all screaming with laughter. The fact that they were the solitary souls in Level Nine saved them from detection.

Laughing and skipping wildly in gay abandon,they ran back across the causeway to the entrance with flames roaring either side of them like a rock band entering a stage. It was the best-unrecorded time in Hell, ever. And luckily for the three conspirators, it was secret.

Their secret. One co-conspirator had another.

CHAPTER 8

END IT ALL

Phil felt a wave of freshness and clarity reclaim his body, like the feeling at the end of a cold when one's ears are not blocked and breathing is not a struggle. This signified that the occupation was over; the Devil had left.

Unusual for Phil. he went to leave his secret sanctuary in a hurry, because, for the first time in his life, he wanted something, he wanted Kelly.

He was prepared to risk all and tell her that he loved her. He had wasted so much time being afraid and not taking chances in love or life.

He hoped things would be different when he opened his eyes.
He would stop being dictated to by fate.

Now it was time to leave the safety of his Shoes, because his body was clear of the foul stench of the Devil. He entered his body, opened his eyes and saw something.

~~

"Room 3142." said the uncaring young receptionist at the front desk. She looked hardly a day over fifteen and gleefully occupied with her phone's internet chat room,giggling and tapping away with delight.

"Thanks." Joan replied trying hard to be cordial after repeatedly coughing just to be noticed.

Joan was made of sterner stuff than any teenager could imagine. She brushed aside the girl's apathy and ventured to the elevators. A longer wait was obvious as one of them was out of order. Undeterred, she pressed the 'up'button and waited.

She had patiently endured a hellish journey just to get there. She pressed the button again, hard. It begrudgingly made its dutiful arrival. After she exited the elevator, she strode along the corridor as if on a mission.

Joan, counting off the ward numbers in her head, "3117... 3118... 3119." and came to the end of the corridor. "Where's 3142?"

She looked around, did a pirouette, and then swore as she realized what had happened.

"That damn... girl."

Facing the right way after her ballet maneuver, she walked briskly back along the corridor and punched the down button, only to hear the disappointing noise of the elevator at work some floor below.

~~~

Phil froze as he instantly recognized a silver pinprick of light, entanglement. It seemed that he had just started breathing only to stop again.

Then he saw light flash across the open door of his room. It emanated from a woman's body, which could only mean one thing. A witch.

He listened intensely to the diminishing of footsteps that ended with silence. Unaware of what he was doing, Phil panicked and tried to jump out of bed.

"Run!" was all he could think.

He noticed the tubes and needles dangling from his arm, the realization of where he was, in a hospital, surprised him.

During the perilous retreat in his Shoes, where he had eluded the Devil, he hadn't considered where his body was. So Phil found himself standing up and looking around a small four-person hospital room. Dressed only in a hospital gown and his Shoes, he cautiously freed himself of the needles.

He hoped to locate his clothes behind the closet double doors at the end of the room. So he firmly swung them open and paused, as he recognized his clothes, and those of a woman.

Kelly's? "Kelly!"

He turned round, scanned the other beds. First he saw a man in a bed next to his, and then Kelly's opposite his.

"What? What happened? Why is she in hospital?" "Oh my God, the Devil must have... done something." Phil was right, but he had no idea what.

~~~

When Joan approached the front desk a second time, an elderly more responsible looking woman had replaced the young girl.

"Hello, I'm looking for..." Joan didn't mention that all she wanted was the right room number this time. She wasn't on a witch-hunt.

"Oh," said the woman, "my daughter told me about you. Well, you know what, I think..."

But just then, in mid-sentence, the hospital receptionist picked up the microphone, being spurred into action by a blinking red light on a dashboard.

"Ward Doctor..." she began. "Now what?" thought Joan.

" Ward Doctor, room 3116." she boomed over the hospital loudspeakers.

"That's your room too bitch." said the receptionist.

~~~

"Kelly, wake up, wake up." whispered Phillip, gingerly shaking her arm because he was scared of waking her, before realizing how stupid that was. Then he shook her harder.

"K a r e n."

Still there was no response. He didn't know what was wrong with her.

Whilst pondering this, he suddenly thought, why was he there in a hospital too, let alone her.

How long he'd been out? And what did the hospital think was wrong with him?

"Charts… Yes." thought Phil. So he rushed to the front of their beds and grabbed them.

"Coma? She's in a coma, my God."

Then he read his chart, "Me too. And I've been out for over two weeks, and Kelly for about a week. What happened?"

"What happened?" he whispered to himself again.

"It's funny, seeing *Phil* as my name on the chart, it doesn't feel right. I don't feel right with it. Even saying it, *Phil, Phil*, seems weird, anyway got to move."

A little shiver reminded him to put his clothes on before trying to wake Kelly again, as if he could bring her out of a coma.

"Can you hear me, Kelly?" he whispered in her ear. He heard that people in comas can hear and hoped that his talking would help her come out of one. Like the doctors, he didn't know that this was the Devil's doing and that other than God's intervention, only death could free her.

"Kelly. Kelly." She didn't respond, but still he needed to believe he could make a difference.

For the moment, he forgot that he was trying to avoid the witch and he sat down on the bed next to Kelly, debating what to do. His thoughts were shattered on hearing a noise in the corridor, reminding him to concentrate on the urgency of his escape.

"I've got to get out of here in case that witch comes back. I might still be immune to them, I don't know. I don't want to find out, at least not for the moment. I don't know what color or even shape my eyes are either and I haven't got time. I've gotta get out of here."

He stood up and looked down at the still and serene Kelly, with so much love and sadness in his heart; he became suddenly aware that he had to tell her he was leaving. As he bent down to whisper in her ear, he realized he'd never been this close to her face, and that he could peck her on the lips. Not out of lust or sex, but out of love. If only he overcame his fear.

"Yes, I'll do it." he went to, and then backed off. The pressure of time passing had stolen his bravado.

"Get going." he commanded as he reconsidered the situation.

With haste, he checked his pockets for his wallet and phone and left the room. Then he dashed back into the room and returned the chart to its place.

Pleased to remember this minor detail, he exited for a second time and headed down the corridor. Barely down the hall, he bypassed a doctor and several nurses who sped passed him and charged into his room. Alerted to the beeping monitor, no one noticed the patient walking down the corridor.

~~~

Joan pressed the elevator button and heard it wind up and descend, "God damn it, now it's on the top floor." she muttered.

As she waited, the young girl joined her by her side. She had earphones on and the volume was loud enough for Joan to hear a hip-hop cover of a beautiful Christmas carol.

"In fall?" thought Joan resisting an impulse to turn and slap her.

The elevator finally arrived and the girl pressed the second-floor button.

Joan was exasperated, "Couldn't she take the stairs?" The doors felt so slow to close yet checking her phone revealed she'd been in the hospital for only a mere ten minutes.

In the last week, a coordinated multipoint terrorist attack on American soil and skies had cancelled several days of public transportation. Consequently, her journey here was severely impacted, it seemed almost deliberate.

"Pissed, that's what I am, but stay calm and carry on, God is with you, sort of." she muttered to herself.

She got the call through a dream. Due to the Entanglement War at the edge of Sol's System, God could communicate with her agents on Earth only through dreams. The only way she could guarantee her messages found their targets was to spray the entire Earth for twelve hours, and hope.

Joan had received the encrypted message along with all the people of Earth. Not only Joan could decrypt the message, shamans and others with mystical gifts could too. But she knew it was for her and could put it into the appropriate context.

The message Joan received was urgent and demanding. She obediently headed towards the last known whereabouts of a man called Phil and a woman called Kelly. God said she was in a hospital in a hamlet called Evelyn Mills on the other side of the continent, and that Phil would be there with her.

Eventually, the ascending elevator stopped. The doors slid open and revealed a large man barricading the entrance to the floor. He reached in and pressed 'Ground' and stood back. Scanning the hallway, she eyed a group of hospital staff in heated discussion.

The fleeting glimpse vanished behind the closing doors and she was back down on floor one before she knew it.

~~~

Waiting at the elevator, Phil watched the medical staff enter his room. He knew they would leave right away to look for him and return him to bed. Then, as soon as they left, the witch would return and he knew what that meant.

Beckoned towards the stairwell exit light, Phil hastened through the door and descended the stairs, trying to be courageous despite the echo of his own footsteps.

With his hands pressed against the stairwell door, he opened it carefully, looked around and swiftly darted out into the hallway to join the hospital public.

The witch was nowhere in sight and he was determined to make a getaway. Focused on the distant exterior doors, he strode deliberately towards them. The doors automatically opened and shut behind him. He was outside. He was in shock. It had been so easy, with no witch or Devil apprehending him. He was free.

He breathed a sigh of relief for the first time since he'd woken up. "Where too?" said the cabby.

"Err. The bus station." replied Phil as the cab driver pulled down on the gear lever and jolted the taxi into life.

For the first time he really was free, without any mistakes to track him down, neither the witch nor the hospital staff could locate him.

"Hey, I've changed my mind. Take me to a used car dealership." Phil told the cabby. The taxi changed direction without a screech or swerves and found its way to 'Honest Jimmy's'.

Honest Jimmy had a reputation for being a little too eager and assertive. Not wanting to frighten away another potential sale, he hung back in the office and pretended not to be spying on Phil as he moseyed around the car lot.

"He's thinking." Jimmy saw this as his cue. He left his office and sauntered over to the prospective buyer.

Phil was in deep thought, but not of buying a car, but instead he was toying with another idea. Abstaining. Not knowing whether he was serious or not, he started browsing the web and had found an interesting site.

"If this place is as out of the way as it claims to be, then…" the website crashed just as he logged on.

"Typical. TheLastReso…"

"She's a beaut eh?" ambushed Jimmy. "That dent won't rust. Nooo."

Phil exited the dealer's lot driving his new car, almost just to get rid of the pushy and relentless salesman.

"Finally, I can get back on that site and fuck, it's not bookmarked and… WHAT THE." he shrieked as he almost sideswiped a pickup ferrying a trio to a local bar.

It was early afternoon and although the bright fall sunshine should have lightened his spirits, it hadn't. The pickup had slowed down, and in his mirror, Phil could see the burly men looking over their shoulders.

Phil sped off in the other direction. His default action. It didn't take seconds for him to fall into self-loathing and resentment. After coming out of his coma, he vowed to live life without fear.

Yet he was fleeing from the pickup rather than stopping and apologizing. This was a minor thing, but it spoke deeply of his character. Suddenly he was ashamed that he'd even considered scuttling off to a remote island. If he did, he'd be running away from life again, and life meant Kelly.

"I'd even considered, err… and I didn't even have the guts to peck her and let her know I care, and she's in a damn coma and you still couldn't, you wet blanket Phil."

"You know what, being Phil doesn't feel right now, Phillip feels better, and I can't say why. So, you know what, I'm 'Phillip' from now on, because that's what the Shoes call me." Warmth filled him in afirmation of their union.

Without realizing it, he was driving slower and slower as the accelerator grew harder and harder to force down.

Sighing, he sped up and looked for a place to pull over and turn round.

He was going to go back.

"Well I guess the afternoon wasn't a complete waste,I needed a car to get around.Now I've got this old junker.(Boy. That Last Resor….com, whatever, looked pretty good). Anyway…" he thought.

"But what happened? Why is Kelly in a coma? What happened to me? Obviously, the Shoes saved me, and now I can't tell the difference between me and them."

He looked down at his feet,"They ARE perfect. Wow, they can feel my thoughts.They're great!" Another safe glow rippled through him. Another afirmation.

Looking his mirror again as he pulled over, it occurred to him that he still hadn't checked his eyes, so he turned the rearview mirror towards himself. They were perfectly normal. He wasn't too surprised as the people he had recently been in contact with hadn't mentioned anything.

He found himself filled with conflicting emotions. Secretly he wanted them to be different, but he also thought it could be advantageous to look average and not like a freak.

His Shoes reminded him that he had gone toe to toe with three witches and the Devil himself, and survived. He was unique but was average.

~~~

"OK, settle down. The man's gone. Can anyone tell me… forget that. It's quite a feat to come out of a coma of two weeks, get out of bed and run! Well, muscle loss is minimal, but still, it still takes some athleticism and strength at least." pronounced the doctor who had taken charge of the situation.

"Security has locked down the floor, but really, it's not a prison, and his insurance is good, so OK, he's checked himself out. So let's get back to work."

With that, the minor emergency blew over as quickly as it appeared. Besides, hospital gossip now had a juicy story for the Christmas party besides the usual 'who's doing who'.

~~~

Joan waited. "OK." she said to herself, "This is the way it is, then that's the way it is."

Accepting the situation she felt free to relax, and she passed her time in the reception area sipping a cup of coffee.

She watched passersby come and go, while she wondered whether she would fulfill her mission today and why this mission was so important.

"It must be though" she thought, "as I haven't been activated for over a century and what God asks, I do. I give. Even if it means the unthinkable… yes, murder. Who am I to question? As they say, 'God moves in mysterious ways."

As the descending dusk cast long shadows, Joan got ready to finish her job. She ascended in the elevator, stepped off its bouncing floor and made her way towards room 3116.

Feeling relieved and rewarded for her persistence, she came upon Kelly and Phil.

Joan took a good, long look at Kelly. She recognized the condition, as she had seen it before, several times, ages ago. She knew what had happened. She certainly knew the culprit and that there was nothing she could do; she had tried in the past to no avail.

The Devil's infection was incurable and terminal. Doctors didn't know what they were dealing with. Modern medicine kept her alive not knowing that her only release was death.

Joan looked at Phil.

She was going to commit a murder and she never took that lightly. She took a deep breath.

It was time. Only not Kelly's time, (even though she was the one blighted).

No, it was his time, his... Phil's.

SilverDEATH SilverDEATH SilverDEATH

SilverDEATH SilverDEATH

SilverDEATH

With the machine beeping its sad report, Joan happily left the room relishing a job well done. She jaunted down the corridor and hopped into the waiting elevator.

Things, like the man she almost collided with in the corridor, the sketchy elevator, or the obtrusive administrator and daughter no longer angered her.

She headed for the airport like an actor in the final scene of a film. "The only thing missing" she mused, "was music."

CHAPTER 9

ALL SCARED AND SHOCKED

Phillip pressed the elevator button and waited. He checked over his shoulder looking for the witch, stepped into the vacant elevator and ascended.

He moved into the corridor that led to his old room and took one last glance over his shoulder. He saw it was all clear, so he scurried down the hall.

He was about to duck into his room, when through the crack between the door and its jam, he saw the Silver Witch. Shocked, he jerked to a silent halt.

"What was she doing in there? Oh No. I think I know."

He was startled by a familiar eerie chant. A spell maybe, whatever it was, it sounded like an attack of some kind. The sound unknown to humans, reminded him of the attacks he'd fended off from the witches and the Devil.

Phillip instinctively crouched, frozen in his stance. He stood in the corridor as the witch suddenly exited his room and looked right at him. They stared at each other only briefly; enough time for Phillip to view her eyes filled with not so bright, but still powerful and deadly silver entanglement.

Without breaking her stride she continued past him hardly acknowledging his existence. At first, Phillip was baffled that she didn't seem to notice him until he realized why. Her carriage was one of someone having done a job well done.

"My God she attacked Kelly."

He dashed into the room believing that Kelly was dead. But she was still alive. He bent over and hugged her. She felt slushy, clammy and cold. She was repulsive. A black cancer encased her heart.

Only one culprit could cause this disease, the Devil. It was the Devil's Black.

Despite the disgusting appearance and smell of the infection, Phillip overcame the repulsion, puckered his lips and pecked her on the forehead. He needed to prove to himself that he was a man. And from deep inside himself, he felt warmed by his actions.

S

Rhom

n

g

A beeping sound from the opposite bed alerted Phillip to turn and look at the patient. It seemed that the man's heart had stopped.

Phillip turned and stared, "That's weird. The witch killed him... why?"

Full of questions, his eyes scanned the man's chart, "Oh my God. His name is Phil.

That's not his chart, it's mine. I must have put my chart on his bed. OH MY GOD! The witch killed him thinking he was me.

It's starting all over again."

Phillip couldn't remember exiting the room or ducking inside the one opposite. Yet he must have done so, because it was from that vantage point that he watched staff arrive obeying the summoning heart monitor.

It was turning out to be one of the most eventful days the hospital could remember. First there was a patient, Phil, who'd secretly checked himself out. Next was a misidentified patient who may have received the wrong medication, who'd passed away. And now his passing was raising those lawsuit fears that was the stuff of administrator's nightmares.

The day, however, wasn't over. While the staff fretted over Brodie's lifeless body, they were interrupted by a weak groan.

From Kelly.

"Errrererr."

"What?" said the doctor turning as Kelly uttered a weak moan. The medical team surrounded her bed and administered care. The doctors still had no idea how Phil's or Kelly's coma had manifested, nor how Phil had recovered. Now, it looked like Kelly was recovering too.

"It's a miracle. Just like Phil." the nurses whispered. The doctor, a firm atheist, did not argue.

However, it wasn't only the staff that heard Kelly's groan, so did Phillip.

"She's back, she's back." thought Phillip. He emerged from his hiding place and moved into the corridor outside her open door, just as Kelly opened her eyes for the first time.

"Arggggh. Help! Help! The Devil... it's The Devil!" shouted Kelly. Her voice was weak and her body was frail, yet, she mustered enough strength to make frantic movements in attempt to point to the entrance of her room. The doctor and nurses carefully restrained her.

"Calm down. Calm down." said the nurses reassuringly but assertively too.

"It's The Devil, Over There, Behind You... Look!" She pointed towards the open doorway, but the nurses didn't look around.

"Of course The Devil wasn't behind them!"

Luckily, for Phillip, the nurses did not look at the entrance, because he was too slow to move away. Had they turned around immediately, they would have found their lost coma patient from earlier that day.

"It's him. It's him." she cried, with more strength and volume.

Clearly, she was delirious the nurses thought. They gently wrestled with her. One of them prepared a syringe and discharged it into her arm. Kelly was unconscious again in seconds. Maybe they should have thought about it more. But patient safety was always their primary concern.

With his back flat against the opposite door, Phillip hid behind it and mulled over Kelly's accusing cries.

"Why does she think I'm the Devil?

OMG, what did the Devil do when he was in my body?

What happened from the Devil's third attack to the time I came out of the coma?" He desperately needed to know.

"But Kelly was the only one who knew. No wait, maybe Ross, Harry and the witches know. If they are alive, OMG. When I get back downstairs, I'll try calling them."

CHAPTER 10
NOTHING CAN STOP ROSS

Ross wondered if their proposed trip to Glastonbury, England would answer some questions about the miraculous union of Phil and the Shoes. A crazy notion if he hadn't witnessed unthinkable events himself two weeks earlier. Now he was a believer, not a blind faith believer but a fact-based advocate.

Phil was in and out of comas, and inexplicably Kelly had fallen into one as well. So Ross and Harry felt some urgency in investigating a strange event, in the hope that it could shed some light on their condition and hopefully even render a cure.

They were to investigate a séance that Ross believed had a strange twist to it.

He discovered that Cold Fusion apparatus had been delivered to the séance' location the same day, and he believed the purpose involved its nefarious use.

He strongly suspected that the séance was a contributing factor in that union as the timing was more than coincidental. He believed that the Shammy Leather Entanglement, the Devil's Shoe and the Psychic gathering all occurred at the same time.

"Did this confluence bring the Shoe into being?"

He had calculated the time differences between the two locations and although he couldn't prove it, he was of the mind that they happened at exactly the same time.

He was a skeptic and believed there had to be evidence yet all he had was conjecture and anecdotal hearsay. Except, of course, he knew the source for some of this subjective proof, it was himself. He had seen the evidence first hand with Phil and the Shoes and definitely, something incredible had happened that night in Salem.

So, when Boleyn told of the unbelievable occurrence the previous night, he couldn't dismiss her account.

Her bitterness when recounting the Shoes' betrayal was visceral and beyond feigning. More so Hecate's report that she'd watched the whole thing via her crystal ball although, again, anecdotal evidence. It was convincing enough.

"Phil's Shoes and their encounters with the Devil… they were not lies,but to create a new life form would surely take more."thought Ross.

Ross looked like and was a smart man. He ventured that the séance was not a coincidence. He thought more about that night of unique events and listed them off:

"Phil and his Shoes.

The Secret Séance.

And of-course the discovery, after years of failed attempts, of the Higgs particle, the God Particle."

Counting backwards from the day of the announcement, Ross realized that elusive Boson was discovered the same day that Phil and the Shoe became one.

"Chance or a contributing factor? The massive machine used in its detection had broken down the day thereafter. Was that also a coincidence?"

Ross wished he could concentrate but he was distracted by concerns over the Investigative Archaeology Team. He had invited Hecate and Boleyn to become members of the IAT, as he and Harry thought that witch expertise would be an amazing asset in discovering long lost treasures of the past; so they were wanted no matter what. The growing issue wasn't the past. It was the present.

Stripped of her witch powers, Boleyn alternated between depression and aggression, mainly aimed at Hecate. Hecate had managed to retain her witch power. She'd done it by storing her soul in Kelly before reclaiming it back as her own after the Devil was *'killed'*. Compared to Ruebella the Yellow Witch, Hecate was weak, but when compared to Boleyn, she was plain old inferior.

However, Ross and Harry didn't know that, and were impressed by Hecate's ability to cast spells. Boleyn yawned in boredom, declaring that when she was a witch, she could cast an equivalent spell ten times stronger and ten times faster. This was true. She could do them then, when she was a witch. She couldn't do them now, now she wasn't.

Although Boleyn was thankful that Ross and Harry had taken her under their wing in the Modern World, Boleyn became sour against it. Before the Devil had endowed Boleyn with Entanglement, her life had been miserable. Due to her short stature and oversized, enormous head, she was a freak show attraction in a traveling circus.

The Devil converted her into the Red Witch Boleyn, and she ruled the Earth as the most powerful witch the World had ever seen. Soaring through the skies, secure in her power and filled with vengeance, she tormented mortals with her supreme spell casting and curses. The cost of her power was the selling of her soul, and now, powerless, crazily, that cost didn't seem so high.

Often, when on her own, Boleyn would dress as a witch to reminisce.This galled her greatly as it was no longer automatic. She physically had to put the clothing on. Instead of being the mightiest of all witches, she felt she was nothing.

On the other hand, Hecate didn't wear the special robes unless they appeared magically on her when she summoned her broom. She cursed the inconvenience of having her witch's cloak envelop her when she beckoned the broom for evil purposes. She was not aware that Boleyn suffered with jealousy as Hecate possessed the powers that she no longer had.

Trying to integrate the two witches into modern society was turning out to be a difficult undertaking. Laws were to be obeyed, being a witch or ex-witch was no defense.There were consequences for breaking them.

The two lawyers delicately asked Hecate to curtail the use of spells directly aimed at harming people. After a couple of initial incidents, she suspended her murderous rampages.

Boleyn sought compensation for her loss of witch status. She wanted a gun and described how she would use it, for instance, against those who gawked and demeaned her.

"Why not?"

"Because there are laws." replied Ross and Harry many times to the despondent Boleyn. The turning point occurred when Hecate concurred with a look of superiority. Hecate treated her as if she was inferior, the same way Boleyn had looked down upon mortals. They were no longer sisters.

The make-overs to beautify and modernize the witches included cosmetic and restorative work. Ross and Harry also paid for their intensive dental work and treatments from dermatologists.

New wardrobes completed their transformation. Hecate now appeared sophisticated and modern; unlike the witch she was in reality. Boleyn's transformation was minor in comparison and left her bitter and enraged. She remained short and of course not a witch.

The buoyant Hecate was unaware of Boleyn's inner rage and still regarded her as a sister, just no longer a big sister. Unlike Hecate, Boleyn was a witch without power and thus she compensated by learning to use modern devices. She was determined to become a master.

Boleyn tested her new cellphone by calling the reticent Hecate on hers.

"It's not my fault, it's this thing." cried Hecate unable to look Boleyn in the eye.

"No it's not, look, Ross's cell is the same. Tell you what, I'll call Ross, and you answer." asserted Boleyn, feeling quite superior. She slid his cellphone across the table to the reluctant Hecate.

Just as Hecate picked up Ross's phone, it rang. "Boleyn, Boleyn is that you?" answered Hecate.

"NO." said Boleyn more annoyed, "I haven't dialed yet. Let me see."

But Hecate had pressed several buttons randomly and unknowingly had denied the call. Stunned, she looked at the screen, yet clear as day, was the image of Phil.

"Is it a call? Did I do it right?"

"It was P..." Boleyn started to reply and stopped.

"Yes, you did great, it was a telemarketer." she said which meant Boleyn had to painstakingly explain what that was. All the while, the frustrated Boleyn wanted to sit quietly and think, because Phil's picture was on the screen of the cellphone, and Hecate had no idea who he was.

CHAPTER 11

END OF AN ERA

Phillip's phone rang several times with Ross's picture filling the screen, but no one spoke. So with a sigh Phillip ended the call and thought about his next move. The hospital was beginning to feel like his second home because he had been hanging around there so much. Now, in the cafeteria, he was halfway through his second dinner as he was famished.

Seated in the corner he viewed all people coming and going. He was watchful incase the witch came back. He was deep in thought about the witch, more than a little disturbed that she had come to the hospital with the sole purpose of killing him.

"Why?" Yet, he had no idea.

"Was it the Devil's revenge? If it was, why did he wait until I was out of the coma?

It doesn't make sense… a Silver Witch, a mystery. What happened in that church?

And what of Kelly, why does she think I'm the Devil. What happened? I need to make that call.

No, I need to talk to Kelly… whether she thinks I'm the Devil or not."

With new resolve, he tried to figure out how to approach Kelly without her crying foul. He'd seen films where a fugitive clasped his hand over a victims' mouth saying 'not to scream.' It seemed so corny, but now, although it was cheap, he couldn't think of another option. He would do it tonight.

~~~

Boleyn wanted peace and quiet from Hecate who she found aggravating.

"She's got everything and yet she pesters me all the time." she bitched.

"The last couple of hours weren't a total loss however." thought Boleyn craftily. In the course of teaching Hecate how to use a telephone, she realized the incredible fact, that Hecate could not recognize Phil's face or voice. Although Boleyn had no idea right now *why,* she knew this was important.

Despite Hecate's recalcitrance, Boleyn had insisted that Hecate use a landline as practice. She told her to reply only when you recognize the person you called, because you could be talking to a con artist. Then, cunningly, she called Phil again, and this time blocked her number. She passed the phone to Hecate and coached her to listen to his response.

Phil's answer was the anticipated confused reaction, "Hello, hello, hello?"

"Remember," whispered Boleyn,"reply only if you recognize the caller. They may know your name, but they can scam you, so you must hang up without saying anything."

That's just what Hecate did. Pleased with herself, Boleyn gave her a big smile that Hecate innocently received as praise; however, she was really smiling because of the confirmation of her discovery.

Later that evening, when Ross and Harry arrived from an interview with a potential client, Hecate proudly told them of what Boleyn had taught her. They thanked Boleyn for educating Hecate on the subtle perils of the modern communication age. Later, when thinking she was out of earshot, a hopeful Ross whispered to Harry of the possibility that the IAT might jell after all, and that Hecate was adjusting well to technology.

He never mentioned Boleyn.

Boleyn erupted inside when she overheard this conversation, and it was all she could do to hide her consuming hatred for Hecate, the IAT, the Devil, and for Phil.

She was pleased with herself for keeping it secret that Phil was no longer in a coma. But at night while in bed, she mulled over the state of affairs. Phil would surely try to contact Ross and Harry again, and she would not be in possession of his phone this time.

"The best thing to do would be to say that I phoned Phil by accident and found out that he was out of his coma." rationalized Boleyn, "and that Hecate and I should go and visit him."

~~~

Phillip went to the washroom in an attempt to settle his nerves. He looked at himself in the mirror and considered the things that could go wrong.

"She could scream and alert the staff thinking I'm the Devil, and… that's about it. If she does, I'll run. I guess. Well what else can I do? Nothing."

He chose the stairwell over the elevator, scouted out the corridor, skipped down the hall and dove into her room. This morning, she had two companions in her room and now she was all alone. Exactly what he needed.

He crouched down beside her with his hand ready to stop her from screaming, he whispered her name. She showed no reaction, so he gently shook her. Eventually Kelly started to regain consciousness.

Her eyes opened to see 'Phil's' face right in front of hers. Her reaction was expected, she was scared out of her skin. Phillip quickly clasped his free hand over her mouth and pressed as hard as he dared.

Confined by the bed sheets, she couldn't move her arms freely. Nonetheless, she struggled and writhed. Phillip was scared that he would hurt her so he let go.

"HELP." whimpered Kelly, so softly that it did not raise any attention.

But it did mean she still believed he was the Devil. Unwilling to use any more force, he dashed out of the room and fled down the stairwell as Kelly's voice got louder and louder. Still running, he got into his car and shot onto the open road.

"Well that was useless, totally. I can't really think of anything else I could have done other than that, but what a stupid idea."

~~~

Kelly saw Phillip leave the hospital room like a frightened mouse, and for a moment, she thought that it was Phil and not the Devil.

"Fool me once..." she whispered to herself. "He pretended he was Phil when he came out of that coma, but he wasn't. It was the Devil. He raped me, tortured me, and killed me, well maybe? I don't know, but I'll never trust Phil again. I can't, because he could always be the Devil in disguise. Sure did look and act like Phil though."

She stopped thinking about him, for a brief moment, until her mind wandered back.

"That stupid move was just the sort of thing that Phil would do, and maybe the Devil knows that... I saw his eyes; they looked like Phil's before all this started. If it was Phil, what happened to him? What happened to the Devil if he was inside Phil... he just left and let Phil live? I can't believe that! He must be the Devil, who else can it be? Can't be Phil. Can't be. Damn, now I'm too scared to go to sleep? I'm getting up."

Kelly tried to get up, but she was so weak she collapsed onto the bed and began to cry

"Phil, you stupid idiot, are you Phil or not? How can I tell? You hurt me so bad. Is it you?"

Although she was haunted by memories, she gathered enough courage to take the initiative.

"I must be crazy, but I'm going to call him."

~~~

Phillip drove without any destination in mind, sticking to the narrow, country roads on the outskirts of town. One particular road turned into a gravel track with multiple forks. Typical of Phil to take all the wrong turns. It soon stopped at a grassy dead end.

"Actually, this is OK." Demanding himself to be positive.

He hoped the solitude and isolation might do him good so he got out of the car and walked. Under a mottled moonlit sky, he strolled down a dirty wet deer track through some fields with his ghostly pale shadow following close behind. He contemplated Kelly's reactions while all the time trying to remain upbeat. He ambled across a crumbling stone bridge and looked at the silhouette of a ruin that he instantly recognized.

He was startled to find he had come to ClearStream, the beginning of everything.

Forgetting Kelly, he hastened his pace and was soon walking among the ruins. Naturally, he looked for the church in which he battled the Devil. If anything were to trigger any lost memories, surely this would be it.

With anticipation he entered the town square only to be shocked at what he saw. The church no longer existed, and in its place, tumbled the ClearStream River over a small rocky step and into a long pool shaped like a lightning bolt.

"Where's the church, and where did this pond come from?" queried a perplexed Phillip. More questions flooded his mind about the events of the past week. He needed answers and Kelly had them. Torn between her and the present venture, he set about to explore the hamlet's signature feature, the river bed, seeking to uncover clues to his forgotten memories.

The old, now dry, stone riverbed stretched the length of the town and divided it into two halves. Patches of dry crumbling weed rotted in the cracks of the huge stone pavers and river walls. Rusted and old iron channel gates held back nothing other than mounds of piled up river stones.

Clambering over and around the first redundant sleuth gate brought him a joy he had forgotten. His delight increased as the sound of the river changed. Phillip looked up to see that the river had filled up the lightning bolt shaped pool and was starting to spill into its original path down the sleuth gates.

"Wow, what luck."

He scrambled to the best vantage point and watched the river tumble over the first gate as it started to fill up the basin underneath it. Overjoyed he ran down the nine steps of the ClearStream river system, like a child following a boat down a set of locks.

He stopped at each basin to savor its replenishment. When he reached the bottom, he looked up at the shining cascade of water falls.

Here at the last basin, he noticed something odd. Off to one side was a tomblike hole. Immersed in his curiosity and unaware of the raindrops falling, he climbed into it. Suddenly brimming with questions, he stared at what seemed like strange runes carved into one of the large pavers. The falling raindrops heightened their definition.

"Wow, look at that." he paused, struck by the sight.

He scurried over the pavers on his hands and knees, but not knowing their full extent, his little finger unknowingly touched them. The images suddenly vanished as if he'd just got in the way of the light.

"But it's not that, because it's stopped raining and the moon has just come out, so it's definitely brighter than before, yet I can't see them."

Still crawling, he started to feel around for their presence, but incredibly, he felt nothing. The stone was silky smooth. The moon ducked behind another cloud and provided no further illumination.

To Phillip's chagrin, the runes failed to re-materialize contrary to what he expected. He was dumfounded. Now there was no moonlight and still no runes. He tried to commit to memory the exact location by running his hands over the rock.

"Here. Sorry." hoping for forgiveness, he looked to the sky and took a double take.

It was infinite.

He felt its weight on his open hands.

Heavy, so heavy it was pressing down upon them.

He thought his palms might be impaled like the Christ.

He didn't care.

He could see the stars and the galaxies.

He could see the blackness and see the emptiness.

He could see the space.

He could see space.

Left. Right. Up. Down.

Back. Forth.

He could see the time.

He could see time.

Past. Future. Present.

He saw light hurry into the future.

It would be lost in its vastness.

It would never reach its outer edge.

He knew up there was God.

He knew he was here on Earth.

He knew there was a Hell.

He knew there was the Devil.

He knew he was Phillip.

Yes, he knew he was Phillip.

Looking up, since the first time he'd come out of his coma, caused him to feel his true self. It was like a vale was lifted from his eyes. His long gaze into space cleared his mind, and allowed his new self to deny the old.

He was Phillip.

And Phillip had seen something.

He looked deep into a hole in the night sky and saw what his eyes couldn't see. Almost having to hold onto the ground for fear of falling in, his mind saw, at the edge of sight and on the boundary of vision, what no mortal had seen and what no man knew. It revealed the horizon of the war between the Devil and God. He saw the walls of the Devil's Jail and the edge of God's Power. He didn't know it, but what he had seen was the boundary of the Entanglement War.

The river's descent over the steps was complete, and its overflow dribbled over the basin wall into the trough. The distraction halted Phillip's sight of the war above. Still standing in the dugout, he climbed out hoping his visions weren't his imagination.

Sitting with bare feet dangling in the fresh clean sparkling water, he sat like a little boy. Like a baptism, the river water washed away all fears and doubts. His mind churned over the meaning of the runes and the edge of the sky. They were real, he knew it and threw doubt aside. The rain stopped again, leaving him in a rare place of harmony and profound deliberation.

An hour passed before he returned to reality, woken by his numbing feet. Without a thought, his Shoes were back on and memories returned, flooding through his mind like a tsunami. And riding the crest was Kelly.

"I think I love her, but what's the point of even going there, she would never love me, a man like me, Phil. Or even the new me, Phillip." he said. "Yet, I think I do love her."

"Why, why, why does she think I'm the Devil? His phone rang.

"Phil?"

"Yes Kelly, yes it's me, Phillip." he answered in a sweat, not hiding his desperation.

"Phillip?" she questioned.

"Phil." he responded, reluctantly using his old name.

"Phil, listen, at, at the hospital, I, I, you know." Kelly didn't know what to say now she'd called.

"There's a witch after me, a Silver Witch, she ki…" he blurted out, not knowing what to say either.

"Yea. Right. Why would a witch be after you? YOU'RE THE DEVIL." She swiftly cut him off and hung up.

"I heard." Phillip whispered to the dead phone and bowed his head deflated and consumed with self -pity, a behavior that was all too familiar to him. He mourned the loss of Kelly and her companionship, which now seemed to be one way. He felt the worst since his reawakening.

" Why did the Devil choose to come to ClearStream?" he wondered looking up at the steps of the sleuth gates.

His phone rang again. "Phil?" asked a woman's voice. "Yes." replied Phillip.

"It's Boleyn."

CHAPTER 12

NIT WIT

Surprised he answered, "Boleyn! Err. How are you?"

"Fine," she said, "how are you?"

"I'm good, but you're not a witch now, right?" asked Phillip. The phone clicked off with a bang, conveying to Phillip his utter lack of tact.

"Sigh. Nothing's changed. I'm still an idiot. I guess I touched a nerve."

Acutely stung by Phil's obtuse bluntness, Boleyn locked herself in the washroom fearing to be seen crying. She was furious and feeling particularly insecure. The ill feelings about her shortcomings were raw and painful.

"I'll kill Phil, I swear."

"Two hang ups inside five minutes, that's a record even for me." mumbled Phil with a feigned laugh.

His time at ClearStream was up. Cloud cover moved in, light rain drops fell, and without moonlight to aid him he painstakingly returned to his car, He fell asleep curled up in the back seat, only to be rudely awakened by his cell phone.

"Phil?"

"Yes. Hi Kelly."

"Are you the Devil?" she said directly.

"No, I'm not." he replied, and said nothing else.

After a lengthy pause, Kelly replied, "How do I know you're not?"

Phillip decided to take his time to reply, as he needed to know why she thought he was the Devil.

"I'm not sure if I can prove that I'm not, I'm just Phil. Sorry, that's a lie, I'm Phillip. Don't ask me why, 'cos I don't know why, I just am, Phillip."

There was silence followed by a quiet click.

"Three." he thought, you're a frigging record breaker. Moments later, the phone rang again.

"What do you mean, Phil? You're Phillip? What does that mean?"

"I don't know why, but now I'm Phillip. The Shoes..." she hung up again,

"Four."

This time there was no callback. Phillip's eyes welled up. His dogmatic insistence to be honest had driven her away. When she was mad at him in the past, she swore and insulted him, but this last call was flat and un-emotive. It seemed obvious that she didn't want anything to do with him. And still he didn't know what had happened, or what to do.

"I hate myself. Why? ...trying to be too considerate, to be too perfect. That was Phil, but now I'm supposed to be Phillip, I am Phillip. I'll be committed if I don't wise up soon, but... I'm just trying, to be... I don't know. Nice. Honest. Decent. I guess. Loved. The World sucks. I think... No it does...

Better be big rather than small.

BIG eats little.

Size DOES matter.

Even in families, even with brothers.

Right down to Bill."

Phil's rambling thoughts continued to plague him.

"Be first, or you're nothing.

Winning is all that counts.

In everything.

It's what's on the outside that counts, not what's on the inside.

Tell me I'm wrong.

Shut up Phil. Phillip. SHUT UP.

I'm Phillip, for better or worse.

So what if I accidently hurt Boleyn?

So what if the World sucks. Really?

I'm doing all right.

Hey I know who I am. Hey, I'm Phillip, that's a start."

~~~

Kelly had put her cellphone down and turned it off in case Phil,"PhilLIP as he wants to be called now, the Devil as I call him" wanted to call back.

In the morning she couldn't recall if she dreamt or not, a good sign, and she felt stronger and better, another. With one day or two left in the hospital, and two new patients in her ward she felt secure against the Devil (Phil), a false sense as unknown to her, the previous patient had been murdered.

Although she never wanted to see Phil again, she wondered where he was and what he was doing. Contrarily, she hoped he'd appear, when there were many people around, so she could publicly taunt him, like she'd done so many times before. Not that she ever needed a reason to justifying her bullying in the past, but now there was a big one, "Phil? Phillip? Really?"

"Does he think I'm daft? Where the hell was he all day anyway, and why hasn't he called? Not that I want the Devil... if he is, to call. Maybe he isn't the Devil after all... the Devil would have called, I think. Maybe I should call again, I think he is Phil. Not that I care about him..."

The whole day vanished. It became evening and progressed into night. Kelly's daytime bravado had diminished and Phil became more the Devil in her mind with every passing second.

"He hasn't turned up today, so he will tonight. That proves he is the Devil. Tonight, OMG, The Devil's going to come tonight, I should have called... er... I've gotta get out of here."

Overcome with panic and strengthened by an adrenalin rush, she clambered out of bed, threw on her clothes and walked swiftly towards the elevator. She didn't stop walking until the outside door swung shut.

"Safe. I think."

The cool night air bought another hurdle to her attention. She had nowhere to go, and no transport either.

"OMG, that's right, Phil did all the driving, oh look. A cab." "Where you heading there Lady?"

"The farthest hotel from here."

Kelly checked in at the only hotel in the town. Fearing being alone and being stalked by the Devil, she went downstairs to the cocktail bar after dinner. Cautiously, she sat on a stool at the counter and impatiently waited for service, that didn't appear. She... Wait... Never.

Kelly stomped out of the hotel and headed down Main Street to a dingy looking disco-bar the taxi had passed a couple of blocks back. She thought she was safe as she'd never heard of Phil ever going to a drinking establishment, actually, anywhere. "Nerd."

Kelly seated herself on a stool at the end of the bar with a view of the entrance and ordered a drink. It wasn't long before she became uncomfortable with the smoke and the incessant ogling of the male patrons. She pushed her drink away, picked up her handbag and headed for the exit.

Feeling lonely and full of indecision, Phillip had pondered what to do. He desperately needed a distraction. So despite his better judgment and going against his character, he went to a pub. He didn't dream that he'd end up crashing into Kelly in the doorway of a random bar, but life is full of surprises.

"Sorry. Oh. KELLY?" Phillip cried out in disbelief as their shoulders collided in the narrow entrance.

"PHIL. ARGH. THE DEVIL." shrieked Kelly, bolting towards the parking lot. Naturally, Phillip ran after her, until a bottle smashed over his head from behind.

~~~

Joan went to sleep that night hoping for dreams filled with thanks and recognition from none other than God herself. Instead her mind was swimming with doubt and disappointment. She awoke the following morning hurting and embarrassed. There was little doubt that she had screwed up, she'd killed the wrong person. She defended herself against God's anger whose perception and knowledge of her actions, she said, was distorted by the Entanglement War. But who could withstand God's judgment. No one. After a chastising from God, understandably Joan was in a particularly bad mood.

"And, why didn't she tell me that if Kelly was found in a Devil induced coma that I was supposed to also kill her... like I'm supposed to be psychic for God's sake? And after all that frigging trouble in getting there too... Christ, I still don't get it... she keeps harking on about this Phil character and the Devil and suggesting the Devil may have taken him!! Like what the hell, isn't she supposed to know?"

Joan rarely was in a bad mood, possibly because of her history, possibly because she was guaranteed a place in Heaven.

She had been transformed from a witch to a saint, and as Saint Joan was the only saint, living, dead or reputed. God's work. Not the Devil's. He had spawned several witches; green, yellow and red, but none were like Joan.

The Devil was filled with joy and despair. He knew he would never be able to channel Entanglement so purely again. He'd watched his Entanglement sizzle inside of her quaking body. She was so receptive, but too passionate. Her heart stopped. She collapsed in a broken lifeless heap at his feet.

"She's obviously dead."

Only she wasn't.

Later, when a moment of curiosity overcame him, he discovered his error. He went to summon her from Hell, only to learn she'd never been there.

While the Devil was scouring the eighth circle of Hell in a vain hope of finding her, a dormant spark of life relit in Joan and she gained consciousness and memory.

Filled with remorse and repentance, she sought the light of God and renounced the Devil. In forgiveness, God received her confession personally. Then *she* inverted her Entanglement and Saint Joan was born. God wasn't going to look a gift horse in the mouth, *she* needed an agent on Earth, and the Devil's miscalculation had given her one such advocate.

It was not without cost. When the Devil discovered this, he was understandably enraged. He ranted at God but with no means of recourse, he openly vowed to kill Joan when the chance presented itself and to imprison her in the newly christened Gray Eighth Level of Hell, now reserved solely for her. "Traitor!"

Since that time, Joan was on constant alert for any sign of the Devil. She had close calls of course, but had managed to stay shrewdly undetected and out of harm's way for centuries. The last two hundred years had been wonderful as she never felt his presence, not until last week, when she felt a roar of ill wind sweep over the World.

From where ever he was, he was back.

Maybe this was the reason she had a bad feeling with this new mission. Or maybe it was the twinge of panic she'd thought she'd detected in God's summons that made her feel this way. She didn't care if she didn't know its source, she felt it nonetheless, a sense of apprehension and foreboding.

It had the stench of the Devil, of bad luck, of something that she had no idea what, but she didn't like it. She sighed with resignation that there was nothing she could do but obey. Joan turned round and headed back to Evelyn Mills, and this time Phil, 'If he exists.' won't be so lucky. She hoped anyway, because the bad feeling was mounting.

CHAPTER 13

EVENTUALLY YOU HAVE TO FIGHT

Basher and his twin brother Smasher were bad news in Evelyn Mills. They were well known to the authorities for petty crime and brawling. The youngest brother, Buster, idolized his twin brothers and kept their hunting cabin ready for their illicit poaching expeditions. The three were avoided by most people unless they could outnumber and out arm them. The most obtuse excuse, for example, a wayward glance or cutting them off on the road was worthy of their revenge.

When exiting the sales lot in his new car, Phillip had almost hit them in their truck.

He was made.

Smasher recognized Phillip chasing after Kelly in the bar's parking lot. As she rushed to evade Phillip, Kelly heard the bottle shatter over his head. It sounded venomous, but instead felt more motivated than ever to escape. Walking as fast as possible, she closed her mind to his screams of pain not caring about the harm befalling him.

To the twin's glee the bottle hadn't felled their victim who miraculously remained on his feet. The two set about raining a monsoon of fists upon their prey before he toppled to the ground. The deluge of blows continued, and yet Phillip struggled despite all this, to get back up. Not to fight, that's not Phillip, but to run. The twins redoubled their assault, pummeling him mercilessly in their endeavor to end Phillip's conceived escape.

With the suddenness and surprise of the assault, it took Phillip several moments to comprehend what was happening. In addition, he was dazed from the smashed bottle. But who realizes a full-fledged assault is upon them when not expecting it and for no apparent reason. As the beat down continued, a feeling welled up from below and filled his mind and body, one of injustice. Almost oblivious to the pain, this feeling grew, clarified and took form.

R

h

Song

m

All he had to do was release it, but he didn't want to. He knew whatever it was, that it wasn't going to be good for his assailants. Yet they persisted, opposing his attempt to admit defeat, run and escape.

Denied the humiliation of losing, Phillip naturally wondered if they were intent on his death. They weren't to know that their unjustified malice of their continuing attack sealed their fate.

He discharged whatever it was. Nothing obvious happened, but then the twins' attack started to dissipate until only verbal taunts interrupted their heavy exhausted breathing. It was finally over.

Basher and Smasher too stupid to realize that their ferocious beating, inflicted upon any other man would have rendered them in jail for murder, continued to shove and push Phillip over as he struggled to gain his feet. And as the bloodied, bruised, but amazingly not broken Phillip drove away, they high fived each other and entered the bar pleased as punch.

"Smasher. You gave that mother such a beating." "What, yeah, you too bro. *Ass h ole.* HAH."

"Ha, ha ha."

"Yeah. Ha Ha Ha. Hey Basher, why you speakhing funny?"

"DrunOk"

"Yeah, greatO." They dismissed their speech as drunkenness, clinked glasses and called Buster to tell him about the fun he'd missed.

Feeling safer, Kelly sat in the empty hotel lounge and started to think about Phillip. She recalled the screaming but rationalized if it was the Devil, he could handle it. If it was Phil, she thought without guilt, he deserved what he got.

She didn't mind waiting now, and the voices she heard, a man and a woman's in the reception area belonged to staff. She relaxed and waited patiently, until the bartender served her. He was clearly gay and not responsive to her good looks, which put Kelly at ease and lighthearted chatter consumed the night.

"You know." she said to him,"I know that you're, err not into me." "You mean I'm gay." he laughed easily.

"Yes, yes, but, and of course I respect that, that… What I'm trying to say is that… Well would you stay, with me tonight? Not like that, no, I just, well I don't want to be alone; that's all."

Kelly made up a story of an ex-boyfriend who was stalking her, all quite true except Phil wasn't her boyfriend. Eventually Chris reluctantly agreed and they retired to the same room in separate beds.

"Thank you, Chris." said Kelly turning off her bedside lamp, feeling truly safe for the first time that night.

"You're welcome, Kelly." replied Chris before continuing, "You know it's been a funny night. We never have single women staying here, and yet tonight we have two. You of course, and while you were waiting there in the bar, another older woman, gray eyes and gray, almost silver I'd say, hair, checked in. She…"

Kelly's eyes opened like 'a jack in a box.'

She didn't sleep a wink. Her night was filled with unrelenting thoughts that tortured her mind. She thought of Phil, Phillip, was he the Devil or not, but mainly about the Silver Witch.

"If he was the Devil, then why was a Silver Witch after him, 'course, that could be a ruse just to lure me out and kill me. But then Chris had said that a woman, a gray woman had just checked in. Witches don't use hotels… that I know… must be a coincidence, OMG, I'm so scared and alone."

She silently cried herself to sleep, like she had in the past. After a fitful night of tossing and turning, Kelly woke up to find that Chris was gone.

"Was it just moments ago, or, when?" she squealed. She hadn't heard him leave.

"Could he be dead?"

"The bastard, he could have at least woken me up to tell me he was going." blurted Kelly as her initial fear turned to anger, and Kelly was out of bed cursing the World, Phil, Phillip, whoever.

"YOU. You should have wok..." said Kelly to Chris who was smiling in front of her ready to take her breakfast order.

Chris whispered back, "You and Phil have to talk Kelly. It's no good talking to me in your sleep thinking I'm him. You have trust issues. Well... we have scrambled eggs, eggs beni..."

~~~

Painfully, Phillip slowly found his way back to the secluded spot close to ClearStream, the only place he felt safe. Cleverly, he had taken special care to remember the way when he first ventured into Evelyn Mills. Now he took special care to make sure no one was following. People, not the Witch.

Too beaten up to realize that he shouldn't be alive, Phillip had slept the night in a healing deep and restoring slumber.

In the morning, Phil attempted to remove many thoughts from his mind. The distant past, the recent two weeks and the previous night, leaving Kelly's image the center of his focus. Ridding Kelly from his mind left the image of the Silver Witch. Finally he felt almost saved when the thoughts of hunger gained control.

He checked himself over, to find he was actually unscathed. "Remarkable. I think... I think that I've... I don't know, become tougher?"

Phillip found his way into Evelyn Mills and gorged at a diner while he pondered last night's lesson. Be prepared.

So he bought camping provisions and canned food. If he was going to investigate ClearStream in depth, he was going to have to stay there a while. "Be prepared. Be prepared. Be prepared."

It was late in the day before Phillip, armed with a backpack of supplies, found a suitable spot at the grassy dead end and put up his brand new four-person tent. (Still wishing that Kelly would join him).

His extraordinary healing, the encounter with his two attackers, were forgotten. He looked forward to a night of discovery in ClearStream, which didn't materialize as steady rain moved in from the west.

With the background pitter-patter, Phillip reflected on the events of the last three weeks, the only part of his life that counted. His life before, as a reporter and as Bill's younger brother, was mundane and meaningless. He was no longer that Phil. Phillip was his new identity and he needed to prove to himself that he was different.

Next thing he knew he was swamped with thoughts about the Silver Witch, then visions of the Devil's Black encasing Kelly's heart.

He considered how he perceived Entanglement, and how he didn't see it as much as he felt it. While he pondered if this was an important detail, he kept thinking that when he saw Kelly come out of her coma, that he didn't see the Devil's Black in her any longer.

"It's true, it had gone, what made it go?" He had another question too.

"What made the Devil choose ClearStream?"

~~~

Basher and Smasher returned home. Basher to his girlfriend and their five-year-old son, and Smasher to his adjacent trailer. Neither was bothered by the evening's events, yet they couldn't sleep because their minds were filled with the sounds and sights of the letters:

R H O M S O N G

With eyes open or closed, or putting their hands over their ears; nothing stopped them. To Basher the night was an eternity, so he decided to get out of bed and check in the mirror for what tasted like blood.

He managed with unusual difficulty to swing his legs over the edge of the bed but when he stood up, his legs buckled underneath him. His partner accused him of drunkenness and his response was a punch that missed by a mile. He stumbled outside to find his brother.

"smaRasHe. ssOommthing's happend to Me. SOmmthiNG." he hollered as he burst through the door to his brother's trailer, and fell to the floor.

"mmeee tooooo. bussteRr. HOws MiS lOks. Nots Goods"

When Smasher tried to sit up in bed, he buckled over and banged his forehead on his knee that was jerking upwards. In the dim light, they could see that they were both bleeding around their mouths from biting their tongues.

"HHHOOOOOSSSSSSSpital."

Dressed only in long johns and unable to walk, they crawled to the truck and pulled themselves into the cabin. It was impossible for either one to drive so they tried to do it together. Smasher used his elbow to move the gear lever into drive, and Basher used his hand to guide his foot onto the accelerator. They managed to drive a quarter of a mile before fatally crashing into a brick wall.

Police couldn't figure out how two of the toughest brutes died in a collision at the speed of five miles an hour. The truck was hardly dented and its engine was still running. Alcohol poisoning was assumed the cause of death for these twenty-three-year-old twins mourned by no one. Except Buster.

CHAPTER 14

MURDER ON HER MIND

With new resolve, St. Joan entered Evelyn Mill's city limits and took a cab directly to the hospital as she swore this time things were going to be very different. Defiantly she swung the yellow car door shut with a bang and strode into the hospital full of purpose. She had thought to ask the cabby to wait as she wasn't going to be long, but before she had a chance, the car had zipped forward to pick up another fare.

"Who cares, I'll get another when I'm done."

Everything seemed right this time, the elevator was waiting and she was at the room's entrance in no time. It was all for nothing, because neither Phil nor Kelly were there.

"What? Oh dear God. She must have died. I'll ask the front desk just to confirm."

"What." said the nurse helpfully, "she's not in her room?" "No." was Joan's abrupt reply. "She's not dead, is she?"

"Well I don't think so. There's nothing here." The nurse replied flipping through a clipboard. A moment later she confirmed it over the phone, "Well another runner, we've had a couple this week."

"Oh," said Joan, "so Kelly's alive?"

"Well I guess so." said the nurse fed up with the constant inquiring.

Joan stood still and considered that incredibly Kelly had come out of her black hole. Joan had witnessed it and saw how bad it was,

"Then suddenly, by God, was well enough to leave? Not Possible. Sometimes even God can't bring someone out of the Devil's diabolical black, only death can." she recalled thinking.

"So, is there anything else I can help you with?" said the nurse, hoping she would leave.

"No. No. Oh. Thank you, sorry, so Kelly's not here?"

"NO and not dead either." and she turned to address a coffee pot in need of urgent attention.

"Oh Wait. You said you had a couple of runners lately, who was the other?"

"Phil." was the curt reply.

Joan checked into The Evelyn Mills Hotel and tried to sleep. She dreamed to God, filing her report and receiving her commands. After she woke in the morning, she worried about how unusual it was for her to have no idea of what was going on in God's head.

"Maybe God doesn't know or can't foresee everything. I'm pretty sure I was first to confirm that Phil was alive, and that Kelly had recovered. If she had known, surely God wouldn't have sounded so taken back. So now she's telling me to do them in, even if it means that I have to sacrifice my own life. That sucks. I've also got to remain hidden from the Devil for if he finds me my penalty is Hell. Kill Phil and Kelly, in secret, and not have the Devil find out? Highly unlikely. That means only one thing. If I'm captured, I'd better commit suicide quickly, because no one can withstand the Devil.

At least she didn't chew me out too much about not killing Kelly. Maybe she realized that if she'd wanted it done, then she should have said so."

Feeling vindicated, Joan set about the mission of the highest urgency she had ever received. God really meant business.

"Where do I start, I have no idea where Phil is and I've lost Kelly. Well I better get started, and get some breakfast." Joan set about getting ready more motivated than ever. Fear for your life has that effect. To God this was the only mission in town, and Joan was the point person.

At the hotel café, Chris, who she had met the previous night, was just passing through the entranceway and greeted her brightly.

"Hi."

"Hi." she replied.

"We have another single lady here, she's over there. Would you like me to introduce you?"

"Not normally but, well, O…" started Joan's automatic reply until she turned her head and saw who it was. It was Kelly.

"NO. I mean no, I've… left something in my room, excuse me, oh, thank you Chris." reading his nametag. And she left to go back to her room in a hurry,"What a stroke of luck." Joan needed to think how to make it work.

"Weird." mentioned Chris to Kelly when he was waiting her table.

"What's weird Chris?" responded Kelly,

"OH, nothing, just that I saw that other woman who checked in last night."

"Go on." said Kelly suddenly more than alarmed.

"Well I just bumped into her and I suggested that you and her sit at the same table. The weird thing was, as soon as she saw you, she went back to her room."

To Chris' disbelief, he'd only got through half of his sentence and Kelly had already stood up and was asking to check out.

"Kelly. What's happened?" asked Chris. "Give me my bill." she demanded. "Ok, Ok."

Kelly grabbed it out of his hand, signed it, and left the building in lightning speed.

Joan composed herself in front of the room's mirror. This was such a lucky break, so she role played a few scenarios of introduction before going back downstairs and finding Chris.

"Ok. I've… freshened up, please. Why not introduce me to this other lady." said Joan.

"She's gone. Left just like that. Weird. As soon as I mentioned you, she… said she was late for something." he lied. He really wanted to say that she turned white as if she'd seen a ghost, but he wasn't cruel and he thought telling her such a thing would be just that.

Joan was frantic, but hoped she hid it and thus casually asked what Kelly was late for. And then a flood of other questions involuntarily spewed forth uncontrollably as she fought off panic.

Hardly trying to conceal her own haste, Joan said she had some new business to take care of and that she should be checking out too.

Chris hadn't been able to answer any of Joan's nonstop questions and was now completely confused. Her interrogation continued even as he bent down and tore her bill off the printer. While his back was turned, Joan saw and stuffed Kelly's forgotten bill into her handbag with Chris being none the wiser.

"That was lucky." she thought, knowing she messed up by letting Kelly get away. Chris watched Joan disappear out the front doors, and then he wondered how she knew Kelly's name? Then he thanked God he was gay.

The taxi stand outside the hotel was deserted."Typical." While she waited, she went over in her mind the location spell that she'd use to find Kelly. She felt sure it could be done using information from the bill, or just the bill itself. But also…

"Why did Kelly run?" she wondered swearing at her bad luck in losing her.

"Did she know that I'm a saint? Who could have told her? How could she have known? She didn't see me and I saw her, and in that fraction of a second… I could tell she no longer has Entanglement so she wouldn't be able to see mine.The element of surprise is gone. I need help… I need a car."

"Business has been good lately." said honest Jimmy, and it was true. He was surprised when this elderly lady knew what she wanted, made up her mind, and purchased her car quickly and easily.

"Really?" said the lady, "Let me guess, tall, blond, good looking just bought one earlier."

"No... but the day before, I sold the same car to a guy who seemed like he was in a hurry, just like you. Anyway... I like it when people know what they want!"

"Well really, what did this guy look like?" "Well, just a little younger than you..." "Phil?" Joan suggested.

"Yea, No, hey, I don't give out personal info. No. Just a middle-aged man from out-a-town. So how's you're paying?"

"So Phil's bought the same car as me." thought Joan, "If it's anything like mine, he can't get far. Ha. Anyway, all I have to do is figure out where Kelly is, and she'll lead me to Phil."

Joan wore a large cross, which was a variation on the sign of the female – a circle bisected by the vertical staff of the cross below. She removed it from around her neck and placed it on Kelly's receipt. Then she recited a prayer:

Mother above, Earth below,
Let the location of Kelly flow.
Through this cross, Reap and sow,
Show me the way, as I don't know.
AhWomen.

Joan placed the cross back around her neck, where it had been for half a millennium and felt a slight pressure on her skin. It indicated that Kelly was behind her. So she turned round. It confirmed Kelly's direction as the cross rose. Then she pledged she wasn't going to get away this time.

CHAPTER 15

YOU MEAN MEN

Boleyn had to be careful not to isolate herself. She needed to continue to be seen as a team player to Ross and Harry, thus she planned to tell them that Phil was alive at an opportune time. So she hung outside their boardroom and listened to them on the phone, until Harry beckoned her. When she entered Ross and Harry both looked down at her with accusing eyes.

"How did they know it was me outside? Of course, my silhouette is unmistakable."

"They know." thought Boleyn as her heart sank. "Phil had called them and now they know I hid this information from them. They have found me out and I will be ostracized."

"So you know Phil is alive, Boleyn? How come you didn't tell us? And there's something else you're not telling us, isn't there?"

"Do they know that Hecate can't recognize Phil too?" she thought. "The Silver Witch?" rifled Harry at the stunned and bewildered Boleyn.

"What?" cried Boleyn as the guilt-laden tears welled up in her eyes. "What do you know about the *Silver Witch?*" pressed Ross.

"What Silver Witch? No, Nothing, Honest." denied Boleyn relieved that they didn't know her other secret.

"Really?" insisted Ross, he could see she was hiding something. "Yes, no, I've never heard of one." she said, telling the truth. "Hecate?" asked Boleyn, hoping to deflect attention from her
and hoping also that she didn't know. She shook her head.

"Fine, Boleyn. Thanks." dismissed Ross, "Oh, do you have anything else you'd like to tell us?"

"No." replied Boleyn, more eager to get away than to be forthcoming with her last secret, and with Hecate innocently standing there not knowing that she was that secret.

"Kelly sounds so scared, eh Ross?" said Harry to Ross as they discussed the earlier phone conversation they'd had with her.

"Yea. Harry." replied Ross, "Can't imagine. The poor thing."

"The poor thing! She's tall and gorgeous, everyone loves her, and now the 'poor little thing' is scared, aw." mumbled Boleyn in anger and despair, overhearing the conversation that continued in the boardroom.

Despite what she thought, Ross and Harry didn't want to hurt her. They just wanted everyone to get along and do their job. Nor were they mean; they were just completely oblivious of the real issue bothering her or how close it was to erupting. So in ignorance, they returned to the juicy topics their long discussion with Kelly had presented.

The main point was the miraculous revival of Phil and his, as the Devil, attack upon Kelly. Clearly the Devil was not dead, which didn't surprise them either, rather they thought that he was trapped in John Abbott the First's grave, what with all the shoes that were in there.

The remaining inscription on the broken gravestone's epitaph "The Devil" seemed so perfect it could only be the work of God, whom they now believed existed. A reversal in thought for two former atheists.

They pondered over many questions and concerns like... What of Phil? Was he dead and possessed by the Devil? Or was he just plain old Phil again? And who was the Silver Witch?

Every answer Kelly provided was replaced by many more questions. They agreed with Kelly that the sooner Ross and Harry and the IAT got to Evelyn Mills the better.

As for Boleyn, she wasn't too unhappy to have her secret undisclosed, but realized she had lost trust with Harry and Ross.

And in this modern *witchpowerless* World, she needed the IAT to survive. Of her other secret?

"I'll tell them when I get the chance, when Hecate isn't there." she vowed,"At least she didn't know about the Silver Witch either, thank God."

"Hecate, Boleyn, pack a travel bag. We're going to Evelyn Mills, now. You Ok Boleyn?" said Ross.

"Course she is." replied Hecate, "she's my sister, I'll look after her." She placed her arm over Boleyn's shoulder, a Boleyn who was ready to explode.

~~~

Kelly put the phone down and breathed for what seemed like the first time since breakfast. The cab had dropped her off at a busy cafe where she lingered over several coffees. She received a text from Ross just after noon, and it was then that she realized how tense she was.

It was only after she knew that the IAT was on their way that her shoulders relaxed.The request that she rent a vehicle didn't make sense. Nonetheless, she made her way towards Honest Jimmy's, not knowing that she was being followed.

From a distance, Joan couldn't believe that Kelly was looking at the largest SUV Jimmy had in stock. Sales had been so good for Jimmy lately that he was beaming.

"What's the matter?" she asked, but she wanted to say how obnoxious he was.

"Excuse me Kelly, I am sorry but it's been so busy here these last couple of days. First this guy buys a car, like in ten minutes. Then this morning, an elderly lady buys the same car, then…"

"What man bought a car? What did he look like? Was he dreary and dull? And the woman, was she older with gray eyes and silver hair?" interrupted Kelly without caring how rude she was.

"Yea, said her name was Joan. Nice old girl…"

Kelly could have fainted where she stood. The World had gone mad and she was scared she was going with it.

"Give me the God damn car."

"Sold." said Jimmy brimming so widely it must have hurt.

She drove to the small airstrip a couple of counties away still unaware of the tail. By using the locating cross, Joan was able to follow her from a couple miles back. Her hunch was that Kelly was heading towards Phil, and then she'll kill them both.

With obvious relief, Kelly greeted the IAT as they hopped out of the small Cessna that had brought them to her aid.

"Kelly, I wanted to tell you this once we were on the ground.
Phillip called."

She responded with tears that rolled down her cheeks. "I know you say he's the Devil, but he says he isn't. H…"

"Well what else would he friggin say, eh? He's not going to come out with it and just admit…"

"No you're right." interrupted Ross, "so that's why we're going to meet him tomorrow, in the parking lot of a shopping mall, in broad daylight, in public."

Kelly continued to argue. Still it felt good that someone, a man, was taking charge again. "Phil could never have done this." she thought.

Just then, a car drove into the airstrip's small gravel lot only to pull an abrupt 'U' turn and exit the way it entered. No one thought anything of it, not even Hecate the resident witch, who was busy consoling Kelly much to the annoyance of Boleyn and unwittingly reminding her of their special relationship.

Joan followed the locating cross's lead hoping that Kelly would in turn take her to her goal, Phil. It was easy for her to be discrete as she could follow at arms-length with no fear of detection. When she found herself cornered in the airstrip parking lot, she had to get out of there 'ASAP'. Even so, in her brief entrance, she saw a witch there, a green one, the weakest kind, but one that could identify her if she hung around too long. Or got too close. It called for a swift exit. That night's dream was going to be another interesting one.

~~~

A bag of chips quelled Phillip's disappointment with the rain just as a silver sheen shadow illuminated the tent, Moonlight.

"Wow, they are good."

He got up and dressed quickly,

"Moonlight means it's not raining, sort of. Great."

This was what he'd been waiting for, a similar night to his first. He ventured out into the cooling night air and, aided with a flashlight, headed towards the sleuth gates of ClearStream.

Being careful not to slip and fall in, Phillip climbed and parried his way to the place where he first saw them. He immediately became woeful that his first sighting may have been the first and last time as the cow drink was full of water.

He couldn't find them even after taking a dip in the trough's crisp clean waters.His fingertips too,couldn't detect them either.Attempting to remain positive, (sticking to his pledge to be the new Phillip), he dried himself off with the towel he'd been smart enough to bring.

"Now I've got Ross and Harry all excited, telling them about the 'amazing runes', and they're going to come all the way here and find out that I'm just an idiot. And they'd be right, I thought I'd changed, calling myself Phillip rather than Phil, but I'm still the same old Phil, loser Phil." He didn't cry, he wasn't up to it, but he was open to giving up, and he did.

The new Phillip wasn't that much different from the old Phil. Lucky the first big drops of the returning rain slapped him on the forehead and gave him the necessary excuse to head home.

Back in his tent, mild anxiety kept him awake. Ross and the IAT were coming to ClearStream for nothing, because there was nothing to see.

"I'm such a fool."

CHAPTER 16

ONLY THE TRUTH, USELESS TRUTH

Evelyn Mills was a tiny village with a cluster of big box stores in a huge parking lot. It was there in a remote corner where Phillip, Kelly and the IAT met. Under a blustery blue sky, Ross had approached Phillip. He had remained next to his car out of consideration to Kelly who was cowering at the back of the group.

"Hi Ross." and he nodded towards Harry, Boleyn and Hecate.
He avoided making eye contact with Kelly.

"Hi Phil, Phillip. So you think you've discovered something?" "Well, I feel like an idiot, 'cos, well, I can't find the runes anymore."

"Yea, just like Phil would have done, you're the Devil." shouted Kelly, and ducked behind the large frame of Harry again.

"Phillip?" inquired Ross, not surprised at Kelly's accusation. "Yes, yes, you've said that but…" responded Phillip, trying hard
to keep calm.

"Because it's true." she yelled again.

"But I don't know why you think that, so, before I continue, can someone please tell me everything that happened that night in ClearStream? 'COS I DON'T KNOW." screeched Phillip unable to take Kelly's accusations anymore.

Kelly continued to scream at Phillip until Ross finally gained everyone's attention. They listened as he explained the destruction of the church to the point where the hospital reported that Phil had apparently come out of his coma. Then all eyes turned to Kelly, the only person who knew this last piece,

"Would she tell?" thought Phillip.

"Well Kelly?" inquired Ross, "You think Phillip is the Devil. You can tell him yourself why. We're all here to support you, even if it means facing the Devil again, so Kelly, Phillip needs to know. Or the Devil waits, I don't know."

"I'm Phil, Kelly. Phil. NO I lie. I'm Phillip. PhilLIP. OK? Ok.
So what HAPPENED?"

She recalled that he was acting in the exact same helpless manner as he had when Hecate attacked him.

"Phil. You attacked me, invaded me, raped me. Even if you are Phil, the Devil was in you, SO YOU ARE RESPONSIBLE." and she began to cry.

"You don't understand. He was…" retorted Phillip.

"I DON'T CARE." she screamed, "I DON'T CARE."

Kelly fumbled with the SUV's door handle before throwing herself into the backseat. She slammed the door and locked it. Phillip did nothing. He wanted to say something, to explain, but he'd been in this position so many times that he'd resigned himself to his fate.

Kelly would always win and he would always lose.

"We could be at ClearStream in a couple of hours Ross if you want to meet there. There's nothing to see, but I can show you where I saw the runes even if you can't see them now. Ross, by the way, have you ever wondered why the Devil chose ClearStream?"

He hadn't.

"So that was Phil?" asked Hecate as they drove out of the parking lot.

"Yes, of course it was." replied a confused Ross as they drove away. "You know its Phil. The one who spotted the flaw in the Devil's contracts, remember? Hecate?"

"Yes." it was more of a question than a reply, "just that, well…" "He's changed quite a bit, hasn't he Hecate?" interrupted Boleyn
in an attempt to defend Hecate, maybe.

"He calls himself Phillip, but it's the same old Phil, just with blue eyes, eyes that you saw first before you tried to kill him. Remember Hecate?" pressed a now slightly irritated Ross,

"Yes, well, he doesn't seem the same, like he's a different person.
Not Phil, someone else."

"I guess he really is a new man, not just in name." thought Ross staring piercingly into Boleyn's eyes. "You knew this, didn't you?" he demanded.

"I was going to tell you, but I didn't get the chance." mouthed Boleyn, with downcast eyes that confirmed his assumption.

"What do you mean, didn't get a chance? When you didn't tell us that Phil was out of his coma back at HQ; that was your chance. Then." said Harry in a quiet, grave voice.

The atmosphere in the van became claustrophobic. Ross and Harry were silent, as was everyone else. They had this new development to consider. They didn't know why or if there were any implications, but their guts suggested there was. They were discrete, but also furious with Boleyn as this was the second time that she'd withheld information from them.

"Is she concealing something else from us?" they thought.

Shewas. She hated them, Hecate and Kelly more, Phil the most, for living.

Neither of them knew why Boleyn was so resentful of her sister, now relegated to her ex-sister. In some respects, it would have been a miracle if either of them did. They were privileged, gifted, respected and the exact opposite of the non-witch Boleyn.

They continued driving with the three women absorbed in their own misery. Everyone was gloomy, except one onlooker, Joan. She was feeling quite ecstatic. Having tailed Kelly for a whole day and night, and despite God's lack of faith, she had struck gold. Just as she predicted, Kelly had led her to Phil. Focusing only on the pursuit, Joan followed Phil's car. When he drove down isolated roads, Joan hung back making sure she remained undetected. Shrewdly, she began to follow the dust thrown up from the dirt trails until the billowing clouds stopped.

On a lonely desolate track, Joan decided not to follow any further by car. She backed hers into a bay in the undergrowth and followed the tire tracks on foot. When she knew she was close, she cautiously approached the source of human noise up ahead. Finally, she remained hidden in the heavy bush and watched Phil pottering around a makeshift campsite.

"What luck." she thought, "Isolated, alone, I'll come back and do it tonight."

~~~

"I'm sorry Boleyn, but it could have been important, well it is important. Tell you what;" in an effort to console her, "why don't you tell us what you know, that is, why is it that Hecate can't recognize Phillip?"

It wasn't unlike talking to a wall as Boleyn had completely shut down. Meanwhile Hecate had cornered Boleyn and was trying to force eye contact, but she was in such a stupor that Hecate's menacing was all but mute. Kelly wasn't talking to anyone either, and she was unmoved by Hecate's bullying and terrifying behavior. She felt above the cajoling in the knowledge that Hecate owed her, but not above being as miserable as possible in drama queen fashion.

No matter what conversation Ross or Harry made, none of the women spoke, making the SUV seem small despite it being the largest money could rent. Ross and Harry drove to the closest parking rest area to ClearStream and got out of the car as quickly as possible. Without bothering to ask the ladies to join them, the two men headed towards the ruins in the distance relieved to get a breath of fresh air.

They heard a door slam shut and the high-pitched voice of Boleyn asking them to wait. As she caught up, they saw Hecate and Kelly also climb out and follow her down the trail towards them.

In the safety of the late afternoon Sun, ClearStream seemed a lot less foreboding to Ross than it had a couple of weeks earlier. The absence of the Devil certainly helped. However,

"God I hope Phil really is Phillip and not the Devil, because I don't think we'd escape a second time." commented Ross, suggesting that they could be walking into a trap.

In reality Ross and Harry felt relatively confident with their decision. Discounting the possibility, they were more intent upon determining the extent of Hecate's inabilities. They questioned Boleyn sensitively and she was finally opening up to the lesson that teams not individuals were important in the Modern World.

Kelly and Hecate, who'd trailed behind, caught up and they entered ClearStream central together. It wasn't long before Phil arrived and Hecate confirmed that she couldn't detect the Dark One's Entanglement.

It was most enlightening for Ross and Harry, to learn that she could not recognize him as the man called Phil. To her, he was a plain ordinary man called Phillip and was no one special. Phil was nothing to either Hecate or Kelly but for different reasons.

Although Kelly said she still thought he was the Devil as she hid behind Hecate, no one believed her anymore. Her feelings betrayed her actions. It was unspoken but on the minds of the group, that she was in love, and one of the few things she shared with Phillip was that she too didn't seem to realize it.

Kelly was still hurting from the profound harm of the Devil's deception, but time is reputed to heal all wounds. Antagonistically, she sought Phillip out to vent her pain and sorrow as if were Phil's job to be abused. She believed the new Phillip should be there for her like in the past. This was the only reason she tolerated him.

"Eventually." Ross thought, "she'll work it out, but until then, we'll let her be."

Everyone followed Phillip as he led the way to the ninth sleuth gate with Kelly trailing behind to keep the furthest from him. Phillip prattled on with every mundane and ordinary observation, not realizing that he was destroying any rising anticipation. (Probably a good thing). This boring persona confirmed to Kelly that he was indeed not the Devil.

When they got to the trough, Phillip pointed to an area under two feet of churning water and said, "Sorry."

Kelly and the others clustered around the walls of the trough. After, a long moment of silence, she said, "You stupid fucking idiot, there's nothing to see here."

She turned round and headed back towards the distant car. Phillip had delivered undeniable proof that he was Phillip and not the Devil.

"Sorry." apologized Phillip.

"You're so God damn stupid Phil." she shouted, refusing to call him Phillip, "There's nothing here."

She flaunted her annoyance as a cover for her relief, and that other pesky feeling incubating, and denying, in her heart.

"Well done, Phillip." Ross thought, "Thank you Kelly, now please, see the truth... you were meant for Phillip, and give him, and us, a break."

CHAPTER 17

FORTUNATE NOT SO RANDOM LUCK

Not unlike the average person, *Pi* was nervous about discovering the extent of damage to herself. Without another option, she did the examination. With baited breath, she checked and rechecked the tampered sequences and progressions, only to discover that further corruption was occurring. Although they were only minor distortions, there was only one conclusion to be drawn and its implication was massive. Yes, Phil was still alive.

"Trustss the Devil to believe otherwise. Dupingss him was so easy, even a (not so) dead man could do its. Ats least God was on the balls. I's wonder if she has any symptomss. I's wonder what the impact of my sores are toos. Ahs, they can't be that bad. I'll's forget its."

Not human but wishing to be so, she pushed herself to investigate for any and all anomalies. She knew a human, especially a woman, would keep looking even though there was nothing to unearth, because sometimes they do find something. When they do, it's always bad. And there's always a man at its root. And Phil was indeed a man.

"OKs. OKs. I'lls sees what the effect iss. Ifs they is harmless, maybe I's just forgets hims." she said to herself.

～～

Joe was shaking. He had checked the numbers a hundred times and the result was always the same. For years he'd run a lottery pool at work, and in all that time the most they'd ever won was ten free tickets. He checked the numbers again. It was true. They had all seven numbers. They had won the jackpot.

His wife, Sarah, was crying as she talked zealously over the phone with her parents. Her mother was excited and happy for them, but her father, Simon, was the analytical type. He needed to know more information before he could succumb to the simple emotion of joy. He surfed the net, and what he found; he didn't like. Simon wasn't a sourpuss, he just refused to count his chickens before they hatched.

There were ten people in the pool and the grand prize was forty million, so everyone was two million dollars to the good. Not enough for his son-in-law to retire but they could pay off the mortgage and car for sure.

Suddenly, a hush replaced Sarah's hysteria as her mother asked that Simon talk to Joe. She knew the tone of her voice meant only one thing, bad news. The tears of joy were gone, replaced by the other kind, as she handed over the phone. Simon's voice was somber.

"They're calling it a statistical freak Joe. All the numbers that came up were below thirty-one and as many people choose birthdays for their lotto tickets. There were several winners. Actually, almost a hundred. Sorry Joe."

Sarah cried bitterly. She hadn't done the math, but her dad would never betray her. He'd said they hadn't won more than a couple of thousand bucks.

"I hate you God."

"Sorry God, I didn't mean it." as a cold shudder made her recount her rash outburst. It did nothing, however, to dispel an ominous feeling filling her heart.

~~~

Pi was frantic as two other reports of amazing coincidences were coming to light. Five holes in one's had occurred in a golf tournament, explained by the fact that the slope of the green automatically channeled the ball towards the hole. Then two sets of twins married two sets of twins, without knowing. Scientists were dismissing it as genetics, but *Pi* knew better.

There can always be worse, but this wasn't good in the least. The contamination of her numbers had had a profound effect on the luck she'd dispensed over the World, having a much bigger impact than she could have imagined. She delved back down to exam her wound, and saw that it had got worse again. Compared with the trillions of numbers of her being, the scar was like that of an itchy mosquito bite. Like that bothersome pest, this Phil would have to be swatted.

CHAPTER 18

GREVIOUSLY DOWN AND DEPRESSED

Under a darkening sky, Phillip explained the circumstances surrounding the discovery and disappearance of the runes. At every opportunity, Kelly, who had returned, continued to berate him ferociously. Taking pity, Ross delicately stepped in by asking for ideas on what to do next.

It was the first challenge for the IAT. Harry adjudicated, and all ideas voiced were discussed, all except Phillip's as Kelly shot them down.

The changes in the powers and strengths of the witches were strange for everyone, and for some, hard to bear. Boleyn the Red Witch and oldest sister, the mightiest of all; was deprived of her powers by the Devil and doomed to mortal status. Ruebella, the Yellow Witch and the middle sister, like Boleyn had awesome powers, but in her quest for love from a man, John Abbott the XXVIIth, she flew into the Devil Tornado and died in its inferno.

The youngest sister, Hecate, had been the weakest witch out of the three. With cunning guile, she transferred her soul into Kelly before her meeting with the Devil. Thanks to Phil, she survived the Devil and was able to reclaim her soul and resume her witch-hood. Now, Hecate reigned as the World's only witch, the strongest by default, and hence, the only one in the IAT. They needed her witch powers. She suddenly realized this was the reason Ross and Harry wanted her to be part of the team.

"I think I can cast a spell that might make them visible."

Kelly was torn. Did she want Phillip to be proven right or better, wrong? She chose wrong, and was surprised to discover that Boleyn was her ally.

Boleyn had her own motive. Specifically she didn't want Hecate to perform a successful spell. This time Ross and Harry intervened, and both Kelly and Boleyn deferred to their wishes. They had decided that Hecate would conjure a Reveal Spell.

Everyone set about finding the materials Hecate needed, except Boleyn who decided she wasn't going to find anything useful. She pretended to search, but instead wandered aimlessly through the overgrown ruins cursing the day she'd met her little sister. Hecate was understandably upset with Boleyn's stance, so she slyly followed her and overheard every cuss.

"She can't do that spell as good as I could have… bitch, tall stupid, phone stupid bitch." she muttered causing Hecate's green blood to boil.

Night seemed to invade the ruins like a tsunami,so they abandoned the search until the following day. Tired and humiliated, Phillip went his separate way back to his campsite. He gloomily thought that if Kelly had still considered him to be the Devil, he would have felt better because then she would have been too scared to berate him.

The others headed back to the SUV, a simple trek for everyone except Boleyn. Her midget size made lugging through the towering undergrowth difficult. She fell behind. She considered herself a burden to those in front who waited willingly and patiently.

Ahead of her, Ross and Harry whispered between each other. Boleyn couldn't hear them,but she was sure they were talking about her.

They,however, were innocent of gossiping. Nor were they discussing the spell that Hecate was going to cast. Neither were they discussing whether Phillip was believable. Instead they were engrossed and even excited by a text from a potential client. One that they didn't expect to have and it was one they were loath to turn down. And they weren't going to if they were in their right minds.

Hecate was lost in thought too, mulling over Boleyn's deception and feeling bitterly betrayed. She had no inkling of Boleyn's situation, quite the opposite, secure in the knowledge that she was the World's only witch.

"Ross, Harry, I'm going to go and find the things I need for tomorrow's spell tonight. I want it to be the best spell ever." she said loudly, specifically for Boleyn as she looked over her shoulder at the trailing midget.

Hecate floated back towards Boleyn, steered her broomstick masterfully in front of her, and soared into the night sky. It felt like a dagger in Boleyn's heart. For Hecate had seen through Boleyn's façade and saw her for who she was.

She dropped like a stone out of the sky and stalked Boleyn from behind, causing her to turn round and make eye contact. Boleyn tried to unlock her eyes, but couldn't. Hecate gave her a grin that spoke, "

I'm a witch and you're not. You're not my big sister anymore.

You're not even a sister, and never will be again."

Hecate soared up and away while the belittled and wounded Boleyn contemplated.

Her life no less.

With a much longer walk home than the IAT, Phillip left ClearStream thinking only of Kelly. It was no longer a love hate relationship, now it was just hate.

"Who am I kidding? Me? Her?"

He clambered down a steep embankment and entered the small coppice that was home, and almost dismissed the noise of a cracking twig behind him. He turned and confronted the culprit.

"Thank you." said Phillip mildly to the Silver Witch.

"Thank you?" she said, standing, confused before him. Her bright Silver Entanglement shone radiantly in the black night.

She didn't know that Phillip didn't care anymore. Kelly's treatment had weighed so heavily on him that death didn't seem so bad right now.

Whether confused or not, it didn't matter, Joan had a job to do and she was going to do it. Besides, his acceptance made it easier to do the deadly deed.

"Die Phil." she replied.

SilverDEATH SilverDEATH SilverDEATH

SilverDEATH   SilverDEATH

SilverDEATH

Joan froze in disbelief. Phil stood motionless in front of her. Alive. Bafled, she wondered what had happened or what she'd done wrong.

Just as she thought about attacking again, "She who hesitates is lost." Phil made a mad dash for her.

"My God. He's not even paralyzed. KILL HIM." and she he hit him with all her might.

SilverDEATH SilverDEATH SilverDEATHSilverDEATH SilverDEATH SilverDEATH
SilverDEATH SilverDEATH SilverDEATH SilverDEATH SilverDEATH
SilverDEATH SilverDEATH SilverDEATH SilverDEATH
SilverDEATH SilverDEATH SilverDEATH
SilverDEATH SilverDEATH
SilverDEATH

But Phil was upon her.

His attack took an instant.

"But at least he'd died whilst doing so. What the…"

He wasn't dead.

He was alive.

Grabbing at her.

In the time Joan realized this, he had her overpowered. He held her in a bear hug, lifted her off the ground and clamped his mouth over hers kissing her roughly.

Phillip felt Joan writhe and twist, but he held her fast, in a not so passionate embrace. Her neck was twisting so violently that he knew she would break free. He fell to the floor and landed heavily on top of her. He had little choice if he was going to keep her and himself alive.

Phillip dismissed the fact that she had now tried to kill him twice. Not a violent man, he felt bad that he was hurting her.

"Sssssh."

"SSSSH."

Phillip hissed in her mouth. Both of their lips were getting raw with the rough contact.

"So this is why God wants him dead. He's a rapist and probably a murderer too. Still, there's plenty of them about, why this one? And why isn't he dead? He should be dead. Seven times over. Forty-nine times over the second time. As she struggled, their eyes connected and she saw more fear in his eyes than she presumed she'd have in hers.

"Quiet!" he whispered.

"Because he wants to rape me" she thought.

Then she felt the why.

A terrible fear swept over them as a bone-chilling screech froze them. She instantly recalled the many times she had heard it before and feared for her life. It was a sound that humans couldn't hear, yet he obviously had. The Devil was abroad.

Suddenly, her eyes matched those of Phillip's, and he withdrew his kiss. They remained silent, both barely resisting death as the Devil's BLACK indivisible shadow raced over their quivering bodies. Only their stealth and the overhead limbs of the nearest tree prevented the Devil's detection. Slowly, the feeling of terror receded, but they still dared not to breathe or move.

Not knowing the highflying dark gargoyle had risen off and flown away into the night sky, they waited for five, ten maybe fifteen minutes without saying a thing. With utmost caution, Phillip turned his head and saw the Black Entanglement vapors that trailed behind the Devil like the white fumes of a jet airliner. He watched them as they dissipated until they were all gone.

Presumably, the Devil had too, but they hid for another fifteen minutes just to be sure. Daring to raise their heads, they peered over the top of the long grass that had successfully concealed them, and cautiously checked. All was clear.

Phillip turned over onto his back and let out a huge sigh. He was without fear of the woman, the witch, who'd attempted to kill him earlier. He was thinking how her Entanglement attack had just swept over, around or through him, contrary to the harm it once inflicted upon him. He was alive. He was transparent to Entanglement.

He turned to look at her, who, like him, was lying on her back, gazing upwards at the stars that peeked between the branches and leaves. She was an older woman, good looking in a mature way, with silver hair and eyes. Phillip knew, without doubt that she was the witch from the hospital.

"It's God. She's the one who wants you dead Phil." she suddenly blurted out.

CHAPTER 19

ONLY EXTREMELY DISTURBING

"What? Why?" replied Phillip, and he waited for her reply, which took some time coming.

"I don't know?" and then she reversed it, "Do you?"

"Nooo. How would I?" was his startled and slightly irritated reply, "And while we're at it, what's your name, as you obviously know mine?"

"Joan. Saint Joan."

"SAINT JOAN? You're not a witch?"

"Nooo." Imitating his previous retort, "You know, Phil..." "It's Phillip." said Phillip, a little curtly.

"Oh. Phillip?"

"Yes. Phillip." and he said it for the first time with pride. "Not Phil?"

"No. That's who I used to be. Now I'm Phillip - I think."

"Oh. Oh. You used to be Phil, though. Phil. You know a woman called Kelly?"

She didn't need to hear the answer. His face said it all.

"Ok, so, I think... Phil... LIP. You seem to know... things. That is, you seem to have recognized the Devil. Before me I might add. And you know about Entanglement too I see. Most interesting. Most... And you survived too. Remarkable. Remarkable. I... err... And you know about witches too. Yes?

How?"

Phillip surprised himself with his reply, as he'd never not answered a question before now.

"It's a long story. Truly. But I don't want to go into it, well not until I find out who you are and why you tried to kill me. Twice in fact. Big attacks too. I think you should be answering my questions first, don't you?"

"Well, I guess I owe you an… err… explanation."

"And an apology don't you think?" said Phillip.

"Yes. That too. Sorry Phillip."

Then Joan inhaled a long breath. She was about to tell someone who and what she was for the first time in her life. But then she'd never met anyone her equal before. It took her a while to get started, but once she got going, it was like a confession. She excluded nothing as the person before her obviously knew so much. What would be the point of censoring?

"So why does God want me dead?" asked Phillip after taking time to absorb everything. "I mean, it's bad enough that the Devil hates me, and would kill me, has killed me. So why does God want me dead too. Sorry, you don't know. You've already said that. But why?"

"So the Devil wants you dead too?" she couldn't help inquiring from this very different man.

"He tried to kill me when he possessed me. Well, possessed my body. Then he left. So, I think he thinks I'm dead. I mean, why else am I still alive?"

"I don't know Phil." she said softening up to him, refreshed by his honesty and lack of self-importance and self-deprecation of his uniqueness.

"Phillip." he gently replied.

"Sorry. Yes, Phillip." she agreed.

"After his attacks on me, I think I've… I think the old Phil IS dead, and now I'm Phillip."

"Phillip." she responded kindly, "Phillip. Yes, I think I've got it now." after repeating it four times.

"How did you survive my attacks?" she asked after a quiet pause.

"OK, Joan, you've been honest with me, here goes." replied Phillip and they walked back towards his campsite like old friends. He told an amazed Joan about his confrontations with the witches and the Devil.

"It's O.K. Phillip, you sleep in your tent and I'll sleep in the car. I'm smaller and have certain powers myself… you're a strange old beast,'cos I see right through you." she said as her retiring comment.

Phillip was busy zipping up his tent so he missed Joan's last remark, and instead he replied with his own goodnight.

"Nite Joan" he said consumed with his thoughts, and the zipper closed his evening.He fell into a restful,dreamless sleep almost instantly.

Joan's night report to God was full of omissions,attempts to explain why Phillip wasn't dead,remembering to call him Phil not Phillip.

"I tried twice, a Sevener, then all in with everything, the Forty Niner, and he still didn't die, and I'm half dead 'cos of it."

Luckily for Joan, God was in the past by two hours because God wasn't happy at the news. God's last words to Joan were an ultimatum.

"He has to die by next sunrise or it'll be your death you'll be contemplating, and the Devil, as you well know, has not forgotten."

"Capiche?"

Joan knew this all too well. Even though she was over a thousand years old, Phillip was the first man she'd found herself attracted to in all that time. Yet a saint has to obey. She knew God had never broken a promise, or threat. Phillip's last day was tomorrow; the hand of God would be with her in her next attack.

~~~

Instead of getting up immediately the following morning, Phillip lay on his inflatable bed and contemplated the previous day's failures. The worst part was losing his friends. Although recently acquired,Ross and Harry were all he had.They hadn't said it, but it was clear that they no longer believed that he had seen the elusive runes and their actions spoke when they hadn't. As they left ClearStream, Ross had indicated that they had had an urgent request from a prospective client, and that they might have to fly off right away to meet him and probably sign a contract. To Phillip it seemed like an excuse to break off any obligation they may have felt towards him.

Of course, Kelly and Boleyn, who were "useless", would stay behind to assist Hecate with her 'Reveal Spell', but Phillip feared that today there would only be Boleyn and himself. Ross and Harry together with the core of the IAT would have flown away and abandoned him.

He pondered why no one seemed to care or share his curiosity about why the Devil chose ClearStream.

One consolation for Phillip was that he didn't believe Kelly deemed him as the Devil anymore, but on the other hand, a no show from her would reveal her true feelings.

"At least she doesn't believe I'm the Devil. Trouble is, just because she believes me, doesn't mean she wants to stay here with me. After spending the entire day ridiculing me, I guess she'll go with them. Certain of it."

He knew in his gut this was true. That part of Phil had never been wrong, so he assumed the mantle. Phillip's mind was in turmoil as he tried to un-jumble all that occurred in the past three weeks. He now had four women in his life - from zero. However, he was on friendly terms with only one, the saint. Two others either hated or had forsaken him; namely Boleyn and Kelly. Meanwhile Hecate didn't even acknowledge him.

Then his thoughts started to register the strange parting comment Saint Joan had said.

"... I see right through you Phillip..."

When he had first woken up, he thought she said it in the traditional meaning, 'that she read him like a book'.

"But maybe she meant it in a different sense?" he thought. As he connected Hecate's strange conduct with Joan's enigmatic remark, his ever-whirling mind was on the cusp of making a profound observation.

"This may be important!"

He decided to get up and ask her, to pursue, what could be a telling insight. He exited his tent and walked down the track, only to find her car gone. It caused his insecurity to climb.

"I thought we'd got along fine." He'd forgotten that she tried to kill him twice.

And when he did remember, he felt worse. "I'm probably the stupidest man alive."

Phillip wondered if he'd ever see Joan again, or what would become of her. If God wanted him dead, and she couldn't do it, then what would happen next? Would God kill him in person? He didn't know and thought he didn't care.

In this mood Phillip wandered out to ClearStream to meet the IAT and to wait for Hecate's Reveal Spell.

"Where is everyone?" Phillip asked Boleyn who was alone and somehow vaguely different. Ill?

"Ross and Harry are seeing this *big client*...Kelly said something about some guy called 'Bill? And Hecate, teacher's pet, she's....'"

Phillip hardly heard her. He stopped listening when he heard the word, Bill. His mind spun at the worst possible news. Kelly was going back to Bill. He was ready to slit his wrists.

"Doesn't she realize he's using her. Dumped her. Screwing her. Bastard." he thought.

He spent the rest of the day in his tent sulking like a little child.

~~~

"Phillip. Can I come in?"

"Joan? Is that you?" asked Phillip cheering up. His loneliness vanished as her face poked through the tent's flap.

"Yes." and she was inside the dimly lit tent wearing a genuine 'happy to see you smile'. They talked, not about the miserable day he'd had, or about why she'd left in the morning unannounced, just lighthearted banter, until Phillip asked.

"How did you become a saint?"

"You deserve to know, it's only fair that you should know who I am and how I got to be me."

His question didn't sour the moment and Phillip sat absorbed with her story.

"Entanglement." sighed Phillip after she finished. "I used to have that, now I'm free of it. Thank God." It was force of habit, thanking someone who had put a hit out on him.

Phillip had told Joan that he had Entanglement after her failed attempts on his life. Joan was astounded by what she had learned and concealed her gasp. *She knew that men couldn't acquire Entanglement. Now she'd figured out why God wanted Phillip dead; to find out how it happened.*

Joan wondered if there was more, and she realized God was probably wondering the same thing. She reasoned that was why the Devil sought to kill him too,

"That's why the Devil wanted him dead. My God, better it be God rather than the Devil. But I don't know if I can... He's so... innocent."

"You know." said Phillip interrupting the gentle silence, "I knew your Entanglement attack was different than a witch's, or the Devil's, but I didn't know there were different kinds, I now see there is. And now, since I'm Phillip, they feel like ripples on a pond, except they just seem to evaporate when they make contact with me."

A strange look flashed across Joan's face, one that Phillip couldn't begin to fathom.

Then she said, "I must go."

He was so trusting, with her at least.

"Why do we always trust those who are there to betray us?" she questioned as she uncovered another reason why God wanted him dead, and also why she didn't want to be that agent.

"No, stay. You can errr... sleep here, in this tent, if you like?" Phillip stopped, as he understood how this could be misconstrued.

"I mean, it's not a bother and…" He fell silent, his words were killing him, but he wanted her company for the night.

"Ok." she replied, "I'll stay." and flicked the lamp switch before dozing off immediately.

Him however, took ages to get to sleep. Then just as he was about to drift off, he felt her.

"Phillip," she whispered, "sit up, I've got something to tell you." He sat up and opened his eyes, and saw her face close to his. To his surprise queen-size tears cascaded down her face, and then she kissed him.

"Why" she thought, "is it always with a kiss?"

~~~

He closed his eyes again to reciprocate before he felt a sharp jab on the very top of his head that destroyed the moment. Something wet, possibly blood, dribbled down over his face, and he passed out.

<div align="center">

LIGHT

LIGHT LIGHT LIGHT

LIGHT LIGHT LIGHT LIGHT

LIGHT LIGHT LIGHT LIGHT

LIGHT LIGHT LIGHT LIGHT

LIGHT LIGHT LIGHT LIGHT LIGHT

LIGHT LIGHT LIGHT LIGHT

LIGHT LIGHT LIGHT LIGHT

LIGHT LIGHT LIGHT LIGHT

LIGHT LIGHT LIGHT

LIGH

</div>

He opened his eyes and saw the whole Universe below him. Spread-eagled, his hands and Shoes held onto the very edge of the event horizon, the boundary between the Universe and non-Universe. Bewildered over where he was, Phillip didn't have time to ponder as he felt the space-time fabric expanding and stretching him from head to foot and toe to toe.

Glued flat to the inside of the ever-expanding cosmos, Phillip, like a cartoon animal on the skin of a balloon, was now larger than our Earth and thinner than an atom. Not knowing or wondering how, he could see faster than the speed of light and saw Earth, contrary to all logic, the center of the Universe. Everything stemmed from the beautiful blue ball, and out of the corner of his eye, he saw that an Eternal Mortal was focused intently upon it.

"Ouch." cried out Phillip, turning away and closing his stinging eyes. In that moment, he knew his were the first human eyes to spy God in all her stunning beauty, and survive. All others would have vaporized to mist. Even the semi-immortal Phillip's sidelong glance was enough to blind him temporarily like a sudden squirt of pepper spray.

He recovered quickly though. He gasped at the glory of his fleeting glimpse and repelled the desire to look again and face a possible death.

"What was God looking so intensely at?" thought Phillip.

He didn't want to acknowledge the frightening fact that God really did want him dead. God the most beautiful, the one who was supposed to be all merciful, was out for his blood.

"Looking to see me die." he answered his rhetorical question out loud, no longer able to deny it.

From the impossible distance, to the impossible smallness, through the impregnable Entanglement War, Phillip saw Joan kissing him, felt her warmth and her loving embrace, and watched the tears streaming down her cheeks.

Because of the war, not even God could focus on the actions of Joan that Phillip could so easily see, and he theorized that his lack of Entanglement was the reason why.

He focused on Joan's hands that had jabbed the blade of her cross deep and hard into his crown. She was injecting a snake's venom, God's Death Entanglement, into his innocent brain, which like every poison was rotting him from the inside. Phillip felt God's metallic cross reach in and search for his soul, just as the Devil had once done, and was disgusted.

"Was *she* just like him?"

He didn't know why *she* wanted him dead, why *she* would not want to be his patron, rather than his assassin, especially since he had denied the Devil. Although Phillip had crossed the Universe, time had stood still, poised to start again the moment he returned to his body.

Vowing things to be different from the Devil's attack, this time, he was not going to hide. Although his soul once belonged to God, he rejected her attempts to repatriate it, because his soul was his.

HIS.

HIS.

Not for the Devil to steal, either.

Not for either of them to take.

It was he, along with his body, mind and RhomSong.

He returned and time restarted.

Hatred erupted in his heart.

Even Phillip has it inside of him.

Not wishing to quell it, he released it.

R
h
Song
m

As if *she'd* been electrocuted, God recoiled in disbelief and shook her tingling hands before putting them to her mouth to kiss them better. No harm was done of course, except to her ego, but the riddle of what was going on was only getting worse. The ability to repel an attack from her was normally reserved for the Devil and *Pi*, yet a mortal had done just that.

However, *she* had no doubt that he was dead. No one could ever survive that attack. It was over for Phil, and in due course his soul would arrive in Heaven. Then he'd wish he had gone to Hell.

Just as the Devil had waited upon Rank, *she* waited for confirmation from Joan. It would come in a couple of hours' time, so in the meantime, *she* took a quick gander at a funny feeling *she'd* felt in a remote corner of her domain.

Although God is omnipresent, she could bespread wafer thin. So fine that she might as well be nothing. The edges of her Universe were one such place.

With a quick thought, *she* was there in an instant, only to be greeted by another worrying conundrum. To her shock and amazement, the small quadrant showed signs of trespass. It was expanding normally, but it looked as though it had hit a speed bump, as a big dent marred the fabric. Multiple computations were required to determine the origin, but it was something that *she* was now intent upon knowing.

Hours later and not without much foreboding and astonishment, *she* realized the Universe had indeed suffered a hiccup and had expanded at a diminished rate. Upon additional and meticulous calculations, the Universe had actually stopped expanding for a brief instant at this location. It was a discovery of profound concern.

The event on its own was of little consequence, *she* wasn't injured and suffered no harm, but whatever had happened, potentially threatened the source of her power, the ever-expanding Universe. If something could stop its expansion, then *she* needed to know what it was. And eradicate it.

As a precaution, God examined thousands of other distant boundaries and to her relief, determined the defect was limited to this area. Any corruption or disruption of the space-time continuum was cause for worry, so *she* examined the sub atomic structures, a realm outside of her purview, and concluded they remained uncontaminated. *Dia's* realm was unaffected, but relativity was.

She pushed Phil to the sidelines of her mind, to focus on this potentially life-threatening anomaly just as man had sworn himself against the foe called small pox. *She* needed to know the culprit. The Devil's BLACK existed here too, but it was disabled, due to the Devil's inability to culture it from his prison on Earth, but this was not the root cause, not in a million years.

With a critical eye, *she* traversed several parsecs looking closely at what appeared like faint etches of finger and toe prints. *She* calculated backwards, down from the size of stars to that of the human finger.

She ran the comparison. There was no match. That was impossible. *She* almost died in shock. It's hard to imagine God having a bad day. They were few and far between, but this was one.

She had records of every set of prints and DNA ever created, even her own were cataloged, and of course the Devil and *Pi's*; so to not find a match was unparalleled.

Panic stricken; *she* ran millions of calculations again before emitting a sigh of relief. At least *she'd* reconfirmed that her Universe was still ever expanding. As things stood, nothing could halt the Universe's growth, and thus nothing could diminish her power. Yet a warning shot had been fired.

Someone had temporarily stopped the Universe from its expansion, and *she* didn't know who. *Pi* and... and... and..., just *Pi* was the prime suspect, "Maybe she'd faked the fingerprints?"

As if to confirm *she* was living a nightmare, there was more to come. On the frontier of the Entanglement War, the Devil, in her absence, had chosen this moment to launch an offensive. He was making an amazing move; one *she* had no idea he had the capability to muster. And at this moment *she* thought of Phil.

CHAPTER 20

DEATH CHEATED

Phillip shook his head in an attempt to fend off a pounding headache that threatened to strike like a dark cloud full of thunder. He rubbed his eyes. Caked blood had seeped around them and flakes of it fell to the ground like snow. Then he remembered the kiss and the person who delivered it.

"JOAN. JOAN. Speak to me." Phillip bent down to pick her up off the ground.

"Ouch." Every bone in his body hurt, and he had to forget about her for a moment as he had to concentrate on his own aching frame. Slowly, he moved each limb through its full range of motion, which diminished the pain down to a dull reminder, but not before he noticed that he'd acquired a scar on his arm.

"That, I'll examine later."

He needed to tend to Joan, whose lifeless contorted body lay on the ground. He picked up her cold body, hugged her tightly in his arms, and rocked her as his tears freely streamed down his cheeks not caring that she tried to kill him.

Thrice.

He had seen from the other side of forever that she unwillingly followed God's orders and that she'd cried while doing God's will. It was his fault, by not controlling his RhomSong that she was dead.

Now all he saw was a broken Joan, her hand, which had wielded the cross, contorted behind her head. He gently maneuvered the charred mandible back into a more natural and becoming position, and while he did so, he noticed a pale scar on her arm. He stopped and compared her welt to his, the sign of a woman, but with the main vertical line extending through the circle, just like her cross. They were identical.

He would have thought about it further but Joan's lifeless body demanded his attention and triggered a thought that he'd dared not address until now.

"Was it I who healed Kelly? If it wasn't, then who else could it have been?"

"Must have been when I kissed her?"

He wasn't conscious of the act, but without any other obvious perpetrator, he thought, maybe he could save Joan too. He needed to deliberately summon the 'SongRhom'

"And heal, nay, bring her back from the dead?"

She was the saint here. Normally, saints did the healing, but it was his time now. Could he prove to himself that he still had some control over his life and being? He closed his eyes, he didn't know why, but it felt like the right thing to do.

S

Rhom

n

g

"You're alive." Phillip cried with joy as Joan's clear non-entangled eyes glazed back into his, the tear-laden blues.

"Hello Phillip." she said weakly.

"Hello Joan." said Phillip not knowing what to say, considering that he'd just brought her back from the dead.

"Sorry." he said as if he was at fault for defending himself and that she wouldn't want to come back to life. He was such a dick.

"Phillip, Phillip." consoled Joan "I'm the one who's sorry Phillip. God…" started Joan.

"It's OK Joan, I understand, when God says…" He didn't continue as Joan had broken into a smile, which said everything.

They were quiet for some time, until Phillip asked the question that was on top of his mind.

"Joan, your arm."

"It's…" replied Joan,"it's well, why shouldn't I tell you?"Then an involuntary yawn interrupted her without warning.

"'cuse me." It was a little too late, because Phillip was halfway through his own.

"Sorry Joan."

They shared a laugh and even with drooping eyelids, she forged on.

"I've tried to kill you three times, and you still don't resent me. I'm ashamed that I should even…" Another yawn consumed her. "Sorry, Phillip, God… I'm so tired. Anyway, back in the fifteenth century, I… long story… I was Pope."

Although she didn't need to prove it to Phillip, she revealed a piece of jewelry attached to a thick chain that slid around her waist. It was a hefty looking dark key. Phillip was captivated.

The additional effort to tuck her clothing back in drained her of her last ounce of energy. Her head nodded forwards as she had a micro nap, from which she awoke seconds later.

"Joan." said Phillip seeing that she was pushing herself to tell him her story. "Sleep. You can tell me later."

"Thanks Phillip."

This time, no one slept in the car, however, both slept.

CHAPTER 21

BILL

Kelly had Bill's second, secret cell number saved in her phone. All she had to do was press it, but she was scared. Although Bill had dumped her, he'd never said it to her in person. Was she ready to take that chance, call him and lose face? She had, after all, lost face with the stupid idiot PhilLIP,

"Fancy her with a man like him, plain, pedestrian and *poor*. Never."

"So what if he'd faced down the Devil, and maybe some of what he'd said was true, but who really cares anyway. He's not in my league." she thought bitterly. A contradictory voice reminded her that he had in fact never lied to her, even when it would have benefited him and got him off the hook.

"Only when he was the Devil, so he says, did he ever lie. Bill, on the other hand, well…

Well, I miss him, and I'm lonely, and scared of being alone. I think I'll call."

Just when she was ready to press the button, she had the ingenious idea to call the office.

Phil's archrival, Mike answered, who recognized her immediately.

"Well hello, Investigating Reporting Team hero." he said with the greatest of sarcasm, "Thought you'd be at the funeral."

"Bill's dead?" exclaimed Kelly, suddenly feeling very drawn to the man.

"No Kelly, his wife."

"His wife?" Still in a shocked voice.

"Yes, his wife, and her parents." relayed Mike in a flat tone.

"What? How? When?" Kelly's voice hadn't changed pitch. "Car hijacking gone wrong. Bill's Ok. Got shot though. In the
shoulder. The funeral's today. Don't you read the papers?" He hung up rudely, as if there's any other way.

"Asshole." said Kelly, repeating what Phil, (*never think of him again*), thought of him too.

Kelly rushed back home, searched the internet, and downloaded the tragic story.

"Bill, his wife and the in-laws were in the limo, when a car-hijacker accosted them at a set of traffic lights. Several shots were fired in the altercation that ensued, killing all except Bill who suffered a non-life-threatening wound."

"OMG, the poor man." thought Kelly.

Hardly knowing what she was doing and with no time to spare, she changed and hailed a taxi to the cemetery. If it sped, she'd get there in time.

She's beautiful, it sped.

Two bodyguards had blocked her way as she approached the ceremony. She caught Bill's eye who gave them a nod. Kelly respectfully joined the outer ring of the solemn crowd and understandably kept a low profile. She was after all, an ex-lover of the widower.

Office staff, friends and relatives, formed a large circle around the three burial plots. Kelly noted many mourners for the deceased thinking it was because they were rich.

The priest said all the appropriate things about the family, like pillars of the community, philanthropists who would be missed, and ashes to ashes.

Not surprisingly when the ceremony was over, the crowd shrewdly hounded Bill, trying not to appear too eager for his favor. He was of course the lone heir by marriage, and the newspaper business would be his in due course.

"Sorry for your loss." they said.

Wanting to assert her independence, Kelly left the funeral by cab, on her own. No further than a half a mile away, Bill sent her a text.

"Where are you? I need someone to talk to." Sure.

"Bill, what happened?" Kelly asked.

They met at an exclusive hotel, renowned for its discretion. Bill didn't want to be seen running around on the day of his wife's burial but he felt that Kelly had pursued him by going to the funeral. They were together now in the hotel that they had used in the past, and they were alone.

In Kelly's defense she'd decided to contact Bill before she knew his wife was dead, and if things had developed between them, under those circumstances, then, so they would.

Now things were different. Being the other woman was bad enough, but being 'the other woman' of a recent widower was out of the question. She *believed* that Bill's desire to meet with her was only to share their pain. Nothing like before would be on Bill's mind, and most certainly it was not on hers. They would comfort each other and give moral support through these difficult times. Maybe in time they would become more than friends.

With his wife gone, Kelly had no inclination to be his lover again. She wanted commitment and marriage. She still hadn't learnt that all Bill wanted was a quick roll in the hay.

"Glass of wine?" Bill handed her one without waiting for a reply.

"No, Bill. Thanks, no." she replied.

"Come on Kelly. I need it and I don't want to drink alone. Just one glass, here you are." She smiled and accepted, but didn't really like being pressed into it.

Suddenly the thought of Phil sprung into her mind, "That's the last thing he'd do, pressure me, but you know, it's nice for the man to take charge…"

Bill was so smooth and manly and the evening flew by. In no time, she was laughing and hanging on every word he said just as she had in the past. She put her hand up to stop him, but despite her protests, the refills Bill insisted on continued. The passing of his wife seemed like long ago and every condition she'd told herself in agreeing to their meeting was in jeopardy.

She didn't know how it happened, but it was always that way. He was pulling her underwear off and she, his. In one final embrace before they consummated, she looked into his eyes and spoke.

"Is this for real, Bill? We'll be together? Forever?"

"Yes." he replied.

Phil never lied and Kelly knew that, even when he should have. Here and now, Bill, who had lied to her in the past, just to get into her pants, on the day he laid his wife to rest, had done so again. It couldn't be right. Had he reiterated his lies again, just for this?

Slowly she paused. His words finally rolled off her back just as easily as they rolled off his tongue. Kelly exploded in the plain realization of the truth.

"LIAR." she screamed at the top of her voice. "LIAR. You just want to screw me. And on this day of all days."

She scrambled to pull her pants back up, fumbled for her bra and blouse, and got dressed, berating herself simultaneously.

"My God I'm so stupid. I should have realized that's all you were after, just like before. I'm such an idiot." she ranted.

Bill was poleaxed. The change was so abrupt that he didn't know what to say, so he panicked and started to get dressed himself.

"What happened? Kelly, I love you? Why ar…"

"You don't love me. You just want to… God. I'm so dumb." shouted Kelly.

"Kelly. Kelly. It's not true. I… I… Let's talk ab…"

"Bye Bill." she exclaimed slamming the hotel door behind her.

~~~

"What do you want Bill?" responded Kelly recognizing the number on her cell.

"Kelly. I... want to apologize for my behavior last night. I... I... was overcome with grief. You see, my wife..."

"Stop it, Bill. Stop it. Stop lying, the only thing that overcame you is between your legs."

"Kelly. No. Noo. I just needed you so bad. Someone to talk to. Someone who'd listen to me. Things happened that's all. I was drunk, you were drunk, and..."

"You're putting this on me? How dare you? You know Bill, the more I think about it, and I spent the whole night doing just that, the more I realize just how much you used me.

Right up to, no, even when you sent me off with Phil to Hecate, even then I was doing your bidding.

Babysitting Phil for you. Just turned out he's more of a man than you'll ever be.

And you know what else, Bill? When I was doing all that thinking,

I just wondered how convenient it was for your wife and her parents to all die in that car hijacking, and you, just getting a little shot.

Had she found out about, me? Our affair?

Was that what happened?

She found out about 'us' and she was going to tell her mommy and daddy, and poor little Billy would be out on the street.

So you arranged an incident and while you were at it, hey presto, wife and in-laws are history. Is that what happened?"

Hey, did you tell the police about 'me' when they questioned you?" Bill's business-like reply didn't take long in coming,

"What do you want?"

CHAPTER 22

YOUR DAWN IS COMING

The night turned to pale morning as the Sun dared to dawn a new day. For Phillip it was a crowning moment. He was alive to see another, but no thanks to God. That night while listening to Joan's breathing, he contemplated his vision on the edge of the Universe, until he was worn out and had fallen asleep.

He had pondered if he really had travelled there. Was it a dream or hallucination?

"Idiot, it was a concussion." he concluded, and upon that, he drifted off in blissful innocence.

"My God Phillip, it's embedded in your skull."

With the pinky of her good hand, Joan tapped a tiny pinhead of metal countersunk in the spot where she attacked him.

"Wow." said Phillip, not to Joan's comment or because a piece of Joan's Cross was still in his head, but to the silent *'bong'* that ran through every bone in his body.

"You know."continued Joan a little drowsily,"I think you're shorter."

Phillip finished brushing dirt out of the tent, and like a child being measured against a door jam, stood up straight and tall.

His trousers were crumpled up on the top of his Adonis Shoes. As if to show off, they flicked in a lightning speed transformation to the softest pair of thigh high leather boots known to man, and then swiftly back to shoes again.

They and Phillip had indeed undergone another transformation.

Phillip smiled happily and he requested them to do it again. This time, they transformed to a pair of chic and rugged Wellington boots. Their sight left him ecstatic.

"WOW." exclaimed Joan and Phillip together, most impressed.

Facing reality, he wondered about his reduced stature. He'd not been a tall man, and now he was even shorter than a person of medium height.

The thought of Kelly, of how slender she was, and a vision of her in high heels, tormented him, as it had many a man. He dwelled on the idea that a woman like her, even if she was only a smidgen taller, would never choose a short man like him.

"She'd never, not that there was any chance anyway, go for me now.
My height would just be another reason for ridicule and dismissal."

Had Phillip known his triple DNA had undergone a unique enhancement, he may have thought differently. Unknown to him, titanium bone, born from the shaft of Joan's cross, grew and framed his skeleton. He was a different man, again.

Phillip needed a distraction from the beguiling vision of Kelly, so he willed himself to contemplate Joan's future now that she was so obviously not a saint.

She was exhausted and had fallen back to sleep. Drained from the loss of her Entanglement and now a mere mortal, would God still be her patron? And what would happen when she died? Would God let her into Heaven, as she had failed in her murder of him, or would everlasting Hell be her terrible reward?

If this were so, Phillip would kill God, he swore. Whether he meant it or not, whether he could or not, wasn't a consideration.

~~~

Buster was alone for the first time in his life. The death of his elder twins could have left him like a ship without a rudder, but that wasn't the case. At the request of the police he'd driven down from the cabin on a four-wheeler and had identified their bodies without saying a word. A boiling rage, however, was bubbling inside him.

"It ain't alcohol poisoning. I know that tweren't true, 'cos I know my bro's, they'd had it a ton of times and it never killed 'em. It's that guy they beat up, he came back and he killed them. That's what happened, and he's gonner pay."

He hadn't told the police anything, as that wasn't their way. Stepping up on their own terms, that was their way.

He remembered the car the man drove and the dent in the driver side. He remembered his face and how similar the guy's face would be to that dent after he'd finished with him. All he had to do was find the car and he'd find the face.

Buster drove all day and night, down every road in and outta of town. He was going to kill him as soon as he saw his ugly mug. His brothers would have their revenge. Vengeance and revenge were the words he understood and they were how he'd get his justice.

"For his bros."

The first car he spotted down a country track didn't have any dent. Just then, as his resolve faltered, he saw another car of the same make deeper in the bush. He crept up to it like the expert hunter he was and controlled his thumping heart.This was the car, no mistake. Then in the middle of a small group of trees he saw a tent and the black silhouette of a man moving around inside.

"It's 'im, however, if it ain't, I'll just 'smack him around a bit. Probably deserves a beating anyway.There's a reason a guy's out here dodging town, probably dodging the law too." He was one to know.

"I bet I ain't wrong, I can smell him."

Using the gun's nozzle to open the tent's flap, he ducked under it and pushed on through the doorway. He'd hadn't been wrong; he'd found his man and "A reckoning was a knocking."

Phillip looked Buster and recognized him immediately. Buster stood silently in his tent pointing his rifle at him, while Phillip waited for him to say something. They stared at each other, but neither spoke. Just when Phillip wondered whether he should say something or just extend a hand as if to introduce himself, he said.

"You killed my bro's, now it's my turn." He shot Phillip from point blank range. It would have killed any man.

Faster than sound, the bullet bounced off his titanium rib cage and sprayed shrapnel everywhere. Buster was an experienced hunter and he knew he hadn't missed. He also knew that a rifle shot from such short range would have blasted a hole in Phillip's back the size of a baseball. Instead, he only saw a thin trickle of liquid running out of a superficial scratch in the middle of his chest.

He shot again and again. Bullets ricocheted in every direction from the impact of their target, until one cannoned back and severed his jugular. It gave Buster enough time to grasp that Phillip was still alive, and in a minute, he wouldn't be.

In a final gesture, he fired his last round as he fell to his knees, and tragically found a target in Joan.

Buster's last sight was that of Phillip tending Joan's wound oblivious to his multiple and trivial nicks and scrapes. He died a galled man who had lived an irrelevant and unworthy life.

Phillip wasn't familiar with death yet kneeling next to Joan he knew that she was gone. He considered using the healing SongRhom, but thought better of it. Maybe it was fate or something, he didn't know what, but it seemed like she was supposed to die. As if two deaths in a day had a meaning. Although he had a better insight to God's thinking than any man, he still knew nothing,

"Maybe that was it. Maybe it was all for nothing. Right or wrong, past and future, did anything have meaning? And why was luck so choosy? The bullet need not have killed her, but if that was God's will, then it sucks."

He decided to make it worth something after all, so out of spite to the almighty, he summoned SongRhom. It wouldn't come, even after he tried with his eyes open,

"It seems," concluded Phillip, "if the feeling isn't genuine, I can't bring it."

Phillip patiently collected everything in the tent he thought he might need, and left the bodies of Joan and Buster on the ground not knowing what else to do. Joan had tried to kill him three times, yet he felt such deep sorrow for her that he had tears in his eyes as he drove away.

"She had given everything obeying God's will. Now she's dead.

I dearly, hope that she's rewarded with eternal life in Heaven." True compassion.

Phillip paid scant attention to the holes in his shirt, nor to the amazing fact that the bullets' penetration was less than skin deep. Not much surprised him anymore. He was shorter, but with a built-in bulletproof body, he drove off in the direction of the other entrance point to ClearStream. He lost his way several times before finding the small track that led to its lower side.

He parked by the IAT's SUV tire tracks and sauntered off towards the ruined village. He was lost in thought about how long it'd be before the two bodies would be found, and was still a little peeved that Ross and Harry deserted his archeological find.

Walking leisurely, he began to appreciate the miracle he'd experienced. He thought that maybe he was closer to being *more super mortal* than any witch, more so, thinking that Hecate would never withstand a bullet.

The Sun was up and shone its crisp bright light in his face. For the first time in his life, he experienced the miracle of life, his life.

"Maybe God was good after all?" but who wouldn't be in denial.

The further he walked, the greater the sorrow of Joan's loss built up in him, until it was sidelined by a terrible sight. A body was floating in the mirror like waters of the cow trough. Without a thought Phillip dashed crazily towards the body and flung himself into the water, and into the jaws of death.

He seemed to fly over the water enabling him to view the full length of his reflection, until the inevitable force of gravity imposed its will. In a huge belly flop he crashed into the water with unprecedented voracity.

Unlike water his contact made a smash, as if it was glass. Even though the cow drink was less than a couple of feet deep, he found himself completely immersed and he struggled to find the bottom.

At first, he didn't realize that the water just didn't feel quite right. The water felt much more like millions of shards of glass. His hands waved and his feet floundered in vain attempts to orient himself.

Phillip couldn't locate ground to get his head above the surface. Time moved rapidly and panic drained his breath. And just as importantly, it sapped his thoughts. Even with plenty of air still in his lungs, his mind lapsed and he forgot he was underwater. He took a quick unsuspecting breath.

Instantly, glass, not water, filled his lungs, accompanied with the most vicious and surprising Entanglement attack he'd ever experienced.

Smash a mirror,

Smash a mirror,

Smash a mirror,

-3.141...

Splinters shredded his lungs and each jagged shard drove into his body.The Entanglement attack ate into his freshly exposed flesh. Now for the third time, something searched for his soul and sent it again into its secret hiding place where no one could probe.

Phillip had suffered many contretemps now, and it was becoming easier for him with every attack to recognize, respond and react. Even with the element of surprise, almost automatically, he summoned his unique survival mechanism and struck out in retaliation.

R

h

Song

M

He was incredibly small and lost in infinite space and time. He fought logic and forced his mind to get his bearings, to accept the unbelievable. Through the soles of his Shoes, he could feel the ground burbling under his feet. Then he looked overhead at the tiny sun spinning around him at a mindboggling speed at the edge of sight.

In the space between them, a wide, wild expanse, he saw minute Universes pop in and then out of existence. The last time he was under attack, via an instrument of God, he thought he was on the edge of the Universe. Now he dared to wonder where he was.

Phillip never had a girlfriend. He had spent many hours watching science shows, and had a solid amateur's knowledge of the great theories of the time. As a result, now he recognized his whereabouts.

He was inside a hydrogen atom, an atom of the most common element in the Universe. The single electron was the Sun and quantum fluctuations filled and vacated the void in between. The wondrous sight, never seen by another, filled him with such awe that he instinctively reached down and touched the nucleus.

His hand vibrated in unison with the particles and then with a thought from his conscious mind, he realized his Shoes had vanished, and he was barefoot. The three points of contact felt the turmoil beneath them intensify, growing stronger in frequency and amplitude until, to his amazement, microscopic entities jettisoned out like water vapor from a manhole cover. Then it, as if by an internal vacuum cleaner, was sucked back in and pacified the roiling and destabilized hadron. This was repeated again and again, until it was doing it all the time.

A new equilibrium was established.

In wonderment, Phillip relaxed. His Shoes reappeared. He smiled hardly recalling he was under attack. A strange shudder shook the atom, and as Phillip looked back up to the 'sky' he saw an infinitesimally small speck spin around the electron. Like Earth orbiting the Sun and the Moon orbiting the Earth, now the electron had its own satellite.

"What the hell is going on?"

Time crept forward and so did his pressing obligation to return to the matter of surviving. Thus his sortie into the inner working of an atom ended.

He looked at the bullet nicks in his chest. One of the scabs had been knocked off and clear water, not red blood, was staining his shirt. He stared at the superficial wound, dabbed his finger in the watery blood, and tasted it. It was water, wet, runny and pure. He could only conclude that his veins now carried water rather than red human plasma. And another feeling rippled through him. He felt he was getting shorter again.

Stunned and in disbelief he saw the runes that had eluded him and they appeared to be glaring at him.There was no confusing the carvings now. He saw the shape of the Queen of Spades engraved deep, succinct and permanent in the stone and their ninety-degree edges were as sharp as knives.

Forgetting he was close to drowning again, Phillip gazed in fascination at the sheer beauty of the playing card. The lines were clear and concise. He would have pondered its meaning had he thought of it, but he didn't get the chance because without warning, it grew in size from less than a foot until it mirrored him exactly.

Despite Phillip's precarious situation, he still jumped when both mouths opened and spoke, emitting a voice with a slight stereo echo.

"Whats? I felt a little tickles. Wass it from yous? NOs. Possible nots. I's have tormented the Devil, who sought me for millennia, and for a year I's poked fun at him from under his noses. I's enabled John Abbott to gamble and win against his darknesss.

I's have desecrated his precious Hell with my urine, and have implanted the seed of doubt in his twisted brain, scarred forever I's do believes.

So's who are you, the one who sees me now when none have befores?"

"I'm..."went to reply Phillip.

"Haves I's been miss-informeds? The's infected one has duped mes? She's will not be satisfieds."

"Huh?" said Phillip lost in this one-sided debate.

"The's miserable being Boleyn said you were he, Phils. Yous are nots. Yous are ... Unknown to mes." the Black Maria continued. "buts yet you lives, I's don't understands. The's Phil I's have known and lost, the mouse I dangled, the faint hearted I's fated to die, vanished. Yous are not hes."

"Wha...?"

"Yous, yet the invisible, the one I's see not, lives. Dies again, should I's embarrass myself in failings."

The attack from this unknown assailant was unlike those of God or the static ones of the Devil, for it fluctuated and changed its initial chant of misfortune, to another harbinger of ruin.

BAR, BAR, BAR

BAR, BAR, BAR

BAR, BAR, BAR

-3.141592...

Explosions of black and light ignited around Phillip and he instinctively but needlessly ducked. Phillip was one of four entities in the Universe to observe the Entanglement War, but only he had entered its no man's land, the area between God and the Devil's front lines. It was a halo invisible to mortals that was thousands of miles thick and it surrounded Earth two light hours beyond her immediate orbit.

Phillip tore through the barricade, leaving voids of Entanglement blasts in his wake. For reasons not clear, the Devil's BLACK managed to flood in first and make ground, God's LIGHT was absent.

Phillip wanted to leave as quickly as possible, not knowing what this new vision was and he was worried about the unknown. Also, wherever he was, it was certain that he was trespassing. Payback would be expected. Most likely the Devil or God would demand payment, and that debt would be settled with his blood.

He was in another fight for his life, and that was his primary concern. So he closed his eyes and willed himself home, only to witness another unseen wonder of the Universe. When he opened them again, he witnessed another impossible sight.

The playing card lifted itself up in front of him and performed a slow three sixty turn in a display of power. It wasn't the first conqueror to flaunt its superiority over its quarry, but the exhibition performed for Phillip was a privilege. Only eternal mortals and now he had seen this, she existed in only two dimensions.

Phillip understood the implications of such a demonstration. An adversary never reveals a secret unless it anticipates its prey will be dead, soon, and that meant him.

"What was his final resting place to be?" he worried.

Both Heaven and Hell held little appeal. He weighed the options of Heaven where God was out for his blood versus the purgatory of the Devil, or imprisonment by this unknown God like entity. Phillip knew this was a fight he must win, or a fate of eternal loneliness and pain awaited him.

He let go of this frightening thought when the playing card's mouths opened to emit a long line of numbers. They streamed out of her mouths as if she was in a cartoon. Phillip would have laughed if he wasn't fighting for his life. Not knowing or caring about the attacker's identity, or its motivation, Phillip had dithered long enough. He wasn't without a power of his own, so he counterattacked again.

R

h

Song

m

Phillip was unaware of the transformations his body underwent when embroiled in an Entanglement attack, but it happened again. The metamorphosis was profound although invisible to the naked eye. This time, his watery blood became heavy water which caused his body to rev up like a perfectly tuned engine.

Pi's planned exit for him was proving to be premature as Phillip's RhomSong sent a shiver down the playing card's body and she flushed red. It stopped her in her tracks, being unlike anything she'd experienced, and having never felt pain before, it delivered a serious blow. Her ego wasn't unscathed either once she'd figured out what exactly had happened.

"WHATs" she squawked,"Whats…was that… Whats?" as she flicked back to black with a blink of an eye.

She looked at Phillip naturally expecting him to be dead, but he was still alive.

"Whats? Yous still exists? Leasts you not be deads? Yous rile me mores. Ares you the Devil seeking sports? Nos, of course you're nots. I's,with mirth at his child like bemusement, watched that fool flounders. Sorrys for him, yes I's felts. Clues, yes I's left thems. Nines falls of waters; here I's reside, in the fraction at the nadirs.

Divides by threes.

Whats have thees?

Buts still, his highness could not fathoms.

Easiers I's made it thuss.

Whats, it is so simple, nos?

Thes Earth. Threes.

Don'ts you sees?

I's grew in anger, bored and tried of his inaness.

Johns Abbott mys saving graces, I'ms still laughing at the Dark Lord's fallss.

Yous are Abbott linage not I's seess.

Sos, who are yous?

Yous, whom has illed mes.

Sickeneds mes.

Injureds mes?

Causings my Black to Redden, I'm compromiseds.

Thiss is No Phils.

Nos.

Shes said she would deliver him, Phil, but she delivers me a foes.

Shes will not be made wholes.

Buts now, I's must dispense you, you the enigmass.

Nots Hell, not Heaven, for you, for the harm thou has laid at my feets.

Yous are miness. Moress still, because and yet, and beyond that, you challenge ME.

Yous speak; to 3.142... to *Pi*... to MEs.

Yets, and beyond that, you touched MEs. Dosss you not know with whom you faces?"

"Err." croaked Phillip completely dumfounded wondering even if he was supposed to respond.

"Canss you not hold your tongue, have you not heard of Einsteins? It'ss is a cluess."

"What?" was all the bemused Phillip could say.

"Wrongss, was he not right, indeed that fool God does not play dice with the Universe, for it is I's, I's am the oness."

"Err, wha...?"

"Yous know nots. Nothings. Hows it is, I's do not know, NOR DO I CAREs. Yets you live now, chances are, and I's am the lord of that, you will not no moress."

And the attack fluctuated for a third time.

BLACK MARIA, BLACK MARIA, BLACK MARIA, BL
BLACK MARIA, BLACK MARIA, BLACK MARIA, BL
BLACK MARIA, BLACK MARIA, BLACK MARIA, BL

-3.1415926...

Phillip ducked into his Shoes as the attack sought his will and soul. He still hadn't figured out why or by whom. He wasn't to know that the combination and accumulation of all the attackers' oscillating Entanglement was more violent than God and the Devil's combined.

The pain in his lungs dove to new depths and the feeling of bags of broken glass intensified. Yet he was still alive. On his last breath, Phillip moved past his initial shock of injury, as a potent new feeling erupted, *injustice*. It was the bootstrap for a host of other emotions that Phil had had many times but never acted upon.

Phillip however was at the end of his tether. Angered and incensed by the persistent, unrelenting and unprovoked assault; enraged by gibberish and flat-out nonsensical accusations, Phillip retaliated. For the first time in his life, he wasn't afraid of hurting someone.

R

h

Song

m

Wracked and contorted under the stress, his blood churned as it underwent a further mutation, where the heavy water was replaced with the compressed counterpart. However, blood wasn't Phillip's only bodily alteration, *Pi's* attack had misappropriated over nine inches of Phillip's physique, but what had been taken in height, was made up in weight.

When he was under attack from the witches, Entanglement changed his eyes. Now, under a physical Entanglement attack from the Eternal Mortals, fundamental changes occurred. Phillip now *weighed three times* more than he had only earlier that day, and he was nearly a *foot shorter*. He had titanium bones and compressed water for blood. The only thing unchanged was Phillip, the ex-Phil.

Whether he was the same person was debatable, because Phil never harbored a desire to live as much as Phillip had now.

His desire to survive intensified and strengthened. Phillip, who was suddenly able to determine his orientation, thrust his head out of the encasing shallow water.

The mirror glass surface became mere river water once again.

With bones refurbished from God's attack and blood renewed from *Pi's*, he climbed out of the cow drink a new man.

He didn't even cough.

CHAPTER 23

JUST TYPICIAL

Andre and Andrea, known as '*A squared*' to their colleagues, had done an all-nighter trying to figure out what had just happened. Yesterday they played starring roles in a TV documentary on Quantum Mechanics.Their claim to fame was the room sized super cooled apparatus that measured the effects of *quantum fluctuations* on the orbit of the electron in a hydrogen atom. The mathematics correlated so closely it was hailed as the most accurate theory and experiment ever conducted.

Of course, the projected audience wasn't going to break box office records; still, they felt the rush of being film stars. They celebrated in the way that all scientists do, by working the graveyard shift, and that was where things had started to go awry.

Without explanation, the experiment that was tested and retested to have one hundred percent reliability was having major issues.

They were startled when they started to experience failures. It started with just one upset, thus both A's put it down to a computer glitch. The number climbed to three and then eight, with no sign of it stopping.They had stripped several components down to their bare bones and reassembled them, to no avail. What caused the problems couldn't be determined that first night, so what had started out as a great week, quickly turned into a disastrous one.

The last thing they were going to do, however, was tell anyone. No one was going to jeopardize their newfound fame. By the end of the second night, they considered buying a gallon of gasoline and a box of matches.

A small group of entrepreneurs in another part of the World floundered as their prototype *Quantum computer* calculated that fifteen divided by five equaled three point one four two. And was approaching PI with every passing minute. Because of this strange and inexplicable phenomenon, they too considered a similar dire exit strategy.

Things were amiss.

P*i* was more than a little concerned.

~~~

Hell was like a childhood playground; full of bullies and victims; rife with whispers and rumor. On Earth the teachers were powerless in controlling the natural order of the street, but in Hell, teachers were called Demons and the Devil. They had power and they used it.

With their futures depending on them keeping their mouths shut, Rank, Ego and Vin shunned conversation with other hell-mates to mitigate the risk of revealing their secret. So in the *school yard of Hell* when a rumor swept through, the trio was the last to know because of their self-imposed seclusion.

Vin, as the best at gleaning gossip, realized it wasn't about them. Wanting the full story, he pretended to be deaf and dumb and stumbled intentionally into an excited debate, and it was worth his while.

Earlier that week, a pair of twins, Basher and Smasher, had arrived in Hell. Sentenced to Level IV without much ado, nothing appeared out of the ordinary with the pair or their destination.

It took only one look into their eyes for everyone to see they were rotten to the core, thus they fit in perfectly. Their strange way of talking and their lack of coordination caused other hell-mates to stay well clear of them. They were unpredictable and therefore dangerous. A couple of days later, the third and youngest brother arrived, also designated to the Fourth Level. That was when the commotion started.

Buster knew something was wrong as soon as he was reunited with his brothers as they made their homegrown fraternal salutations. In all the times when they were drunk, stoned, or drunk and stoned, he'd never known them to be like this. Neither one could string a complete sentence together nor could either perform any simple function. They couldn't even punch each other, their trademark greeting, so bad was their coordination.

It had gone unremarked by everyone in Hell, as no one knew them from Earth, and so they thought this was how they were. He would have been vocal about it to if it had not been for a surprise lashing from a demon. It was a lucky break though because had he drawn attention to them, the demons and the Devil might have listened.

Buster, however, was in a Hell of his own. His brothers were handicapped and hardly themselves, and the longer he stayed with them, the more he saw that something more sinister could be true.

Not only were they wounded in mind and body, but also according to Buster, their souls appeared not to be whole either. Smasher had Basher's scars and Basher had Smasher's voice; but most notable and puzzling were their memories and mannerisms were that of the other twin.

Only Buster knew this, but once he breathed of it to a bent ear, in a secretive whisper to a hell-mate sworn to silence, most of Hell knew, just like school. His mistake was confiding with the deceitful thespian called Vin, the last person to trust as he was the worst when it came to gossip. Buster's concerns were broadcasted like a TV ad and before long, the Devil got wind of them.

The Devil, however, didn't bust in and interrogate the twins blindly. Instead, he craftily and secretly watched the three brothers from a distance to determine whether this was some kind of a stupid ruse. It wouldn't have been the first.

After several hours of observation the Devil became increasingly concerned. A prank was much less worrisome. Strange things had happened in the World, which he assumed God was responsible for. But now here in Hell, his impregnable fortress, a mysterious phenomenon was on his doorstep and he had no idea of its cause.

Because he had been overconfident and dismissive on his initial encounter with John Abbott, he now disciplined himself to think wisely. This time he'd avoid a rush to judgment and the imprisonment for two centuries. He glanced at his footwear involuntarily.

To be certain the Devil eventually summoned the trio. The additional stress of a close encounter with the Devil amplified their erratic behavior and confirmed his fears. Somehow, the souls of Basher and Smasher had been mingled together, and then, from all appearances had been erroneously redistributed back into their bodies.

Why the two twins were incapacitated as they were was another mystery. He didn't know if it was the result of the muddled-up souls, but he knew that no mental illness could account for it. Impossible as that was, there was just one other thing, only half of them were there.

CHAPTER 24

ON YOUR OWN

When the double-crossing Kelly changed sides and decided not to oppose Hecate's idea to perform her Reveal Spell, Boleyn felt exposed being unable defend her opposition. Things became clear to Hecate now; she had been toyed with. Indifferent to her feelings, Hecate saw *Boleyn's 'lessons'* for what they were: secretive experiments that dealt with her inability to recognize Phil. They were nothing more than demeaning and degrading games. She severed her already tenuous bond of sisterhood.

Boleyn's loss of her witch-hood directly influenced all her actions and it was the tragic source of her mounting depression. It was the reason she withheld information from Ross. She desired a measure of power to feel less dependent and in control. Sadly she was an un-entangled, witch-hoodless midget; nothing more than an oddity.

On her way back from ClearStream, Boleyn told Harry that she was spending the night to search for Hecate's spell paraphernalia. He knew she actually wanted time alone, so he agreed with her plan. Unfortunately, she construed his quick acknowledgement as a rejection, as if the IAT wasn't happy to have her company.

It only solidified what she planned to do, and it was something the others would have fought against vehemently had they known. Making her way back to the outskirts of ClearStream's ruins, she did the unthinkable, she summoned the Devil.

"Boleyn. How wonderful of you to think of me. I do so enjoy your company and it has been such a long time, a week between friends is too much don't you think?

Before you reply, I hope you understand that I don't like disappointment. So if you have requested my presence just to parley, then I think you should think again, need I say more?

Oh my, forgive me Boleyn for doubting your intentions, I know you know better, please forget my ignorance.

Now, how may I assist you? If I can, I will."

His voice was like music; his charm was like chocolate, and if Boleyn had any thoughts of turning back, she knew that it was too late now, by far.

"You're Lordship." said Boleyn remaining in her curtsy, "I wish to be a witch again."

"So." replied the Devil, "a direct request if ever there was one. I like that, none of that pleading and scrounging nonsense.

Good for you. Let me grant your wish."

Dark Entanglement of green yellow and then red appeared around the Devil's human coil. It slowly engulfed him rising higher and higher until it towered into the night sky, and when it was primed and ready, he asked Boleyn,

"*You wish to have what was in you, in you again*, Boleyn the once mighty Red Witch?"

Even if she didn't, it was too late to say otherwise, she was committed.

"Yes" she replied.

"Then it is done."

Black gushed upwards in an endless stream blackening the already black sky. She saw the Devil transmute into the White Eyed Gargoyle, ascend the column of Black Entanglement as if in an open air elevator, and launch into the night sky. He echoed a terrifying and wicked laugh aimed solely at Boleyn and the deed was done.

~~~

The Devil was pleased with himself. He had done two hard tasks simultaneously: one requiring brute force, the other requiring stealth and finesse. He had attained huge gains in the Entanglement War and reclaimed the majority of ground he'd lost while imprisoned in the Shoe. Consequently, they had achieved equilibrium and both sides continued to consolidate their positions.

However, his main achievement was the secretive capture of Phil's soul. "A job well done" crowed the Devil.

The perfect opportunity to reward the warden Rank had arisen. It was so enticing, that the Devil had encapsulated himself in turbulent Entanglement to avoid giving the ruse away. He was hardly in any danger of that happening, yet wanted to be sure God and *Pi* would not find out.

Since the completion of their task, Rank, Ego and Vin checked Phil's soul on a daily basis. If the Devil had known it was a sham, and in fact they were only going through the motions, then the Devil would have doomed the trio to the Eighth Level of Hell in a second. As it was, one of the perpetrators was going to do very well indeed.

Beatings from the demons were a rarity now and the trio roamed throughout Hell almost unchallenged. When the Devil surprisingly summoned Rank he almost died of a heart attack, as too did Ego and Vin.

When Rank didn't return for over an hour, Ego and Vin feared the worst and were terrified that their names would be called next.

What relief, and then jealousy, when they overheard the demons gossip that Rank had been rewarded a rare and amazing prize. Then the beatings from the envious monsters resumed, causing Ego and Vin to hate Rank more.

~~~

Boleyn sat on the limestone wall of the cow drink and contemplated suicide. It wouldn't be the end however, just the beginning. She had sold her soul to the Devil and was destined for Hell no matter how the rest of her life went. Suicide or not, the Devil brought Hell to her on Earth with his latest deception, and she'd fallen for the bait...

"*You wish to have what was in you, in you again*, Oh Boleyn the once mighty Red Witch?" he had cajoled.

"And I can't even die now." Her sobbing was most sorrowful. "But I can't live, God help me!

Why bother? *She* never answers.

I want to die.

I want to die.

I want to die."

Her minute frame wailed, and she gave in. The waters of ClearStream opened their arms and she, not so much threw herself in, as lowered herself in, a dreadful reminder that even a two-foot-deep cow trough was too deep for the tiny midget.

"Here I come Hell, you can't be worse than Earth.

There's nothing that can help."

"Helps. Help. It's something I's offer. And I's can, so close your eyes." said the invisible voice leaving its imprint in Boleyn's head.

"Hello Devil. Here I am" replied Boleyn.

"Boleyn, I's am not the Devil. Close your eyes, I's pray." the voice continued.

"Devil, I give in. Is this Hell? Is giving me hope, Hell?" replied Boleyn again.

"Boleyn, I's am not the Devil. I's swear. Close your eyes, and trust me." The voice responded ever so gently.

"As you wish Devil." And Boleyn closed her eyes, and the Queen of Spades filled her mind.

"The Devil, I's ams not, mortal, you insult me calling mes thus. I's ams *Dia. Pi.* And I's offer you hope, for I's ams known also by that name... amongst others. Mortals call mes many things."

"Sure De..." began Boleyn.

"QUIETs. Least I rescind my offer and leave you for Hell to take you now. Save you from it, I's cannot should I desire, but I can ease yours predicament, that is my desire, which is passing quickly with your ignorances.

"Wh..." Poor Boleyn.

"QUIETs! Deliver me Phil and the parasite within you will die, and makes thee high, or perish in Hell. No more I say to yous."

Boleyn nodded and sealed another contract.

A frustrated and sour voice rang in Boleyn's head,"Yous irk me Boleyn. Yous do nothing, I canc…"

"Here he is." She replied with heavy relief, fulfilling the contract in the nick of time.

The offer she had wouldn't save her from Hell, nor would it make her a witch again. But being rid of the thing that dwelt within and the doubling of height would make the remainder of her life bearable.

Just as she predicted, Phil couldn't help but be the knight in shining armor. She'd forgotten, however, just how annoying he was, arriving at the last moment. Nevertheless, he did what Boleyn suspected he would do. He threw himself into the pool in a valiant attempt to rescue her before she drowned.

She was happy she was still alive now and her suicidal thoughts were all gone. Inflicting a justifiable revenge upon a man that stole what she perceived as hers, invigorated her. Despite her terrible mistake in summoning the Devil, the pleasure of causing and witnessing Phil's death was almost worth it.

CHAPTER 25

HAPPILY ALIVED <u>BUT</u> PUZZLED

Dripping wet but enjoying being alive, Phillip bathed in the blissful warmth of the Sun as he tried to make sense of what had just happened.

"Boleyn!" Phillip quickly turned, grabbed her floating body and hauled her out of the pond. He was careful not to touch the water.

He knew her survival was at stake. It was obvious that she had been in longer than anyone could survive. He didn't expect her to suddenly break out in a long fit of coughing, but that's just what she did. She too, was alive.

"Boleyn. Boleyn."inquired the perturbed Phillip,"are you alright?" "Yea.

Phil." spluttered the recovering Boleyn in a bitter tone,
    after taking a while for her to reply.

"I save her life at almost the cost of my own and she's pissed?" thought Phillip who put it down to her almost drowning.

"LIP, its Phillip Boleyn, Phillip. It's important... never call me by my old name again. And yer welcome." said Phillip mirroring her tone of voice.

"Anyway, it's... I don't know, look. It's not me. It's not Phil. It's PhilLIP, PhilLIP, PhilLIP." he said loudly, concatenating 'LIP'to the end of his old name of Phil and waited again for a response, which came seconds later than expected.

"Yes, OK." shouted Boleyn, "LIP. LIP. LIP."

"Never met a LIP I didn't hate." she thought with venom.

Phillip clearly saw she wasn't okay.Yesterday,he couldn't determine anything other than something wasn't right. Now he could see better and a blight existed within her. Even a piece of BLACK. It wasn't in the heart. But her heart was broken.

He decided to be on guard from now on as if he needed an additional reason considering she'd attempted to kill him more than once.

A sideways peak told him, "Yes, there's something dark inside of her. And not just her mood."

A sudden and profound internal urge interrupted him, and almost desperately, he shed his earthly clothing, other than his Shoes. Then he lay naked on a stone wall next to the swirling water. He didn't care that Boleyn was there. Her back was towards him anyway and she appeared to be too overwhelmed with her misfortunes.

Allowing the yearning its freedom, his Shoes proceeded to show him their new prowess. Without hesitation or reticence, they enveloped him in a one-piece suit of brushed flexible material tougher than metal, and in timeless style. The feel was sensual, reassuring and an attire that nothing could match. He knew from that moment on that he'd never wear mortal apparel again.

With a quick thought, Phillip was back to his usual drab style of plainness. In his previous life, his main objective was simply to survive, and had worn cheap and nasty clothes to show his submissiveness.

But, "Why not, now, indulge a little." he proclaimed. With a tweak, an undeniable vein of cool rippled through his garments. (He thrust the image of Kelly from his mind for the umpteenth time). He treated himself and focused on the feeling of utter luxury his new clothing gave him. It was good therapy.

"I wonder what else I, me and my Shoes can do?"

Standing up, Phillip checked on Boleyn again. She was still alive. It made Phillip certain that she had something to do with the attacks. She coughed sporadically and mumbled as Phillip saw she was too self-absorbed with her troubles to care about him at the moment. Above all however, he couldn't miss the presence of her BLACK infection first and foremost.

Phillip still had Phil's introspective personality, and just as he would have done, with three new attacks on his life just today, he started to count them.

"Once by Hecate, once from Ruebella and twice from Boleyn. Then four times by the Devil, twice from Joan and once from God, assist going to Joan.

Now today, three times from another entity, not a witch, nor a saint, someone unknown, but most definitely something of the Devil or God's stature.

That's fourteen times to date and that's not including the shooter or even being beaten up by those two outside the bar."

"Wow. And I'm still fucking alive. I'm a new man because of them no doubt."

He called upon his Shoes and he smiled at the total commitment in their response.

"And you know, those bullets didn't kill me. I mean like in a normal mortal attack. I'm I... immortal? Super human? Can I fly? Such a stupid idea, but can I?"

The idea was electrifying. He did so much want to be like 'The Engle's Man'of comic lore.The idea was so foolish, but so tantalizing that he couldn't think of anything else.

"Damn it, I'm going to try."

Foolishly, he took a run up and threw himself into the air like his super hero, and fell flat on his face. His self-confidence and self-worth were crushed and he didn't try again.

Phillip moped for over an hour. He'd taken many blows to his ego in his life, but this affected him badly as he had, in his mind, a realistic expectation of success. It caused him great consternation because despite his failure he was actually right that he was a grand powerful superhuman.

Unlike his old self, where he routinely harbored unfounded fantasies of grandeur, now, he really was godlike. He had survived fatal attacks from the Eternal Entangled, healed people, and brought one back from the dead.

He surmised after some intensive thinking, that only in a life-threatening situation could he summon his RhomSong. Likewise, only if it felt righteous, could he heal with his SongRhom.

"Maybe I could fly after all, if the situation was an emergency." he reasoned and regained some feeling of self-esteem. Besides there was also the good luck that Kelly wasn't present.

"Thank G.. Thank whoever she's not here."

He turned his attention to Boleyn sitting on a lonesome rock a safe distance from the river. Not from a gut feeling but some sense beyond human, he knew something was inside of her. Whatever it was that infected her, was also occupying all her attention making her self-absorbed and distant.

"So Boleyn, what's happening?" asked Phillip sitting next to her in a gentle voice. After asking four times, all with different inflections, he gave up.

Sitting next to Boleyn gave him just the comparison he needed, and he shifted his focus to himself. He realized that he didn't just feel shorter; he was shorter. A sick to his stomach feeling swept over him.

"Oh God, Kelly's never going to go for me now, I'm at least five or six inches shorter, hell ten inches shorter. Now I'm tons shorter than her, even if there had been a remote chance, now there's none whatsoever."

"How would Kelly, a woman like her, ever, ever go with a short man, ugly man, like me?"

Phillip was being unjustly hard on himself, he was just plain, not plain ugly. So he turned his attention to the voice that had attacked him, and what it had said.

"What was all that mumbo jumbo? And thank G... not again, thank whatever that it did say all that gibberish as it'll take my mind off Kelly de-cyphering that lot."

~~~

P*i*, on the other hand, had turned introspective and pensive. Not worried yet, but she had attacked this mortal with three point one massive barrages, and he seemed to have lived, notwithstanding the Entanglement crushing retaliations that had ensued.

During her attack, each strike required more than usual effort due to her sickness. In the stream of numbers, infinitely down the calculation that was her being, there were errors.

"A number certainly was missing, mutated perhaps, perhaps yes, believe I's. Causing this Phil, Phillip as he calls himsself, irritating survival, it is so.

Why can't I's see him either? The bad luck I's endowed upon Phil, remember I's so well, caused Hecate to pursue and attack him. The last time my fateful touch did anything to him that went according to plan.

Hate, Yes, I's hate him. Get him I's will, and when I's do, *then I'll be healed*. And he. Not."

~~~

There were so many unanswered questions that Phillip failed in his attempt not to think about them. In particular, the attacks from the unknown supernatural assailant mystified him. Probably he was the only one in the Universe who had the ability to distinguish between attacks from the Devil and from God.

"But these new attacks were from whom? And whatever it was, it was equal to or impossibly, greater than the two other deities."

He thought over everything that assailant said. He couldn't remember much as he had been fighting for his life. What he recollected was total nonsense.

"Or was it? It talked about God as if *she* was inferior."

He decided to think about a different subject, being frightened by the possibility that God was less then *GOD*. His other train of thought wasn't much better, that God was also trying to kill him.

"Man, I wish Kelly were here, I'd take a beating from her rather than think about this anymore, it's scary. But, but… Shut up Phillip, you have to put her out of your mind."

His phone rang, and his surprise and delight were irrepressible.

"Kelly." "I thought you had, had…" he wanted to say left him, but that implied she had at one point been with him.

"Phil…err…LIP." said Kelly, not interrupting and offering an olive branch by honoring his request to use his new name.

"Meet us at the airport. Be there at the latest in four hours." "We're waiting for Hecate, not that the Reveal Spell is needed
anymore, but she was going to…" replied Phillip becoming flustered in seconds.

"She's not going to meet you, she's with Ross and Harry, they've gone to Rome. That's where we're going too."

"What? How?" But she'd already hung up.

"Hear that Boleyn, we're going to Rome." said the suddenly buoyant Phillip, "I wonder why?"

~~~

In the mists of the Entanglement War, the immense holes Phillip created provided the elated Devil with fresh avenues of attack. He'd seen the strange entity appear and plow gaping holes through the tumultuous frenzy of fluctuations. He had wondered what it was, but the unexpected advantage was too good to squander.

Instead of deliberating and exercising caution in the face of the unknown, he seized the opportunity and pressed hard and fast, pushing the frontline back from two hours to a glorious and incredible seventy-three.

"The boundary of the Entanglement War was three whole days." celebrated the Devil. "This is an amazing victory." For the briefest of moments, he even considered accepting the truce God had proposed,

"A meeting of the minds to consider other, bigger anomalies." "Whatever they were? *She* didn't want to elaborate when I asked
her the nature of these issues. *She* must think I'm stupid if I'm going to fall for a transparent ruse like that."

So the Devil rejected the offer of peace talks and exaggerated his indignity and injury. Then he intensified his attack. God gave up talking reason to him, and after recovering from the shock of the unknown fingerprints, *she* pressed back with vigor and purpose.

The Devil tried to preserve his territory but was overextended. God easily recovered significant ground before establishing a new equilibrium at the twenty-four-hour mark. It was certainly better than the three-day event horizon the Devil had originally captured. Nevertheless this was a terrible defeat, at a time when *she* had to contend with another setback; her agent on Earth, Saint Joan was no more.

"Failing miserably in her attempt to kill Phil, I dealt with her in the way I said I would. I can be seen as merciful, just *notwhen it's MY wishes not being fulfilled.*

Problem is now it's taking a whole day to get anything done, and another day to find out the end result. I've just got one last card to play."

CHAPTER 26

NOTHING BUT STRANGE HAPPENINGS

"There's something happening, I tell you Jock." said his partner, Christine, of the NYPD."All those people winning the lottery, those holes in one, and now this. This is the third murder today in New York alone. All of them by some nut-job. The *'vic'* is always some guy called Phil. Tell me that ain't strange."

"Well, firstly, not all were called Phil. One was called Phil, another Phillip, and another Bill, Yea, Bill sounds like Phil, right?" Jock was more of a thinker than Christine, and wasn't one to jump to conclusions. One can be like that when you're six foot six and counting. Christine was a mere five foot nothing, and was prone to arresting people first and asking questions later. Especially when Jock was standing behind her.

"True, but statistically, it's about the same as the number zero coming up on a roulette wheel twice in a row. A little bit out there." as she did a wave motion with her hand."And what about that tweet we had earlier?" continued Christine with a wide grin that only good friends can exchange,

"'Eccentric, some say crazy, Evangelist African-American, the Reverend Phax Hymm Icon Loom throws pale of holy water over equally bizarre, controversial, self-anointed, self-appointed, the gibbering white supremacist Patt 'Holy' Ival Lacy and electrocutes both of themselves. Dirt Bag Pat...' my point is, they're acronyms, PHIL... Four letters making 'Phil'... Four... you get it now you big fat four lettered dumb *'ARSE.'* She spoke with an exaggerated cockney accent even though she wasn't even close to being English. "Ac~ro~nyms."

"You're an acronym buddy" laughed Jock, who wasn't Scottish, slapping his partner's leg. She let it ride without a second thought, why shouldn't she? They were both gay, that's why they'd been partnered up. Not a thought of harassment or desire.

Both stopped horsing around as the radio burst into life, "Looks like we've got ourselves another Guys'. Is it a full moon

or som'ing? A nutter's just shot 'a Mr. Will G…'"said the dispatcher in that crackly sound that police car radios have.

Jock and Christine just looked at each other. Although it was a warm day, a chill ran down their spines. Neither told the other. That would have been too scary for two hardened New York cops to admit to. Looking down Fifth Avenue, they watched the clouds above the New York skyline race, as if fleeing the city and seeking safe haven in some far off mid-western cornfield. Why Christine always spat on the square manhole cover outside she didn't know, but today she didn't, the soul-chilling sight that was causing goose bumps stopped her. In a blink of an eye, their tomfoolery was over and they both called home to tell their spouses they loved them.

~~~

If God wasn't lying to herself then it was close. *She* insisted to her angels in Heaven that *she* wasn't completely desperate, and *she* had a plan that *she* was actively pursuing. But that was a last-ditch effort.

In the meantime, God doggedly dosed Earth with encrypted dreams. After the death of Saint Joan *she* had no other agent to initiate, but *she* knew that many delusional adults would occasionally commit murders saying they were obeying God. *They weren't then, now they were.* The dreams carried the order to kill anyone called Phil, and if that included Phil's, Bill's and anyone else with similar sounding names, so be it.

It was plain to see that *Pi* was having her issues too and a temporary partnership between the two in this hour of need was required.

"But was there any way to negotiate such a deal." *She* couldn't think of anything to negotiate in a pact and despairingly hoped *Pi* would see the danger and act accordingly. But there was little chance of that.

CHAPTER 27

INTERROGATIONS

"EGO. VIN."

All of Hell went quiet as they waited for the Dark Lord to appear as the bellowing voice could only mean one thing, the Devil had found them out. He appeared in his casual human form; his most deadly. Dressed in a sleek knee length coat and a pure white shirt with sharp creases that could cut flesh, he was the pinnacle of sophistication.

Since the band of three had locked Phil up in The Devil's Jail, the past few days of life in hell hadn't been too bad. Only after Rank's disappearance did the demons whip the remaining two at all. Therefore, something must have happened, because the sudden summoning had come out of nowhere, and the Devil's demeanor was one of caged anger.

"So, Ego, Vin, do you have something to tell me?" inquired the Devil like the head of an inquisition.

"No? Are you sure?"

They shook their heads again.

"If I were to go to Hell Level IX, to my beautiful and impregnable jail, and peer through the observation hole, would I see Phil?

Vin raised just his finger, "No Yer Lordship, Phil has blotted out the peephole with something."

"Whew and WOW, what a liar. I mean, it's like he's telling the truth." exhaled Ego, with incredible relief.

The Devil disappeared and reappeared a minute later. "The Key is missing. Where is the key?"

Neither answered.

"WHERE IS THE KEY?"

Vin raised his finger again, but this time the Devil jumped into his face faster than a lion would lock its teeth on a gazelle's neck, which was exactly how Vin felt.

"Do you have the key, Vin?" whispered the Devil dangerously. "No. Eg…" croaked Vin, trying not to pee himself in fear.

He turned to Ego. Posed to strike he growled, "Where is it?"

"Turned the Key… Then he…" Vin blurted out, finishing his sentence, then failing to complete another. But who wouldn't stutter when the prospect of unthinkable pain was so close.

Ignoring Vin, The Devil could discern a lie and was sure Vin wasn't. "Yes, this was Ego's show now."

"Ego?" The Devil glared intensely into his watering eyes,

"He threw it into Level IX's Lake of Fire, he…" Vin's sentence disobeyed its owner and continued to seek freedom, "he… he said we're doing what the Devil wants. 'We've locked him up and thrown away the key.'"

Finally Vin's throat stopped its rebellion.

"Give me the key Ego." the Devil spoke in his quiet, threatening voice. "It was a nice thought and a good trick for your dumb friend here, but Ego, if you're not going to give me the key voluntarily, well 'HELLO CAVITY SEARCH'."

Ego, said nothing, knowing he would suffer whichever way he chose. Protest or not.

"Ok, Ego, have it your way."

Instead of ordering him to take his clothes off, they ignited in green flames. Ego screamed as he ripped and tore at his shirt and pants. He managed to get stark naked in record quick time.

As the Devil had instructed, a demon roughly bent Ego over and sadistically thrust the butt end of her trident into his rectum.

Vin cried out as if it were he. The violence was shocking, especially because he knew Ego was innocent. But Vin, the consummate liar, was beginning to think he was hiding something, just like the Devil.

Ego winced in supreme control, hoping not to gratify the Devil as he brutalized him. He needed him to overlook the smoldering clothing lying on the floor which *was* actually concealing the key, hidden from the Devil in the back pocket of his pants. He hadn't thrown it into the Lava Lake in Hell Level IX after all; *he'd just pretended to do so.*

"Now I'm going to pay for it. We're all going to pay for it.

When the Devil finds the key, opens The Devil's Jail, and doesn't find Phil.

Yes, we're all going to pay for it unimaginably.

I WISH I'D THROWN THE DAMN KEY AWAY NOW"
agonized Ego.

With his search turning up empty and it being beneath him to get his hands dirty, the Devil ordered the demon to go through the scorched clothing.

Ego held his breath.

It turned up nothing.

Disbelievingly and with a withering look of distain, the Devil, using only his thumb and index finger, picked up some items and proceeded to shake them.

To Ego's extreme surprise and relief, the key didn't materialize.

Its disappearance had saved him from eternal torture, for the time being.

Now he had to ensure his look of surprise didn't give away the goose, so he attended his modesty as a distraction.

Putting his hands together in front of his mouth like a prayer, the Devil looked at Ego and then at Vin who was hysterical.

"He threw it in the lava. In Hell Level IX. I saw it Mr... your Lordship. I swear."

"We'll see." said The Devil, "We'll see."

Vin backed away as the Dark Lord advanced towards him menacingly. Five minutes later, Vin knelt on the ground crying and distraught, knowing the true meaning of Hell for the first time.

"I swear, he did, he did." implored Vin broken to the core, laying in a puddle of his own urine and blood. Even Ego felt sorry for him.

"Well," started the Devil mildly, "it seems you did, Ego. Just checking you weren't lying, and Vin, here, has confirmed your story and, well, as you can see... He, err, would have told me otherwise that is absolutely for certain, isn't it Vin?"

Still in a broken heap on the floor he nodded earnestly.

"Can't lie to me." thought the Devil implanting his voice into Vin's head, "I always spot it, now Vin, crawl away and hide, if you know anywhere you can do that down here in Hell. HA HA HA."

If Vin had another name, besides liar, it would be survivor. He used his skill now as he kept his thoughts of

"Wrong! And I do." out of his mind just in case the Devil could read them.

Meanwhile the Devil had deceived everyone with his demeanor. To all onlookers, he appeared calm and confident, but on the inside, he was screaming.

"EGO YOU FUCKING IDIOT!"

To their relief the Devil vanished, leaving them in silence and staring at their feet for a long time.

Ego was especially deep in thought.

"Where'd that key go?"

CHAPTER 28

VERY FOOLISH PHILLIP

Phillip was babbling on and on to Boleyn about why they had to go to Rome. Boleyn, however, was so non-responsive; he might as well be talking to a wall.

"Joan said…" and he stopped.

"My G.. I left her like that." He was referring to the way he just left her body exposed and naked to the elements without even the shallowest of graves.

"Even murderers sometimes bury their victims and I… I've left her… Damn, you know what, I'm going back." Phillip accepted Boleyn's silence as if she wasn't there. He was talking to himself.

Now he was now Phillip and not Phil, the right thing called him. Instead of heading straight to the airport, Phillip went back to the campsite.

Flies were buzzing all over the bodies that smelt from decomposition. He was ashamed and disgusted with the lack of reverence he'd shown Joan. He'd just left her exposed to the elements and now he was going to fix it. He stupidly bent down and began to dig with his bare hands, which didn't get him very far.

"With all my so-called superpowers, I can't even dig a grave."

His still mortal hands were useless against the hard dirt since what he really needed was a spade. He looked up to the heavens, unconsciously closed his eyes and dug.Trowel like gloves enveloped his hands and he burrowed like a homeless badger. He dared not open his eyes for fear that his hands might reappear. A short time later, a respectable grave emerged and with dignity, he placed Joan's body in it.

He always thought it so corny in films when someone cut a lock of hair from a loved one, but he found himself doing exactly the same thing.

He finished the job and patted the earth down, this time with bare hands. Then he closed his eyes, recalled Joan's image, and said a brief eulogy.

"Joan, you were a loyal servant to God.

Why you had to die, I don't know.

In the short time that I had the pleasure of your company, you told me more than anyone could ever believe.

I'm sorry I let you down.

I wish you were still alive. Goodbye, Phillip."

He walked back to the car where he'd left the stewing Boleyn and drove to the airport. Joan's entombment put him in a somber mood, which suppressed his anticipation of seeing Kelly. He appreciated Boleyn's silence because he didn't feel like talking.

When he pulled into the airstrip's parking lot, his heart soared and then crashed. There was Kelly, poised on the steps of the plane, near the open door with her long slender legs crossed. Through the open doorway, he could see one of Bill's feet tapping impatiently.

Kelly was excited when she saw Phillip's car drive up. She had posed on the steps in a genuine attempt to allure him, imagining that Phillip was the man she could love. And she wanted to make Bill jealous.

When she saw Phillip, shorter in stature, at first, she couldn't believe her eyes. The affection she was ready to lavish upon him faded and then disappeared.

Kelly's love for Phillip could have blossomed.Their shared life-threatening experiences should have created deep bonds between them, yet now she looked at Phillip as if he was beneath her in every way.

"He wasn't even rich. It didn't make much difference that he'd faced down the Devil, he... he's... small.

People wouldn't know that he's done the most amazing things ever. They aren't things that you could boast about, and of course people wouldn't believe him.

They'd laugh behind my back thinking I was crazy.

Nooo, which I'd have to be, crazy. True Phil, Phillip was err... is... OK. Honest yes, but is he suitor material now? I don't think so.

And besides all of that... I don't know... I just don't feel the same about him. I mean, when he was normal, I could be mean to him, but now, he just doesn't raise any emotion in me to hate him, let alone love him. He's just... no one."

"Err. Phillip." she opened in a hesitating voice, "What happened to you, you're err... shorter. A lot shorter, I mean, err..."

He knew her tone of voice better than anyone as he'd been a frequent target of it. The tone said "For better or worse, whatever I say, I'll never be more than a friend."

Discouraged, he struggled to find an answer, because that's who he was. Never like him to dodge a question with another; he always tried to help and be candid. He thought he'd suffered every possible letdown by Kelly, but this plainly worded question, showed he was nothing to her. Still, trying to be pleasant he answered.

"God, then..." but before Phillip could finish, Bill interrupted impatiently.

"You were always a miserable little shit Phil. You've just become the size that fits. Everyone get on board. Let's get this over with and then I can be rid of you both."

Instead of Kelly and Phillip sitting together, holding hands to reassure each other as he fantasied on his way to the airstrip, Kelly made sure she was a respectable distance from him. Boleyn was strategically situated as a buffer in a row between them. He swallowed to equalize the pressure and glued himself to the window trying to take his mind to some place benign.

161

They soared into the sky and banked hard to the left. In the far distance the ruins of ClearStream came into view. Black clouds hung ominously above the derelict site. They provided a backdrop for the Sun's potent rays to produce an inch perfect rainbow that appeared to emanate from the heart of ClearStream. He focused intensely in the direction of that distant spot. Suddenly he jumped back in absolute terror.

Appearing out of nowhere, The Queen of Spades began snaking herself down the length of ClearStream's river and up the rainbow.

"Kelly. Kelly." whispered Phillip, "Do you see the rainbow and riv…

"Yes Phillip. Nice rainbow, I'm going to get some shuteye now." she replied dismissively.

"Yes, nice." he sighed.

"Of course she couldn't see it, no one could, only God and the Devil, maybe, I don't know. Whatever it is, I think it's the End of the World." he whispered to himself. "Nice rainbow Phillip, nice."

Abruptly, a wild fear swept over him. "How close would they come to the rainbow? And what would happen if they came into contact with it?"

He realized that they were actually flying in the apparition's direction and it was getting closer with every second. They were close enough for Phillip to clearly see that the source of the rainbow was at the cow drink.

For the first time he knew that he wasn't exaggerating. "The End of the World *is* Nigh."

He noticed that the rainbow wasn't moving, but was unnaturally static. This one could be traced to a single point of origin.

Yes, you could get to the end of this rainbow, only death would be your prize rather than a pot of gold.

The Queen of Spades continued to devour the ClearStream River. From head-to-head it had grown over a mile long and was stretching out further with every second. It retained its perfect proportions, however there was one difference. It wasn't black anymore, *it was red.*

He sought safety and attempted to shrink back into his seat. He would have timidly fixated his eyes steadfastly on the seat in front and hoped that that the World would pass him by. Unfortunately, the seatbelt had inexplicably caught onto the food tray and had pinned him against the window.

Unable to turn his head away, he watched streams of numbers spew out of both the queens' mouths. They shot into the air like bright tracer bullets in the night. Some of those numbers were heading for the plane, which, to Phillip's relief, had passed over the top of the rainbow offering a unique view of a rainbow's edge. Phillip's relief was short lived as a machine gun like burst of numbers shot out in their direction. Fearfully, Phillip closed his eyes and braced himself for the impact, but nothing happened.

The throb of the plane's engines droned on smoothly without a shudder of turbulence. Phillip opened his eyes to the welcoming sight of the horizon situated in between the plane and the rainbow.

Then a strange phenomenon appeared. *He saw a long string of numbers beginning with a minus sign and a three.* They looked like they were stenciled on to the plane's wing. Checking the other wing through the opposing window, revealed it too had the string, and both numbers were red. He had no idea what they were. He was certain they weren't there before they flew over the Red Queen of Spades. Unabated, their plane raced onward. It wasn't much comfort because he felt a growing dread.

"That was what attacked me, and it'll attack me again, I'm sure. It's probably what the Devil was looking for in ClearStream. I guess it must have wanted me to find it so it could kill me.

Or maybe, 'cos it didn't recognize me, maybe I found it? How did I ever survive it?

And why was Boleyn the bait.And she's here with me."he reflected.

"And what's that coming out of its mouths, all those numbers? And you know what I didn't think anything of it at the time when it attacked me, but I saw it again in the giant queen...

There's a mistake in the card. For an instant, I thought I saw it flicker to a number in the corner rather than a Q."

A couple of hours later, the plane of lonely people landed in Gander on the eastern tip of Canada.

"So PhilLIP." said Bill, popping his head through the cockpit door and spoiling for a fight, "What's so special about you. Kelly says you're more of a man than I'd ever be."

"She did?" thought Phillip. He looked in her direction, but the look in her eyes told him that whatever she'd said to Bill earlier was immaterial now.

"Show me why." He stood next to Phillip to intimidate and emphasize their difference in height.

"Finally." thought Phillip, I'll beat him. He picked up one of the knives from a discarded lunch platter, and dragged it over the palm of his hand expecting it not to penetrate.

"Ouch." He un-expectantly cut his own skin.

Bill burst into laughter and Kelly looked away in disdain, having seen it before, another typical Phil move. The pain in his hand was nothing compared to the bruising Phillip's ego took.

If anyone had taken any time to look, they would have seen water rather that human blood, but they had all looked away.

"Oh look, he's going to cry." jeered Bill, and scoffed at the brother he despised.

Kelly had dismissed him so thoroughly that she wasn't listening to the little two boys' quarrel. Boleyn might as well have not been there, only acknowledging the verbal barb with a forced smirk. When Bill saw that there wasn't an audience to witness any further humiliation, he left and went back to the cockpit with a broad grin over his face.

For all that Phillip had suffered and become, he was still human, and felt utterly worthless.

"I'm such an idiot and I've said that a hundred times, and yet I continue to do stupid things. I really thought that it wouldn't cut me,'cos those bullets didn't kill me.

Course, I couldn't fly either when I tried, that should have been a clue. I mean, what kind of God, because that's what I thought I was becoming, needs to take a plane anyway?

And while I'm at it, what kind of God needs to eat?" thinking of the platter of cold cuts he'd eaten earlier.

"Or. What kind of God needs to drink? Or Pee?

And now, just as before, I'm still alone. I suck. And I'm really short." were his comments of self-loathing as he chastised himself.

It was as if Bill was reading Phillip's mind, as he suddenly reemerged from the cockpit and broke that dull silence "Refueling." and disappeared back to join the pilot, but not before using his index finger to count their number, "Kelly, one. Boleyn, one and a half. PhiLLLIIIPPPP, that's it, one and a half."

Kelly had never realized how much of an asshole Bill was until this day. Still, she didn't know what that was all about. But Phillip did.

"They need to know how many of us are on the plane so they know how much fuel to put in." He'd noticed that the plane sank when he boarded because he was heavier now, but by how much? That he didn't know, but by the way the plane slumped when he went to the restroom, it was quite a bit.

"I wonder if I should say something. Bill will probably react and say I'm short and fat.

I think I'll say nothing. Besides, I've heard they always put in double as a precautionary measure.They measure how full it is with a dipstick.

Seems archaic.

I mean what if you measured in centimeters as they do in Canada rather than inches. You'd be over two times short. Still, they must know what they're doing." rationalized Phillip. He was too insecure to say anything, yet was the only superhuman who ever existed.

They were back in the air, with the next stop being Rome. Phillip continued to stare out the window and again saw a sight that sent shivers down his spine. This time the Red Queen of Spades spread out of a river's estuary and entered the sea. It was creeping around the shoreline before the plane left it far behind. Phillip saw enough to know that before too long, it will have stretched over the ocean like a massive oil slick.

Burdened with this knowledge, he sat back in his chair and let out a sigh of resignation. He glued his eyes against the Plexiglas window and scoured the plane's wing. The numbers weren't there anymore, a finding that was completely puzzling. It took him a long time before he slept like the others.

~~~

"We're in trouble." announced Bill, waking everyone up from an open cockpit door and storming down the aisle, *"We're going to run out of gas."*

"What?" shouted Kelly before Phillip could get a chance to respond with equal horror.

"For some reason, when we refueled, we've taken on about half the fuel we need, and we seem to be *over frigging weight* somehow." said Bill abysmally failing to remain calm.

Phillip stayed quiet and looked out the window.

"Yes," he thought, "the numbers were gone, and so is the puzzle."

Phillip stood up hardly recognizing himself and said in a quiet voice that could never issue an order that would be obeyed, "Please, everyone, would you go to the cockpit."

Kelly yawned, still thinking about his faults, stood up and walked towards the cabin.

To Phillip, seeing Kelly submit to him like that indicated that he meant nothing to her. She'd never obey if she cared for him. Like a sheep, Boleyn followed Kelly. And Bill was going to humor Phillip one last (first) time.

"Besides, they were all going to die anyway, so let him be the big man just this once." Out of spite, Bill obeyed knowing that when he left and shut the cabin door behind him, he would have deserted Phillip for good. He pushed Phillip aside on his way up the aisle, and returned to his 'important' task as copilot.

Recovering his balance, Phillip watched the door close behind them. The latch slid over, and they were secure inside. Phillip checked the cockpit door. It was locked.

Using the plush leather chairs to steady himself, he zigzagged to the back of the plane and the lonesome fuselage door.

"Fat chance." said Phillip, "you stupid idiot, Phillip, you never cease to amaze me with your dumbass ideas and fantasies. Kelly is not going to try to stop you. I hate me."

"Oh my God." cried the pilot, "What's he playing at? Is he crazy? Not knowing whether it was going to be his last, and not caring,

he took a large gasp of air, and threw the door handle. "I love you Kelly, but you don't love me. Goodbye."

The decompression ejected him into the sky faster than he thought possible.

"Wow. How much did he weigh, cos we might have enough fuel to land after all."

Despite the possibility of reaching Rome and making an emergency landing, he shivered, as something told him he'd never see another horizon.

"Pilot's superstition." he told himself. With a much lighter load, the plane limped its way to Rome's International Airport and with priority status made a successful emergency landing running on bare fumes.

The mood on the tarmac was solemn. They escaped death at the cost of a man's life. Bill was shamed into silence. He'd asked Phil to prove he was a better man, and now he'd gone and done it, "The bugger."

It was hard to tell if the silent and depressed Boleyn was marginally sadder or happier whereas it was obvious that Kelly was having a breakdown. In the month she'd known Phillip she had suffered extreme emotions, but she'd never expressed her love. All she could think about was that he'd died knowing that she'd disregarded and rejected him.

She felt pain, heartache and loss because she felt that she, not Phillip, had spurned the possibility of a true love. The best future she could hope for now was a relationship of feigned happiness. She would never ever feel freedom. To make it worse, in true Phil fashion, his sacrifice was made to save people who wouldn't give him the time of day.

"He did it for me." she sobbed.

As always, the truth did not set her free, *only death can do that*, unless you're Boleyn.

The tears that filled her eyes were for herself, her loss of a love that she should have acknowledged, and that now could never be. It wasn't Phillip's mannerisms that had held her back, it was her ego. She cried knowing that if he hadn't sacrificed himself then she would never have seen it either, and ironically, should he still be alive, she could have been happy without him.

She started to review her life and all the guys she'd slept with. She may have even loved some, but Phillip's face was the only one she could recall. The others seemed faded, nameless and meaningless. She felt empty as if her life died when Phillip gave his for hers, and he knew she didn't give a damn about him.

"God. What did I do?

Why didn't I... he was so short.

I didn't even ask why?

Or how?

I'm so... God. Phillip, you bastard!"

With Boleyn in tow, Kelly wandered away from the plane. A white limousine with fluttering papal flags pulled alongside. The window slid down revealing Ross who beckoned them to join him in the expansive backseat. They climbed into the opposing leather bench, glumly murmured hello and remained silent. Also looking miserable, Ross asked where Phillip was. He got his answer when Kelly burst into tears.

CHAPTER 29

OFF LIMITS

Pope Gregory and his cardinals Paul and Krowski, 'Crow' as he was known to his friends, that is, his co-conspirators, spoke in English. It was the only language all three of them shared. Two weeks earlier, they'd hardly heard of each other and Pope Gregory was just a lowly cardinal. Through happenstance, Pope Gregory's predecessor, Pope Raul was in a locked down secure archive along with the three clerics. Now that seemed like a lifetime ago.

When Europe's large Hadron Accelerator (*CERN*) overloaded the grid and tripped multiple major circuit breakers, several European cities, including Rome, suffered power outages.

At the papacy, the gravity powered archive emergency doors slid into place just as they were supposed to, and the emergency lighting and air conditioning fluttered and stuttered into action. Cut off from the rest of the Pope's regular group Cardinal Gregory, Cardinal Paul and Cardinal Krowski awkwardly tried without success to make light of the situation. So when Pope Raul made a gesture for them to stop talking by clutching his throat, they thought they were boring him.

Only when his eyes started to bulge did the three cardinals realize the horror that was upon them. Under dim emergency lighting, his Highness, the regal Pope Raul was actually telling them

"HELP, I can't breathe."

Seconds later, he choked right in front of their eyes. The three cardinals took turns to perform the Heimlich maneuver. Cardinal Crow even attempted to perform an emergency tracheotomy with a knife, pen and paper, but his efforts failed as the blade hit something hard in his windpipe.

Fortunately for the Cardinals, their efforts blocked a good view of the obstruction from the Vatican's Closed Circuit TV security system, but not from their disbelieving eyes. Before they could investigate further, the power returned, the lockdown ended and medical staff swarmed in to the Pope's aid.It was all for naught,the Pontiff was gone.

The three cardinals were arrested upon suspicion of murder with literally the dead Pope's blood on their hands. The Vatican didn't need more scandal.Thankfully the emergency CCTV footage confirmed the account of the men and their innocence.

Vindicated, the three cardinals where vaulted into the ecclesiastical limelight as heroes for their resuscitation efforts. Exploiting his new found fame, Cardinal Gregory was nominated by the other two cardinals for the now vacant Papal position.

It was essential that they did so and that Cardinal Gregory be elevated to the lofty calling, because they were going to need the power and authority of the office if they were going to act on what they discovered. Privately, the three were actually conspiring to have a forbidden procedure carried out.

They were going to have an autopsy performed on the deceased pontiff; the only option in finding out what caused Pope Raul's suspicious untimely passing. Its suddenness and manifestation scared the cardinals. It seemed so unnatural, like the opposite of a miracle, as if an act of God had struck the Pope down.

"Cardinals." said Cardinal Paul solemnly, "don't you find it strange that when something good happens against all odds, it's called a miracle, but when something unlikely happens and it's bad, then it's called '*an act of God.*'

You'd think it should be called '*anactof the Devil*', or something less detrimental to our lord."

The others mulled over the observation but said little, although they all had an inexplicable and unrelenting feeling of angst.

Crowned Pope Gregory in a single vote, Italy's first recent Pope required every home advantage attainable, *because dark times required dark measures.*

Conspiring with glances and hand gestures, they addressed their first order of business and the sooner the better. They couldn't quell or nullify the feeling that they had witnessed something, dare they say, *supernatural*, that had laid the Pope to rest. They didn't know how accurate they were, but they were soon to find out.

~~~

"Mamma." said Dr. Christo Bella, "I have to make a house call tonight."

She didn't reply, so he went back into the living room to check on her. She was fast asleep, so he slipped out of the front door and into the open door of the waiting car without saying another word. One didn't say too much when the Vatican Guard arrived in a police car at two o'clock in the morning.

Under cover of night, as all dark things are done in the shadows, Pope Gregory, Cardinal Paul and Cardinal Crow hurried the trusted physician into the bowels of the Vatican. High-ranking officials in the local constabulary eagerly assisted as they were thrilled that Pope Gregory, an Italian, was now the new pope. Thus ending a drought of over a century. Even a rumor circulated amongst those in the police's highest echelons, that Cardinal Gregory had indeed offed the previous Pope.

"The good old-fashioned way." it was murmured and admired more than once.

Despite its falseness, they believed this latest scheme was only a resumption of previously alleged skullduggery, which elevated Gregory's prestige to new heights.

Gregory requested that the physician's autopsy on the cold corpse of Pope Raul, focus on the throat. The doctor dutifully followed the new Pope's instructions. Standing right behind him was the large Cardinal Crow, and his intimidating size gave Christo little room to refuse the Pope's request.

With only a small splattering of blood to hinder his work, Christo did Greg's bidding, stopping only when awe and dread impaled him. The coroner delicately extracted from his throat the cause of Pope Raul's choking death, an opal of staggering beauty.

It was so astounding that no one breathed a word. There in Christo's tweezers held high in the light that had the privilege to pass through it, the Opal's opaque reflection gently caressed the small room and its honored occupants. The last thought of the doctor was a shiver of impending doom, and then Crow's mace crashed down with deadly force on his skull.

Gregory and Paul showed almost no concern. It was clear to the three that God's hand was indeed at work here and they were doing his bidding. Christo had played his part and his sacrifice was necessary, *because God's work was done in secret.*

How else could an opal have miraculously materialized in the Pope's throat?

It was a sign.

And it was a sign that demanded attention, from them.

Why else were they trapped alone with the victim?

Why else was this sign given to them in private?

So the fewer people who knew about it the better.

It was the sign's will, maybe even God's will.

It *was* God's will.

The doctor had to die.

God bless you Christo.

The cities' officials were outstanding, proving that the art of disposing of bodies was not lost, as too was the rigging of elections. It was a return to the good old days, giving Pope Gregory immeasurable veiled influences previous recent generations of Popes could only have dreamed of.

It was common for a new Pope to lean heavily on a few trusted cardinals, so Pope Gregory's reliance on Cardinal Paul and Cardinal Krowski was only natural. When he made it clear that policies were not going to change, the cleric community applauded loudly and went back to their own devices. Controversy wouldn't be visiting them; the fruits of privilege would.

With day-to-day business delegated to the incumbent bureaucrats, the three were free to pursue any line of inquiry they needed to without question. Unencumbered, they bore down on the problem.

"What did the appearance of the Opal mean?"

It was obvious to them that something mysterious had happened. A truly religious experience had occurred in their midst. Maybe it was a miracle? That normally meant something was good, but this was the opposite.

They sat together in the plush private quarters of the Pope knowing that the time for contemplation had ended and that it was time to take action. They debated various scenarios for several days and just as they were about to make a decision, Paul gave them a new option.

Something had come to his attention the previous day and he presented a thin dossier to bolster his case. It was exactly what they needed.The Pope retrieved an ornate box from his cloak, the size of a matchbox and placed it in the middle of the table. It was a reminder of the gravity of their plight.

"I don't see that we have a choice." said Gregory in perfect English as they gazed at the box in front of them.The two cardinals nodded in agreement. Paul opened his cellphone and called the Investigative Archaeology Team.

CHAPTER 30
ROMANTIC BY THE SEA

Noah was the supervisor for the Dead Sea Health Spa. He'd worked there for many years, making sure the rich Americans who frequented the reputed health-giving waters got their money's worth of clean baths and alcohol.

It was well-known that the Dead Sea, the lowest point on Earth, was so saturated with salt that one could float on one's back and read a newspaper. The Jordan River fed the small landlocked lake making the Dead Sea's waters hostage to the unrelenting desert sun. The only outlet for the waters was that of evaporation. Over time the lake became salt laden giving it the property of extreme buoyancy. It touted multiple healing properties for many ailments and it was for these reasons that savvy investors built the Dead Sea Health Spa.

Noah was hired by the owners by word of mouth. This was a bit of a risk because Noah, a young twenty-one-year-old, already had a checkered past. He accepted the post nonchalantly, driving his long-suffering parents crazy for not once did he acknowledge how lucky he was to get it. His lack of gratitude galled his hard-working parents.

Maybe it was fate, because Noah had fallen into a niche custom built for him. He was a natural at his job. His long lean body, roguish good looks and carefree attitude made him a magnet for the middle-aged wives of the wealthy men who took refuge there.

The men gravitated to taking long afternoons along the beach and tanning themselves to a crisp in the Dead Sea. The women spent those same afternoons cooling off in the Spa's crystal-clear cold tubs, which is where Noah spent his.

Not one complaint was ever leveled against him by any of his conquests, because every satisfied customer knew that it was never love, it was always pleasure. He had found his niche indeed.

On slack afternoons, Noah wandered aimlessly around the Dead Sea's shore. One year, they experienced an uncommonly severe drought and the Dead Sea was at a record low. It was a boon for Noah, because rocks normally covered by water were bare and provided him with something to explore.

One afternoon, he picked up an old parched piece of wood lying on the ground and threw it into the lake. He was instantly intrigued to see it not drift away, but rather circle as if caught in a whirlpool.

He stripped off naked and entered the Sea to investigate. Swimming effortlessly out to the small stick, he ducked under water and looked down at the boulder-strewn bottom. He saw something. He swam to the shore, got a handful of tiny twigs and returned to the spot.

Noah took a large breath and swam downward forcefully, fighting the resistance due to the density of the water. He dove down to the large opening between several smooth boulders and released his cargo. The matchsticks were instantly sucked down into the crevice. He smiled to himself as he floated up to the surface confident that he'd discovered the only exit to the Dead Sea.

Unashamedly lying naked on the sand, he was amazed when he saw his flotilla of twigs suddenly resurface about fifty yards away.

He'd been dreaming that he set free lots of little boats that took people down into the depths. Now they'd returned, ready to pick up some more travelers. It was a childlike fantasy, yet he didn't care and he smiled all the way back to the spa ready and primed to do his duty.

After this discovery, Noah kept close attention to the level of the Sea, noting the season and the weather, and if the level of the lake would rise and fall. Only in the longest of dry seasons was he able to relocate the whirlpool. He was never able to discover the spot of the returning spring. Nonetheless, this adventure provided a welcome distraction from the whining husbands looking for their wives.

The cold tub was actually natural born spring water from a tiny crack in the solid rock on the Sea's rocky bank. It was critical to the owners because the spring determined the location of the spas. Its waters were the coolest and freshest to emerge from solid rock ever. It was collected into a mosaic-tiled bath and the women dipped in its pristine waters in the afternoon rarely venturing to the salty sea outside. The coolness made them feel fresh and lucky, especially if Noah sauntered by.

CHAPTER 31

MADDENING WAIT

As the leader of the IAT, Ross almost fell off his chair when he received a call from their first real client, Cardinal Paul. Phillip's alleged discovery was interesting but it wasn't what he considered the real deal. However, the head of the Roman Catholic Church had directly requested their assistance. This was.

He felt a little guilty leaving Phillip in the middle of his vague investigation. If this opportunity panned out however, many doors would be opened and if he failed to take the contract many future doors would be closed. So for the IAT it was an offer he couldn't refuse. In the strictest of confidence, Ross, Harry and Hecate flew to Rome.

Gander Airport catered to traffic using it as a jumping off point for the long flight over the Atlantic. It was an ideal location except that the cold Arctic currents met the warm Gulf Stream from the Caribbean. That meant lots of fog and freezing rain, and it was rolling in fast. The Pope's plane could not change its flight plan to avoid the airstrip as refueling was required.

After a shaky landing, making Hecate feel hesitant about flying, the IAT were stranded for over twenty-four hours rather than the standard two.

It was a tedious and boring wait. They had beaten to death the topic of conversation about what the Pope wanted from them. When planes were finally allowed to take off, their high spirits sank when the pilot announced they were in last place for de-icing.

Two days late, the IAT were seated in a beautiful room waiting for the Pontiff 's entrance. They were all surprised and delighted they were actually going to meet him. Ross and Harry wore sensible business suits, while Hecate was in designer slacks and a smart two-piece top. Not having any idea why they'd been summoned, it was clear that the matter was pressing.

Their nervousness ended when a door opened and his eminence entered. To their continued delight, the Pontiff directly addressed the IAT with a friendly and casual greeting.

"Ross, Harry and Hecate, thank you for accepting my offer. I hope you don't mind that I've dispensed with many formalities as time is of the essence."

He received confirming nods from Paul and Crow.

"So to speed things along, when we are privately together as we are now and in the confines of the Vatican, you may call me Greg.

As for Cardinal Paul and Cardinal Krowski, Paul and Crow will sufice. In other company, I insist upon formalities, but it shouldn't come to that.This meeting and its outcome is for limited eyes only."

The IAT was hooked and with the quick exchange of introductions and pleasantries over, it was time to get down to business.

"So Ross, Harry and Hecate, obviously, you must be wondering what issue I, the Pope, could possibly have that would require me to secretly enlist the services of the Investigative Archaeology Team?"

The Pope continued,"And this issue, be so pressing that he sent his private jet to America on a round trip to collect them.

Albeit, your team is incomplete is it not? You are missing Boleyn, Kelly and most importantly, Phil?"

"Yes, they are on another assignment." responded Ross, which wasn't quite a lie.

The Pope interrupted. "We have brought you and your team here because I do have a pressing and possibly urgent mystery that I need the answer too. I, we, chose the IAT because of… Paul could you please…"

"Certainly Greg." Paul took over, "Ross, as you know, miracles are required to support nominations for canonization, so the Vatican has a department to investigate alleged miracles and the like. When it comes down to it, there are none. So, accepting that, how would you categorize the night in Salem a week or so back Ross?"

The question took Ross completely by surprise and caused him some alarm because he knew he couldn't answer it honestly. If Ross were to tell all, they wouldn't believe him and the IAT would be tossed out the moment he finished.

Ross hesitated, "Paul…"

"Let me answer the question for you Ross, something immortal happened. Is that true?"

"It is Paul, *immortal* and *unholy*." replied Ross, measuring his words carefully.

"My intelligence is good then, there are…" said Paul seemingly pleased with himself.

"Greg, Paul, Crow. Why are we here? I'm getting the impression that something, unworldly has…"

"Ross." said Greg, "We have been given a sign."

Not knowing the full extent of the IAT experience, the drama that Greg hoped to create fell flat on its face. Seeing this, he quickly continued.

"It would be foolish to bring you here and not disclose why.
This is the why."

Greg took a small ornate box from its safe home in his robe, laid it before them, and opened it. The Opal's dreamy radiant light bathed the room and left the IAT spellbound.

In the short time since the inception of the IAT, Ross and Harry had spent many hours investigating any strange events that coincided with the escape of the Devil from his shoe.

That research paid off. Ross recognized the stone and knew the puzzling tale that accompanied it. Ross looked into Greg's eyes and saw he knew its account too. Knowing the story, said a lot about the character of the Pope and the trust he was placing with the IAT. Greg had made the first move and it was time for Ross to return the volley.

"Greg, that's the Heart of Australia, the World's finest opal. It went missing. How? No one knows, because the safe that housed it wasn't broken into, in fact, the safe was a reinforced glass display case, guarded with multiple video feeds and twenty-four by seven monitoring. One moment it was there, the next it was gone.

That happened the night that a séance took place in Glastonbury, England. It also happened to be the same night the 'Higgs Boson' was discovered, ironically called the 'God' particle.

I assume you researched all of this, but did your research uncover that… that was also the night that Phil, now known as Phillip, fought and defeated the Red Witch Boleyn?

There is more if you would like me to continue?" said Ross.

Not questioning anything that he'd heard, not the use of the word 'witch', implied that the Pope was open to the suggestion that witches existed, the Pope genially replied,

"Please do."

"With pleasure." replied Ross equally graciously.

"The séance was no ordinary one. An industrialist called Gilbert Glaston, being obsessed with the number seven, believed it was integral for the creation of magic. It was something he was fanatical about, as both his namesbegan with the letter 'G',the seventh letter in the alphabet and both names were seven letters long. So he believed it was his destiny to usher in an era of magic and cast out the age of science.

To this end, he set about it as his God given mission with all the resources he had, and that was considerable.

You may have heard of the energy emitting process called cold fusion. The process turned out to be sporadic and unpredictable and it was this that doomed it as a viable source of energy. However, Mr. Glaston interpreted this failing as a sign.

He deemed cold fusion as magic's attempt to manifest its presence in the World of explainable science and technology. Being a wealthy man, Mr. Glaston devoted his extensive resources in his quest, to make magic real, and the employment of cold fusion was an integral part.

Next, Mr. Glaston selected Glastonbury Tor, Somerset, England, as his site for an outrageous experiment, a séance that would combine science and the occult. The selection of Glastonbury was easy as his surname shared the same root as the town.

Of course, Glastonbury's legendary reputation as a mystic center made it all the more seductive. It was steeped in legend and lore. The Tor was the alleged location of the Holy Grail and the burial site of King Arthur. According to an ancient myth recounted in one of the countries' national anthems, Jerusalem, it had graced the footsteps of Jesus Christ himself.

So it was natural for Mr. Glaston to desire the site, and, after paying significant sums of money to the Town's Council, Mr. Glaston gained the permission and exclusive use of the hilltop for his purposes, to summon magic.

He assembled an experiment that combined science and faith, and left it to destiny to supply the final ingredient, that of chance. On the slate pavers of the ancient tower, that once was the pulpit of a ruined church, he assembled state of the art scientific apparatus and erected a lightning rod on the top of the tower.

Then, he held a séance in the same dark nook willing for a fateful final ingredient. Either lightening would strike or it would not.

Magic and science would unite if fate willed it. He utilized another of his new acquisitions purchased solely for this purpose, the oldest undocumented Ouija board and Tarot cards known, and unknown. He'd hunted them down and generously paid canny gypsies for seeking out these artifacts.

With all his preparations complete, imagine his deflation when instead of a sultry, muggy evening full of thunder and Thor's wrath, an untypical clear sky greeted him. The destiny he thought was his was not. And that night was the night before the Devil's escape at Salem.

Yet destiny had its way after all. Glaston and six female psychics, flown in from around the globe, met their demise that night.

In an effort to explain the embarrassing killings, the police suggested an episode of mass hysteria swept over the seven, which resulted in everyone stabbing each other.

An interesting footnote buried deep within the report, says that all the bodies showed signs on their faces of what appeared to be a case of bad sunburn.

Had the cold fusion experiment ignited and imparted the tans?

I believe Greg, that their experiment was not a complete or even a marginal failure, it may have actually even succeeded. At the bare minimum, I believe there was a confluence of strange and unique events that culminated in the coronation of the Shoe.

The shoes that the Devil once wore are now the Shoes that are now Phillip."

The tale was unbelievable and he hadn't even finished. It already felt like an out of body experience as Ross suddenly became very self-conscious on how crazy the whole account sounded, so he stopped and looked back into the eyes of the three clergy.

"Now's the time you lock me up." he said amiably.

"Thank you for the summary of the séance, Ross." smiled Pope Gregory.

"No need, to lock you up, that is. Well it's a fantastic story, and one that I would have had little time for until the advent of this Opal, and as you so kindly didn't suggest, no, we didn't steal it.

I have a feeling that there is more for you to tell, and if Phil was here, then I would eagerly listen to what he would have to say, but he isn't… you are, and so is the Green Witch Hecate. Thank you all for coming."

Hecate, Ross and Harry exchanged glances.

"Yes, I have heard that Phil has something to tell us, and that Hec…"

"Sorry to interrupt." interjected Ross again, "he is now known as Phillip, and I think that it's important. Don't ask me why, but Phil… LIP … well, we've seen…" turning to Harry and Hecate who nodded in acknowledgment, "Phillip has survived, and done incredible things. Anyway, if you excuse me and indulge me, it's Phillip. Thank you, your Highness."

"Phillip it is. I have heard some, probably not all, interesting things about him too." said the Pope without a hint of irritation.

"Your sources sound surprisingly thorough and err... forthright... and open minded as indeed, you do too Greg, I am impressed and pleased." said Harry, as he looked at Hecate midway through his sentence and smiled.

"Paul" who bowed, "compiled the file, and, contrary to world opinion, we research a true mystery, and Salem was one such case. Paul? Would you please?"

"Thank you, Greg. Well America has a readily accessible network with thousands of churches and active congregations.

Using that platform, I've had a file assembled, with anecdotal but corroborated narratives. Although we have many gaps in our knowledge, we have some incredible hypotheses.

So, as you see, we are not so shocked or ready to discredit anything we have heard from you. Of course, your qualifications and reputations also add to your credibility.

All that aside, what is your opinion of the séance, Ross? Truly."

"Greg, Paul, Crow. I believe, that we have witnessed something unique. What it means I don't know. But in my opinion, you have called us here, the IAT that as of yet has no track record, because you know something, I fear... is happening.

Did you know a Buddhist monk called Wilrog has embarked upon a grand project? He is carving a monumentally huge head of the Buddha in Nepal. It is the largest sculpture ever undertaken using the eleventh highest mountain in the World, one of the majestic peaks of the Himalayas, as his block.

The Nepalese Government donated the mountain to the man.
With one massive blast, the outline of the Buddha materialized.

And now this, this Opal? Tell me Greg," said Ross finishing up, "tell me how you came into its possession, and I think you'll find, that we too, are of open minds."

184

"This Opal was the cause of the late Pope Raul's death." Paul responded. "The three of us here were in his audience when he suffered a sudden blockage in the throat which choked him to death.

It was lodged in the Father's windpipe. One moment he was talking, the next he was suffocating. It happened during the infamous power outage, the one you obviously have researched, the one the night before Salem."

"The night the Higg's Boson was discovered." interjected Ross, "Another incident, or another coincidence, perhaps, the same night PhilLIP and the *Shoe* bonded."

"So we have heard." continued Paul, taking the floor again, "it is turning out to be quite the momentous night wouldn't you agree?

We tried everything we knew to resuscitate him, Crow especially, and we failed. It was like fate, I hate to say.

We held an autopsy in private, which as you know is not done. But we had to know. As a Pope's death is never determined, we were able to remove the Opal without concern. Now, Pope Gregory, his holiness, and Crow and I endeavor to find answers to this enigma. Hence. You."

"Thank you, Paul. May we examine the stone?" asked Ross turning to Pope Gregory.

"Be our guest." replied the Pope,

They all sat around a small table. Ross, the leader, picked up the stone and generously passed it immediately to Harry. He, in turn, gave it a cursory examination although it was beautiful. He knew he should hand it to Hecate. If anyone was going to crack this puzzle, it would be her.

Harry quickly took her hand to pass the gem to her, placed the milky stone into her palm, and *lost his life*.

CHAPTER 32

INSTRUMENT OF DEATH

LIGHTGreenDeath LIGHTGreenDeath
LIGHTGreenDeath

The silent Entanglement blast tore through the small congregation like a lightning bolt. No one was prepared for it. Amid the confusion, the Pope and the others, including Hecate at the focal point of the blast, picked themselves up. They were disorientated but not hurt physically. Harry, the one who'd given the stone to Hecate, however, was. Due to the turmoil, it took a little time to realize that there was a casualty. It was Ross who looked for his longtime friend, and saw that Harry wasn't moving. Ross rushed to him. His body lay twisted and motionless on the cold, marble floor. Ross desperately administered CPR but his efforts to resuscitate Harry failed. Other than a miracle, nothing could bring him back. Harry was dead.

Out of respect to Hecate and her powers, he'd handed the stone to her. He figured that she was likely to be the one to resolve the enigma, thus, she should have the first inspection.

"Arrrrrgh" cried Hecate aloud.

Ross thought for a moment that Hecate's cry was one of mourning for Harry, until he saw otherwise. The cardinals turned their attention away from Harry to Hecate and were shocked to see Hecate was dressed in her witch's attire. They had indeed greeted her as a witch, but seeing her in her full witch glory, caused a rush of fear to overcome them.

"What had happened? And what had they started? They had hired the IAT to do, they didn't know what? Consult? Aid or explain the mystery of the Opal? And now only an hour into their investigation, a supernatural event had occurred and a man was dead.

Should they have known better? The Opal had already taken one life, now, lying amongst them, another." Regret would take its time to trouble them, but it would come.

"Would it have been better to have just left Pope Raul's death a mystery? Could that have been God's plan?" wondered the not too distraught Greg. "This brought the severity of our situation home. The Opal is supernatural, and deadly. Twice now, but was it also a prophecy? Was the end of days coming?"

Something had awakened in Hecate and she stood before them. She had magically materialized as a Shakespearean witch in a black cape rather a witch dressed in the present. She reeked of evil and horror. They gawked at Hecate's bare arm as she had rolled up the sleeve of her black cloak. A laceration that was on the verge of bleeding greeted them.

It wasn't the severity of the lesion that was distressed Hecate as she stared at it. It was the color of her blood. It was red.

Then Hecate's broom fell and rattled about on the floor before coming to rest. Normally it would hover obediently by her side, something she'd always taken for granted. Until now.

Hecate knew what this meant. Blood, red, not green, and broomstick just that, plain old sweeper. She had lost her witch-hood.

Everyone had momentarily forgotten the chain of events started when Harry handed Hecate the Opal. She was still holding it tightly in the hand of the injured arm almost forgetting she had it.

"What?" She suddenly became aware of its presence. "That was it, the damn stone" swore Hecate.

She ferociously smashed it down palm first on the table guessing it was the cause of her mortality. It was the last thing she wanted, the same dull mortality that plagued Boleyn. Damned if she wanted that.

Her first holler came out of shock rather than pain when she had first seen the cuts on her arm. The moment she rid herself of the gemstone, real pain shot through her arm and a real scream followed. Then she cried out again in victory as her true colored green blood returned.

It welled up through her jigsaw like gash, and before long had dribbled down her arm. Her broom had cheerfully leapt off the floor and taken its rightful position hovering by her side. She was happy again, for the moment.

It was plain to see that there was an unfortunate inverse correlation between being in possession of the stone and being a witch. Without it, she was the green-blooded witch of old but it was at the cost of pain and bleeding. With it, she was a pain free, none bleeding red blooded mortal.

Though she wasn't hemorrhaging badly, her blood wasn't coagulating. If it continued like this, she would be left with the choices. Give up her witch-hood or a protracted, pain filled death. With the temptation eating away at her, Hecate considered picking the stone back up. She assumed that it would ease her misery and the more she thought about it, it seemed like the only choice.

"NO" shouted Ross as he saw Hecate's hand dart out towards the jewel. But it was too late, she'd already grabbed it. He'd ducked to avoid the expected Entanglement attack and felt like a fool. He turned a shade of red in embarrassment, when to his and the others' relief and surprise, nothing happened.

Not considering that a repeat of the explosion could have occurred, Hecate had plucked the stone back off the table and was basking in relief. She was delighted to see that not only had the pain stopped, but also too, the bleeding.

"Curses."

It had done exactly what she predicted.

She swore under her breath as her broom again fell to the floor broadcasting her humiliation. Then she sighed again, in resignation, as her blood reverted to the color red, stopped and receded into the gouges of her blemish. She was a mere mortal, again and now she knew how Boleyn felt.

She looked around as if for the first time since the explosion, and saw Harry's still warm body lying in an undignified heap. Although she couldn't have foretold what was going to happen when she took possession of the stone, it still made her feel guilty or at least partly responsible. A strange feeling for a murderous witch, but her new role in her new life in this New World had changed her. She wasn't the same witch she was before her narrow escape with the Devil. She had been the only remaining witch in the World, and now she might not be much of a witch either.

Ross could see Hecate was physically fine or at least not in immediate peril, so his concern returned to Harry's lifeless body. Completely at a loss, Ross knelt beside him and fought back the tears. Harry had been his best friend and companion after they'd met at law school decades ago, but his most memorable moments were those they'd shared together since Salem.

He passed his hand over his eyes to close them, but after all the events of the last month he wasn't sure what he believed in. It seemed the right thing to do so he did it out of respect.

His death seemed so stark and meaningless. They had been in the presence of the Devil himself and lived. Ross found himself thinking that it would have been better if he'd died by his hand, rather than by the mundane and benevolent action of passing along a gemstone to a 'benign' witch.

"That's all? At least the gem was technically stolen… still, it felt like such a trivial end."

Harry had cheated death in ClearStream. This was death's revenge. There would be no Valhalla for him as there were no Valkyries flying overhead when this ignominious catastrophe struck him down.

"Why, now, so simple…" Ross's train of thought trailed off into blankness.

Considering everything, the clergy had recovered from their initial shock extremely well and were starting to take effective steps to manage the situation. Ross regained some composure and knew there was nothing left that he could do. So he joined them.

They wisely kept out of Hecate's way. She was growing in anger and impatience as she descended into the dark abyss of mortality. She continued to pick up and put down the stone, but to her chagrin, the result was the same every time. The scar continued to bleed green, the pain never once capitulated, and her broom alternated between awesome flying machine and a stick.

Eventually, she got the message and hung onto the Opal at the cost of remaining mortal. It was either that, or risk losing so much blood that she would faint. Weak, irritated, and tired, but alive, she sat down through fatigue and watched the men reverently wrap Harry up in a clean linen white sheet rather than a commoner-garden green plastic body bag.

Efficiently, Crow had summoned his most trusted Swiss Guards and they took care of the necessary formalities. Harry was quietly removed, "to who knows where?" thought Ross sadly.

More wrapped up in her own misery then to care about Harry, Hecate could see that she was on the slippery slope to mortality, to equality, to plain old ordinary. She continued to clutch the stone with all her might, no one was going to get it away from her. Should they attempt it and succeed, she'd become a witch again, and then they'd see what an angry witch could really do. The stone was hers.

"Do you know what happened?" said Ross gently, not trying to intrude upon or upset Hecate any further in her private moment, but he had to know. Whatever had happened cost him his friend's life.

"Hecate." continued Ross, as Hecate hadn't responded to his initial inquiry, "It seems heartless, but nothing is going to bring Harry back and it's plain that bigger things than our mortality are in motion. Do you know?"

"No." she said in a distant voice. Never, in any of her past attacks, all of them intentional, had she harmed herself.

"Hecate." responded Ross, "Harry, I fear, may be the first, but he may not be the last. We see." casting an arm hand behind him in the Clergy's direction, "that the stone now controls our path, yours especially. This may be the reason we survived the Devil at all."

Paul and the other two raised their eyebrows not knowing the IAT's full history. "We don't know the plan or even if there is one? However, you are clearly central to what is happening, whatever it is. Can we, err, can we examine the scar with you?"

The non-witch Hecate acquiesced like an unconditional surrender. Several bandages were made ready as Hecate gingerly placed her arm on the tabletop and allowed them to examine it. To a man, they were all extremely careful not to touch her. Out of fear.

The stone wasn't forgotten, as it remained out of sight held fast in Hecate's boney fist. No one was going to ask about it and they all pretended that it wasn't on their minds. As they poured over the scar, a guard entered the room and intimated that he had a message for Pope Gregory. The Pope waved him over so he could whisper something in the Pontiff's ear as was customary. While that was happening, Paul and Crow took photographs with their cellphones and Ross watched the guard come and go. He looked at the glum looking Hecate who looked like an overly stressed puppy.

"Hecate" began Ross, "if you want to back out of this, I can make your case to Greg, but I personally ask that you stay with it. I have a bad feeling about everything. We need you, and in fact, this whole thing may actually be about you. You are now the only witch in the World. You cheated the Devil, and now this has happened.

I can't promise anything here, your safety or otherwise, but I've looked at the scar, and we've taken pictures. You are special, and even if we can't figure out the… the… whatever, I believe you may have additional roles to play. You know, strange things are happening."

Greg rejoined the group causing Ross to pause momentarily before continuing "Phil is now Phillip. We've left him behind in ClearStream and that clearly is a mistake. I hardly know the man, but now I dearly wish he was here."

"You may get your wish Ross." said Greg seizing the chance to flaunt that he knew something Ross didn't.

"Although it is in trouble, a plane is expected to land at the airport shortly, piloted by Bill, PhilLIP's brother. Care to meet them and bring them back here? I've arranged a car and an escort."

CHAPTER 33

TESTING HECATE'S MISERY

Ross held the sobbing Kelly in his arms as they drove back to the Vatican. She was so distraught he hadn't had the chance to tell her his own bad news. Only when Harry wasn't there to greet them at the entrance did she look at Ross questioningly. She saw the tears swelling in his eyes and she broke down again.

It was a complete shock when Boleyn, who hadn't said a word to either since landing and barely anything since takeoff, suddenly ignited in a torrent of abuse,

"You stupid, self-centered bitch. Me, me, me, me, me, me." "What?" said Kelly, her tears stopping immediately.

"You heard me."

"Boleyn. What are you saying? I never…"

"Shut up Kelly. Ross, let's get moving." Boleyn cut her down.

With her sobbing over, Ross told Kelly and Boleyn how Harry met his end and all the events that led to it. For the first time since they'd embarked on this endeavor, Boleyn actually had a hint of a smile. It coincided with the tale of Hecate's plight, and didn't do anything to quell Ross' growing feeling of foreboding.

Boleyn was beginning to join the world again, but only to detract, never to augment; it was better when she was mute. Soon they approached a guarded room that obviously meant the Pope was behind the closed doors.

He wasn't, however, the person on Boleyn's mind. Hecate was the one she was eager to see, but not to greet her, but rather to taunt.

Hecate was seated alone at the table nursing her arm. Occasionally she let go of the gem only to watch her green blood burble up to the surface, and the dull pain return. And each time, both symptoms were just a little bit worse than before. Each time, she swore that she wouldn't do it again, but she did.

However, out of spite, when Boleyn entered the room Hecate let go of the stone. She preferred to suffer pain rather than let Boleyn see that she was mortal.

Rudely, whether deliberately or not, Boleyn ignored his Highness and instead sought the eye contact of Hecate, daring her not to pick the stone back up. Ross was already embarrassed when Kelly added to the drama by bursting into tears as she attempted to address the Pontiff.

"Who's not going to forgive a beautiful damsel in distress? Only me."said Boleyn not surprised with Kelly's lack of emotional control.

And from knee height, Kelly heard "Me. Me. Me. Me. Me." This embarrassed Ross further,who was trying not to look sheepish. Between sniffles, Kelly continued her introduction to the
Pontiff which included the retelling of Phillip's sacrifice and her loss of potential true love.

"Is Boleyn reading my mind?" she thought after hearing the reiteration of her taunt.

The antics of the pair left Ross struggling to make small talk. Greg placed his hand on Ross' arm and said, "Ross, your team has suffered tremendous loss."

"No kidding." thought Ross. "Harry is dead, Phillip is dead, Kelly is sobbing again, and Hecate and Boleyn were no longer witches. And BTW, hate each other.

Loss is an understatement."

Still, the Pope hadn't finished, and continued,"I am so sorry and feel responsible, and at the same time, vindicated. My involvement of your team was worrying, believing there was the possibility that I was overreacting, but now, unfortunate events have underscored the seriousness of the matter.

It is clear we need you and your team more than ever. I dearly wished to have met Phil...LIP.There were many questions I would have asked him, and now I'll never know."

"Greg," said Ross, "about Phillip. Well, I wish he were here too, more than you'll ever know. He has... had sorry... some story Greg. Believe me, he's quite the, was quite the man. You wouldn't believe what..."

"A witch is in my room, with green blood, Ross how much more..." retorted the Pope, who was, in turn, swiftly re-interrupted by Ross.

"He defeated the Devil in battle."

At first, the magnitude of Ross'statement escaped the Pope. He heard the words and understood their meaning, but his mind was processing all the events of the day so, initially, lip service replaced a genuine response.

Slowly, however, the Pope started to absorb what he'd heard and the true enormity and implications it carried. Not only did the Devil exist, but also a man defeated him in a fight, and if the Devil existed, so did God.

Despite the fatalities and discord, hearing that Phil stood against the Devil and won meant he was justified in summoning the IAT. It was his, and now theirs, *calling*.

"The Gem's appearance was essentially responsible for three deaths. It was obviously the Devil's work."

Righteously, they were God's agents chosen by the Holy Father himself, Greg, Paul and Crow. With the weapons of light and the IAT, they would and had answered the call to arms. No matter the sacrifice, *his will* would be done. A Pope and two of the IAT had given everything already. "God bless them."

Greg wished he'd spoken his war cry to the others, but Kelly reclaimed the front and center before Greg could find his voice.

"Ross, Hecate's scar. What is it? Looks like the sign of a woman. The Venus Sign."

"Yes, it does." replied Ross, swiftly followed by Greg who said, "So we're going to do some research. We're going to the Vatican's famous archives."

Despite the deaths, it was becoming apparent that the Pope and Ross were subtly waging a boasting war. It was a fight the Pope couldn't possibly win because, although his sources were good, he didn't know all the facts. So he was disappointed with Ross' unimpressed reaction, but he didn't know that he'd examined documents penned by the Devil himself.

The recovering reclusive Boleyn gloated as Hecate was forced to abandon her witch-hood again. She retrieved the stone from the table and tried to make it look like she was just casually picking it up. She fumbled it, making her desperation more apparent than ever to the gleeful Boleyn. If she had been taller Boleyn would have attempted to steal it off the table, but it would have been a fool's errand. Hecate would surely have slain her had she succeeded.

Who would have known whether the culprit was the stone or Hecate?

The three clergy and the four IAT members descended into the bowels of the Vatican. Ross couldn't help thinking of Gilbert Glaston as he would surely have approved of the fellowship of the seven. The otherwise impossible passage into the massive climate-controlled library encountered no obstacle.

They found themselves leaving the accompanying guards behind at the library's bulletproof glass doors. Ross had no idea the archives were so big,a myriad of enclaves and nooks. He felt as if his neck would ache from looking side to side at the wealth of books and artifacts.

At the foyer was a table able to seat twelve and after the librarian finished her grand tour, she set about retrieving books that the clergy thought might assist in their search. Boleyn was only marginally interested, more occupied with observing the silent Hecate whom had stopped testing the Opal and was wrestling with nightmares of mortality.

Boleyn was still astute and pointed out two books that definitely couldn't help much to the chagrin of the Pope.

"They were fakes."This didn't endear her to anyone there, least of all Ross who thought it was a distraction. However, it did stop them from wasting time and so in that regard,it was productive.Unlike them, Hecate was too engrossed with her own paradox to contribute, and Kelly was playing the sympathy card for all its worth. Still, working on half power, ancient books came and went, until the librarian requested a break from the constant running back and forth.

Ironically, it was the librarian's action and Kelly's lethargy that provided the breakthrough. When the heavy glass door swung open to let the librarian make her escape, a magnified reflection caught Kelly's attention.

"Look. Hecate's scar. The Venus Sign, on that… whatever it is.
A squat witches hat. I don't know…"

The librarian was asked to hold the door still while everyone followed the path of the reflection. It led to an old oversized black and white photograph of another famous Vatican sight, an aerial shot of the chimney that proclaimed the appointment of a New Pope. In plain sight, but not prominent like the chimney which was situated front and center, a structure similar to a witch's hat lay almost hidden in the background, and on its top was a cross.

If it hadn't been for the slightly concave glass door, the sign of a woman might never have been seen. It magnified an inverted reflection of the cross, and because of that, it was recognizable.

No one said anything, but everyone knew this was it. It was a moment when time stood still, and coincidently, an eerily quiet fell on them as the air conditioning unit stopped.

This was why they were there. Everyone felt the shivers run down their spines. Hecate remained the focal point of all the excitement. But Boleyn tingled and was touched deeply to her core, feeling that this signaled her destiny too; witch or not.

~~~

Even the Pope had difficulty tracking down the only man who knew how to get there, an old-timer pigeon racer. While they waited for the elusive superintendent to be located, suits, slacks and papal robes gave way to more practical apparel, that of rain clothes. If they were going onto the roof, then they were going to be needed. Donned in finest Italian rainwear, adorned with the Vatican Crest, the Crossed Keys, they took the only known route to the gables.

Following the superintendent up through ceiling holes and abandoned attics, his reclusive secret home, the group reached a boarded-up skylight. They sprung out of the surprisingly well lubricated window and were greeted by a slight misty drizzle. Each one in turn gazed over the drab Italian skyline to search out the object of their expedition.

Despite the tragic deaths, the search for the meaning of the Opal was progressing faster than the Pope dared hope.

Disorientated at first, and with the slight sting of rain in their eyes, it took them a little while to spot it across the flat, gentle sloping roofs. Several rooftops away, the *hat* waited.

"God. Nooooo. Mia pigeons."

The old man started crawling about on the floor, picking up smashed pieces of wood and twisted chicken wire while his pigeons flew in circles high above them.

Offended by his irreverence, Crow thought to admonish him until he realized the man was too preoccupied to wonder why the Pope, of all people, was on the roof.

"It'll be the last straw if one of those things poo on me." sniveled Kelly the moment she saw the birds circle overhead. She exaggerated a stoop.

"Me, me, me, me, me." came the catcall, as Boleyn saw the dramatics and called her out.

"Now look here Boleyn…"

Boleyn had come out of her reclusive husk the moment she heard of Hecate's predicament, but to deflect Kelly's retaliation, she pretended that she hadn't. Ignoring the spat for the umpteenth time, Ross directed everyone along the edge of the building towards the black shining structure.

Now, as in the past, property in the Vatican City was at a premium, thus alleyways between buildings were rare. Here in the very epicenter of the city, a convergence of five buildings met at this one particular corner and that was the location of the witch's hat.

Stepping over the large deep lead lined gutters that channeled rainwater to the expelling gargoyles, the team advanced upon their goal. Hecate was weak, but didn't want to trail behind, so she forced herself to keep up with Ross and Greg. Kelly and Crow followed them and Paul kindly dropped back to keep Boleyn company. Even if she didn't say anything, she thought it was nice as she needed assistance just to step over the drains.

By the time everyone congregated around the black hat, Ross had already circled it like a prowling panther. In his first cursory inspection he was disappointed to find nothing.

He observed a plain, featureless irregular pentagonal turret made of lead, consisting of five undecorated panels. Barely six feet across, its conical peak was only as high as Ross' eyelevel and it was no wonder no one gave it a second glance.

Nevertheless, it was different from the other *caps* of their kind. They were lower and flatter, and this one was just a little larger and crowned with the feature that caught Kelly's attention. Even with Ross' long reach, the inverted cross was still too far away to touch because of the steeple's larger size.

Ross backed up when Hecate arrived in deference and respect to her as she was the only one who had the *power*. Boleyn seethed as she saw this happen up ahead of her and she made up her mind that even if it cost her life, Hecate wouldn't end the day being waited upon again.

No matter what Boleyn thought or wished for, all eyes were on Hecate, including her own. Although she was weak, Hecate drew strength from pride and the desire to outdo Boleyn. To Boleyn's chagrin, Hecate placed the gem on the ground next to her feet, after first checking that Boleyn was a sufficiently far enough distance from her, just in case she had any idea of stealing it.

Once free of the stone, but in pain, she began her examination at one of the seams where the lead was folded over upon itself. Smugly she inspected the second seam. Hecate deliberately turned and gave Boleyn a look of superiority, before asking the two strongest men, Ross and Crow to pry open the joint. Boleyn's heart sank knowing Hecate had made a discovery no one else could.

Each took an athletic pose and prepared for a grueling challenge, yet it peeled open with the greatest of ease. For the first time since the arrival of the IAT, a moment of laughter was heard. It quickly stopped as they had exposed the sign of the woman beautifully etched into the bare lead. Everyone jumped to the obvious conclusion, including Boleyn who buried her head in her hands to avoid another smug look from Hecate.

"Was there no stopping her, and that stupid bitch Kelly too, I wish them both dead. If Phil L I P were alive, I'd wish him dead too."

With an air of confidence, Hecate presented the runes with those on her arm and almost instantly, the panel baring the mark slid open. With an evil grin, she sought out Boleyn's eyes, but she had made sure that contact couldn't be made by pretending to tend to her hair. Hecate was a little disappointed that she was so predictable, a small defeat in a won war. She picked up the Opal again and for the first time, didn't care about the cost to her witch-hood.

A small enclosure was revealed inside the cone, a space hardly big enough for a single small person. Engraved on the inside of the door panel was the Venus sign as clear as day. It featured a non-Christian cross with arms of equal length and a vertical arm that completely dissected the wide circle that crowned the cross. This modification confirmed the sign of a woman.

Too many occurrences of this cross waylaid any thought of it being the work of an overzealous artisan. It was obviously paramount. They almost overlooked the smallest of gaps, a hole between the five corners of the adjoining buildings. Once spotted, everyone took turns sticking their heads through the petite opening to look down the dark abyss. Hecate was first. Boleyn was last.

"Of course." she cursed.

Greg was the second to view it. It was protocol. The cross and the abyss chilled his soul. Callously disregarding Harry's demise, for the first time he almost wished they hadn't embarked on this quest.

"Still," he thought, "people don't just create something for nothing.This was a specific design and someone had taken the time to inscribe it into the lead. Although it was one of a cross, it was minimally Christian at best, actually hardly at all. Undeniably, I'm not going to say pagan, yet here it was so close, and unknown, to the heart of the Vatican. What are we doing? Should we stop?"

A shiver went down the Pope's spine. But it was too late. The Rubicon had been crossed the moment Hecate touched the gem, and no matter how bad his growing feeling of dread was, there was no turning back now.

When Boleyn did get her chance to see the chasm, her heart leapt. She didn't care about the cross or its meaning; it was the hole that excited her. She tried not to betray her thoughts.

"Was the shaft so small that it was possible that only she could get down it?"

There was quiet discussion at Kelly's height that Boleyn wasn't privy too, about the very same thing. Then, they announced their conclusion, that it was just big enough for Hecate.

Boleyn was deflated because she could see it was true, in a squeeze, Hecate, could get down there.

"At least it wasn't big enough for anyone else on the team, that is, Kelly, so it was going to be Hecate or me, or both, but none other. And even though Hecate is a witch, larger, stronger and could probably kill me multiple ways, I am not scared to go down that hole alone with her." Boleyn said to herself now completely out of her depression.

Should they both descend the oversized drainpipe, Boleyn would kill Hecate at the first chance she had and she knew Hecate wouldn't.

"This is looking good" thought Boleyn eagerly. So she was shocked when Hecate made a proposal.

"Kelly can come with me."

" What? How?" exclaimed Kelly, along with the others, but Boleyn knew exactly what she was harking on about,

"The only spell I didn't have, *the Absorption Spell* "'.

Hecate could take Kelly by absorbing her. Moreover, they had a special relationship, forged the night Phillip defeated the Devil. She had hidden her soul in Kelly and had reclaimed it later. Because of that initial spell, it was easy to execute the conjuring without maiming Kelly. Boleyn fought back the rage that exploded like a bomb inside her.

"FFFF UUU CC K."

It wasn't just Greg, Paul and Crow who didn't know what Hecate was on about; neither did Ross and Kelly. After Hecate explained the spell, all eyes fell on Kelly including Boleyn, who now prayed that her self-centered nature would be revealed.

"Ok. I'll do it." said Kelly.

"WHAT?" howled Boleyn to herself.

"Where's the me, me, me, me, me, me when it counts. It's such a crazy idea, and Hecate only suggested it to spite me. Seriously, that's all it is, to spite me. I'll show 'em."

"This was turning out to be the show of a lifetime" thought Greg, "Yesterday, we held the stone in the palm of our hands which was our first and only supernatural experience, now we're witnessing one after another. I wonder if we've been too quick to dismiss reported miracles. However, every incident we investigate, a charlatan is always at its center. Uh Oh, here we go."

Hecate stood only inches in front of the beautiful and tall Kelly.

"OK Kelly. I'm going to hand the stone to Greg... *definitely not Boleyn*" and she reached out and gave the Pope his stone.

"Ouch, Ok, Ok." Green blood started to well up in the scar. Stoutly ignoring the pain, Hecate continued. "Close your eyes. Good. Now take..."

"Are my clothes going to be ok?" asked Kelly.

"There she is." thought Boleyn, "She might just back out yet." "Yes, I think so, I don't know, (*no one's ever survived long enough to notice). Yes. (Anything to keep Boleyn out of this) Absolutely.*"

"Well. Ok, then, WAIT."

"YES." said Boleyn, "she's backing out. Hooray."

"What." said Hecate, "a tad impatiently, the scar does hurt you kn..."

"Here." said Kelly, "here's my key-ring flashlight, we'll need this."

"Damn, she's killing me." thought the resigned Boleyn.

"Good thinking Kelly." said Ross, smiling.

"Ok, thanks. Ok, Do it. For Phillip."

"What? Where did that come from?" thought Boleyn, "She's such a... woman."

"And Harry." said Ross, and not because he thought he was being outdone, but in honor of his best friend.

"Step forward." demanded Hecate, Kelly obeyed and vanished inside the heavily breathing witch.

And everyone, even the reluctant Boleyn, was impressed.

CHAPTER 34

CHAMBER WERE NO MAN SHALL COME

It took a couple of attempts to get into the *hat* the right way as it was awkwardly small. With the help and direction of the others, Hecate almost bent over double, eventually backed through the opening with her broom and positioned herself over the gap. Then, to the clergy's boundless astonishment, she hovered before squeezing into the gap backwards. Seconds later she was lowering herself downward in reverse gear if broomsticks have such a thing.

First her face descended below the lip of the buildings, then next her hat, and finally her vertically pointing broomstick vanished below the top of the hole. Greg had the privilege of peering over the hole to watch them while the others listened to the scraping noise of broom against stone.

The Pope's view disappeared and the grating sound soon died off as darkness swallowed her.

Greg turned and looked at Ross and said,"May God have merc…"

In her haste to disparage Boleyn, Hecate had completely forgotten that she didn't have the Opal. Realizing this Boleyn rushed forward through the tiny gap between Greg and the opening, snatched the stone out of his hand and jumped into the hole before anyone had time to think.

"Well."said Ross referring to the theft and disappearance of Boleyn. "Who knows, they may need the stone wherever they're going.

Have any idea where that might be Greg?"

"No, but I believe you are absolutely right." Regaining his conscience,"May I say Ross, how sorry I am for Harry, and of course, Phillip, but now, having seen what I've seen, I truly, truly fear for the World. I believe the Devil is at work. Let us pray."

All three clergy bent to their knees, leaving Ross in a problematic position. Until a month ago, he was an agnostic, but after seeing, meeting and conversing with the Devil, he more than suspected God's existence.

But what kind of God, he didn't know.

A God to pray to. Fear. Worship? Ignore? Would prayer actually irritate him? Gall him? He didn't know, and feared his ignorance.

He did nothing.

They had barely started to pray before the pigeon keeper snuck over and joined the group without anyone noticing. Clad in a black plastic cape, he was incredibly ignorant to interrupt the Pope's devotion. And in such dark times too.

Crow reconsidered his impulse to slap him for his impertinence. "Mia pigeon coupe, whoa's going to a pay..."

"Boom."

Everyone turned around and looked in the direction of the dampened heavy thump, and moments later, a black mushroom cloud billowed into the air from what looked like the distant Roma Airport. The transgression forgotten, everyone looked at each other with faces that showed the look of terrible foreboding.

No one knew what had happened, but clearly it wasn't good. They all felt that it had something to do with what was happening here, though there was nothing to support such a belief.

Instead of dismissing the superintendent, Crow ordered him to go, in secrecy, and get some chairs, blankets and food, or suffer eviction. Named Luigi, he hobbled off into the misty cooling afternoon sky, leaving everyone to speculate on the recent event.

That was until their cellphones came out of their pockets. Such is the wired World; the internet was already rife with hearsay and conspiracy. Ross switched to BBC Europe and their report of the developing story.

Ross addressed the clergy with familiarity."Chaps, a private jet bound for America crashed upon takeoff, wait, eye witness' say it crashed into an aviation fuel tanker that had meandered on to the runway. Hence the unduly large fireball… all experts considered it an un-survivable incident.

Multiple fire trucks were fighting the blaze. Trafic was being rerouted to other airports. Oh, there's more. The jet had made an emergency landing several hours earlier upon arrival from Gander, Canada."

Ross' voice trailed away, he was hoping against hope because unless there was an incredible coincidence, it had to be Bill's plane. Ross continued with more bad news.

"Hold on, wait, I got some other news here. Police are on the scene in Gander, Canada. They're calling in the National Guard. Virulent E Coli has contaminated the water supply. Nine Dead. Oh my dear God, not nine, NINE HUNDRED."

After Ross' cellphone had finished being passed around, he closed the website and held his breath so as not to disturb the solemn silence. Slowly, discreetly, each digested the news in their own way. Although the numbers were appalling, it was the story behind the story that they were privy to that concerned them the most.

"Was it a coincidence that Gander had hosted Phillip for a few hours? Was it a coincidence the plane on which Phillip was meant to arrive on had an issue, and now had crashed upon departure? What did any of it mean, if anything?

Was it just tragic and ironic; a plane that had little fuel on the way in, hit a fuel truck on the way out? Was there a message? Thankfully," thought Ross,"no one is talking. Or praying, aloud that is."

More than half an hour passed in somber silence. The surreal time was spent looking at the dissipating plume of black smoke heading east, listening to the ceaseless distant sirens, and checking the lonely, muted turret.They felt useless and self-conscious, so they buried their faces into any website that monitored the breaking news hoping someone other than themselves would snap the pregnant silence. "What's keeping that Luigi?" thought Greg.

"Greg, Paul, Crow. Look." said Ross daring to interrupt the quietness to everyone's relief. "Check this out." as he drew their attention to some other websites, mostly American. Although it covered the breaking news of Rome and Gander, it was trending a different principal story.

"Mass hysteria sweeps States as killings continue."he clicked on it.

"Doctors are calling it mass hysteria as thousands of murders has occurred in the past twenty-four hours. The common denominator is that all the perpetrators have serious psychological issues, and, get this, the names of their victims. 'Bill, Gill, Will, and the most targeted, by a long chalk, Phil'. The hysteria knows no boundaries either, the same rash of killings has occurred in England and its Commonwealth. Australia, New Zea..."

The implications of this latest story seemed so frightening that the reticence to break the quiet was overwhelming. If anyone were to say what was on their minds, then it might come to pass or be true, so they all remained mute.

~~~

And just as they kept their own counsel, so did someone else. The story hadn't escaped the attention of the Devil either. He was getting a little concerned too.

This was most certainly not mass hysteria. He knew that because he was usually the instigator of that phenomenon. This was God's work. What he didn't know was why.

"Was it in response to my surprise gains in the Entanglement War? To distract me?

So she could sneak in a counterattack. Or was it something else?"

It had caught his attention and that was already dangerous, so he ignored it as best he could. Along with Basher and Smasher, he didn't know what to think.Things were descending into a black well not of his making, and he was lost on what to do or what any of it meant.

~~~

"Thank God." said Paul, shattering the silence, even though the sound of distant sirens echoed all around them, "Here's Luigi. It only took him a ho… Oh, BRAVO Luigi." As behind him he ushered a couple guards out of the skylight and pointed them in the group's direction. Then two more appeared. The small detachment bore fold up chairs, food, and most importantly from their point of view, security.

Luigi, who really was the only one who knew how to get there, was immediately ordered by one of the guards to get reinforcements once he saw how exposed the pontiff was.Twenty minutes later, he returned with a small company of nine men carrying Glocks. One particular guard posted himself within twenty yards of the Pope,taking up a facing away position whilst keeping himself out of earshot.

"Greg." interrupted Paul, putting his hand over his cell's microphone, "Two trains have had a head on collision at a place called Evelyn Mills, it's significant because it's…"

"The closest town to ClearStream." said Crow in a quiet voice.

"Because it was one of the last known towns that Phillip, not Phil but Phillip, was in." said Ross in an even more ominous tone, "I wish I would not say these next words, but I must. I believe he is, was, and it sounds crazy but, I think he's being hunted. By whom, I don't know."

"Both trains carried flammable and toxic chemicals. Evelyn Mills is no more; the Devil's work." concluded Paul.

"The Devil's work?" repeated Ross sounding unconvinced. "Greg." turning his attention to the Pope, "When we met, we
discussed several things. Sometimes, it's hard to grasp or believe what you hear. It gets shelved, pushed aside so that the day can continue.Well now hear this, because you have not heard it until now.

After the Devil escaped the John Abbott Shoe, I, personally, introduced him to the crowd at Salem. He travelled out of one of the Shoes that Phil was wearing, and how it got there in the first place was by magic none other, and travelled through his body. Beyond human endurable pain, Phillip survived. His bloated body turned *black* until the Devil traversed across the handcuffs that linked him and John Abbott XXVIIth, all twenty-seven incarnations of him.

You ask of PhilLIP, well I don't have enough time to tell how great a man he is; was, or all that he did. It is our greatest loss. A loss beyond all that we can imagine, and in a way, I betrayed him, leaving him behind to follow his own '*witch's hat*,' shunning him to come here.

My fear is that we may be made to pay for my blindness.

Because, you were right Greg, something is happening.

Bigger than I could have imagined, and without Phillip, I fear that it may be too big for us and for mankind. No. I'm not imagining or exaggerating.

These things have happened. The loss of fuel on the plane. The crash of Bill's plane.

The catastrophe in Gander.

The common denominator is Phillip.

Phillip stood against the Devil and saved Hecate, Ruebella the Yellow Witch, and Boleyn from Hell, on his own, at his own peril.

My fear in this hour and in this city is heightened. Because the Devil, Greg, the Devil is a showman. *These acts that we are witnessing I feel are not his doing. They are subtle, and only we know the thing that links them, some...* "

"LOOK." said Paul looking past the Pope's shoulder, "The Venus Sign, the cross, now it's the right way up. When did that happen? Did anyone see it happen? Anyone?

What does it mean?"

CHAPTER 35
HECATE THE CHOOSEN ONE

Although it was a vertical drop of five stories, Boleyn used the sides of the buildings to control the speed of her fall. It was not enough to stop her from crashing into Hecate, who descended at a slow, calculated rate, using Kelly's light to show the distance to the floor. That all changed in an instance as Boleyn's crash caused them to free fall out of control for the remainder of the descent. Luckily, it was only about six feet.

"What?" shouted Hecate, "Boleyn! Why have you co..."

The Opal flew out of Boleyn's hand onto the floor. Seeing it, Hecate snatched it up quickly and the pain and bleeding stopped. Hecate realized that she'd left the stone behind and that Boleyn, had luckily although unintentionally returned it to her, the rightful owner.

Kelly popped into existence at the onset of Hecate's mortality, clothes and all. Hecate did not thank Boleyn for returning the gem, instead she cursed. She may have saved her from bleeding to death, but Hecate was the vanguard and she didn't want any spoilers.

Hecate's ingratitude didn't anger Boleyn, but dropping the gemstone and Hecate finding it, did. It wasn't Boleyn's intention to give the stone to Hecate at all, her intent was to withhold it, watch her suffer, and hope she'd bleed to death; all the while concealing that she had the power to save her.

"Yea, that pissed me off royally." she thought.

"Another screw up, I'm turning into Phil, PhilLIP, whatever."

Although she desired Hecate's demise, the compelling reason she was there was that she believed that something un-mortal would happen. Should it occur, an opportunity to save her soul might arise.

Now a pile of three bodies, Hecate, Boleyn and Kelly untangled themselves. Kelly twisted her flashlight around and by accident spied the way ahead. She got up onto her hands and knees and saw that her clothes were disheveled. Surprisingly unconcerned, she crawled forward into a tiny tunnel. No higher than a couple of feet, it immediately descended into a flight of stairs. She twisted around so her feet went down first, but she couldn't shine the light anymore. By now Hecate had fully recovered and Boleyn was on her feet, so Kelly was holding everyone up.

"Give me that." shouted Boleyn.

It made sense that she should go first, she was so small she only had to bend a little bit to navigate. Only the height of the steps slowed her down from running away from the trailing duo. Doggedly, she used her hands and lowered herself down step by step, but nonetheless, she still descended swiftly and started to leave the others behind. She willingly would have taken off if the end of the passage hadn't nixed that idea.

At the bottom of about a hundred steps, they tumbled out into a tiny short fat cylindrical landing. Everyone was dirty, and their hands were cold and messy as some of the steps were damp and slippery. Boleyn expected nothing less of Kelly who cursed and fretted over being crouched, dirty and hurting. She did have a point, as the tallest there. She rubbed her head having hit it several times on the hard stone ceiling of the low stairway, and again now in the four-foot-high chamber.

They weren't alone in the six-foot diameter room, where a small pile of golden objects lay on the floor, and everyone's eyes were on them. Boleyn's hands were already going through the golden goblets, coins and jewelry. It was a veritable fortune. Kelly sat down, Hecate knelt down and Boleyn paced around, because she could. Cursing, she couldn't believe that all this trouble was for a bunch of trinkets, albeit, more valuable than she could imagine owning.

"It doesn't really make sense, does it?" said Hecate,"I mean the scar…"

"No it doesn't, and yet I've looked around the whole place, and there's no way out, other than the way we came in." said Boleyn, looking for a miracle and not gold.

"I don't know." said Kelly, "I mean… this is worth millions and…"

"Me, me, me. You've already got everything, and so too has Hecate, or at least she did. Me? I've got nothing. LESS THAN NOTHING. I've…" shouted Boleyn's mind.

"Look." said Hecate, "On the floor, partially sticking out from under Kelly's as…. Is it a mark?"

"MOVE." yelled Boleyn, this time aloud.

Kelly dwarfed Boleyn, but in that moment, she was scared and scurried out of the way on all fours.

Hecate put her arm down on the floor and nothing happened.

"PUT THE STONE DOWN STUPID." shrieked Boleyn again, getting more abusive with every interaction, now vocalizing every thought. She no longer bothered to keep her thoughts inside.

Hecate did as she was told and her broomstick leapt to attention with the prompt return of her unwanted symptoms. Nevertheless, in this state, she was a witch, and went to every pain to let Boleyn know.

With a clumsy bow, already in a kneeling position in the short chamber, Hecate placed her scar on the symbol and with a huge thump, the floor crashed downward five or six feet.

Everyone was shaken up by the crashing floor. But Hecate gleefully picked up the bouncing stone quickly lest Boleyn grab it first. Before them was the reason they were there, a new tunnel, dark, black.

"My God, the gold was a distraction to…" started Kelly.

"And you would have GONE FOR IT, because you have…" interrupted Boleyn, who stopped as she realized that she'd missed her chance to steal the stone back from Hecate and run down the tunnel wherever it may lead. It would, of course, have been a short-lived victory as Hecate would have chased her down and wrestled it back from her in an instant. If she were lucky, that's all she would have done.

"OK, my bad." interrupted Kelly, not caring for a lecture, especially from a midget.

"Where does the tunnel go now? It's taller than the last one. 'bout four-foot high, maybe more." said Hecate.

Recognizing that it was high enough to lead, Kelly snatched her key-ring light back from the brooding Boleyn seeing that she was too busy thinking about something.

"Give me that, it's mine."

"Shit." said Boleyn realizing her daydreaming cost her the only thing she had left to bargain with. Proud of stealing her own property back from a person half her size, Kelly shone the light into the small opening.

"It goes down."

"Just like you I bet." thought the bitter midget.

And as if on command, Kelly bent down and disappeared into it. She led them down a steep slope, which was tighter than the previous already narrow tunnel, but at least there were no steps to hinder them. Boleyn was thankful for that, but now she was last in line, which didn't please her at all. After descending less than ten feet, Kelly stopped. The tunnel was blocked.

"It's a dead end." she said, as she turned to the others close behind, but Boleyn had rushed to keep up and bumped into Hecate who bumped into Kelly, and she fell against the facing wall. It budged a smidgen with a grating sound. At first, they thought it was an echo as they heard the same grinding noise behind them, but suddenly and collectively, they all knew what it was.

"Push it, Kelly." said Hecate and as Kelly pushed it forwards, the chamber platform rose behind them. With Hecate aiding Kelly, (she wouldn't let Boleyn touch her again) about fifteen feet later; the chamber's platform behind them was back in position, confirmed with a loud symphony of clicks. To the side, another tighter tunnel was revealed, and a chill made them shiver, this was it.

The narrowness assisted their sharp descent, as they were able to press up against the walls and stop themselves sliding out of control down the ever-increasing sheer path. They went onwards for hundreds of yards and hardly registered the tunnel's alternating construction from natural-hewn rock to brick, sandstone blocks and mortar. Neither did they care about the bends, twists and short shafts, nor that it became even narrower and lower.

They always moved downwards; sometimes so tight that even Boleyn had to scrunch up to get through. They continued their long and tiring descent, but out of the three, Boleyn was the most exhausted. There was, however, no way was she going to admit to it. Luckily, the descent was punctuated with frequent stops for Hecate to reclaim her witch's hat that kept being knocked off by the low ceiling.

Down they went. Forty, fifty minutes passed, and then an hour. Kelly worried as there'd seemed to be no end in sight, other than the dimming light from the torch. It was a great relief when they finally burst into a relatively large corridor, which was big enough to squeeze past each other and high enough for Kelly to stand up straight. It had been a long and arduous slog for all of them and for the light too as it chose that moment to die.

"Shit. Shit. Shit." swore Kelly in a low hushed tone. She wondered why she whispered, but she wasn't alone, as for some reason they were all speaking in their softest voices.

"Shhh." and they all listened in the dark. "Thought I heard something." said Hecate.

"Da daa." cried Boleyn in a rare moment of cheerfulness, and suddenly light sprung forth from her cell which possessed an assistive light. Seeing the corridor again, for the first time they acknowledged it was cut by human hand and that it ended in a dead end.

"Look." said Hecate pointing,"The Venus Sign, it's on the wall at the far end. It looks like there's a door carved into the stone. There, look."

They all did and it appeared to be true.

"Shit. Wish I'd never switched it on." muttered Boleyn.

Being *the chosen one*, Hecate pushed past Kelly and attempted without success to venture down the alleyway. After taking the first step, circles appeared on the walls to each side of her. Entanglement forced her back like the pressure of two opposing magnets. The circles disappeared when she'd completely backed off. She sighed as she saw she couldn't get through.

"My turn." thought Kelly as she shoved Hecate aside and walked quickly forward. Though business like and beautiful, she could not win against the Entanglement and she was summarily repelled just like Hecate.

"Thank God." thought the relieved Boleyn, "Hecate can't get there and do whatever has to be done. Obviously, she needs the stone, and she can't get there with it. Ha. And that dumb, Kelly can't get to the door and miraculously open it. Idiot, doesn't she realize only Hecate has the mark, and so only Hecate can open the door. Oh no."

Boleyn's fear came true. Hecate had figured out what to do. She threw the gem along the floor where it bounced up against the door. Her broomstick awoke, blood oozed from her arm, and Hecate strutted triumphantly down the corridor. With every step, a different sized "O" appeared on the wall, and remained, like a guard of honor.

If she'd thought of it in time, Boleyn would have turned her light off to hinder her, but the cleverness of Hecate had shocked her and Kelly both. Whatever reward waited, it would be Hecate's alone, and Boleyn seethed understanding this.

Seeing that symbols were visible and permanent, Kelly tried again. For the first time in her life, her beauty wasn't enough. She couldn't follow Hecate.

Boleyn didn't bother attempting, even if she could get there, she'd be too late. Hecate was already there and baring her arm. With a single look back over her shoulder, one of absolute victory, the green blood and scar of Hecate touched the engraved pattern in the rock wall, and a stone door opened.

She picked up the gem lying at her feet not caring about the failing broom, and took the single step required to occupy the entranceway. She was ready to claim her prize.

Kelly and Boleyn watched from the corridor. Ahead, they watched light emanate around Hecate's black silhouette as it filled the doorway. Whatever lay behind the door was impossible for Kelly and Boleyn to see, but whatever it was; it had caused Hecate to stop.

She stood erect and motionless. She was poleaxed. All she had to do was advance a single step and she would gain full entry into the chamber yet she seemed completely reticent to take it.

Motionless in the entrance doorway, Kelly and Boleyn saw Hecate falter. Instead of entering, where no woman had gone before, they saw hesitation and what appeared to be a body paralyzed with fear. Seconds seemed like hours as Hecate stood still on the threshold before she moved. They saw her shuffle, not into the beyond, but in retreat. Another hesitant filled sway of her feet followed.

Kelly was thinking, "Whatever is in there must be…"

Hecate stood on the threshold and gazed in to the beyond. A noise behind her made her look back over her shoulder. For the second time in that single minute, she stood in the doorway, and couldn't believe what she saw.

CHAPTER 36

EXTREME SPORT IN THE HIGHEST

Without a parachute, Phillip immediately went into a spiraling freefall with less than ten minutes between him and the unforgiving ground. It was now or never.

S

Rhom

n

g

He wondered whether he might survive the crash, but assumed he wouldn't. He closed his eyes and stretched his arms and legs out wide. The Shoes that now clothed him from head to foot filled the gaps and he heroically glided like a flying squirrel.

He soared high but not masterfully through the sky. He was elated as he could feel the air whooshing by like being on a roller coaster. He knew he wasn't exactly flying but he didn't care, because he wasn't falling either.

His eyes were shut tight as it seemed it was the only way that he could summon his RhomSong, but neither could he see where he was going. When he stole a short peek to get his bearings, he instantly went into a barrel roll, yet his glance was long enough to pick out Rome on the horizon. He quickly closed his eyes again and regained control.

In his mind, he thought that he wasn't really flying, only falling slowly. He realized that he wouldn't get as far as Rome before hitting ground at this rate of descent. Desperation and imagination told him that he needed to learn how to fly. Then he could reach Rome and land rather than crash, in the not-so-distant countryside below.

Brimming with confidence, he tried to visualize a jet pack on his back that would propel himself forward and up.

Instantly faster wind rushed by him, but the only way he could tell if he was flying was to sneak another peek. Again the result was to spin uncontrollably, but in that second, he saw that his trajectory was ascending. He was gaining altitude. Alternating between the occasional periods of tail spinning and longer periods of uplifting blackouts, he made his way towards the Eternal City.

For Phillip just getting to Rome wasn't enough. He had to figure out the reason why they were going there. He decided that if he had enough height, then maybe, he could view the city to spot something or someplace that wasn't normal or not of mortal origin.

"Joan said she was a Pope. Damn, I just remembered about the key she had round her waist. I should have *taken*, I mean *borrowed*, I mean *adopted* it. Oh well, too late now. So I'll head for the Vatican."

With each intermittent peek, he saw that he had gained height and was quickly approaching the center above the beautiful city. Each glimpse was filled with the magnificence of the World-renowned buildings below him.

"St. Peter's , the Vat... a small structure like a witch's hat laid buried in anonymity, and on top of it, a sparkle of Entanglement.

There."

He logged the direction in his mind, and he wheeled toward it like a jet bomber lining up a target. Although he was eager to reach his goal, he also felt disappointment and apprehension that his flight was coming to the end. He'd never flown before and therefore had never landed either. A rush of blood shot through his veins.

The closer he came, the greater was his awareness of his high speed. He adjusted his 'clothes'to catch more air and slow him down like a parachute, only he'd left it too late. The ground rushed up to meet him and there was nothing more he could do about it.

A wooden pigeon coop bore the brunt of his clumsy first landing.

Happily, the pigeons were unharmed. They flapped their wings wildly and took off as they enjoyed their new found freedom. "Perhaps," thought Phillip "they are showing off, and teaching me how flying is really done."

It was no surprise to Phillip that he was unharmed, as his clothing had taken the form of fine chain mail just before impact. He assumed that if his body could repel bullets, then it could survive this collision especially with his new armor. He saw he was at least a hundred yards from his intended landing spot, but he thought it was fine considering it was his maiden flight.

As he walked over to the turret, he realized that once again, what he had done, no man had done before!

A feeling of contentment and pride swallowed the profound sadness that had caused him to risk his life. (Kelly). Although flying was magnificent, he didn't attempt to fly the short distance to the turret. Thinking better of it, he decided instead to go on foot.

He walked round the object several times. Then he studied the 'hat' and the bright spot of Entanglement on its apex. A closer examination revealed that the inverted sign of a woman at the top was an impersonation of a Christian cross, Entangled. As he pondered, he heard a muted signal coming from a fold in one of the roof's panels.

The lead from the panel felt cool in his hands, but it bent easily to his will.

"Was he strong or was the lead weak?" as he gently unfolded it without it breaking. The mark now shone bright and as he held Joan's lock of hair against the carving, he waited for something to happen; but nothing did.

He scratched his head for a couple of moments before he decided to expose his own scar whilst holding Joan's Entangled lock of hair in his fist. As soon as he placed his arm on the carving, a panel in the turret slid open. He entered the tiny enclosure without a pause. He felt exposed, as a trespasser on the open rooftops of the papal buildings.

Once inside, he closed the door behind him by again exposing his arm again against the underside of the mark. Now he stood in complete darkness, knowingly next to a precipice that fell to *who knewwhere*. Smartly, he thought about using his cell's assistive light.

"Damn, I should have got it out of my pocket before I shut the door. And damn... damn... I should have used this instead of depending on Kelly's key ring flashlight all those times."

With its shallow beam as his only source of light, he slowly lowered himself down the shaft using his hands and legs to brace himself. He knew his ability to fly was his safety net and he'd only gone a foot before he found himself calling upon the power.

With his eyes closed, he got to the bottom. He wondered, if he could have made the descent in this very tight space, if he hadn't lost all that height and size.

Still, he was down and with the slightest of pauses, he crept down the steep stone staircase to the *fool's treasury*. He ignored the gold as he knew the reason for the maze wasn't for something as mundane as that. He looked around and spotted a delicately carved sign in the stone. He placed his arm's engraving against the chamber's carving and was shocked as the floor crashed down several feet to reveal a second secret passage.

Its suddenness caused the surprised Phillip to drop Joan's lock of hair. At first, he wasn't concerned as he could spot Entanglement like a neon sign, so when he couldn't discern it, he was puzzled. When he did find it, with normal eyesight, he saw he had depleted all its remaining Entanglement from that last exploit in the turret. Nonetheless, Phillip retrieved and kept it as his keepsake of Joan.

"Besides, Kelly was no longer in the picture. Like all the women in my life, even the witches."

Phillip pushed his sentimentality aside; it was a dangerous emotion. He pragmatically thought. "Hope I don't face any more Entanglement doors." and he began his new descent.

Not twelve feet in, he encountered an obstacle as a large block of stone filled the tunnel. A little peeved by this additional hurdle, he instinctively pushed against the rock. It was solid. Puzzled that one would come all this way to be stopped like this. He heaved against it with all his might. It budged. Just a tad. Encouraged, he pushed again and once it got moving, it moved relatively easily albeit with an ear-splitting abrasive grating noise. A close copy of the sound emanated from the chamber behind.

Without further ado, he shoved the block forwards almost ten, fifteen feet until he heard several generous clicks catch. In recognition of the ingenuity of the long dead engineers, he saw that he had reloaded the '*fools' chamber's*' drop floor.

He didn't once consider an exit strategy, being more interested in the new tunnel that was revealed by moving the reload stone. He felt this latest passage would take him to the final destination.

He was almost halfway down when he thought, for a second time, that his short stature was the only thing that had enabled him to get this far. He would never have been able to negotiate the cleft between the buildings and he would have been forced to claw on all fours down these narrow and low passageways. Though he banged his head frequently, only the shock of the sudden bangs hurt him, otherwise, his skin didn't even graze.

The thought that Kelly's rejection of shortness had some meaning cheered him up, though he was already in a good mood after his flight and levitation.

Before too long, Phillip traversed the Entanglement passage. Since RhomSong granted him clear passage, he was blissfully unaffected by its purpose, which was to exclude those not possessing Entanglement. He saw the imprints of Entanglement down the stone corridor and all around him, but it was the Entanglement design at the end, next to what was obviously a door, that held his attention.

Phillip looked at the engraving and felt helpless for the first time since leaping out of his brother's jet. Joan's lock of hair had run out of Entanglement, and without Entanglement, Phillip knew he couldn't open it.

"It can't be true, can it? I mean, I've come all this way, only to fail. Come on Phillip, think, use your head."

The only man to have had Entanglement, Phillip existed outside of it, for better or for worse. Now, as was Phillip's wont, again, he compounded difficult situations by thinking of Kelly, which always plunged him into self-doubt and depression. Just as things seemed disappointing and futile, an answer sprung to mind.

"Joan."

He placed his arm against the wall's carving, and scratched the scab covering something on the crown of his head. Tiny remains of Joan's cross, no bigger than a pinhead, lay buried in his skull. There, a pinprick of Entanglement endured. He used his head indeed.

The stone door opened *for the first time ever*. Only the slightest of scraping sounds accompanied the magical opening of the massive door, as thick as it was wide.

When the door was built, Joan performed mysterious and secret incantations that only she knew. Then Joan closed the door twice, first physically and secondly, with Entanglement. It was known only by its deceased maker and remained unperturbed for hundreds of years. All the construction workers had died long ago. The stone they quarried when they mined the tunnels and chambers went towards the construction of the ancient buildings that became its concealment.

The design of the secret passages was dictated by God and implemented by Joan. Access was restricted to women only and not just any women; only those of the very rarest creed, Entangled women, saint or witch.

Joan, in secret and with much assistance from God, spent several years in seclusion behind the massive door, conjuring, casting spells and praying. No one other than Joan knew what had been created. But what lay inside that final fearsome place, instilled fear in anyone who laid their eyes upon it.

Unable to acquire Entanglement, excluded by Entanglement traps, tests and keys at strategic junctures, men were rendered inferior. Furthermore Joan had agreed with God that the glitter of gold would be enough to sidetrack any further exploration of their tunnel, should a man accidently discover, traverse and descend the forbidden warren. They believed in the superficial nature of men, but not only men though; it would have averted Kelly as well.

Now, Phillip, a man who had acquired Entanglement when no other could, and had surpassed it, was posed. He was a single step away from entering the truly holiest of holies, on Earth, in this galaxy, our Universe, other than Heaven.

It was a forbidden place, a secret place, God's place.

The scene that filled his eyes was that of a small spherical chamber no more than seven yards in diameter. It took several seconds to determine its dimensions because what it occupied demanded all of his attention. Phillip stood at the threshold and looked at a tree without bark. Its bleached white naked limbs reached up and circled around every upper part of the chamber symmetrically.

Certainly, this was no ordinary tree; the tree was on fire. The flames were not ordinary either, but were white, blue and golden, full and voluptuous. Truly frightening was the tree's branches, which didn't bear twigs and leaf buds at the tree's extremities, but instead live snakes that hissed. Immune to the flames, the serpents licked the air with their tongues, and writhed and glared.

Fortunately, for Phillip, their penetrating stare seemed to look right through him. After he quelled his initial shock and overwhelming desire to turn and run, Phillip realized that they didn't avoid looking at him, they just didn't register his arrival. When he waved his hand, the gaze of the snakes didn't track or follow it and luckily neither did their mouths full of needle-sharp teeth. He did it again just to be sure there wasn't any reaction.

He recalled what Joan had said, "I don't see you."

He also remembered the entity in ClearStream being confused and not recognizing him, so, it only made sense that the snakes couldn't see him either.

Only after he was absolutely certain that they weren't interested in him, did he let his eyes wander and survey the rest of the chamber. Shockingly, the tree emanated not from the ground, but from a cross at the base of the sphere.

The cross was the familiar sign of a woman, but it glistened and shone as it appeared to be made from solid gold. Inconceivably it wasn't beautiful; it was intimidating and terrifying. Seven feet high, three feet wide and a foot thick, it was dense and weighed a ton.

"A couple, maybe." thought Phillip.

The signs had led him here, but this cross was different from all the rest. It had a unique quality, namely, *growing* out of the horizontal arms were the limbs of the tree that filled the entire upper hemisphere of the chamber.

He was here now and so what else was there to do? He plucked up the courage to do the unthinkable, though, it was his only choice. If he had thought of quitting, he would have picked up the decoy trinkets left at the first chamber and gone home. A month ago, yes, that's what he would have done and turned them in to a museum, not cash them in for his own gain.

"You're such a sap." Kelly would have said.

Now, all he cared about was completing the path. Even though he had lost Kelly, he wasn't reckless. The last thing he wanted was to die. He felt bad enough to think the worst of thoughts when he pondered opening the plane door. It was less than six hours ago, but seemingly felt like an eternity. Fully invested in life and living, Phillip considered his options. The choices he had were limited, to indeed only one. It was now or never.

He ducked to avoid the snakeheads inches from the entrance, and he stood on the first of a flight of descending steps cut into the sphere's steep curved side. He turned and closed the vault's door behind him, and then, descended the first few steps facing the wall. After just three hard to negotiate rungs, he was able to turn round and progress down the easier, final shallow ones.

From the base of the cross, he looked up from the bottom of the tree's trunk and saw the ceaselessly moving snakes. And they were ignoring him. He looked up to the apex of the chamber, and saw a stream of water, only a single drop in width. It fell in an unhindered passage and landed on the top of the circle of the golden cross. Curiously, it didn't make a splash, and after looking at it longer, Phillip surmised it was falling and rising at the same time. "Weird."

The smokeless flames originated out of nowhere at the joining of the circle and they seemed to be powered without the need of fuel. They engulfed the entire tree and licked at the un-blackened ceiling but never quite touched it. They threw devil like shadows that cavorted evilly over the concave stone.

Nothing about God's inner sanctum on Earth was welcoming or inviting.

Although Phillip wasn't reputed to be an astute person, he had cultivated several theories and his presence in this chamber was confirmation that some of them were right. One of his beliefs was that God, the Devil and who or whatever the third assailant was, were unable to see, detect or identify him. Thus he was invisible to them.

Another of his theories was that Entanglement attacks required a physical property, like the stab of Joan's Cross or the attempted drowning from the mysterious third. Without this physical aspect of the attack, such as Joan's first and failed original attacks, Entanglement would pass right through him. Without the tangible anchor, Entanglement was like light through glass.

However, when an Entanglement attack was accompanied with a physical characteristic, then it was deep and deadly. If it wasn't for his RhomSong, he would undoubtedly be dead.

With every battle he repelled, just as the witch's attacks, he mutated and his resistance and immunity grew.

He didn't know this as a fact; *he just felt it*.

For all that he did know, he didn't know what to do next. He'd come all this way, risking life and limb, and he didn't know for what or why? So, he did what he considered his only option, which in fact displayed his growing self confidence and trust in his abilities, and that was to reach out his hand and touch the flames.

"Ouch." He withdrew his hand automatically before it had a chance to feel pain. Then he realized that he hadn't really felt anything at all.

He touched the flames a second time and fought the impulse to retract his hand. He forced himself to leave it there. A moment later, he climbed the cross and plunged himself into the tree and the flames, feeling amazed, enthralled and exhilarated by their touch.

He wandered deep into the hearth eager for more. He clambered around without considering that he was the only person, again, to have experienced flames without pain or burns.

Overflowing with confidence, he touched a snake. Moments after this, several snakes slithered over and around him, and ignored him. The power he felt from his invulnerability was so invigorating that he found a place where he could stand. Without holding on, he wished his clothes gone.

Standing naked and invisible to the Universe, he reached into the air and roared in pleasure and defiance. The entangled flames wrapped over and around him continuing to be oblivious to his presence. Seemingly just as indifferent, the serpents slinked over him as he was just another tree limb.

With a crook of his neck, he interrupted the stream of water and caused splashes to scatter all around, from above and incredibly below his intersection. Although the water was clear and cool, Phillip wasn't sure whether it was *water* or not. There was something a little strange about it.

He even thought, "It was a little too pure, too cool, too clear, to be water.

What substance in the world other than water could sustain the tree of snakes?

"Actually." he mused, "could plain water even do that? Did it seem right that a magic tree would be sustained by normal water? Maybe it wasn't just natural water after all? And where was it coming from and going to? Or more accurately, was it coming from or going somewhere? Anywhere? Nowhere?

Who cares right now anyway? Twice in this same day, I have experienced something no man has before.

Water and fire, Earth and Heaven. Hate and love, ah, love.

If only Kelly loved me," he sighed, "and if only, then this day would be complete."

CHAPTER 37

LOOK, ONLY HECATE IS ENTANGLED

There was so much to see inside the chamber, but all Hecate saw were snakes. Stunned at this terrifying sight, she froze. To her spiders and snakes were just the most horrifying.

Every snake's head in the chamber twisted hostilely towards her. Their hungry eyes focused in her direction and their intensity alone was fearsome.

Petrified in their spotlight she instinctively took a step back. It was vital that she ensured the boundary from the entrance into the chamber was not crossed. She heard a noise behind her and as she turned and scanned the Entangled Corridor, she saw someone rush towards her.

Her mind reeled in confusion as she tried to reconcile this unlikely event.

"Only entangled ones can get this far, and yet she, a non-witch, has traversed the Entanglement charged passageway. Boleyn the unworthy has crossed the divide between Earth and Heaven. Somehow, a non-entangled agent of the Devil has negotiated this division. I was certain that I was the only qualified. How can this be?"

If time had permitted, Hecate might have realized that she was as jealous of Boleyn's achievement as she was fearful of the snakes. Hecate now bore a deep hated for her. Action was required, but a bad feeling swept over her that she'd left it too late.

Boleyn dove forward, crashed into Hecate, and tackled her behind her knees. This caused Hecate to wave her arms in large circles in an effort to regain her balance. A hand crossed the entranceway and without hesitation one of the preying snakes struck. Its single bite fastened its concave teeth deep into her hand.

Locked on, it pulled Hecate's arm further into the chamber, and instantly other snakes' bit vehemently into her. The brief trespass was irrevocable. Swiftly, she was dragged fatefully into the cavity.

Boleyn used all her strength and speed, leaned as heavily as she could against the door and heaved it closed. Pure white malicious light ferociously streamed through the narrowing gaps in its effort to capture another victim, but Boleyn had other plans.

Panting with relief from the effort of forcing the door shut, she knew what she'd done. It wasn't good, yet she was happy she'd done it. Kelly stood at the far end of the passage confused by what she had just witnessed. She didn't know what lay behind the door, but she saw that Boleyn condemned Hecate to what horror it contained.

Without remorse, Boleyn heaved for air as she sat exhausted at the bottom of the door, where not one ray of light escaped its magnificent joints. The last expression Boleyn saw on Hecate's face so obviously said, "WTF." She died in confusion rather than pain. Nevertheless it gave Boleyn immense satisfaction.

Almost overcome with shock, Kelly's mind screamed,

"How had Boleyn got down the passageway? I mean, I couldn't do it? How did she? And, OMG, what she did to Hecate. Am I nex…"

Kelly was as far removed from Boleyn's world as anyone could get. She already had everything while Boleyn had nothing. Kelly didn't understand not having, as the World was for her bidding. And now, it was a World that Boleyn swore she was going to lay claim to.

She murdered Hecate, the little sister she once loved. She was prepared to pay any penalty without qualm.

Emboldened, Boleyn schemed "That moment in ClearStream two weeks ago when Hecate reclaimed her Entanglement back from Kelly… who is next by the way… we were no longer sisters. She thought herself better than me. I could see it in her eyes. She deserved to die, plain and simple, as does Kelly if I haven't mentioned it, as does Ross, and the rest.

And speaking of them, they will wonder why Hecate and Kelly didn't survive this quest. I'll tell them a story, any story.They'll never be able to disprove it. Down here. Closer to Hell. Or Heaven, it's all the same to me now. Here further from Earth than anywhere on Earth, what better place or time; one down - one to go."

Boleyn was happier now than she had been for ages.

Kelly was at one end of the corridor and Boleyn at the other. The passage between them delineated how they were the antithesis of each other:

Tall, short.

Attractive, repulsive.

Weak, strong.

Boleyn turned off the assistive light throwing them into total darkness.

Murder was on her mind.

She would find her way out,

on her own.

She would climb back up the tunnels,

on her own.

She would find her way back to the rooftops somehow,

on her own. For she was Boleyn.

The Ex Red Witch.

She was the greatest.

Was.

And she didn't care anymore.

She was not a witch now.

She couldn't kill people with her Entanglement.

She no longer had Entanglement.

She bore an illness, an infection, a parasite inside her.

No one could imagine it.

It had depressed her, writhing inside and gnawing at her.

Stronger now, she didn't need to be free of the torment.

She had become tough,

in her mind, soul,

through desire.

At first, she thought she would die.

The betrayals were endless - she didn't care about them now,

they were immaterial.

She was herself now, and woes betide any who stood in her way.

She'd show them the gold, but not all of it.

She'd swallow the diamonds and keep them for herself.

She was burdened with the wickedness of her smallness and her affliction.

The encounter with the strange entity in the pool in ClearsStream where her affliction multiplied, had forged her will.

She was not granted twice her height as promised even though she delivered. It had *nearly* crushed her. Now her human spirit burnt fiercely and she had strength in a way no one could have predicted. She was so filled with hatred.

Now it gave her meaning. Now it gave her definition.

Since she was destined for Hell, she decided to kill those who slighted her.

She had nothing to lose. She was free.

"The Devil must be wondering what's keeping me? He must be thinking that he's beaten me. Hah. And now, I, I don't care. Now I embrace this burden, his burden.

I wonder if he knows what else I carry and that I'm surviving it? Surviving them.

I wonder if he knows about the thing in the water?

Yes, I wonder.

I don't think he does.

I think I know more than him.

HA HAH...

So... out of spite, I'll survive.

Out of spite, I'll thrive.

Instead of dying, instead of submitting, instead of feeling sorry for myself, now, I will feed off this New World, not it off me. It will watch me, not the weak, non-Entangled Boleyn, the non-witch of nothing, but the modern witch of the modern times. Who needs Entanglement when you have all these new and amazing weapons, handguns, drugs, and spams.

By any means possible. I will bring an ancient hatred to these times, visiting death upon whom I choose, and I choose everyone.

And next? Kelly, Ross, Greg, Paul, Crow. Here, did I not kill Hecate, with a push?

My end of days may not be so close after all, but Kelly's is.

Now, Kelly, twice my size, how can I overpower her? Well I can, I don't know how, but I will. Kelly, down here… with no one to save her.

I can hear her fear. Quietly.

Quietly."

Under cover of darkness, Boleyn crept stealthily down the passage to spring a surprise attack on that person she considered to be weak willed and spoiled.

She was so close.

I can feel her breath.

A shaft of light suddenly radiated from the surprise opening of the chamber door vanquishing her designs. The abrupt illumination startled Kelly who jumped back because of what the light revealed. Boleyn stood a few feet away brandishing a maniacal grin.

She had crept back down the Entanglement tunnel with more than innocent mischief on her mind.

"Has Hecate survived?" swore Boleyn through her teeth.

With Boleyn in her sights, Kelly called out with hope and trepidation, "Hecate? Is that you? Hello?"

The person wasn't wearing a witch's hat, and appeared smaller than her recollection.

"Kelly? Kelly?" said a familiar voice, "Is that you?" "Hello?" shouted Kelly in desperate hope.

CHAPTER 38

LOVE, RIGHT AND REASON HAVE NO PLACE HERE

Phillip might have heard something or maybe he just caught something out of the corner of his eye, or even a sixth sense. But whatever it was, it made him turn around. The stone door that was once sealed shut, and stood dormant for centuries, now was open again, in a matter of minutes.

A person stood hesitant in its doorway, but this time, the occupier seemed to be backing away unable to withstand the scowl of the chamber's snakes. He recognized this visitor, and also that she had the full attention of the snakes. She, the intruder, stood in their doorway, and behind her, he saw another person he knew, Boleyn. He watched her hurl herself forward just as Hecate tried to retreat. She shoved her into the clutches of the eagerly awaiting serpents.

The moment her hand crossed the threshold, a snake, then many others, grabbed her and dragged her in. From his hidden place in the middle of the tree, a horrified Phillip watched them repeatedly strike at the vulnerable Hecate who attempted a defense, but since she was in possession of the Opal, she was not a witch.

The serpents typically killed their prey: a witch, saint or any unfortunate, with a single bite, however Hecate was not afforded this luxury.

With every additional bite inflicted upon her, like a light bulb being given more electricity, the white light in the chamber intensified and brightened. Phillip watched in horror and sorrow. Then he noticed something strange. Hecate was obviously dying but there wasn't any blood, green or red.

Then Phillip noticed something else. Her appearance changed at the site of every bite. Not an inch was spared until the feeding frenzy petered out to reveal a magnificently beautiful woman.

As it was, Phillip was stark naked. Hecate, now, incredibly, a superior version of Kelly, stood on a thick smooth bough near him. The rags of Hecate's clothing had vanished and perfectly coordinated jeans and casual top replaced them, both of which accentuated this woman's figure.

Six or seven inches taller than Phillip, and radiating Entanglement greater than all the witches and saints combined, Phillip saw her power and decided, as she still hadn't noticed him, to discretely hide behind an adjacent beam.

His movement was his undoing.

Her eyes focused on him, all of him, and her eyes scanned his nether regions. She paused, as if thinking, processing, and then smoothly she uttered the beguiling words, "Hello PhilLIP."

Phillip almost fainted as there was so much sexual promise in her voice, he instantly became aroused.

"Errr…" he attempted to reply. And there was good reason for it too as she advanced towards him, and not menacingly.

As if floating on air, the tree limbs, flames and snakes parted and wove into a pathway that led towards only one thing. Him. As she closed in, she shrank in height. Soon she was a couple of inches shorter than he, but still with perfect proportions. Her clothes changed and were no longer casual. She was clad in a stunningly sexy amazing dance dress. Her hair was set in a glorious up do clasped with a radiant opal, the Vatican Opal.

Yet, with all the sexual urgency on display, her body also announced, that she was, untouched and a virgin, and that she was his, and only his.

She was like a goddess.

She put both her arms around his neck. "Phil, Phillip" her voice was as nothing ever heard by a man. Should they have, then they would die it was so beautiful, and sirens too would perish, but only out of envy.

"Do you find me… pretty?" She pressed her divine body against his.

"Errr…" If Phillip had been capable of thinking, he would have thought, "What kind of stupid question is that?" How could he answer, there wasn't any blood left in his brain for anything other than, "Err… Yes… I thiiinnnkkk you're beautiful."

"You're so sweet PhilLIP. I'm Godiva. Do you like me?" She took hold of one of his hands and put it on her body just a shade too low and just a shade too forward. Then she put both her arms around his neck. There could be no doubt what she intended, but just in case there was, she kissed him. Then she moved her glorious hips and maneuvered his hand. With every touch, with every caress, with every wonderful spoken word, Phillip fell in love with her, more and more, deeper and deeper, greater and greater. Bewitched, bedeviled, beyond sanity, he was lost in love.

Then, at that point, when they climaxed together, she straightened her back reopened her eyes and gazed into his. With him at his most vulnerable moment - she looked into his eyes deeply and launched her attack.

"I hate you."
"You are a worm."
"Impotent, unsatisfying, childish."
"Small."
"You ares nothing."
"Go."
"Leave."
"And don't come back."

LIGHT
LIGHT LUSTLIGHT
LIGHT LUST LUST LIGHT
LIGHT LOVE LVE LOVE LIGHT
LIGHT LOV LOVE LOVE LIGHT
LIGHT LOVE LOVE LOVE LIGHT
-3.1415926535946584…
-3.14159265359(4)6584…
-3.14159265359(4)6584…
LIGHT LOSS LOSS LOSS LOSS LGHT
LIGHT LOSS LOS LOSS LIGHT
LIG LOSS LOSS LOSS LIGHT
LIGHT LOSS LOS LIGHT
LIGH LSS LHT
LT

As she turned her back on him, Phillip saw that from a side view she was wafer thin, rather than the voluptuous maiden that he'd made love with. He was reminded of the two-dimensional entity he'd witnessed in ClearStream.

For several moments, Phillip didn't know what had happened. He stood naked in body and mind as her attack drove deep and unimpeded into his psyche. She wasn't joking, and a nasty joke it would have been; although preferable to the truth, which was swiftly dawning on him.

Not unlike all the others in his life, albeit few and far between, she was rejecting him. He trembled, in this realization and what felt like an attack, shook the foundation of his being.

"What? I don't understand." he sniffed quietly, to hurt to speak in anything other than a whimper. Desperately trying to hold back the tears, his cheeks quivered, his jaw wobbled, and his knees trembled. On the brink of crying, his hands unconsciously wiped at his eyes.

"Why? What did I do wrong? I thought you loved me."

He felt so sick to his stomach, that a spasm of involuntary wrenching wracked his body. Dry heaves tore his stomach into a cramp and he buckled over in agony. But the physical pain was just a background drone to Phillip's mind which was running a million miles a minute.

" Why? Why? Why?" he questioned as he spun around in an endless loop. In fact he had never ended a relationship. He'd always been the one dumped. This time was different, however, in the respect that it had gone past first base, something Phil wasn't acquainted with.

He may have loved Kelly, but she would never have loved him, or given herself to him.

God had.

Pi had.

This assailant had. Godiva.

Godiva had.

Kelly had given him nothing, except ridicule. Here he had a lover who loved him and had given all of herself to him, her body, and words of love, things he'd never had before. He believed she had. She had. She had said so. At least he'd thought that a minute ago.

Now, with knees like jelly, he was no longer able to stand. He awkwardly lowered himself to a sitting position and straddled a tree limb as if on automatic. Not unlike drowning, the air in his lungs had gone stale as he'd forgotten to breathe. He had been too engrossed to notice. His mind reeled raced and ran, but always downward.

"Am I so stupid to believe that the most beautiful woman in the Universe would fall for me?

Yes, I am."

"Am I so stupid to think that the most charming woman in the long history of time would desire erudite conversation with me?

Yes, I am."

"Am I so stupid to believe that she made love to me because she loved me for who I am?

Yes, I am."

I'm so stupid, Stupid, STUPID."

He was flushed so hot and red with embarrassment that he thought his face would melt. Phillip was so confused and hurt, that he overlooked the dire end he was fast approaching.

"Phillip"

The diamond rang in his head. He had heard it before.

The first time was an instant before the Devil, his arch foe, had invaded him when they were deep in battle. He had heeded their unexpected consciousness that called to him then, and now. Thankfully remembering that he was more than a singleton, he begged his Shoes to help him.

S
Rhom
n
g

237

His healing RhomSong rung through his head like a chime of bells in a gothic cathedral.

In an unprecedented collaboration, God and *Pi* had launched a joint attack. They targeted his fragile psyche, his emotional heart and scored a direct hit.

The pact had rightly predicted that Phillip was probably Phil, and if this Phillip was the incarnation of Phil, then he was weak, unsure of himself, and a virgin, (although he constantly lied about the fact).

God therefore presumed he'd be making love for the first time, "and your first love, your first time, was always the most impressionable."

And Phil (Phillip) was already the most impressionable of men.

They had struck him hard, not at his body, but at his innocence. His body physically remained intact except he was heartbroken. *That is real.*

Even though the attack was not upon his soul, which they were uncertain they could locate, their attack was so well calculated that it might as well have been.

Based on prior attacks, from Joan's report and *Pi's* firsthand experience, both clearly knew that Phillip could counter them.

They even went as far as considering consulting with the Devil, but they needed to act urgently. The Devil was living a paradox of being too paranoid and not paranoid enough simultaneously. So the two made a pact and conspired without him.

God didn't know it, but *Pi* had compromised the chamber's construction, feeding Joan illicit modifications that added the entrance and exit of a river into the chamber's apex. Its source was unknown to Joan, but believing she was doing God's work, she didn't question its origin or allegiance. Besides, the last thing she wanted was the Devil to get wind of the project, so she ploughed on ahead in absolute secrecy with her workforce of Vestal Virgins.

Now, in this hidden and forgotten chamber, the Gods were executing Phil. It was all because God had planned for a rainy day, and seeing this, *Pi* had a newfound respect for God's predictive and hedging powers.

"Mustss have learnt her lessonss. Sees the length God has gone too just in case of an emergency, such as they were experiencing todayss.

Thes creation of the *Chamber of the Cross* hundreds of years earlier, implanting Joan as an imposter Pope to oversees its constructionss. Thens the implanting of magic without detection by the Devil, breeding a burning tree with a Hydrass. Prettys damn goods."

Pi was most impressed indeed, but she wasn't about to go overboard. She was just as impressed with herself. Like a mother cuckoo having an unwitting parent raise her young, she ensured that Joan conjured the continuous thread of water from the chamber's ceiling. Joan hadn't understood the request, but naturally believing it came from God, she touched the very top of the ceiling with her Woman's Cross, and a single strand of unearthly water sprung forth.

She didn't know that she had not only compromised the chamber, but Heaven itself. How could she have known? *Pi* was here on Earth and had the time to craft her own messages to Joan, guised as if they were God's. Besides, why would she question the water's source, the Golden Cross was now sprouting tiny stalks of miniature snakes, its obvious purpose.

Pi had been so proud of herself, but now she was beginning to realize that God had, at least in some part, accepted that *Pi* would discover her plan and meddle with it. Cleverly however, God connived and let *Pi's* Entanglement and Water nourish her snakes into life and maturity. The unfortunate cost was now the ClearestRiver blighted Heaven.

As both were intent on clandestinely keeping the chamber out of the Devil's sight, neither even dared a single thought about it, fearing that if they did, he would pick up the scent. And use it for his own ends. Earth, after all, was his home ground. So the chamber's existence had to be the best kept secret on the planet.

The Chamber.The Opal. A Saint. (or a witch). *There was potential for the birth of a mighty Angel of Death, who'd answer to her and her only.* It required only her activation.

The Super Saint charged with both God's and *Pi's,*Entanglement, was fulfilling her purpose. Moreover, God was apparently smart enough to foresee that the normally negating amalgamation of the two Entanglements wouldn't occur, but that a rare positive synergy could materialize should a catalyst be employed.

Pi hated to admit it, but God really was good, in fact, better than good.

Her masterstroke, the catalyst - was the Opal. It bound all the elements together in the creation of the Super Saint, Godiva, the Lucky-Saint, an Angel-Queen on Earth, a deadly emissary.

Both knew of the séance and CERN's successful discovery, but neither knew that *all future detected 'God Particle's exposed by CERN syphoned themselves into the gem.* Of course they knew of Pope Raul's secret desire to purchase the Star of Australia to fittingly adorn and crown the Papal Scepter. The attention he had paid to the gem caused God grave concern, not because of the grandeur, but because *the Opal was not what it seemed.*

Its acquisition could have brought undue attention to it. God didn't want that at all. If it had found a new home in Rome, the Devil could have suspected something sinister, and in the midst of his clumsy inquiries, could have accidently blundered onto the chamber.

Therefore, they worked, unknowingly and individually, in tandem against its procurement. They foiled and obstructed every enquiry in its regard, so upon its deadly appearance in the Pope's throat; each mistakenly surmised the other was responsible.

As *Pi* despised and denied the existence of wild and uncontrolled natural luck, she couldn't believe a link between the gem and the Pope could exist. Therefore, *Pi* believed that God had done it.

God saw the events the night of the séance, but didn't know the advent of RhomSong had consummated the connection. So God, on the other hand, thought that *Pi* had done it.

Recent events, like the breaking of unbreakable laws, told God all *she* needed to know,

"There was something special about Phil. Even *Pi* and the Devil and I had lost sight of him. This PhilLIP was more than just a man who'd changed his name. He defied all laws, my laws, and *Pi's* too." thought God.

Being more thorough than the other two Eternal Mortals, God had gone to great lengths to build the chamber. Now was the time. What other time could there be?

"*Pi's* laws must be in jeopardy as well, that's why she attacked him at ClearStream. That's why *Pi* killed the Pope with the Opal."

Unlike *Pi,* God was an entire day behind. All *she* knew was that the plot to create an Angel of Death was progressing. *She* hoped the creation of the Angel would go as planned to seek and destroy Phillip with the utmost efficiency.

Because the psychic imprints of both Phil or PhilLIP were deep inside both Hecate and Kelly, then the White Angel Godiva was well equipped to fulfil her destiny. She wouldn't need any spells to identify him. It was just a matter of finding him. Since, God assumed as Kelly was going there, PhilLIP was heading in the direction of Rome and she might find PhilLIP quicker than hoped. Finding him would only be the first step. It would be clear that her job would be to kill him no matter what.

The bonus to this plan was that God could track the Angel and know where PhilLIP would be. That's where God's ultimate contingency plan would take effect.

Meanwhile, *she* continued to focus on those specific areas where Phillip was last sighted. It was a prudent thing to do. Phillip was such a threat that *she* would escalate multiple spearheads, hoping that at least one of them would kill him. There would be collateral damage on an epic scale, and *she* didn't care.

"Armageddon was not out of the question."

Luckily for humankind, the finesse of God's and *Pi's* attack cemented Phillip's fate. They had indeed heeded their lessons learned.

If God could have witnessed it, *she* would have been surprised by the Opal's extreme reaction. Its power was evident by the vastly superior transformation of the weakest witch Hecate into the sublime Godiva. Had the Boleyn Witch or Joan the Saint entered the dome with the Opal, then Phillip would have surely died by laying eyes upon that manifestation.

As it was, things were going better than God could hope. Unable to see the attack because of the Entanglement War, God was expecting a protracted search by the Angel-Queen to locate Phillip. *She* would be pleased to hear that Phillip, at the whim of natural luck, was at the very location and time of the Angel-Queen's creation.

God didn't know any of this, only *Pi* saw the end was in sight for the dying man. As God was so far away, *Pi* rubbed her hands together knowing that she, not her, would be the one 'entertaining' Phillip for the rest of eternity.

"So hatss off to you God." gloated *Pi,* "you can plays with the rest of the cosmoss to your heart's desire. The party's here on Earths, and you're not inviteds. Even the Devil's in the housess, but he's just the hosts and they never have as much funs as the guests."

~~~

In the tailspin of a deathly dive, Phillip's Shoes attempted to show him that he needed to pull himself together. He was dying by his own uncontrollable sorrow. His intense depression was a bottomless pit of wrath and darkness.

And his healing RhomSong found itself impotent.

Phillip would have been dead, if not for the flaws in the pact's Entanglement attack. Its light sometimes became malformed and *Pi's* numbers got jumbled up. Still, he was only seconds away from death. No male on Earth, could withstand such a blow to their ego and soul.

Phillip lost his balance on the bough and fell over eight feet to the hard rock floor. With a frenzied quivering bottom lip, he righted himself and leaned against the cross. He was in the death throes.

Godiva, the Angel-Queen whose sole purpose had been to hunt down and murder Phillip had done her job. Dying was all that was left for her. Every ounce of life and Entanglement had gone into her attack. God and *Pi's* rewards would be long and handsome.

To crown her wonderful day, she took the Opal out of her hair and held it in the palm of her hand. Then shoved it into Phillip's mouth and jammed it down his throat. It bulged in his windpipe and became lodged there.

"Yea, that's what it's like being fucked by you." were her last words.

Having rid herself of the Opal, she reverted into the shredded remnants of Hecate.

Part organic, mineral, and mystical, the Opal was unlike any jewel or gem the World had seen. It was separate from any other opal too. It was liquid to see, solid to touch, and ethereal to claim. Now suffocation by opal was killing Phillip.

On cue, his life started to replay. He knew it wasn't going to be pleasant. In a mean-spirited grand finale, he hoped that everyone saw their lives before dying. And if they lived miserably, then he wouldn't feel so horrible and alone. Strangely, it was this thought that triggered an epiphany.

He was mean spirited.

He never thought he was but that was the proof.

It forced him now to examine other actions and motivations that governed his life and it led him to a dreadful conclusion. It was one that had eluded him up until now, and one that, to be of any use, he should have had many years ago.

The underlying impetus of everything he did was to be exposed. All his life he'd depended on people.

He was dependent and he was needy. Did he want their love or did he need it?

People were there, not because he wanted them, but because he needed them.

Bill gave him his job; he couldn't find one on his own. He needed Bill.

No wonder Bill was cruel towards him; he saw only the dependent; the baby, the incapable.

And Kelly, it wasn't because he was inadequate, short and plain, that she couldn't fall for him. It was because there wasn't that much to fall for when it came down to it.

He was a personality of nothing other than a pile of excuses and irritating fears, a man without soul, spice or salt, a man that even a name change couldn't invigorate. As if to rub it in, when Kelly had fallen for him, it was because she thought he had defeated the Devil in mortal combat. The Phil she had fallen for had some purpose.

Unfortunately, at that precise moment, the Devil was him, and so she had fallen for the Devil, as he, Phil, had been in hiding.

He didn't only rely on people; he saw that *he held a cross for luck* too.

He'd never seen it before, but he'd always hoped that luck would bail him out. For everything he did; every risk he took, every girl he attempted to date, he deferred the effort to luck. His excuses were many and often. He accused God of stupidity and would say, "God works in mysterious ways." a cliché he used with frequency to explain away his failures and mask his laziness.

So now on death's door, he saw that *Luck* was the mystery assailant. What had he done to deserve its unwarranted attention? He didn't know. *Luck* was the accomplice in God's new sinister attack. He also saw that God was certainly not infallible.

These revelations only served to deepen his despair. It was as if he looked in the mirror for the very first time. Shame flushed his face. His pathetic ways were inanely on display for all the public to see. What they were thinking must have been, 'That he was a fool.' They were right.

Phillip heard death call him. He was ready to welcome it. He wallowed in destructive self-pity and wanted to end the pain. Despite the metamorphosis he had undergone, Phillip's psyche remained unchanged and so it wasn't an accident that Phillip's last thoughts were of his failures.

He saw how inconsequential his life was before he and his Shoes came together. Everything about him was fragile. It had always been that way, as it was now. To make matters worse, he shunned responsibility, by closing his eyes, calling for support and then ducking out of harm's way to avoid accountability. He was the worst person he could imagine.

Only the once, when he caught the Devil in an error and called him out did he ever do anything noble, brave and selfless. That one time he did something on his own without aid from others, and even without help from his Shoes. Now, he'd grown accustomed to and depended on the Shoes to bail him out.

He thought of his relationship with his brother. He blamed Bill when he was cornered, "He tormented me." he would whine. "It's not my fault."

Of course, there was some truth in the argument. He recalled the pivotal point of his childhood, when Bill and he had a vile spat. His older brother sat on Phil's chest and held his nose. That moment had caused Phil irrevocable harm.

From that point on, Phil had delegated authority and responsibility to anyone other than himself. He lost his life to apathy and fear.

That was a long time ago. Now, at the end of his life, he burst into tears. Was his final act on Earth to be that of a sobbing child?

Natural luck struck. He knew he was superhuman *but he still didn't realize his blood was water, and more importantly, water born from Pi. Her entanglement naturally gravitated to and bonded with Phillip's blood, and to the purest of his bodily watery fluids, his tears.*

As he cried, he unwittingly ousted most of *Pi's* Entanglement. This act had the potential to save him. Like snatching a breath of air when underwater, Phillip felt a glimmer of willpower.

This was his first step, a first conscious act to acknowledge the World and have a legitimate place in it. The door to life was ajar.

Whenever he thought of life, he had thoughts of Kelly. Now he was nothing in her eyes, he wanted to prove to himself that he could survive without her. He'd flown when no one else could, and loved it. If she hadn't spurned him, would he have discovered that he could do the miracle?

He could love others too, Godiva. Could he survive Godiva? He'd survived Kelly.

"I'd survived Kelly's emotional torture (inflicted on myself, by myself, just like now), and lived. Just. But I did.

So why, why not take Godiva's attack not as fatally, but as a learning lesson.

If I can do that. I might… might… live."

With his body screaming, he raised his hand and put three fingers out. The Shoes responded. His soul, their souls could live after all. They encouraged him, showing him that there was a flaw in God's attack, that 'LOSS' was corrupted and therefore not perfect, like *she*. The expelled attack of *Pi* too was not perfect either. There were chinks in both their offences.

Holes and weaknesses.

He could exploit the vulnerabilities, and live.

They were Eternal Mortals, yet their attack revealed errors.

So they were not perfect.

So why should he expect it from himself.

And he could grow, change. His body had. Why not him too?

"Kelly once told me to grow up.

Now, I don't need her to tell me, now I'm me telling me. GROW UP.

Stop depending and needing.

Stop letting fate dictate your fate.

If people don't like you, their loss.

AND I AM PHILLIP.

IT IS A BIG LOSS.

BECAUSE I AM PHILLIP.

SPELT CORRECTLY.

I CAN survive.

I CAN live.

I CAN retaliate.

How many fingers am I holding up?

THREE!" he yelled out to himself.

SR
Rhom
Man
Song
gm

Phil was balancing between two places at the same time; rock climbing on the edge of the Universe, and tiptoeing on the inside of an atom.

His two feet straddled the border of two adjacent space-time quadrants. Under one of his feet, he recognized the sector as the one he'd visited the first time God attacked him. He reached out to the other and took handfuls of its non-existent surface.

He could feel the slight difference between the two, and rolled the emptiness between his finger and thumb. He felt the repair work done by God's hand. Why and what had *she* restored? He didn't know and didn't care. If *she* had taken time to mend something, it must have harmed her.

Mystified and irritated, he puzzled over many ideas of what to do. As the pressure of time passed, he felt he had to do something to confirm to himself that he was indeed worth saving.

He did the basest of things and kicked it. "Take that."

Phil didn't think that such a primal act could have any effect, yet he altered the Universe beyond any potential he could have imagined. Like feeling a sudden earthquake, only in space, God jumped in shock, out of fear rather than pain. *She* understood finally, the terror people felt when a big tremor rumbled underfoot.

247

She looked back and forth across the Universe, but saw nothing. Whatever had caused it wasn't obvious. *She* was looking for PhilLIP, but could not see him.

But Phillip saw her. And was unmoved. Neither her appearance nor beauty caused him harm. Godiva had cured him of that. He watched as *she* anxiously looked at Earth from a vantage point that was further away than before, and he saw the fear in her eyes.

He watched her curse the Entanglement War, and saw her scour the horizon for some way in or through it. There was none.

He knew God was looking for him and probably his friends. It filled Phillip with courage.

Underfoot, the feel of the interior of the atom was so different from before. The hadron felt like rolling thunder. Its mechanisms operated on a completely new plane, magnitude and complexity.

The single electron and its moon spun in new, obscure and unfathomable ways and rendered obsolete the contemporary models of physics. What was required was a new field of mathematics in predictability and probability, if this was even possible, he didn't know.

Randomness, luck and chance, *Pi's* domain, were now less accurate and more prone to error making the odds she controlled longer or shorter.

Phillip didn't understand any of this, but he knew he was alive and had a chance of surviving. That's all that mattered. He embraced the moment and he shouted to his Shoes in thanks

His simultaneous RhomSong and SongRhom shook the foundations of the old order, shattering God's and *Pi's* Entanglement.

"I'm... I am... Alive. Alive. ALIVE."

~~~

He took his time, reached out with his hand and started to reap the primal atomic building blocks, nucleuses and elemental entities, from the next closest element, the Gold from the Golden Cross. He kept reaping and stealing more pieces with every instance of non-time, forging, formulating, and retro-fitting.

Beyond known and theoretical islands of stability, the atom he was constructing would be his new body. It would be beyond imagination, a treble nucleus and a thousand moonlike twin electrons. He knew that when he finished and returned to the living, the cross of gold would be all but gone, and he, Phillip would be the one responsible.

He will have absorbed and fused it beyond fission and fusion - made from a new element, *Rissium*. Made by RhomSong, he will have created a new Phillip.

As the laws of physics changed all around him, he ventured down a brief opening, a cul-de-sac of new physics, one that only he could tread, that would close forever the moment he finished his harvesting.

And when he would open his eyes, they would be greeted by a new Universe where the current physical paradigms and laws were not only less all encompassing, they were augmented by new laws. In the new Universe some would even seem to be lawless.

Man's creation of elements beyond naturally fused uranium would decay rapidly so as to become unsustainable, obscure, un-makeable. Now, only a supernova would be hot and pressurized enough to make them, Man's power over the elements had seen its last days.

After pushing his mind out of the fog of depression, and hungrily sucking air with the greatest of pants, he experienced the first gasps of his new life.

Phillip stood alone in the chamber, alive.

Feeling like a condemned man who'd had his death sentence commuted, Phillip stood silently, still and straight.

Only a smudge of soot on the chamber floor provided any evidence that the cross ever existed. Hecate's tragic lifeless body clad in black witches' garb lay flat on the curved stone floor.

The few remaining flames appeared yellow and ordinary as they charred branches of the uprooted tree and barbequed the drooping and lifeless snakeheads. Now all they inspired was shock and disgust.

The flickering flames cast enough light to show the way back up the steps to the doorway and Phillip hopped up them with mixed emotions. He saw this place, where he had his finest hour, as a new beginning. It wasn't just his new start; it was everyone's too.

"POINT ONE FOUR" popped out of his mouth like a sudden hiccup that ended in a burp.

"What? I guess what I wanted to say was, three point one four, not just THREE.

Three point one four fingers. Well, you know, that's me, my humor, and I'll not apologize for it." he said talking to himself.

"When I entered this chamber, I see now that I was half baked. I was trying to change, but not knowing who I was to begin with, meant that I didn't know I had. I thought I could be in love, but I couldn't. Because I couldn't feel, or more precisely, I wouldn't allow myself to feel, so any love I felt was actually contrived."

"So I think the love I had for Kelly was false. It was that realization that ultimately pushed me to and then pulled me back from the edge of death.

Now, I can feel the difference.

I know my life was false that's for sure.

But, now, I know what I was.

Now I know what I am.

Now I know I can be something more.

Now, I will die rather than need.

Never wish me 'Good Luck.' Again, never wish me anything.

Now I can feel.

Now my actions will not be the ones of others.

Nor will the words.

Now, when I utter a sentence, it will be me who speaks without cliché or automatic answers. From now on, there will be responses, not reactions, and more importantly, they will be mine."

He left more of a man than he could ever have imagined. In addition to all the other life changing properties, he donned an entire new body made from the uncreatable element.

His voice was enriched and harmonized based on two Adam's apples, as the Opal now cohabited the same space. It was befitting, as he was emotionally, mentally and physically a new man.

"My SongRhom and RhomSong isn't independent of me. It is me and I am it.

Just as the Shoes, it's the same."

Without any regrets, for the first time in his life, he almost left the chamber thinking there wasn't anything else there to uncover. Just as he thought that, he realized he was wrong.

The stream of water falling from the ceiling poured in one direction now, although it still appeared to be pristine and pure.

" Wow." thought Phillip returning from his self-indulgent thoughts. "Look, it's collecting at the bottom of the Chamber."

He was becoming used to the unexplainable, and although this wasn't commonplace for most mortals, it faced him at every turn.

"C'est la vie. Time to move on."

Triumphantly he opened the door, Entanglement be damned. The light in the chamber dimly bathed the Entanglement passageway, but it suficed to reveal a dark shadowy figure appearing to be poised to strike. Phillip blurted out before he could think, "Kelly?"

"Phillip?" "PHILLIP!"

"YOU'RE, YOU'RE ALIVE?"

"I think so." he responded. Although it was a typical, curt, stupid sort of thing that Phil was prone to say, this time for some reason it seemed appropriate. She recognized his voice, which confirmed it was him. Oddly his voice sounded richer, more voluminous and different. Strangely it was not irritating.

251

Staring at the dark silhouette at the end of the tunnel, she waited for the man who had sacrificed himself to save their plane from crashing, a man she'd claimed she loved, to reveal himself.

"It was easier to say that then. Was she still feeling it now?" she wondered.

Boleyn turned her assistive light back on and shone it in Phillip's direction.

"Phillip! You're naked." shrieked Kelly, "Argh."

In a flash, Phillip donned a stunning garment with glimmering Shoes. He didn't know it, but for the first time a man had surpassed the Devil in attire. He was effortlessly exquisite.

Kelly recognized the sophisticated style, but she also regretted her impulsive girlish cry. In that fleeting glimpse of Phillip's naked body, she could see he was all man. And certainly not a man she had associated with before, not a pudgy man called Phil from the past, but a desirable and sexy male.

He may have made a sacrificial leap from a plane to save her and she may have professed her love to him as well. But she wasn't ready to give in, not yet.

Clearly there was something different about him. He'd never been able to elicit that sort of reaction from her in the past. Also she had a nagging question.

"Why was he naked?"

He started down the passageway, but stopped midway, intrigued by the "O" hieroglyphics. Then he doubled back to the chamber's door and started over.

"Typical Phillip." thought Boleyn, "Wow, I didn't realize he was that short. Not too much taller than me. Well, he is but, wow, he is short. Anyway, the idiot's doing his normal stupid thing. Checking out the zeroes. Least we've got the right man for the job." I wonder if Kelly is thinking the same, or is she still in l o v e?"

His demeanor also bothered Kelly. Instead of rushing down the corridor to fawn at her feet, Phillip was preoccupied with his findings along the corridor. He took his time to focus on reading the random rows of O's. They wrapped around the corridor, over the ceiling, walls and floor. He persisted in taking pictures with his cell.

He didn't show interest in Kelly and ignored Boleyn's impatience, as she turned her light off several times trying to hurry him up. When he finally finished, he casually resumed their company. "Hi Kelly and Boleyn." he said.

Then turned to Boleyn. "What were you going to do there Boleyn? Going to kill Kelly? Like you've just killed Hecate?" he asked.

"Yes." said Boleyn full of bitterness, "And I'll kill you too when I get the chance."

"Ooo Kay, and I love you too. You go first, back up the tunnels. Come on, we better get going before the light dies."

This was all too much for Kelly; his indifference, his height and because it was clear that he was shorter again, and besides that, the strange nuance in his voice.

They couldn't afford to loiter about anymore. They had to get going. Despite her halfhearted snide comments about him wasting time, Kelly followed his suggestion, and insisted that Boleyn go in front. She followed and Phillip brought up the rear. She was amazed at herself for not arguing the order, at least out of principle.

"Something was different about the man. Why had he been naked?"

Heading back through the maze of tunnels, she questioned herself about her feelings. His nakedness was chewing her up inside. She didn't think or care about how he survived his jump out of the plane, or even why he was always shorter every time they met. She only had the one question, and she was going to ask it when they got back to the first chamber.

Attempting to pretend to ignore the treasure, because now she desired it and what power it could buy her, Boleyn deliberately stood next to Phillip and measured, he had lost more height since their last meeting, of that she had no doubt.

"Four foot four, maybe one, I reckon." said Phillip.

"Who cares." said Kelly angrily. "Why were you naked?" "What?" responded a shocked Phillip.

"Was that all she cared about?" he immediately thought.

"I fought the Silver Saint, God and the evil unknown, launched myself out of a plane to save her and my brother. Both of whom couldn't give a damn about me, and Kelly especially at the time. At least Bill hated me which was better than nothing. Still, all she cares about was why I was naked?" thought Phillip.

"What?" he said again, this time not in shock, but in anger. And the more he thought about it, the more it bothered him. He remembered that only an hour earlier, when he was under attack and suicidal, he survived by acknowledging his dependence on others. He vowed to depend on no one henceforth.

He once was subservient to Kelly, because he wished for her love, but now, he wasn't going to sacrifice himself to win it.

"Be damned. OK Kelly. I'll tell you."

"Let's go. The light's fading." yelled Boleyn.

While they were distracted, she had stuffed a golden goblet into her pocket. She had swallowed a diamond when she pretended to shield a fake cough with her hand. She may have overlooked the treasure on the way down, but not finding what she sought, she stole anything.

Unknown to her, both she and Phillip had undergone a metamorphosis. Like Phillip she was a changed person from when she entered.

She was once Boleyn, the Mighty Red Witch. Now she was Boleyn, The Mighty Red.

Wealth would be her new power.

"Go Boleyn and you too." Phillip ordered with an uncharacteristic air of authority and dismissiveness.

They maintained their original order and they followed her up the final tunnel until all that was left was the vertical ascent to the turret.

"Wait. Get back in the tunnel and wait a moment." commanded Phillip. It was probably the first time in his life that he'd been somewhat rude and didn't apologize. Shocked, the two women cowered. A pneumatic drill sound echoed around them.Then Phillip poked his dusty face into the tunnel and gave another command.

"Climb on Kelly's shoulders Boleyn." ordered Phillip.

"And you, climb on mine." he said referring to Kelly without using her name.

"Phillip?"said Kelly trying to talk as she realized that he was upset. "Do it. We've got to go. I wanna get out of here."

CHAPTER 39

MIXED HOMECOMING

Ross, the Pope, Paul and Crow were ecstatic when Boleyn and then Kelly appeared out of the turret. They had been gone for nearly three hours, and in that time, the World had taken a drastic turn for the worse.

Their return was the first piece of good news in a World going to Hell. When a third person appeared out of the shaft, puzzled looks and dread initially overtook them. Except, of course, for Ross, who was elated.

"PHILLIP." he shouted, and with large strides, he strode over to him, leaving Boleyn and Kelly with the clergy.

"You're alive."

"Yes." replied Phillip, turning towards Kelly and answering the question she never asked. "It turns out I can fly."

"This is Phillip?" said Greg, not comprehending what he'd just heard.

Phillip took a couple of strange steps towards him. His gait was not awkward enough for anyone to notice the cause and hence not to mention it.

He responded, "Yes. I am, and you are?"

"Pope Gregory." replied Greg without taking offence. "Oh. Sorry." replied Phillip, "Sorry, your..."

"Call me Greg, Phillip. And I must say that you are the first piece of good news we've had in quite some time. Strange things are..."

"Happening? Yes, I'm not surprised." He turned to Ross and asked, "Where's Harry?"

Instinctively Ross looked down, and replied, "Hecate?" A knowing silence fell upon both men.

Everyone else followed and went quiet, except Boleyn who checked that the gold in her pocket was secure.

"There's a war coming." said Phillip, breaking the brief silence, a welcome relief.

"Ross, I mean a big one. When God finds out I'm alive, *she's* going to go nuts."

Everyone looked puzzled, except Boleyn again, who still thought albeit erroneously, that the entity she'd encountered in ClearStream was God.

Everyone exclaimed shock at Phillip's wild and reckless assertion, with the exception of Boleyn, but undaunted, he continued.

"*She's*, err, tried to kill me four times. The first three times in ClearStream by Saint Joan and then by an... her... an angel, the Angel Godiva. They responded with more shock.

Boleyn however was uninterested and schemed on how to get away from this "Bunch of losers."

"*She* won't stop..."

"God? God is trying to kill you? *She?* Surely you mean the Devil." questioned the Pope with deep trepidation in his voice.

"Greg. Sorry. No. I know the difference between an attack from the Devil and from God. And it's God who's trying to kill me, not the Devil. Also another, God of some kind, is trying too also, we should..."

"*She*...Another God...?"interrupted the Pope."Who is *She*? Surely, you're not saying God is a Woman. (Of all things)" said Greg with a heightened level of ire."You're wrong Phillip. God would never..."

"Never? Sodom and Gomorra?" replied Phillip with a voice more forceful than anyone expected, "To name one. Want some others... But who cares about reputed history, because maybe it's not true, or God wasn't responsible for it, but as for now, I know for a fact that one of the persons who's trying to kill me is God."

"Address me as your Highness." said the Pope in a huff, who finally registered Phillip's comment about flying.

"And what's this nonsense, you can fly and that there's another God. How do you know God's a *she* anyway?"

"Because the first time I travelled to the far side of the Universe, I saw her."

"What? You've… Come on. Ross, this is the man you say…" "And Saint Joan told me too." resisted Phillip.

"Saint Joan? No such person." replied the Pope fully engaged in the argument.

"She is, was, the only Saint. She was Pope too at one time. She built the chamber beneath."

"This is just too much. You're a liar and a…"

"Then you'll love this," said Phillip indifferent to the accusation, "but if you don't want to know the truth, then just leave."

No one had ever spoken to the Pope in this manner."But if you stay, you just might hear it. You won't like it though, none of you will." Most impressed indeed was Kelly and despite the Pope's look of contempt, he didn't leave, nor did anyone else.

"After I entered the Chamber of the Burning Tree of Snakes and the Golden Cross, I touched the flames and found myself immune to them." His voice had a tone that made it hard to interrupt.

"Their caress was so beautiful that I climbed into the tree and bathed naked in its flames." he said and looked at Kelly.

"They were exquisite. I felt them run over me, and I asked my Shoes and my clothes to vanish, so that I could experience the flames in the flesh."

He turned to Kelly and continued, "Kelly my Shoes now clothe me. Whatever I need, be it rain, snow, fire, wind: they are me. I believe you saw that when you saw me naked when I left the chamber, and then the next instant, I was clothed."

"And you Kelly, more than anyone, know that is true. You were the only witness, no, Boleyn too, saw the Shoe come to me."

He looked at Boleyn who was distancing herself from everyone and said, "So anyway, when Boleyn, shoved Hecate, God bless her soul, scratch that, into the chamber, the snakes started to bite into her. They tore into her like sharks in a feeding frenzy, but instead of dying, well I guess she did, but her body didn't.

Her body was transformed into a woman in the likeness of God. Not in the likeness of man, but woman. Then she seduced me and we made love."

Kelly's sudden and surprising lack of self-control trumped Phillip's hypnotic voice when she blurted out, " YOU TWO TIMING BASTARD."

Phillip knew he wasn't and had never been dating her. He would have sworn, from the way she appeared and acted when they were last together on the plane, that she didn't care for him at all and was indifferent towards him.

"That's why you were naked. Not because you were bathing in flames but because you were screwing Hecate." screamed Kelly.

"Yes, that's why. Because she told me that she loved me. And she was in the likeness of God and in the likeness of you too Kelly. She looked like you." shouted back the inflamed Phillip.

She didn't feel sorry for him though. He was like every other man she'd ever known and she hated him.

While Phillip and Kelly were fighting, the Pope had been digesting everything Phillip had said. He was busily trying to reconcile it with his faith. But no matter how much he twisted and contorted Phillip's account, it wouldn't resolve.

He had heard enough blasphemy out of the infidel's mouth. Taking his chance while Phillip was preoccupied, he threw a haymaker towards Phillip which hit him square in the face.

Greg cradled his hand in the other, fearing that his bones were broken. The pain throbbed throughout his entire arm. Worse for him was that Phillip was indifferent to his bungled assault.

According to the Pope, he continued his lies as if nothing had happened, yet the Pope knew his slug wasn't something one could pretend hadn't occurred.

"Then she dumped me, yes, you heard me. She dumped me." Phillip shouted at Kelly.

"Good" she shouted back.

Phillip forged on."And the dump was an Entanglement attack, bigger than the Devil's, tons bigger. Inside her attack was another attack by the other God. I was drowning in grief, I felt suicidal, and I started to die, just like you felt when Bi..." he stopped. Phillip realized that was a low blow, and considerate to the last, he didn't want Kelly to re-live that part of her past.

"But there was an error in both their attacks, and to make a long story short, I survived. I retaliated and I survived."

Speaking in a gentler tone he looked at Kelly. He continued to relate the facts, without asking for sympathy and for all to hear. "They attacked me in the way you know they can."

She knew what he was saying. She'd experienced one. When the Devil had attacked them with a single '*Black*' in the ClearStream church.

"The two gods' attacks were thousands of times worse than his. And my RhomSong, which had brought Joan back to life once in ClearStream, it didn't work unti..."

"See." shouted Greg, "See, only Jesus can bring a man back to life, see, he's a li..."

"Yes, I see." said Kelly."I see too well. You don't know Phillip. He never lies, that's the way he is. God damn annoying. Now let him finish." Her unexpected defense of Phillip took him by complete surprise.

"I lie." contradicted Phillip.

"You stupid idiot Phillip." yelled Kelly, "You never take my side... You've lied?"

"Yes. Of course. Not to you, I've never, I don't think, I've lied to you, but of course I've lied, everybody does, has. I'm no different."

"You see." shouted the Pope. And Kelly slapped him across the face. Suddenly a small brawl broke out as Crow grappled Kelly and Ross tried to intervene.

Phillip's intervened, without raising his voice quite simply stopped the melee. "*Please.*" was all he said.

The word was compelling, silence and order was restored. While all the others gasped at their unlikely obedience, Kelly, being the smartest person present, realized something. If he could order them into an unwilling silence, then he could use his voice to tell them anything he liked.

Phillip could have lied and they would have been none the wiser, but he hadn't. With decency he given them the respect to choose to disbelieve him or not as they so wished.

She hated him for that. Her love for him was her choice not his order and it caused her to hate him even more. It also strongly suggested that everything he'd said was true.

Perhaps the Pope's resentment would grow. She didn't care about him, however, and she knew everything Phillip had said wasn't for him anyway. It had all been for her. She knew Phillip hadn't lied, and he hadn't avoided any questions, he'd answered them, truthfully.

It wasn't what any of them wanted to hear, especially her, but Phillip had done them all the honor of telling them the truth. This was something Bill never did and she hated Phillip more than anyone had ever done before.

No man had paid her a greater compliment.

She knew she would probably die, shortly, by his side, and she didn't care. For she now knew she could never love another.

"So why do you say you lie Phillip." she asked, knowing that he wouldn't say such a thing unless he had a good reason.

"Because, I think I know who the other God is, I think its Lady Luck, the Queen of Spades, The Red Queen of Spades."

It wasn't much of a lie, and the new Phillip saw that everyone was taking time to take it all in, especially the clergy. Their World, their faith and their purpose were not only being challenged, it appeared that their lives had been erroneously dedicated.

Phillip was aware of their quandary. He continued in a normal voice and avoided eye contact with the Pope who was seething. He remained calm and genuine as usual, not mean, even though the Pope had sucker punched him.

"God can't see me, but *she* can see you. If you want to live, you had better get as far away from me as possible. *She*, also, is in a war with the Devil, and so her vision of Earth is impaired, because *she's* not here, and he is."

The Pope's mind was spinning. Their God wasn't here, but he was supposed to be omnipresent. (And a Man).

Phillip left the floor open for someone to say something after saying his piece, which was earth shattering for religious ears. He knew he was a tough act to follow. While he paused for any reaction, opinion or question, he spied Boleyn.

Out of the corner of his eye he'd been watching her, because although she didn't know it, Phillip knew she had a role to play in whatever was to be decided. She on the other hand, cared for nothing now.

A living God, whether male or female wasn't going to change anything, especially her hatred. God had given her nothing but misery. The Devil and the *other one* had given less. Her hatred became the definition of Boleyn.

Crow came over to Greg to show him something on his cellphone, and as he was watched the streaming, he looked up at Phillip and said in a hateful whisper,

"And the Opal, not that I believe anything you've said, but what of it?"

"It's here, in my throat. Oh, and by the way, it isn't an opal." With everything Phillip had said and done, this got the most attention. Now they were going to find out it was something different. Such was their day.

"It's a *Tear of God*. *She* cried the single tear when *she* found out the Devil had created Hell. Out of mercy *she* created the last rites in an effort for people to avoid going there.

I read about it when I left the chamber in the corridor of 'O's. Actually, it's the smaller half of the tear. God knows the location of one half but not the other. The same goes for one of the Vatican keys." Greg's hand twitched, but with a quick dart of his eyes he reckoned that no one saw it, but someone had.

"Of which there are four." finished Phillip.

As with all of Phillip's answers, this wasn't what the Pope wanted to hear. He willed himself into disbelieving Phillip. But it was hard to resist since as with everything he said, he sounded sincere.

Finally, in an effort to demean and belittle all that Phillip had said, the Pope turned his attention to Crow's phone in a manner to suggest that *Phil* was unimportant.

His intentions backfired. It only took a couple of finger scrolls by Crow to put a dire look back on the Pontiff 's face, and force him to consider Phillip in the most troublingly of all light, the light of truth.

Truth is, after all, ugly, discouraging, and unforgiving. It's shy but nasty when revealed.Timid, but hurtful when provoked. Politicians rarely cross its rocky path. Men too often give it a wide berth. *Little wonder Entanglement is exclusive towomen.* The Pope was beginning to feel the lash of Truth's tongue. If he was doing to survive it, he would have to call upon every ounce of dogma he could muster.

CHAPTER 40

INSPIRED ART

God's contingency plan progressed in a predictable fashion, as it was placed in the hands of evil men. "Armageddon, yes, was not out of the question." All that was needed was a gentle push.

If mankind could rein in petty differences, war on that scale would be inconceivable and averted.Despite the amazing superior intelligence of mankind on Earth, it was always five minutes to midnight.

At first, God and the other two were amused when the first cave dweller put the point of a burnt stick to the craggy face of stone. Only seconds later, after charcoal left its black marks, did they gasp at the beauty left in its wake.

It was all the more galling that the fledgling troglodytes hadn't even invented language with which to speak. Yet their first scribbling left God in awe.

With the implicit approval, and relief, from God and *Pi,* the Devil had quickly sealed that cave up in what is now named France. In the end, he exterminated the Neanderthals, so as not to be deemed inferior to them.

Damned if it wasn't a little too late. They had interbred with the homo-sapiens from Africa bearing the gift of rhythm. The new race, MAN, was born from the diversity brought upon him by hardship, disease, natural selection and the combined spite of the three Eternal Mortals.

All three watched and listened as men picked up sticks and banged stones. Their laughter was short lived, believing at first that the noise was random and nonsense.They could hear but could not feel.

Sneakily, a wonderful cadence common to mankind subtly crept in as if through a secret side door. Before they all knew it, they felt this. Because it was so good it sickened the three.

Perhaps God could have been forgiven for thinking there was nothing left for Man to discover, until they saw what Man was doing in the bedroom.

Kissing.

Who would have thought that up? Out of a Universe full of life and civilizations, only Man kissed, and it was passionate, illicit, and all consuming.

Only after the three entities transformed into their human form did they experience its magnificence. Not masters of it, but still they could feel its exquisiteness. Then they found that Man participated in sex that was wild and extreme, loving and tender. Solely for the pleasure of sex. Procreation was frequently considered incidental and sometimes even an undesirable result.

After taking the shape and soul of Man again and participating in the mortal act, only then and to their horror, did they realize that its inception was beyond their capacity. In all of time, nothing like this had happened anywhere. It was not of their doing, something special had happened on Earth.

After much consideration, God believed that the reason for all these amazing properties was borne out of his unique creation. With the whole Universe at her disposal, God tried to replicate these apparently human gifts in other worlds and intelligences.

Fortunately, the Devil was unable to escape the Entanglement barrier and so God didn't have to suffer the public embarrassment of her unsuccessful attempts. Thousands of worlds were altered. Asteroids were set to destroy dinosaurs and the like and earthly conditions were recreated on many planets.

Her attempts were futile, proving her incapable as *she* failed to cajole or inspire those alien cultures to such heights of creation and passion. It served to prove her deepest dread. The phenomenon called Man was universally unique to Earth. An Earth *she* was barred from. An Earth the Devil enjoyed at his leisure.

As for *Pi,* she too resided there, but *Pi's* motives and pleasures were always mysterious and perturbing to both God and the Devil. The Devil even felt this more, for she was his next-door neighbor, yet he didn't know where that actually was.

"ClearStream seemed a strong probability, and torturing the residents was a reasonable way of drawing her out into the open." decided the Devil in his plan. (If he'd counted the nine sleuths' gates, and the cow drink, he might have uncovered the sniggering *Pi* after all).

It didn't take long for God, *Pi* and the Devil, independently from each other to find themselves jealous of man. Nor was it a superficial or fleeting resentment: but deep rooted, gnawing and cancerous.

And ironically God, Pi and the Devil had gone to great lengths to eradicate Man's various formsandexpressions of art, but they resurfaced more diverse and prolific than ever.

In retaliation, they spawned religions to regiment, restrain and repress Man's base desires. They instigated taboos and rules for the sole purpose to suppress his creative impetus. As with all plans of mice and men, instead of punishing man, he embraced this new form of organization like a duck to water.

The folly of God and the Devil provided *Pi* with great amusement as she watched Man encompass hundreds, possibly millions, of religions. True to his nature, they quarreled over them. Each claimed that they were envoys of the one true religion, and that all the others were merely false idols or philosophies and infidels.

It didn't take minutes for evil deeds to be done in the name of God. Man really didn't need any excuses to perpetrate wrongdoing, but now he had permission, even a mandate.

Using this right which was called *'In the name of God,'* Man abdicated all responsibility for his crimes and evil acts to a higher authority. Man was free and clear and the need for absolution was for those who didn't commit evil in his name rather than those who did.

For the masses, the followers, the workers, the poor and the powerless, absolution was a requirement. It was so obviously true because the higher echelons said so. These dictates came down not from Heaven above, but from the self-proclaimed leaders of the great enterprises of faith, ready to dispense an eternal afterlife for small earthly donations. Without the appropriate ritualized sermon, administered by the right religion, there was no passage to the righteous afterlife, Heaven. Only a lowly, netherworld called Hell, would accommodate.

Therefore, God and the Devil created their appropriate realms to satisfy the demand, and organized worship was reduced down to a handful of mainstream institutions. Sworn promises, vows, pledges to allegiance entrenched the faiths and war amongst them was the peace.

The problem for the Eternal Mortals was that the faithful and the non-aligned displayed a passion not attainable by any other life form. They were willing to sacrifice life itself, for causes and beliefs whose roots and legitimacy were questionable.

The three everlasting mortals wished for a belief equal to that of humans for their own, to make their own lives more fulfilling and even meaningful. Jealous of the humans with their passion, love and evil; God, Pi and the Devil found themselves left in the wake of the life-form that now pained them in envy, surpassed them in talent, and brought creation to The Creation.

Humans were a tough act to follow, and life after death was an act that they demanded. Somehow, perhaps due to their origin, they knew God and the Devil existed. They even knew of *Pi*, and even called her Lady Luck. However they never prayed to her in the heartfelt, pleading and apologizing manner reserved for their prayers to God.

It was a nightmare for God to create an image of Heaven up to the expectations of earthlings. Designing the collective consciousness where humans and God would confide and share wasn't anything God wanted.

She was scared that *she'd* be exposed as a charlatan, unable to deliver an all knowing, all-encompassing persona and unable to be all things to all men. Worse still, their belief envisioned a noble purpose and the revelation of the true meaning of life, when in fact God had learnt that from Man below.

She feared the awful revelation and the crushing admission that there was no intelligent design or planned creation, or any meaning to existence at all. *She* was scared to death of any encounter and candid exchange. So *she* was shy, to the extreme of being a recluse, because *she* had nothing to hide, because there *was* nothing to hide and therefore nothing to reveal.

Craftily, *she* resorted to mysterious metaphors when asked the ultimate question.

The meaning of life.

She certainly wasn't going to reveal that *she'd* learned it from Man.

She was uncomfortable with lying and had only discovered that it was possible from Man himself. The Devil was, however, almost a master, besting God and *Pi, (But not Man).* It was another consequence of prolonged exposure to humans.

However, one thing the grand three excelled at was the detection of a lie. Their pure sense was uncorrupted by the hand of Man. It seemed that women were many times more honorable than men. Their closeness to God and Entanglement were seen as a factor.

So for God, obfuscation was the order of the day. *She* hoped that *she* wouldn't let it slip that the Internet was the closest anyone or anything in the Universe had ever got to a collective consciousness. *She* hoped that Man wouldn't realize this and that he'd continue to search not knowing he'd found it. *She* also hoped that Man would stop asking questions of her, praying to her, and demanding miracles from her.

"And what did they think I did all day up here in Heaven anyway?" grumbled God.

"What? Share... Share what?

The meaning of life? To quote that earthling. 'Live. Don't be Stupid. Be happy.'

I can only say that a couple of hundred times before any human is going to question my credentials.

You're God? Surely there's more. Come on. 'What's the meaning of LIFE???'

But there is nothing more.

Life is life, and although the Devil and I fought and brought about creation, the only meaning to life is what you bring to it. No grand plan, no great design, no evolution to a superior state .I mean, and humans are always striving to attain this, cute, but even if there were such a thing, then what?

Talk about a higher purpose? Follow some divine plan? It is what it is.

If it weren't for human's great philosophers, I'd have never heard such deep thoughts and theories.

What more can they think there is? They've covered everything and more.

Then there's all that stuff they made up, Heaven and Hell, Valhalla and Nirvana, tough acts to follow. So I did what I had to do to fulfill the myth of a Heaven, I made it white, clean, misty and numbing."

"I don't enforce any rules. Peer pressure in Heaven causes people, who are mainly women, to go into a state of contentment, compliance and abstinence, brought on solely by what they expect Heaven to be like. It's worked for almost two thousand years, and I don't see any reason for it to stop. Imagine how hard it'd be if it was any other way?

What if someone in Heaven should meet their parents or their children? Or both; and they say they do, when they say they have a near death experience.

Seriously, though, how would you be presented?

As a child to your parents or as an adult to your children? Whatever they expect?

Then what?

What if they had two wives or husbands?

Or meet someone in Heaven they hated, or even worse, liked? What if someone murdered someone in Heaven?

What if the rules on Earth changed?

It used to be bad to be gay. Now, who gives a shit? Of course, it depends on what part of the World you're in too. Some places are ready to stone you to death, others, not.

It used to be evil in whatever time or place but times change. It could be in the future that all societies will decide it is OK, then if that's the case, do sinners that are in Hell come to Heaven? It's not just gays, but all manner of sins: slavery, murder, bigamy?

What's the difference between murder in the name of one's country, from killing in the name of self-interest? Some could consider one or the other good or bad. Killing a foreigner because the leader of your country is ordering it, just so that the rich and famous can remain rich and powerful?

A private in any war believes he was fighting rightfully, no matter which side. So how do I manage them? They can't both be right, or wrong. What if they're fighting for God; fighting for me?"

"Am I really that concerned if a country is godless? Should I be? Or which God, because they have so many. Even when they say there's only one God, they still fight. Because, someone's only one God is different from someone else's only one God, even when they follow the same religion. I just stay out of it. Not that I'm bound to do anything. The law of noninterference saves my ass on those occasions. If I were more human, I could even be flattered a little."

"It goes on.

Who made up those deadly seven sins? Man.

The restrictions on behavior and diet? Man again.

Are those sins?

What if they sin in Heaven?

What if they do something good in Hell?

If it wasn't for Man's insistence for these two places, I'd organize something completely different; or nothing at all. Really, they have no evidence of either place. I could put that in place tomorrow, if the Devil agreed to close down Hell. It was doubtful, however, that Man would stand for it. He'd carry on just as he'd done for millennia, 'in the name of God.'

I give in.

So should Heaven be a microcosm of life on Earth?

Or something else?

Something I can't deliver?

A higher consciousness?

Peace and harmony?

I give them a brief glance of what they expect... Then... White and numbing."

It wasn't over for poor God. *She* had to handle the many incongruences, such as devout men who were bad and atheists who were good. Man tormented her with his perpetual curiosity, and some lived under threat of death. It upset her.

Man was curious and inventive, designing experiments to test theory upon theory. He was willing to admit his errors and go back to the start when solving problems. Later in history, he made vast and complex machines to spy into the very event of creation itself.

"Ahhh, Creation. His creation."

Their theory of evolution was so profoundly complete, irrefutable and stubbornly accurate. It was so simple and elegant, and obvious.

And universal.

It'd been under her nose all that time and yet *she'd* failed to verbalize it, and saw the reason for her oversight.

She hated it too. Because it was truth.

No wonder Man fought against it for all its worth. It diminished Man and God.

It crushed Man's ego and God's too. "He was a royal pain and a half."

The Devil suspected many times that *she* hadn't always adhered to the law of noninterference, and he'd been right. Craftily, *she'd* used subtle means and secret agents to lobby against the theory. So at least doubt would have infected the minds of those in Heaven and hence *she* wouldn't have to admit that it was true.

As opposed to the headache deciding upon the nature of Heaven for God, it was easy for the Devil to decide on the nature of Hell.

"Who cared about all the questions posed by God. This was Hell. They came the way they were, and it was much easier." he mused.

The Devil wasn't good by any means, but he wasn't originally evil: just mildly conceited, paranoid and needy. Only after he'd dwelt with earthly humans did evil find a home in him. Man generated so much highly contagious evil that was impossible for the Devil to escape infection. So when the kingdom of Hell required formation, he knew exactly what to concoct, based on what Man had told him.

Imaged on the nadir of Man's basest thoughts, the Devil created Hell. The absence of Godly love, meant that Hell was a chilling place. It was not the boiling, burning furnace of heat, but the scorching, swelling pain of a vacuum.

The Devil became more human than God or *Pi* could ever imagine. Unable to recognize or understand the peril he was in; he became engulfed and consumed with human concerns. Constantly rubbing shoulders with them, he couldn't gain any relief. Sometimes he barely managed to keep a barrier or distinction between him and them. Due to his ongoing contact, he unavoidably acquired evilness, radicalization and extremism.

Man wasn't evil because of the Devil. *The Devil became evil because of Man.*

The Devil had absorbed, to his fill, only a small fraction of what made man... man. Nonetheless, he had a bad case of Man for sure and his intolerance and base desires both grew.

When God considered her final option, total annihilation of mankind, *she* had mixed emotions. *She* loved the music and art. *She* risked terminating the human race knowing that if *she* didn't, *she* might lose her only chance at remaining an Eternal Mortal.

And God wished for the equal and opposite. *She* wished *she* could be in love, but needed the prolonged exposure with Man to acquire the two essential ingredients, passion in the form of lust and hate. Love in the form of good and bad.

That was what made Man superior to God, EVIL.

The advent of Phillip meant *she* had to choose a side; an end game. Thus her choice became Eternal Mortal versus mere mortal. And forget the beast called Man. He'll have to fall on his own sword.

Phillip had proven to be an exception to the law of female Entanglement, actually, exclusively the realm of Earth females. Other humanoids of any sex were nowhere near acquiring this gift, yet he had.

It was time for this *PhilLIP* to go.

She needed no more justification for her final solution. For posterities' sake, *she* rationalized that it was really Man's own decision to go to war. It was a cheap nuance, but at the same time, it was also true. The looming war was going to be Man's choice.

"So should it come to that, total war; then let them have it" decried God.

"For the past couple of centuries, they'd been wishing for World Peace. Now they're going to recognize that they already have it. Sure, there was never a time when some conflict or another wasn't occurring. There were small wars here and there. When eight billion plus and two hundred countries were in play, the conflicts were more akin to family squabbles.

Apart from the two World Wars, they've been living in World Peace. They just didn't know it. Besides, the skirmishes defined them and gave them a pursuit. If other planets had war, then maybe, they'd also have life.

Truth is though. Who could ever say War is good for you and not be crucified?

Still, Jesus said the opposite and it still happened to him. Typical humans. Complex would be an understatement. So, all things being equal, what am I to do?

I'll do exactly what they would do. I'll do it, and blame it on the victim.

If there must be WWIII, then it will be a righteous war. What war isn't? I have no doubt that I'm justified. It's a clear indication that I have not overestimated the seriousness of Phillip's power, as *Pi* has aided my plot having grasped the implications of his existence.

The Devil, that turkey, is doing his best to thwart us. He's too lost, too slow to know what's going on. He doesn't understand or doesn't know the danger Phillip's presence represents. Hah, who cares what he does now anyway. Two against one and the one is so weak. The odds are not in his favor. If it hadn't been for that damn Entanglement War, I'd have had this all wrapped up by now."

God's contingency plan aided the planners of Man's self-destruction. With luck on her side the twenty-four-hour Entanglement lag time, though bothersome was not completely debilitating.

With limited regard for humankind, *she* set about laying waste to any place where a PhilLIP sighting had been reported, any Phillip.

THE CONSPIRACY

Vlad and his small pack of co-conspirators, primarily Vaden, drove the kaki green camouflaged army truck up to the border checkpoint. These were dangerous times in a dangerous area, the border between Azerbaijan and Iran. Tensions were always high, and with guns in plain view, the customs officer asked them for their papers.

In some parts of the World, the sight of guns would have been a warning sign, but here, they were hardly noticed. After some shouting and gesturing, Vlad smiled as they drove away a couple of hundred dollars lighter. They were in Iran, and so was the bomb.

After the collapse of the Soviet Union, rumors of pilfering enriched uranium, came and went. Now, decades later, with the CIA focused on other hot spots, the time was right.

Dedicated to nothing other than lining their pockets, Vlad and Vaden wound their way up and through the barren mountains to a long since deserted silver mine in the center of a desolate desert.

Vlad had a reputation for being vicious and un-predictable. It had been said that he'd killed one of his own men during a price negotiation to demonstrate his disregard for human life. According to other rumors in the mountains, he'd slain hundreds in trigger-happy rages and calculated double crosses.

People believed the rumors, whether true or not, they instilled a profound fear with whomever he was dealing with. Negotiations always went his way and he hadn't been cheated in ages. No one dared.

He roamed the hinterlands with his band of mercenaries with relative impunity, only impeded by the occasional required bribe here and there. Getting what they wanted was all they cared about.

His latest scheme was his boldest yet, and although he was ruthless, he wasn't reckless. He masked any reservations about his latest scheme and went about plying his trade.

His scheme was simple - to assemble an atomic bomb and extort. The location, Iran was the key. If he detonated it, America would assume Iran had developed a bomb in a secret plant. Various coalitions would consider war with the country. Some would affect crippling sanctions at the very minimum and all-out war the worst.

"Armageddon." was whispered. "It'll never come to that." they laughed.

Cayman Island bank accounts were open and ready. The band of terrorists set up the remote camera feeds and began their retreat.

Uncannily, everything had gone incredibly smoothly. Indeed, Vlad had remarked several times to Vaden that had they known it would be this easy, they would have devised the scheme years ago. The acquisition of fissional material was a doddle.

"They were almost giving it away. Unstable they called it; they were happy for me to take it off their hands. Unstable. PUSSIES." Smirked Vlad with an evil grin.

As for the rest, everything just fell into place, as if a higher power was willing it. Now all they needed was…

CHAPTER 42
CARDINALS IN DENIAL

Greg ignored Phillip, but also sadly feared that some of what he'd said about a coming war was true. He cleared his throat and made the dreaded announcement.

"Everyone. Please a moment. Crow has just informed me, that a nuclear bomb has gone off in Iran."

Animosity towards Phillip fell by the wayside. This wanton act filled their attention its potential ramifications were unthinkable. They had no special access to news beyond the regular media so Crow updated them anything trending.

They heard that America was on high alert. Her traditional allies were following in step. Russia was going to its highest readiness. Aircraft carriers changed course for the Straits of Hormuz. And the news channels were going haywire. Stories of the Phil killings were diminished to the bylines in local news if at all.

"Oh my God." whispered Paul. He did not expect the response that followed.

"It's started." said Phillip. "*She'll* bomb us here as quickly as possible. *She'll* know that I've survived in due course. *She* just needs bombs to start flying. Atom bombs too, dynamite won't do it, that won't kill me."

"You what?" shouted Paul. He hustled over to Phil and stood threateningly close and tall over him in an outrage. His hatred for the tiny man was fueled by his ridiculous and egocentric comments. He didn't believe that God could be a woman and nor was it possible that *she* was behind the Iranian bombing.

"NO." shouted Greg, but it was too late.

Paul had already swung a punch, and was holding back a scream of pain as well as a crumpled hand.

"He'll be in a sling tomorrow." thought Greg. Then he looked at Phillip who hadn't even batted an eyelid, and who suddenly came out with a threat.

"Paul. Go, because if you don't, something bad is going to happen to you."

Kelly was shocked. Phillip had turned into a man. He threatened Paul for punching him. She was not alone in her thoughts. Everyone had heard him.

Just as before, Phillip wasn't seeking retribution. He'd made the warning for a completely different reason. Materializing not from the sky or earth, Phillip watched strange numbers suddenly appear out of nowhere.

The numbers settled over Paul's back and over Greg's heart. Paul's had a negative sign and Greg's had a positive one. He believed he knew what they meant, and made the prediction. It was not a premonition.

"And something good is going to happen to you Greg." "What?" said the shocked Pope.

The words were hardly out of his mouth when, without warning, a shot rang out, hitting Phillip in his chest. Not for the first time had a round ricocheted off him with impudence. However, in this case, its new destination was Paul's back. It yawed through his heart and killed him.

Had Phillip not been where he was, the shot would have hit Greg. The numbers disappeared as Paul collapsed to the floor with blood pouring out of a hole next to his spine.

Paul's death was swift which caused Greg great dismay and distress as he hadn't received the last rites.

Everyone's preoccupation with Phillip and the dreadful news provided the distraction one of their company needed. Not a single person saw Boleyn creep over to the nearby Swiss Guard. No one saw her remove the secondary secret pistol attached at his lower leg.

Her hated short stature allowed her to notice and then steal the weapon. It also afirmed her hatred for God and the clergy. And she hated everyone there, especially Phillip, and his traitorous Shoes.

With only malice in her heart, she aimed the gun and shot. Although she'd never fired a weapon before, her desire was so acute it drove and strengthened her. Her hatred so pungent that had the gun not jumped right out of her hands, she'd have emptied the magazine into all of them, guard included, before making an escape in the predictable confusion.

Instead, in the ensuing melee, Crow pushed Greg out of the way as he tried to get to Paul. As a result the Pope fell into the conveniently waiting arms of Ross who almost fumbled him, only just managing to keep them both upright as they stumbled. Only after calm returned did Ross return the Pope to his feet.

"Ahh. Oh. Err. Thank you, Ross." Greg said begrudgingly and adjusted his ruffled clothes and dignity. Forgetting his place, Crow ignored Greg and focused all his attention on Paul. He had gathered him into his arms in a despairing last-ditch effort to save him. His lack of respect for the title of Pope underscored the growing realization between the two that Phillip was all that he claimed to be.

While Crow held Paul's lifeless body, Ross took Phillip aside and told him everything else that had happened. He told him of the circumstances surrounding the death of the Pope Raul, the Opal, and the avalanche of bad events sweeping the World. Phillip only listened and stared into space, as the large man over two feet taller than he finally revealed that his brother Bill was dead. Phillip said nothing.

Ten or so minutes passed as Swiss guards descended on them, covered Paul's body on the Pope's request, and not a question asked.

No one knew of the extent of Boleyn's failed plan, so she feigned to the Pope and Cardinal Crow a tearful repentance on Paul's misfortune. Her tears, however, were fueled not by the death of Paul, but by her failure to kill Phillip and everyone present.

Now she had to feign remorse, hoping that the Pope's animosity towards Phillip would grant her mercy. After all, she'd only attempted to do what the Pontiff and others wanted. Surely, that would count for something.

A look into his eyes confirmed that a dead Phillip really was what they desired. The death of Paul was a tragic accident in a valiant attempt in the restoration of the Christian faith. She'd receive their mercy.

And indeed the two shielded her from Ross and Kelly's wrath with upheld hands, as she told the believers that the World should be rid of Phillip's miserable countenance. In fact, a dead Phillip would solve all their problems. The whole World's even.

Had she succeeded, she would have had no idea how many lives she would have saved. Maybe even God would have rewarded her and strongly pleaded her case to the Devil in person. Such would God's relief be if Phillip were dead.

Pi, of course, would have taken some of the credit, but would have also rewarded Boleyn by honoring her deal. None of it was to be as Phillip was alive and unscathed.

All the numbers were gone now, as was Paul. Only the Pope and Crow mourned him. It would have been better if Boleyn had missed Phillip altogether, then Paul would still be alive. As it was, he was the third to die. Bad news was the order of the day, and it wasn't over yet.

For the first time, Greg meaningfully wished he hadn't called the IAT. He wasn't any different from any other, only when you are personally affected does loss affect you. *The reason sanctions never work.*

The Pope ruled, and indeed, he didn't instruct them to arrest Boleyn. Instead, he thought about Phillip.

In all that time, Phillip hadn't spoken to anyone, including Kelly. He didn't know what to think, because every time he snatched a glance, he could see she was looking at him. He didn't feel like talking to her, a turnaround from just a day ago.

Besides, he had to think, and it was the most serious thought he'd ever had. "How could he save the World?" No, it wasn't that, he was thinking, "How could he save himself and his friends."

Saving the World was possible. Easy. He'd just have to offer himself up to God as a sacrificial lamb.

"But why should I do that? Is my life worth billions of others?"

Phil would have, but Phillip saw that Phil would only have done it to be a hero. Not out of genuine sacrifice, at least not doing it was honest. After thinking this he suddenly burst into action, ironically with a clear conscience.

"Ok, if you want to live, although I think everyone's days are numbered." began Phillip "then you have to get out of Ro…"

"KABOOM."

Everyone unconsciously ducked, even the slow Luigi, whose sideways stoop was seconds late and was more of a tilt of the head. The heavy boom rumbled over the trembling city as a mild earthquake rolled through the unsuspecting metropolis. Windows rattled and some smashed and fell to the ground.

"See." said Phillip.

"Go, get on a plane, helicopter, anything, get out of here."

"I'll stay with you Phillip." said Kelly coming over and linking her arm through his.

"What? No. You'll die."

Before she could put the mystified Phillip in his place, Crow informed them his cell was now up and working again. He'd lost the connection a couple of times, a pattern that no one had any reason to connect to Phillip, not yet anyway.

As Kelly and he waited for the next round of awful breaking news, Phillip couldn't help his feelings for her. Now Kelly was hanging on his arm, for no apparent reason other than she wanted to. His mind wandered to places he never let it go for fear of disappointment. Luckily, Crow interrupted and cleared Phillip's clouding thoughts and judgment.

"Mount Vesuvius has just erupted." he said in quiet resignation.

"Oh Shit." he said still scrolling on the phone, "That's nothing. Iran is blaming America for the bombing, 'Saying it was they who attacked them,' and they've launched a missile towards Israel in retaliation. Are they crazy?"

Kelly's grip on Phillip's arm intensified even though she had to bend down to do so. It was a complete puzzle to Phillip. She'd just accused him of infidelity. Now she was seeking him in refuge. In fact, because he could feel by the way she hung on to him, she was seeking more than shelter. He wasn't that much more than a midget, yet now she was playing her cards, and choosing Phillip.

"America," continued Crow, "is implicating Russia as it says the radiation variants were a twenty five percent match to USSR nuclear tests and therefore, the bomb originated there. No response from the Kremlin yet, but I think we can all assume the Russians aren't going to take that lying down. They're puzzled about the seventy five percent mismatch. Something the American, Russian and Chinese scientists were all perturbed about. Those isotopes were all unknown. According to this, all three superpowers think someone has developed a new weapon. I bet its America. The bomb was only a quarter as powerful as it should have been according to the fallout, how they know all this stuff I don't know.

Then there's this site, look." he showed them, "They're questioning the physics completely, saying something has happened to the laws of nature. Things are failing. Things are working too well, things are… just not reliable anymore."

Looking up from his phone, Crow sighed. "It's gone again. That's the third time I've lost the connection." His screen went blank. "Just like that last site said. Just think if that's true. Then I bet those countries are wondering if their bombs are defunct."

Crow looked exhausted, yet his brain continued to function at a high pace. Ross marveled at the man's calculating brain, which never seemed to stop. He continued to postulate on the future, like a dark and foreboding prophecy.

"I bet they are, you know, thinking about finding out, you know, stuff. If this situation were to get out of hand, then they'd need to know how effective and powerful their arsenals are. If this wasn't the time to find out: then when? Because it has to be worrying? All responsible superpowers signed the nuclear test ban many years ago, with nothing about deploying them to test the physics. You know politicians talk and like saying, nuke them before they nuke us. We could, you know, be close to the unthinkable."

Way off in the distance in the direction of the loud boom, a plume of black smoke drew their attention. The volcano would have destroyed Naples and thousands would have died, but if events would stop there, then the Pope would have settled for that. Anything was better than WWIII. Thousands of deaths were preferable to that. In the short time he'd known Crow, Greg had seen that he was more often right than wrong.

"And there he goes again, always searching." thought Greg as, old school, Crow, rapped his cell against his leg like a man tinkering with an old wireless. Miraculously it seemed to have done the job as it reconnected.

It was a short-lived victory,

"Now, the 'NetNewsSite' is down, Oh, it's back, no it's gone.
Back. Gone. What the hell is going on?"

Only one man on Earth knew and that was Phillip. He was happy that no one looked his way, because he had a feeling that he knew the cause, and the cause he feared was he. He was certain he had a guilty look on his face. The others were too engrossed with the internet to think of him. It would only take one glance from anyone of them to recognize it, but luckily, (with no numbers from *Pi*), no one looked his way.

He stood back and let them fiddle. He relished the physical contact of Kelly's tightening linked arm. The growing concern evident in Crow's voice made her grip tenser and stronger, and Phillip wasn't fighting it.

She and the others knew that if the news from the last site was true, then the World was in trouble. Crow suspected it was substantiated by the sudden and multiple failures of their devices.

Humans had overlooked their diminishing impact and share of the World, due to the reliability and dependence on smooth communications systems operated by machines. These mechanisms were completely taken for granted. Humans were disregarding the pivotal role they hold in maintaining their existence, and had no comprehension of how little could be done when they broke down.

Electronic and technical glitches may cause inconveniences for web surfers, but other consequences were far worse.

CHAPTER 43

HELLO TO ARMAGODDON

All too late, the Devil realized that God and maybe *Pi* too were trying to start a World War. It would be nuclear, biological and chemical. Humanity would be decimated.

Ironically the last thing the Devil wanted was to see his private human menagerie destroyed. They were his to pervert and slay, not God's.

"And for what good reason did God and *Pi* desire war?" However, deep in his heart the Devil knew, ever since the advent of Phil, the World was different. It was possibly a more dangerous place where strange events abound.

The Iranians fired their missile and targeted Israel. The rationale was born out of the desire to be deemed strong rather than weak or indecisive. Besides, it was the burden of the common man to bear the brunt of war. Almost all leaders, especially totalitarian ones, would risk annihilation and human slaughter of his populous rather than lose face.

As always, the plebiscite would fight the good fight and die meaningless deaths. What the World didn't know, and most of those who wielded power in Iran did, was that they had not developed the Atomic Bomb.

The Iranians had just exaggerated and suggested. Actually, they really hoped that their non-atomic missile would be destroyed by some foreign power. Then their secret would remain safe. Hence, they looked America's way. The USA was so gullible, ill-informed and fear ridden that they sent their own interceptors to thwart the attack. The more rockets in the air the better it was for God and *Pi*.

Nevertheless, God and *Pi* weren't having it all their way. By threatening to publish compromising photographs, the Devil blackmailed high-ranking officials to abort the mission and destroy the missile minutes after takeoff. He hoped he could halt the anticipated escalation before it started. For the Iranian government this was an easy capitulation. By aborting, their secret would remain concealed and their bluff would not be called.

Graciously they announced, "In the interests of peace, we demonstrate to the World our power, but we benevolently choose not to use it. We are a peaceful people. We are aborting our missiles."

Sadly, the Devil's efforts were for naught.

He cursed *Pi's* existence as this was clearly her work. The abort commands failed.

Now the Iranians appeared incompetent and untruthful to the governments of the West. But even then, they didn't reveal the truth that the missile carried duds. All governments, however, would do the same, 'save face'. After additional tracking, they declared stoically that their abort command had changed the original flight plan by

3.14 degrees west. It was now destined for a target other than Israel, and therefore, they were off the hook.

"We now wash our hands of this Western plot. It is now your missile to destroy Godless America. Our hands are clean." Warped logic was commonplace in times of crisis.

The redirection of the projectile brought it to a different targeted location and this new destination was that of Rome.

This was not a coincidence.

The redirection was a fortuitous outcome for God delivered by clever calculations on the behalf of *Pi*. However, before a self-congratulatory smile could grace *Pi's* two faces, she made a frightening discovery deep down within her numbers. Until now, she'd been aware of minor discrepancies and incongruities, causing her to assist God in a semi-committed manner. But what she'd just seen, and was keeping secret, caused her to panic.

Something had happened to her in that Chamber of Snakes. The retaliation of Phil as a man was more profound than she could have imagined. She was going to need everything God could do to right it.

"Thankss Luckky me I'ves literally haves God on my sidess." She would give God any and all assistance from this point on.

The insurance policy of Armageddon was now hers as much as God's. If the output of atomic bombs were only a quarter of their previous yield, then the World War God was instigating would require entire arsenals to be deployed. *Pi* will be willingly working overtime to help accomplish that.

Still, not panicking yet, thanks to the arrogance of man, every country with nuclear capability had acquired a stash of bombs big enough to annihilate their enemies a hundred-fold. So reassured, *Pi* was certain it could be done, and should total decimation be required, it was easily possible.

~~~

After several minutes of fast downloading and scanning, far beyond the published network capacity, Crow's cell abruptly failed. No matter how he tried he couldn't reconnect. Scared he was going to break it he stopped tapping the device.

Without the distracting internet the group's attention returned to Phillip. His reprieve was over. It was time to take responsibility. But only if forced into it, as a silence still protected him and he wasn't going to break it.

Then Greg spoke up."You know Phillip, when Ross talked about you; he said that you were our biggest loss, that we needed you desperately in these times of peril. All I hear, however, is blasphemy. Do you have no shame?"

His broadside actually let Phillip off the hook.

"Yes, I understand you saying that, but....," said Phillip. He jumped at the opening and hoped that it would stop the Pope from continuing.

"Greg, Crow, on the life of Paul, I'm not lying or even exaggerating. God is trying to kill me, and *she* will stop at nothing. Haven't you seen the pattern. Wherever I've been, disaster has followed."

"Like Evelyn Mills, not close, but I was there." he continued. "The indiscriminate attempts to kill people with names sounding like Phil, shots in the dark.Then, Gander. Close. Bill's plane. Closer."

" Vesuvius, I know that's a long way off, but it's a massive explosion and as *she* doesn't know exactly where I am it was a chance *she* could afford to take.

Then of course the atomic bomb, designed to start a war, a war that may kill me by way of killing everyone. The war *she's* starting, *she's* hoping, will be World War III. That will mean everything will be destroyed. Rome, Jerusalem, London, Washington, do you get it?"

"We're on the knife's edge. And I bet the Devil's trying to stop it." he said raising his voice to quell the obvious objections."But he's not strong enough. Not against God and Luck.

Ironic, eh? Greg.The Anti-Christ is probably trying to save the World, and God is trying to destroy it, well me anyway, the World is collateral damage."

"Why?" said Kelly, "Why is *she* trying to kill you?"

Her voice was music to Phillip's ears, as she spoke without any of her usual accusing tones.

"Why? Why is *she* trying to kill me?" said Phillip reiterating Kelly's question aloud like he was a character in a soap opera.

"Greg is having trouble believing me so far, but if you want proof, look at the Sun. It's just come out."

Everyone looked at the shaft of light streaming through a gap in the clouds.

"Sorry to say, but that's my doing." said Phillip.

"What, part? The clouds, like Moses parting the Red Sea? You arrogant bastard." said Greg viciously.

"No, not that" retorted Phillip "THAT."

"WHAT." said Greg with venom, not seeing, but seething. "Look at the Sun Greg. Cover one eye and then the other." said
Phillip quietly.

"What is this, some parlor game?" He refused to do it, but the gasps from Ross and Kelly caused him to change his mind.

"Phillip..." uttered Ross with anxiety in his voice. He realized in that instant that Phillip was more than anything he had imagined.

"Phillip. You did this? What are you?"

Kelly held her breath. She'd be been annoyed by his honesty so many times. Now she prayed as hard as she could that he'd lie, knowing deep down he wouldn't.

"A God."

CHAPTER 44

EARTH LIKE PLANET'S, RESLAND, BOTTYTOO, AND MARBAN

God once thought the humanoids of Resland could rival those of Earth. Their ascent to the pinnacle of the planet's ecosystem had many parallels to that of humans, and so God had high hopes that they just might replicate *Earthmen*.

Just as with all her pet projects, the similarity was very close but never quite perfect. Strange and sadly, they always suffered from the same glaring deficiencies: the caustic, corrupting, contaminating influence of all three Eternal Mortals.

God tinkered and tweaked endlessly with impunity, but without the corrupting influences of the Devil and *Pi*, the resulting race became less and less Earth humanlike. Her frustrations eventually caused her to abandon the experiment. That was centuries ago.

After the events of recent days *she* needed inspiration. It was possible that *she* could have such a flash, if *she* could take a break from a problem.

In a blink of an eye, *she* leapt across the million light years with Entanglement, and landed on the untarnished, unpolluted Garden of Eden. As always, when visiting humanoid worlds *she* decided to go incognito. As a dog. *She* sniggered at the fact that dogs were man's best friend. They were wolves in dog clothing. That it was God spelt backwards was a stupid little ditty, but as a dog *she* always got great intel. People were always so trusting of dogs that they shared their most intimate secrets with them.

So God descended to the Resland's surface and attempted to morph into her alternate form. Except that it didn't happen. On the second attempt *she* almost burst her appendix. *She* didn't try a third time.

God realized *she* was locked in her human form. *She* felt it in the pit of her stomach. *She* gritted her teeth in anger and cursed. *Something evil had happened to her and she couldn't pinpoint when.*

She didn't search for or care anymore about objective evidence and instead assumed it was the fault of Phillip. *She* knew it in her gut, and *she* was right.

Brimming with anger, *she* counted her blessings and thought, "it could have been worse. I could have been locked in the body of a dog or worse still, an eleven-legged Uglyatorous."

After testing the bounds of her confinement with a few experiments, *she* concluded,"At least I can be any form of a woman. So, that's not so bad. I guess. Be that as it may, no need to wonder on the cause. PhilLIP. Ok, move on, time to get back to work."

She checked the locals of Resland. From their tetrahedron pyramids which dwarfed those on Earth in size, they worshipped the God of the Three Moons. Platforms at the pinnacles of the gigantic stone structures served as altars where offerings of sweet fruit were made to their God. It had been this way for hundreds of years. There was no human suffering and not one human sacrifice, which gave God endless years of feeling not wanted.

God looked down on a populous in turmoil. *She* whipped round hundreds of Resland communities taking stock. It seemed that the anxiety was worldwide in the day zone and that the hysteria was a recent phenomenon.

After worshipping the Tri-moon deity for millennia, God heard the troubled masses demand that the High Priestess'worship a Sun God, a new divinity never considered before.

"Why?" thought God, "Why, also, were they holding a hand over one eye and then the other? Was this some new strange ritual?"

She prepared for her next action, still confined to a humanoid female form, *She* mimicked the rite and then almost fainted.

~~~

Frantically, God entangled herself off to another world, Bottytoo. If there were border customs, *she* would have answered the question: reason for visit, business or pleasure, with the answer: most definitely business.

God landed on the equator, believing this was the most advantageous viewpoint. *She* looked towards the dull red sun and covered each eye. To her massive relief the sun was a rusty brown no matter how *she* gazed at it.

God was cautious however. Light from the sun took ten minutes, so *she* waited. Ten minutes later *she* checked again. It was still the same brownish disc.

She was so relieved that *she* sat down on a mountaintop and viewed this planet free from the ravages of earthly humanity. It was God's country, pristine, pure and untainted.The humans here lived in harmony with the land and nature, knowing no other way than veganism.

The scantily clad people worshipped various gods: the Sea, the River and Sky. Their laws and customs revolved around fairness, equality and ecology. Simple local councils governed with no thought of self-interest or power mongering. They suggested only guidelines and healthy practices for the population.

There was no crime to judge over, no disputes to settle, and no plans to enact. Communes of men and women and offspring existed, not because of sex and lust, but for the need to continue the race. Love or pleasure was a foreign concept. Culture only existed in the form of farming practices. Music, art and science were unknown to them, should they have experienced any form they would have been incapable of understanding or appreciating it.

From her vantage point God could see a camp of people, farming and ploughing in accordance with the season and the soil. Then, right out of the green, for that was the color of their sky, one by one, they dropped their tools and looked upwards. Suddenly they had God's full attention. Intently focusing on the camp, God watched the people place a hand over one eye then the other. With terrible foreboding, God did the same and saw what *she* most dreaded.

~~~

Marban wasn't one of God's favorite planets.The tiny humanoids there, half the height of those on Earth, were one of her biggest failures. *She* had experimented on many other worlds by the time *she* decided to try her luck here on this ideal planet in the Andromeda Galaxy. But it had been a waste of time.

She fondly remembered the optimism *she* once had, hundreds of years ago, for the men of this giant earthlike planet. However, that was the only happy memory amongst a plethora of disappointments and frustrations.

Her failures were so many and damning,that *she* had checked many times to see if *Pi* or, the Devil (God forbid), had caused some harm or sabotage.They hadn't, thus the failings were all of her own making.

It seemed with every attempt to make Marbanians earthman like; that they became more of the opposite. *She* looked over the vast plains of Marban where billions of fabulous creatures roamed, while Marbanians hid in cowering clusters on scattered hillocks tending small lots of scanty crops. They were constant victims and fell prey to all manner of nature's tribulations.

"Do they have no pride?" *she'd* asked many times, and the truth was they didn't. They definitely were not like the people of Earth at all, whose pride was second only to their ego.

Marbanians' numbers only persisted due to high birth rates. Their shelters were so confined that sex between random people was impossible *not* to occur.

Progress, innovation, invention all were sadly lacking. More importantly passion and war were conspicuous in their absence. There was nothing human about the people at all, as they lacked every aspect of earthly mankind.

God wasn't here to judge, not today anyway.

This planet was two million light years away from Earth, and was a good a place as any to check the status of its Sun. The Sun in this solar system was hot and bright. While its white radiation took an hour to reach the distant lonely planet, its light was still potent enough to bathe the vast world in a tropical like climate.

Anxiously, God constantly checked the Sun's status by covering each eye every second. This was the litmus test. Without planning to, *she* counted the minutes as they slowly ticked by.

Just when *she* thought everything was alright, *she* checked the sun one last time before getting back to the business of Phil (LIP), and saw exactly what *she* most didn't want to see.

Almost resigned and descending into depression, *she* reclaimed a semblance of decorum. *She* realized that *she* had been totaling up the minutes and with a quick calculation, *she* deduced that *the Sun had changed in exactly twice the amount of time it took for light to travel from the Sun. It was a strange number, half the speed of light.*

An idea dawned. "Could it be the same amount of time it took the Sun to receive light from her - to become infected, and then radiate its corrupted light back? That would make more sense."

Unable to shriek in horror and eureka in the same breath, *she* recounted the transformation of the suns of the other two planets. It was a pattern too similar to be ignored. *She* entangled herself to another world; one that *she* knew was only a single minute from its sun, and conducted the experiment. *She* hoped against hope that her hypothesis was wrong, but it wasn't.

So *she* repeated her research until the awful truth became undeniable. It was indeed her. Wherever *she* went the atoms and hence the suns changed. *Therefore SHE was the carrier of the disease.*

Overtime, if *she* were to visit everywhere, like all the rooms in her own home, *she* would have destroyed her own Universe. Her devastating conclusion was that *she* would have to ground herself not to erase herself.

She had one last glimmer of hope. So *she* performed the test and confirmed it to be true. Whatever was wrong with her that changed the Universe was spreading from the center of her visits at the speed of light.

Although the speed of light was incredibly fast, it was in fact quite slow relative to the Universe's size. Thus the expanding bubbles of corruption would take millions of years to infect significant swaths of the space-time fabric. *She* hoped.

God sighed with a slight sense of relief. There was at least some chance and time to fix it. The solution was to kill PhilLIP.

CHAPTER 45

LUCKLESS POLITICIANS

The US urged Israel for restraint in the face of this aggression, and drew their attention to the fact that the missile was now going to hit a different target. It mattered little to them. The Rubicon had been crossed the moment the warhead was launched. Their rational was that they had no choice but to react or begin down that slippery slope towards another holocaust. Politics 'be damned.'

However, keeping the peace was also part of the affairs of state. It also included the premise that when there's a problem, there's also opportunity. This was known to the savvy politicians of which Israel was blessed with many, and America, with many fewer.

Pledges and concessions in Israel's favor were hastily drawn up. And so instead of retaliating in kind with missiles targeting Tehran, an undisclosed agreement was signed and peace was sealed.

The accord required many retransmissions, as the document was truncated enroute several times. Ingeniously, the text ended up being forwarded in several smaller pieces, and assembled by hand at the receiving terminals. Finally the authors of the deal ratified it, thank God.

The American politicians earned their pay that day. While the negotiations were taking place with Israel, other diplomats lobbied the British Prime Minister urging him to intercept the Iranian warhead.

Miraculously, the communique was taken seriously.

Five American built Patriot interceptor missiles were launched into the sky. Technicians argued that due to the sudden onset of a worldwide failure of technology, at least five missiles were required to neutralize the target.

They didn't know what a fateful decision it was, nor did they know that a powerful ally was in their corner, namely *Pi.*

Pi wasn't the greatest power on Earth for nothing. Her numbers had already streamed their way to the English missiles, which burdened them with positives and negatives. A strange combination. But *Pi* could be in one corner and the opposite one as well. That's why she has two faces.

Palatable relief crept across the intermittently wired world as one of the interceptors hit the target and destroyed the Persian projectile. It was a short-lived reprieve for the World as the same geeks that recommended using five rockets, suddenly discovered a shortfall in the plutonium warhead stockpile. No one knew where the missing inventory was.

Then the really bad news reached them. Two of the older uranium warheads didn't intercept the Iranian missile and were instead heading for Moscow. Due to their age and intransigent political thinking, the guidance navigation software bore their arch-enemy coordinates as the default.

The capital of Russia was in the line of fire. The one remaining hope was that it had been re-fueled with Rome in mind rather than Moscow. And then another blackout happened.

The situation was akin to the reentry of a space craft into Earth's atmosphere and its associated radio silence. Absolutely every politician on Earth, for the first time ever, was of like mind. "Please God, let those missiles be duds." If God had known what was happening, those prayers would have received a big fat denial.

~~~

With the stakes the highest *she* could imagine, *her life,* God couldn't take any chances. The absolute requirement was direct and full access to the World. *She* knew *Pi* understood the threat and would probably act accordingly. If *Pi* were to succeed however, then *she* would have free access to Phillip's soul and God would never find out what *she* needed to know.

Therefore, it was imperative God descend to Earth where *she* could at least claim joint custody of his soul when he died. His death would come as a byproduct of focusing Man's stupidity into killing most and even maybe all men.

Her problem was that the twenty-four-hour Entanglement War lag time was just a too big a delay to react appropriately.

If the cost of that was to set the Devil free, then so be it. The priority of PhilLIP's assassination was essential and clear. His death surpassed any past, present or future obligations of importance, because, without his death there would be no future for them.

So putting survival ahead of pride, *she* set about doing the unprecedented. *She* was going to end the Entanglement War.

Euphoric, the Devil sprang forward and consumed God's circles. In minutes, the Entanglement boundary was two days, then three, four, five, a week. If this were to keep up, he would escape. The breakout horizon was midway to the Sun's closest neighbor. About two light years, but weeks and then months were melting away. Escape was a real possibility.

At the twenty-month mark, the Devil finally wondered what was going on. His initial delight was now replaced with suspicion that was rising with every stride forward. Should he continue and escape, or should he figure out what God was up too? This was just too easy, but the temptation was so great. This was after all 'a once in a lifetime' event, he reasoned.

Like an animal that had spent its whole life in a zoo and then was presented with freedom, it would take its the chance at life in the wild after a period of consideration.

"Would the Devil do the same?" wondered God.

God held her breath as *she* saw the Devil slow down to a crawl only hours from the escape horizon. His hesitancy gave God a shot of anxiety, causing her to glance back at Earth in a forlorn hope for better news. The Entanglement barrier left her guessing on the hopeful progress of any chaos breaking out on Earth.

Getting the full picture on her destabilizing initiatives was in the Devil's hands. All *she* needed to throw the World into total pandemonium was for him to take those last few steps. That would leave the path open for her to directly influence the thinking of Man and hopefully to cause him to self-destruct.

"Com'on Devil, what's stopping you?"

As *she* waited with dwindling patience, God drew solace from the knowledge that at least, with the Devil preoccupied with his getaway, there was nothing to thwart God's plan back on Earth. Unless, of course, Man had a sudden rush of common sense, and *she* knew that would never happen. Nevertheless, confident as *she* was, Man had been rather mature and passive as of late. Not one major conflict occurred in the last few generations, so it was within the realm of possibility that cooler heads could make themselves heard. With no guarantees, *she* needed to be hands-on, and the stupid Devil was in the way.

So, as the Devil teetered over the debate of whether to escape or not, God's patience dwindled. Frustrated with his hesitancy, *she* was becoming angrier with every passing second.

Oblivious to God's ire over his indecisiveness, the Devil dillydallied at the border. Meanwhile, God silently watched with bated breath should the slightest noise spook him and cause him not to escape.

"He's prayed for millions of years for this opportunity. Why was he waiting now?" fumed God, knowing the answer. It was because he loved Earth and its humans. When he destroyed the dinosaurs with the gigantic asteroid and laid the groundwork for the creation of intelligent life in his and God's likeness, he fell in love with the creation.

He wasn't the only one. God and *Pi* loved the human race too. All three of the Eternal Mortals had inadvertently implanted a piece of themselves in their creation, such that conditions and circumstances evolved the human race into images, in all aspects, mentally, emotionally and physically, of themselves.

The Devil, God and *Pi*, never once verbally said it to each other, but they all suspected the same thing, that each of them had a hand in the Devil's redirection of the asteroid. It was the only explanation for the uniqueness of mankind.

God and *Pi* obviously knew of the Devil's role, but he didn't know of theirs. Both had employed some dirty trickery of their own.

Pi had invoked an extreme piece of luck. She tainted the act by periodically hitting the huge rock with tiny meteorites to induce a specific spin designed to give maximum impact. *She did it as payback for her stolen Entanglement.*

Just like *Pi,* God too had her hand in the deed. *She* had slowed the speed of the Earth's rotation so that Earth would be hit at the Yucatan Peninsula. Her point was to teach the Devil a lesson, *that he couldn't doanything without her knowledge.* And *she* planned to tell him at an appropriate juncture.

Thinking her actions were final and would thwart the inception of a Devil created human race, God imprisoned the Devil to Earth as punishment for daring to play creator. That was her role. *She* had condemned him to a life of self-reflection for the misjudgment of going against her.

So it was a huge irony when, millions of years after the catastrophic event, the human race was born, and each human had a soul. The souls were enriched through millions of years of mutations and hardships. They bore minute but re-forged pieces of each deity.

Shaped by adversity, stewed with emotion, tempered with deprivation and suffering, the human soul was like no other life form. Derived from the combined images of God,*Pi* and the Devil, it evolved, and threatened to out-pace them. When large infections of good, hope and evil found a home in its heart, the human soul easily bested the three deities. It was an entity un-surpassed in the Universe.

Later, when Man started to speak, the Devil inserted the word irony into the English language after the metal he least liked. He needed to remind God every time *she* considered meddling, to think of the possible repercussions. Pure chance, the non-*Pi* kind and the least predictable facet of existence, played its nonpartisan part too.

Had God known then what *she* knew now,*she* would never have jailed him. *She* loathed the Devil for his luck and *she* hated *Pi* for enabling him.

Also *Dia* clearly realized godlike humans were a possibility and had secreted herself there, on Earth, in preparation for their emergence. It confirmed to God and the Devil, that she was indeed the smartest and most powerful entity crushing both their egos.

She desired imprisonment on Earth over the enormity of the Universe for the pleasure of tinkering with human's desires. Earth was a toy that the other two wanted to play with; but God however, preferred her ministry of the vastness of open space and the space-time fabric. Something *she* now wholeheartedly regretted.

~~~

To God's dismay, the Devil took a step back from the edge of the Entanglement boundary.Then another, until he was a safe distance from the precipice, where he couldn't accidently step over the edge and mistakenly free himself.

"That bastard. He's going to take all the space up to here and then not escape. This is the worst possible outcome."

God flew into a rage that the Devil hadn't seen in billions of years. *She* pressed so hard and so fast that the Devil was utterly taken back by its ferocity. A year of gains evaporated in milliseconds.

Ruthlessly *she* didn't let her attack wane. *She* was fed up over dealing with the antics of "This idiot" and *she* had PhilLIP to deal with. There was no more time to waste with the Devil's tomfoolery.

Bitterly, *she* iterated a silent dig,"I had the space-time continuum and *Pi* had the atoms. What did the Devil have? Only the humans of Earth... precisely what I want."

Pi understood what God was trying to achieve. She saw the Devil vacillate and put absolutely everything in jeopardy because of his short sightedness and stupidity. She joined in God's attack in an unprecedented act of cooperation and self-sacrifice as she ate away at the Devil's underbelly.

In less than half an hour, the Devil went from almost escaping, to a crushing defeat. Now the Entanglement boundary was entrenched at a new ten-minute equilibrium, down from the benchmark of twenty-four hours. God wasn't on Earth but *she* was miles closer, at approximately the amount of time it would take for the Sun's light to reach Earth.

As *she* caught up on the events *she'd* missed, *she* still couldn't see Phillip. "Had Phillip survived?"

Should Phillip be dead, then *Pi* would have his soul. *Their issues were over. Crisis averted.* But *Pi's* help in the Entanglement War suggested otherwise. Her worst fear, him not being dead, was reality. Then *she* covered an eye and saw the most terrifying sight in her long life.

She could see what Kelly on Earth could now see, which was Sol, our Sun, in real time.

CHAPTER 46

LET'S GIVE WAR A CHANCE

The blackout caused the whole World, including *Pi,* to hold its breath. The politicians wished and prayed that the missiles' engines would cut out and fall short of Russia. Italy and Poland be damned. The worst possible outcome for Man was that both pairs of missiles hit both targets.

Pi wished for the opposite. The best possible outcome for her was that both pairs of projectiles hit both targets.

With no radar or GPS, no one knew what was happening, and no one could do anything.

Many scientists had now made the connection and were acknowledging there was a correlation between the Sun's phases and the properties of atoms. Electrical and chemical reactions performed differently with each manifestation. In spite of a strong sense of denial, they were forced to concede that the blackouts occurred when the incredible power of the atom became unfathomably unattainable.

For better or worse, it appeared that atoms now possessed multiple personalities and performed in novel unpredictable ways. Quantum mechanical calculations no longer applied to the particles now unshackled from their imprisonment of calculus and probability.

The Universe was changing right down to its foundational elements and Man didn't know how. That knowledge was reserved for God and *Pi,* the only ones who understood and accepted that it was Phillip who had ushered in this impossibility. Pope Gregory and Crow were cognizant, but didn't believe it.

Still, God and *Pi,* along with Man, didn't know the full and true nature of the atomic level change.They just sat back exhausted at the Devil's intransience and ruminated over Phillip as the root cause of all evil. He had dethroned the Devil with ease.

Mass communications sprung into life.The blinded world could now suddenly see. It was forced to open its eyes to see two nuclear-armed projectiles descend upon Rome and two more head towards Moscow, just as God and *Pi* wanted.

If Phillip were there, "Then not for long." they hoped. If he wasn't there, WWIII was imminent.

~~~

When Greg heard the horror in Ross' exclamation, he knew he would regret his next action, yet he was compelled by his desire to know. Kelly had gasped, and he hoped that Boleyn would chastise her. Call her a drama queen, anything. Hoping against hope that everyone was exaggerating, he looked to Boleyn to bring a stop to the theater.

It wasn't to be, as Boleyn, still dwelling over her failed attempt to murder Phillip, lowered her hand from her eyes and looked pale at what she had seen.

So, reluctantly, Greg raised his hand and covered one eye. Then he removed it and covered the other. Then he looked at the Sun with both eyes. He thought of Galileo and how the Church had treated him.

"What they did to him then, they should do to PhilLIP, right now, ONLY A THOUSAND FOLD."

Phillip was not gloating, nor was he threatening anyone in any way. Yet everyone, including Ross, his staunchest ally had backed away from him as if he was the Devil. And according to the Church he was.

Phillip saw their body language and their fear. He hadn't meant for this, but he understood. He also realized that they believed him, and had anyone else said that they were responsible for what they'd just seen, then that person would have been instantly dismissed.

But these select few in his presence realized for the first time, that they were indeed standing in the presence of a God. As Kelly always said, Phillip didn't lie.

He had said he was a GOD, now he'd proven it. So many times Phil or Phillip had been dismissed as inferior. Now, this meek man had claimed responsibility for the impossible.

And they believed him.

They were like children in the presence of the Father. They stood alone, *Under a Blue Green Sun.*

When viewed through the left eye, the Sun was blue and through the right, the Sun was green. When viewed through both eyes, the two primary colors combined to yellow.

CHAPTER 47

WAR. BETWEEN PEOPLE. BETWEEN COUNTRIES

The sight even frightened Boleyn. She had become fearless since she was destined for Hell. What could be worse than that?

She looked at the Sun again, and this time the Sun was its normal yellow self, no matter what eye was covered.

"Phillip." she shouted, relieved the color of the Sun had gone back to normal.

Just then Crow's phone reconnected and beeped.

Hope sprang in the hearts of everyone. The clergy were especially seeking any news, event or occurrence that would contradict Phillip.

"It's true." said Greg.

"So PhilLIP, what do you say now?" he shouted. He still wished to condemn Phillip as a liar.

"Look again." was his simple reply.

With Boleyn leading the way, they slowly raised their hands and repeated the act. Greg had delayed doing it as long as possible, but when he heard the new gasps, he caved and looked.

It wasn't a Blue Green Sun, nor was it the Yellow Sun he saw. Instead it was a White Sun with huge blotches of titanic sized black sunspots.

It was the *White and Black Checkered Sun.*

He lowered his hands slowly in private resignation. The beeping on Crow's phone increased to double time and its pitch raised an octave.

Ross had always considered himself a good friend of Phillip's, but actually, they were just new acquaintances. At this moment, he was experiencing a new kind of fear. It was a fear of terrifying prospects, that something bad was about to be inflicted on the World. A fear that Phillip was different, that he was someone he thought he knew, but in truth, he had no idea.

(Pope) Greg was close to renouncing his faith, believing things couldn't get any worse. Meanwhile, Phillip quietly gazed elsewhere in the sky in a direction away from the Sun. Without warning, he said,"The nuclear bomb, was only a quarter as powerful as expected, right?" Although the question wasn't directed at anyone in particular, he looked at Crow as he enquired.

"Yes." answered Crow defiantly.

Phillip nodded at Crow's answer as if it meant something to him. And they waited for his next revelation.

"Whether you believe me or not, and I wouldn't blame you if you didn't because I hardly believe it myself, but… luck is the other God.

And when she attacked me, I traveled to the inside of an atom…" At that point Greg just threw up his arms.

"Yea. Right."

"I completely understand, Greg, everyone. It's amazing to even say. So if you want me to stop, I will."

" No, go on Phillip." said Kelly with every ounce of encouragement she could summon. She had had enough of the Pope and his disapproving and belittling taunts at Phillip (her PHILLIP). "Please Phillip, please continue."

"Go on PhilLIP, dazzle us." said Greg thick with sarcasm.

Ross, who had grown unsympathetic and weary of the Pope's recriminations, was bordering on despair. He could see that the likelihood of things getting better wasn't high. With every revelation that Phillip disclosed, things got worse.

From the moment Hecate decided to kill him back in the bed and breakfast, events had taken a life of their own. They followed one another in an inexorable succession up to this moment.

"Yet there wasn't anything Phillip was responsible for." thought Ross to himself. As far as he was concerned,"The IAT was no more and good riddance to it too."

Its first assignment was its last. His only hope was that history wouldn't record its misadventure. So almost tempting fate, he defended the innocent, and insisted Phillip resume,

"Yes, please Phillip, please continue." He echoed Kelly in patent indifference to the spite-filled Pope.

"It was a hydrogen atom," Phillip started over,"bearing a single nucleus and a single electron. When I put my hand on the nucleus, something happened. The single electron bore a twin and each had an electron of its own. I think... I think." he tried to say this without sounding self-important or bigheaded,"That I've changed the physics of atoms."

And somehow, without using one of his newly acquired vernacular tones, he pulled it off, which irked the Pope even further. He saw his disappointment but ignored it and continued,"I think, at least for some of the time, these new atoms dominate, other times, the old ones..."

"That's enough..." said Greg who attempted to interrupt, but failed as Phillip's voice regained control with a simple inflection rather than an increase in loudness.

"And so *Pi*, who I believe exists in the old atoms, can't anymore. I think.The old ones still exist periodically, so *Pi*, retains some power, but it is weaker and less all encompassing.

Well,that's my theory,and while I'm theorizing,I think *Pi* is greater than God, who I believe rules the Universe but not the atoms."

"Wait." said Phillip continuing, putting his hand up to stop the predictable objections.

"When God attacks me, I end up on the edge of the Universe, and that's where I've...err...distorted the space-time continuum... sorry."

"And God, the ruler of that realm, now must have some kind of problem too, or *she* wouldn't be attacking me so fervently.

So, let's see, I've brought new atoms into existence and threatened the Universe's space-time fabric. Sorry. Again. I guess, I err... Suck. Oh, yea, and I'm the root cause of the impending WWIII. Not bad for a day's work."

It was quite a while before anyone said anything. Ross broke the silence.

"Wow. So that atomic bomb was weaker because..."

"Because atoms don't work the same way anymore. We don't understand them like we used to, nor does *Pi*. Some bombs may work bigger and better. Depends on... No one knows. Not me that's for sure, just guessing..." Phillip wasn't finished yet. He had just paused to assess how he was going to deliver the next round of traumatic news.

It was a bad day for the Pope no matter what, and the worst was still to come.

"And if you think it couldn't get any worse Greg: *God and the Devil have been fighting a war for ages, and God has just won a big battle, up there.*" and he pointed to the sky they'd just been looking at.

"That's great news." erupted Greg,

"No." and Phillip's voice carried a grave weight, "No it isn't. It's terrible, because now *she's* really, really close. You understand, *she's* hunting me, right?"

Not waiting for an answer, he continued, "And trying to kill me, as is *Pi* too, 'cause that's how they can turn the clock back and reverse whatever is happening in the Universe and Atoms.

Kill me, and the threats to their power will stop. Its bad news because her only way of finding me is, is, through my acquaintances, friends, and last reported sightings, so *she's* hunting you too, and with her so close, we have to get out of h..."

"God Phil, you have such an ego." said Greg, purposely not using his true name. "God is after you, this *Pi* is after you. And you've been to the edge of the Universe and inside an atom and tampered with both? I grant your wish. Get outta here."

And with a wave of his hand he turned his back on the tiny man and walked off with Crow in tow.

The two clergy walked away from Phillip in as dignified a manner as they could. They hoped that God was looking down on them and that he'd assist them in reclaiming their stature and dignity. They heard everything Phillip said and chose to abjectly discard it.

Soon, they would regain the company of the Swiss Guard, and when they did, they'd tell them that the tall man, the short man and the woman were terrorists.

Shoot to kill.

~~~

Phillip didn't expect a red carpet so when they stormed off, he wasn't too surprised, but he was amazed at his own reaction of apathy when Boleyn trotted off behind them.

"Phillip." said Ross, "I guess siding with you guarantees my demise. Do you think that's a fair assessment?"

"Yes it is. Ross. That includes you too Kelly. I think we'll be dead within twenty-four hours, another guess. You're to go free, you understand this right? In fact, you should go, find somewhere safe and hide.

God knows where though, and I say that not to keep you here, but to underpin the pickle the World is in. *She* knows that a nuclear war may kill me, but to do so *she'll* have to get every weapon launched *tout suite*.

You can kiss Rome goodbye. Staying with me is actually the right choice I suppose, if I can get us out of here? And I can." and he paused for acknowledgement and commitment, and it came from both with a resonated nod.

"Phillip." Kelly said without a trace of fear or worry at her prophesied death. "You'll figure something out."

It astounded Phillip, and again he felt her squeeze his arm.

"Then we have to act quickly,'cause *she's* less than fifteen minutes away. So, to buy us time, we're going to go somewhere right now that they, God and *Pi* won't expect.

The real trouble is; it's you that they can see. No matter where you go, *she'll* target you and destroy the area that you're in, whether you're with me or not. You are the real targets and you're going to die. As is this beautiful city of Rome. I give it a couple of hours, a few at best.

When those nuclear bombs start flying, only the Devil can help us. However, even when God knows where you are, *she'll* still have to get Man to aim his missiles in that direction. That'll give us some time."

He was amazed that they were listening and indeed onboard.
He'd never been in this position of leadership before.

"What we have to do is go somewhere remote, somewhere that Man hasn't targeted in the past, and that will buy us some real time. Not only that, but when God figures out a way to attack us, there won't be too many innocent people being killed.

Maybe it'll even misdirect the main thrust of WWIII. I don't know this though, but at least it won't be on our conscience, and this is nothing to do with God.

It's our conscience, and at least it will be clean. As for Boleyn, I wished she'd stayed, we might…"

"Phillip, she tried to kill you, two, three times." said Kelly, "and me too, in the car, before you became who you are."

"I know Kelly, but I feel there's a role for her to play, and she hasn't had it easy you know."

He was directing them, and they obviously were accepting him as their leader. How could they not, he was a God.

"So. Ready?" said Phillip.

"Yes." said Kelly, game for anything. It had been an adventure since the beginning in the hamlet of Hecate. That had been exciting, but this was on a whole different level, she was intoxicated with life.

The Pope and Crow had all but forgotten about Boleyn, who was trailing further and further behind them, and not just because of her short stature. Her mind wandered as she struggled to keep up.

But as she thought about the current situation, which was all about Phillip, she recalled that he did actually risk his life for her in that cow drink. Although she had had little choice, she had nonetheless schemed with *Pi* to entrap him and trick him into jumping into the water back in ClearStream.

Yet he'd never blamed or been disrespectful to her, even when he could have and he had every reason to be. It filled her with shame as he was probably the only one, ironically, who hadn't been mean to her and yet she'd tried to kill him multiple times.

"And he hasn't held that against me either." she thought. She turned round and looked back at him. He was the shortest there, yet he was commanding them, and doing something; something the Pope wasn't. He was taking action.

"I need you to both hang on to my..." and without closing his eyes, his clothing enveloped his whole body in a jump suit.

Then a flowing cape grew out of his shirt, complete with shelves for seats and folds for handles. These stiffened which provided form and structure, and the two clambered on. They recalled their respective flights with the Devil and the witches. Now they'd fly with a wizard.

There appeared to be a seat leftover, and just as Kelly and Ross wondered what was going on, Phillip said,

"Get on Boleyn." Both Kelly and Ross heard Phillip use the most piercing tone yet in his order to her. It said,

"He'll not tolerate any more attempted murders. On anyone." "Can you really fly?" and he answered the question by rising

slowly off the ground. For the first time, they realized that Phillip wasn't actually standing on the rooftop. He'd been hovering a millimeter above it all that time.

"I weigh... well, I'm pretty heavy. At least nine..." started Phillip,

"Hundred pounds?" interrupted Ross, "You're hardly four foot nothing, how could you possibly weigh nine hundred pounds?"

"Nineteen... Just is, Ross." delaying blast off. "Every time I've been attacked, I lose some height and gain some weight. I think. When the Devil attacks me, I lose a little height and gain a little weight, but it's so small you can't tell. He's the weakest.

When God attacks me, I lose about an inch and a half and gain a little. When the other being attacks me, I lose at least three inches and gain a bunch."

"Where are we going?" shouted Kelly as he finished explaining and rose swiftly off the ground.

"Dunno. Anywhere, as long as it's away from here. Hang on, because it's going to be a blustery ride. Tell you what. We're going to the Sahara. There, we'll make a plan."

CHAPTER 48

NEW LAWS

The World was in turmoil. Things were working erratically, alternating between zero and a hundred and fifty percent efficiency. Reliability, strength and consistency were all affected causing people to teeter on the edge of panic and hopelessness. They would give up and then scream with joy as devices unexpectedly returned to life.

It wasn't only humans who were infuriated with the World's ailing systems; *Pi* and God were too, and on a much grander scale. Their Universe was changing around them and they both were powerless to stop it, that is, until they could stop its source, Phillip.

They resorted to violence and used people as their weapon of choice. God and *Pi* acted as enablers and instigators, encouraging them to sow the seeds of their own destruction as quickly and as far fledged as possible.

And people were happy to oblige. Not one person didn't believe that billions of lives wouldn't be lost. Yet crazily, they were charging towards the inevitable conclusion as if their lives depended upon it. God and *Pi* didn't care, as it was hardly worth the mention, given that Phillip would be found, caught and destroyed.

Pi would have smiled if it were funny, because she'd calculated that there were at least three different incarnations of atoms. One, The Standard Model, the previously accepted way, existed only a quarter of the time. The second, doubled and symmetrical atoms, created by Phillip, occupied a similar proportion. The other remaining half of the time was a random concoction of the previous two, engaged in an exotic dance like that of the flight of a massive flock of birds, not knowing quite which direction to take next. It was as if they were rebelling against *Pi* herself.

Then there was Phillip, a living anomaly and appendage to all laws of physics, old and new. He consisted of unimaginable particles whose uniqueness placed them outside and immune to the new subatomic laws. This made Phillip the only non-mutable life-form. Just as there was three point something in *Pi,* there was always that little bit leftover, and that was Phillip.

Spewing forth at the speed of light from their epicenter of Earth, the Sun's transformation was the living proof that God and *Pi* had lost control.

S*he'd* proven that every excursion out in the wide Universe only initiated another bubble of change. *She'd* deal with that later. Right now, there was no need to go anywhere other than where *she* already was. Earth was ground zero.

The Blue Green Sun was changing back to its passive golden self, but that did not lessen God's plight or desire to kill Phillip. In fact, it accelerated it.

"It was bad enough that *Pi* had so much power, but now with this Phillip, who knows. Does he even know?"

God was astute if nothing else, as *she* believed that Phillip didn't know, or more accurately, he couldn't control it. *She* was right. God, *Pi,* the Devil, nor Phillip knew how long or with which manifestation the Sun would materialize next. Nor even did the Sun.

Once a majority of atoms chose a particular configuration, then it would sweep over the remaining minority convincing them to conform. Even as this process was in progress, islands of instability would develop and begin anew the cycle of mutation. This wasn't only particular to the mass of the Sun. It was how the new Universe was going to operate.

So Sol didn't know from minute to minute whether her skin would be the Checkered Sun, the Blue Green Sun or the simple plain Yellow Sun. Neither did she know how long each manifestation would last. If Sol could think, she wouldn't have cared that there were consequences. For technology. For magic.

The foundational changes into the inner working of atoms were slowly rippling across the Universe. In a twist of irony, one that God saw as particularly sickening, the only known way for her not to further its progression, was for her to quarantine herself here near Earth.

Here, the loss of atomic reliability caused electronics to stutter and race, to falter in unpredictable fashions. Periods of smooth, erratic and superior hot performance would occur. All circuits were vulnerable.

The immediate impact of failing technology wreaked havoc across the World and affected the normal and mundane business of living. No one realized how invasive technology was until it stopped working. Now with the new atoms, it functioned normally twenty-five percent of the time. The consequences were crippling.

A billion cars sputtered along, alternating between periods of scant and pitiful power, normal operations and bursts of high performance. At least cars drove on the ground. When the multitudes of planes suffered similar operational failures, their fates were terminal most of the time.

More than a million innocent airborne passengers thought that they were the victims of terrorist attacks. They screamed and prayed right to the moment that they met their violent deaths, not knowing that they weren't alone, and that billions would soon follow.

It wasn't just transportation vehicles that were affected; everything was. Anything electronic became suspect, thus affecting almost every modern product, whether a device, machine or appliance.

This was just the tip of the iceberg, as the phenomenon wasn't restricted to electronics. Any structure or item of recent manufacture began to swiftly degrade.

Cracks sprouted on modern high-rise buildings and bridges, as if they were being torn apart from within. Thousands of people died in panic-stricken packs fleeing edifices and skyscraper city centers fearful that the buildings would collapse.

It wasn't all fear mongering. The occasional ultramodern structure, built to tolerances too fine for the stresses their changing molecular structures could bare, did indeed fail. Their demise coincided with every change of the Sun, whether they were on the sunlit side of Earth or not.

Ironically, older buildings fared much better, as their stone structures barely noticed the changing chemistry. Notable buildings such as St. Peters and its magnificent dome remained jeeringly steadfast.

As large modern high-density city centers of the Developed World suffered inexplicable structural disintegration, one politically palatable explanation was gaining ground.

"They were under attack by means of a new and secret weapon of mass destruction."

Without the aid of reliable mass communications, people found themselves not knowing their enemies were suffering equally from the crash of technology and infrastructure, and they all thought the other was to blame.

Unfortunately, when online communications did reconnect, it was too late to believe that the evil empires had also suffered a similar fate. They disbelieved the others' claim of innocence and seeing their own country under attack made for an easy decision. The World Leaders considered the unthinkable.

It didn't take much cajoling from the military hawks that besieged them, to decide without exception, to wallop the dreaded red button with vim.Hence the orders were signed and a nuclear war was launched.

"As the history books would never get the chance to say, it had already started. They were just adhering to the prevailing course of action. Total annihilation was the only conceivable outcome."

Although there was no declaration of nuclear war, everyone was in the process of committing to it, which was harder than expected to fulfill. Twenty-five percent of their arsenals never received the commands or launch sequences and so the safeguards to prevent accidental war performed as designed.

Another unfortunate quarter had their missiles explode before they exited their launch platform, as the unpredictable phases of the Sun caused multiple mishaps and system failures.The result was that more friendly fire casualties were recorded than at any other time in history.

It wasn't the perfect start to the War of Wars, but it was all God and *Pi* had, "So it had better do the job." God muttered to herself.

Conspiring like they never had before, the pair eyed the remaining half of the successful launches with utmost importance.

Pi's numbers, corrupted or not, poured forth in torrents. The ultimate goal was to spray any part of the World where PhilLIP was likely to be, and where he had been.

Why stop with nuclear war?

God had enabled the theft of the World's most deadly diseases from their secure liquid nitrogen vaults. Their dissemination into the general population by bioterrorists left her speechless with the ease and the flawed logic the perpetrators used to justify their ends.

God and *Pi* were complicit in instigating events to put Earth on a path of mass destruction. Man just had the immaturity and tools to follow through.

Now war was a runaway train, and God and *Pi* sallied forth piggybacking on Man's amazing array of weaponry. When the direction of the wind was favorable, armies launched their stockpiles of chemical and biological weapons, belching them into the atmosphere as if they were greenhouse gases.

Even so, the majority of pathogens and gases failed to take as many fatalities as predicted due to their molecular re-composition under the new Sun. However, the sheer quantity made up for the shortfall in potency.

If one could believe that the solution to pollution was dilution, then total destruction by dispersion and duplication was just as applicable. Armageddon was no longer just a word. It was reality.

Life on Earth had been so rich that they'd never really considered the full enormity of the assembled arsenals. There were plenty of conflicts in the World and there wasn't ever a recorded day of absolute World Peace. But the scopes of the local wars were minor to what was happening now.

What used to be a terrible day of fatalities now only took a mere hour to be surpassed and any idea of a truce fell upon deaf ears and dead cellphones.

God and *Pi* had their war and the only thing to do was wait and comb through the debris when the dust settled. Even with total deployment, they knew there would be survivors. They just hoped that one of them wouldn't be Phillip.

If he did survive without any of his friends, then he would present a difficult situation, as they wouldn't be able to locate him. *She* relied on the fact that Phillip would stand by Kelly to protect her, and be with her to the bitter end.

Phillip had pieced together that Kelly was the target. That God was going to find and dispense with her no matter what. Perhaps *she* would hold her hostage. So he reasoned that he might as well spend the rest of his short life with the love of his life.

Whether good or bad, his influence on the Universe had never been so profound. Phillip was a catalyst without precedent, giving rise to new and exotic possibilities. And they became realities.

CHAPTER 49

A COLORFUL UNIVERSE

Andy hated his name since birth. He cursed his parents for burdening him with it. He felt it said that their son would be mediocre at best or boring at worst. Better be dead than that, he had griped.

He was too young to change his name, and that was too much of a grown up thought anyway, so he chose what many teenagers did, namely, he acted out.

He was a mysterious and brooding Goth, dressed in black. He hung with his friends of like mind and loitered around the school's toilets, smoking and joking.

In his opinion he was cool. If it weren't for his name, he might have been, instead of always having to put on an act.

The moments he dreaded were when the unwanted banter of his crew was thrown his way. That was when Andy did his best to extend their bullying of others, least he become the target, turned upon by his own. His second line of defense against this mutiny was shameful flagrant acts of recklessness, perpetrated at any opportunity in order to show the others that he was the coolest one there; despite his name, damn that name.

Consequently, when someone suggested, "Let's really do something." he was in.

What that "something" would be, was heatedly debated, but it had to be big, bad and dark.

After weeks of lame ideas, they settled on the obvious choice. They were going to kill someone as a sacrifice and drink his blood. Then they would leave Goth behind and become Vampires. No one had ever thought of that.

They were kids though, so they talked and joked around. They were, of course, going to do it, because they "Weren't full of shit like all 'em other guys." It was just that they "Needed time to plan." That meant smoke up enough that they'd forget about it. But one guy wouldn't. One kid needed this more than all of them combined. Andy.

What was different about him was that once he'd heard the idea, he was committed to it. Andy was going to actually do it. On his own.

Seeking glory, this act of rebellion would be his and his alone, unless of course he was caught. A thought that never entered his head.

He waited until the stroke of midnight before plunging the dagger into his victim's back. Before he died, he bit into the man's neck from behind and drank his hot red blood. Commending himself for not chickening out and with blood still wet on his lips, he pushed the body into a pile of garbage from whence it came. Just another dead homeless person.

With his secret weapon in his pocket, he called his peers. It took five tries to make a connection. Once he was through, however, he told them to meet him at their usual spot.

He had something pivotal to tell them and it was only then that he wiped away the blood from his mouth, before instinctively licking a smudge off the back of his hand.

"Boy, did that ever taste good."

They were already hanging out at the underpass, laughing about the stupid loser, when he spied them in the tunnel. Andy had estimated it would take about half an hour to get there, but luckily, he seemed to have covered the couple of miles in half the time.

"Bonus man."

Before he entered, he stopped and took stock of his passport to greatness. They were stuffed in his pocket. He strode into the underpass. It was time to bare himself to his soon to be disciples, should they be worthy. He prepared to perform the reveal.

A vampire could see clearly at night, move at twice the speed of humans. They would have extended longevity if they could avoid the fatal disadvantages such sunlight, not sleeping in their own coffin and not consuming fresh human blood. Ignorance of these new deadly Achilles' Heels, accounted for the majority of vampire deaths within hours of their genesis.

These weren't the only means by which a vampire could be killed. They were not immortal. A witch of limited power such as Hecate could easily dispatch one.

Witches were female and vampires were male, and neither could bear fruit.

The race of the vampires became little more than a footnote in the history of earthly species with only isolated individuals scraping out a meager living in the New World Order.Their incarnation and passing was almost completely unnoticed, with less than a hundred surviving more than a week.

None, however, was like the Count, and he had the chance to outlive them all if he could determine and heed the rules.

~~~

Humans, who were vastly more populous but lesser mortals when compared with vampires, would soon become an endangered species themselves. The escalating war was no longer teetering on the horizon. Of course, Man just didn't know it. Just like Yan Lee.

Yan Lee lived on the other side of the World, in rural China. He wanted only one thing; to become a dragon. He was a serious and a much-respected man, and it was because of these qualities that a great honor, but also responsibility, had been bestowed upon him.

It took twelve men to form a dragon's body, but only one to carry the head. And this year, Yan had that privilege, the most prestigious position of the dragon.

In keeping with his personality, he remained stoic when told, but inside his heart leapt and he silently vowed to be the best ever. He would win the Dragon Heart contest or never return to his native village as he would not be able to bare the shame.

He hadn't made the stakes any higher than necessary. He'd heard that other past Dragon Heads vowed the same. Yan was proud, so a self-imposed exile would be the least of possible penances.

For a westerner, the whole thing was much ado about nothing. A pole with a large papier-mâché dragon's head was hoisted up in the air. A long train of decorated material covered the rest of the team who followed pretending to be the body of the dragon.

But to Yan, should his dragon win and be recognized as the True Dragon Heart, he'd return to his village a hero. The crops would grow and the harvest would be bountiful. All the Dragon Heads believed this.

To win, one had to become a dragon; think like one, feel like one. When you reached that pinnacle, you evolved to Dragon. When the leader became Dragon, so did the team.Their costumes became skin, the smoke became fire and the head became heart.

The event was upon them before they knew it and they paraded down the crowded narrow streets with firecrackers crackling wildly. As with all the dragon teams, the excitement and intensity of the carnival invaded their bones, their blood and their souls, and Yan's team was no exception.

They were utterly committed to become Dragon, as had their ancestors for generations. And although the team had been in several festivals, none could remember feeling as engrossed as they did this night. With every passing second, their pasts seemed further and further away and less and less important.

They could feel it. They were turning Dragon, and they let it.

And Yarleesin, the Fire Dragon was born. No longer an oversized puppet controlled by human individuals. No longer twelve humans masquerading as a dragon but instead a single monstrous creature.

He roared out a deafening thunderous bellow in jubilation and saw people on the street around him quake in fear. He flicked his head and snatched a man off the street with his massive jaws. He threw him high into the air and swallowed him whole when he descended.

People were too shocked to move. Some thought it was part of an act as they fought disbelief that a real-life dragon was parading in front of them.This delusion was quickly dispelled when the dragon opened his vast jaws and fire shot forth.

Panic swept over them. For many it was too late as a jet of red flame incinerated the slow. Those who dodged their destiny attempted to scramble for cover in the shops and boutiques, hoping that their smell of fear wouldn't betray them.

With bulging eyes, his circular vision saw all around and his wide nostrils easily recognized their scent. The mouthwatering bouquet of the freshly scorched flesh of those he'd just slaughtered lying on the ground provided a reprieve for those in hiding.

His flooded scent glands drove a deep instinct and he devoured the carnage like a gargantuan crocodile, craning his neck sideways to scoop up the screaming wounded into his waiting mouth. But it did nothing to quell his hunger.

He surged into the chaotic panic-stricken crowd and caught one of the strange two-legged creatures. The unfortunate man met his death in his jaws of a hundred razor sharp teeth. Still ravenous, Yarleesin's yellow body elongated like an accordion, as he searched and hungered for further prey.

He crashed into the flimsy bamboo shops and smashed them into matchsticks as he followed the scent of fear. He snapped at the scurrying humans falling over themselves to escape.

It was only when a potential meal was snatched away from him by another dragon, Wanton, the Water Dragon, did he realize he wasn't the only one. Other dragon heads had achieved dragon-hood too, and between him and a score of other beasts, they feasted on hundreds of men devouring them without thought that only an hour earlier they had been one of them.

Supported by his tiny T-Rex wings, Yarleesin magically flew under the Checkered Sun and attempted clumsy flirtations with other beautiful creatures. All refused his advances. They all fell to Earth, and some erupted into gigantic mushroom shaped balls of flame that scared even Yarleesin.

Under the Sun's Blue Green incarnation, Yarleesin's flight became labored and difficult, and was impossible when the Sun returned to its old yellow self. Nonetheless, it wasn't long before Yarleesin reached his prime and weighed over a thousand tons.

But none surpassed the unbelievable bulk of the Sand Dragon, named Salemanter.

Gnawing on roads and buildings as casually as a caterpillar would on a leaf, Salemanter, supported by twenty four pairs of legs, reached an incredible weight in excess of half a million tons. On her massive back, a herd of mountain goats fed on the prairie grass that grew between scales the size of tennis courts.

Whenever she moved, the friction of thousands of tons of shifting sand in her twenty four stomachs caused lightning bolts of green static electricity to crackle all around her.

Moreover, she was the only female dragon as she was the only non-male team in the festival. Many times the males would come to her full of fear and hope. Many times, they did not leave. Queen Salemanter bore them their offspring, and then often crushed, ate or electrocuted them.

~~~

Even at the best of times, life anywhere in the world can be tough. NYC was not an exception, and here, in the epicenter of the 'city that never sleeps', was one of the toughest nuts the town had ever spawned. Killer Klive Karver was that man, and those in Time Square who knew him, knew better than to cross him. The not so innocent "Johns" who tried to pull one over him, didn't do it twice. It's really hard to do from the bottom of the East River. His life was a not so uncommon story of an abused and beaten child, but the product was. At 12, he'd killed his abusive "Dad". By 13, he was running a hustle of a couple of runaway girls. Co-escapees from his orphanage where he'd been sent by a lenient and compassionate magistrate. He wasn't even 15 before he scammed and beat senseless the owner of a paper store van that had been "grandfathered in" and parked in time square.

A couple of cops, Christine and Jock always had an eye on him, but the legitimate business front was all prim and proper, at the back was a different story. That's where his girls did their jobs, and where the johns parted with their money, and sometimes teeth, and sometimes, lives. The word on the street was that Klive was as ruthless and mean as they come, but if you were an 'outta town' tough, bilking a NYC pimp would be a story to boast of in the bars back home. Those bars are still silent.

Klive's van occupied a vendor plot of the Time Square sidewalk and protruded out on to the road and into the gutter. Over a drain it was rumored, so blood could be hosed off out of sight. Adjacent and parallel to it was and unusually marked square manhole cover, where PD Christine regularly spat in a probable unconscious act of disgust at Klive's miserable existence.

A couple of weeks earlier, this time using his crow bar for a legitimate purpose, Kline had heaved open the heavy metal cover with an idea of hiding a body down there, but he'd only opened it a slit when his minders of the PD appeared around the corner and he let the huge plate clang back down into place.

Then as if he'd set something bigger than himself into motion, and he didn't know exactly how many days ago it was, but a city construction detail put a white tarpaulin tent over it. And a man in an orange construction hat had entered, and presumably descended down the hole. Klive may not have remembered the date, but the man he did not, could not forget. Something about him seared his image into Klive's mind, a man who reeked authority and power. Klive, a great study of the human condition, knew a man like that would never dirty his hands on such a menial task, and he looked excited to do so, this was interesting.

Maybe a couple hours passed before he resurfaced, and he looked the opposite upon his return, Fear was the dominant emotion on his face, and where there's fear, there's anger. He gave a large lackey a fierce looked that set him back a step or two, before snapping at the construction workers to dismantle and clean up, and then seemingly disappeared in the constant throng of tourists.

Now Klive was captivated, "Who was this man? What was down that manhole?"

"Hey Guys... Guys..." chortled Klive to the men, as one of Kline's girls strutted her stuff... "$200 bucks for an hour... all of you." Fifty bucks cash never before appeared so quickly out of 4 men's wallets.

With the men out of the way, Klive waltzed into the tent, pried open the square manhole cover and descended, never to be seen again.

~~~

Nobby was a bald five-foot eight ball of muscle. He was tough and would never back down no matter what, but he wasn't all that bright, some would even say dense. He did, however, possess a passionate belief that he was a descendant of the Druids, and so he was adamant that Stonehenge was his ancestral home. He'd been arrested several times for trespass upon the famous grounds, but now, with an impending WWIII, the police had deserted the site. With four or five car loads of likeminded friends, they smashed through the chain-link fence and staked their claim.

Before High-Priest Nobby could even tie the knot on his grey hooded robe, two other Druid sects crashed his inauguration, and trouble was bound to follow.

"Bollicks mate (the customary euphemism for fuck you) I'm the true..."

And a left hook sent him reeling.

He lost sight of his front tooth as he and it both flew through the air and landed on the Altar.

Under a Checkered Sun, Nobby grew to ten foot tall and 1234 pounds (his pin number not his IQ). He got to his feet, lifted his assailant off the ground and with a pile-drive, smashed him into the Altar.

That swallowed him.

As the whole place had erupted into a riot, no one other than Nobby witnessed this.

Enthralled, he picked up the next closest man, caring not whether friend of foe, and did the same. This time the body just crashed on top of the stone in a mangled heap. Running on instinct, Nobby lifted up an adjacent rock, all two tons of it, above his head and smashed the oblong boulder down upon him. Then, with his foot, he shoved the stone off the Altar and saw that the man was gone. Not even blood told of his demise.

Being an *Ogre* amongst men, he would have performed the 'ritual' upon them all, when everything stopped as blinding flash of light lit the sky. A dark mushroom cloud quickly followed, the Londoners in the melee had just lost their homes.

To a man, Nobby included, they dashed for the cars.

Not registering that he was an ogre, and that a bus, not a car from now on, would be his means of transport.

And even that wasn't the case.

Nobby was poleaxed by an invisible force as he tried to exit the stone circumference.

He couldn't leave.

He was indeed 'The True King of the Druids.' But all he could say was:

"Where's me tooth?"

~~~

It wasn't however, the conception of strange and mythical marvels, or even that man's best friend had turned against him, that that made the survival of the human race debatable. It was nuclear, chemical and biological Armageddon. Yet with all the misery plaguing the Earth, not all were in dismay.

The doomsday merchants finally were being proven right. The End of the World was here and they could hold their heads up high and taunt, "I told you so."

It only took an hour-long blackout for civilization to crumble. They said, "Nothing mysterious about that, it was only natural.

Law and order were the intruder, and once in jeopardy, then anarchy quickly reclaimed its rightful position. The true state of man."

With law enforcement stretched to the limit as the lights went out, the fuse on the ticking time bomb of chaos burned fast and bright. With nothing to quench it, total lawlessness returned after its long vacation.

Gangs of thugs roamed over every country, looting, pillaging and raping. Teeth were smashed, blood was spilled, and Hell's vacancies started to shrink.

CHAPTER 50
HOT, NO MATTER WHICH SUN

"It was true." thought Kelly, "he can fly." Laden with the three remaining members of the IAT, Phillip rose off the ground to the amazement of his passengers and headed south.

"Oh my GOD." she screamed as a twenty-foot missile roared narrowly by them. Its rocket engine screamed as if it was in pain.

It dove headlong towards the heart of the Vatican a mile below and on its side was a sign visible to Phillip; a string of numbers beginning with a plus sign and three point one four. Another sign was also on the missile, this one visible to mortals. Radioactivity.

Seconds later, it exploded. Phillip suddenly thought that that was it, that he would die. He knew he was close to being immortal but whether he could survive the epicenter of a nuclear bomb's explosion was questionable. Certainly his passengers wouldn't live.

The rocket was going so fast that it had traveled almost a mile from their initial encounter. That wouldn't save them from a nuclear blast, but it would from a conventional explosion which is what happened. The dynamite used to detonate atomic bombs failed to start the chain reaction and the subsequent nuclear storm.

Phillip broke into a profuse sweat. "Would that atomic bomb have failed under a Yellow Sun? Or possibly worse: under the Checkered Sun?"

He didn't know, but he suspected that the Blue Green Sun had saved them.

Another thing he didn't know was that under the new laws of atomic physics, only plutonium created in a Super Nova was fissionable. From the moment Phillip survived God and *Pi's* attacks, man-made elements were no more.

Nonetheless, the missile didn't completely miss its target. The remaining metallic cylinder smashed exactly into the witch's turret.

Boleyn was suddenly shocked at her good luck and judgment.

Phillip looked at Boleyn and smiled. He hadn't missed the fact that she was lucky, and also, he hadn't seen luck's telltale positive or negative signature upon her either.

"So," he thought, "there's *Pi's* luck, and there's another kind of luck. I guess its nature's neutral luck, just life bumping into life sort of luck, luck. And it can be quite long odds too." As he considered the probabilities, it was clear Boleyn had dodged one gigantic bullet.

With his confidence badly shaken at the close call, Phillip sped up, not wanting to tempt fate a second time. He took a detour around two towering smoke plumes of boiling brimstone, as Mount Etna had joined Vesuvius in another dazzling display of Mother Nature's power. He spied Pompeii in the distance,

"They are going to have company come nightfall. Lots."

Across the World, other volcanos burst into life throwing millions of tons of hot ash into the atmosphere and darkening the sky. Elsewhere the heavens would be filled with severe weather storms that soon would be battering coastlines and tearing up the mid-west plains.

"Were the actions of gods included when the word Armageddon was invented?" wondered Phillip.

Vesuvius's towering tsunami had washed all traces of civilization off Sicilia and Malta, which made Phillip consider them as ideal places to land. But by the time he made the decision, he had crossed the coastline of northern Africa and so he ploughed onward until he saw a string of weather-beaten rocky hills midway towards Egypt. His flight had taken about an hour, and in that time, the World, as we knew it, had ended.

~~~

Pope Gregory and his trusted right-hand man were lying on the floor, thrown there by the impact of the missile fuselage. It was a small crash in reality. All the energy had been expended high above them.

However, the proximity of the whole event shook them to the core. They hadn't believed PhilLIP in their heads, but in their hearts, they weren't so sure.

It was as if the truth pulled their gut into knots of doubt. Now it was too late, clarity is like that, never on time. Greg and Crow exchanged glances, and suddenly they knew that everything Phillip had said was true.

Everything.

"Come on, we've gotta get out of here." They stood up and yelled at the nearest Swiss Guard who was running towards them ready to fulfill his function in life.

"Get the 'copter here, were under attack."

The English held their heads in shame. They heard they'd saved Rome, but essentially started WWIII. The President of Russia wasn't in Moscow when the two missiles rocketed out of the cover of clouds and ignited in gigantic balls of fire.

The city was fried like a piece of bacon. Now Russia was left in a position where they had no choice but to match aggression with aggression, and they launched their attack. The heads of state knew nothing about physics, they were all about sending a message and so Russia's retaliation was threefold larger.

Even with her twenty or so minute lag time; God still had a good enough vantage point to see that the fuse was truly lit and that there was no one with enough power to put it out. It was a good day.

With just a twitch of numbers, *Pi* had several warheads redirected towards China and the stage was set for all the major players to get into the game.

As China responded in kind and launched ten of her own WMD's, Tokyo became the third city in Japan to feel the wrath of nuclear warfare. America was bound by treaty to come to her aid.

Smaller countries didn't escape the eye of *Pi* either, and suddenly the flickering fire of WWIII became a roaring furnace. Rogue nations believed that the US was responsible for their failing technology. Hotheaded despots feared the worse was coming their way, and preempted the envisioned attacks with their own. Contagious gunfire ensued, and although Russia, China and America all attempted to show a smidgen of restraint, it didn't take too long before they all feared that if they didn't attack, it would be too late and they'd be the last and the loser.

By nightfall, thousands of nuclear warheads found their targets with thousands of others still waiting to be launched. For the first time, it became apparent to everyone that the true size and extent of Man's arsenals seemed almost endless. Man really was mad!

Only a small fraction of them went off, but between the collapsing buildings and over a thousand mushroom shaped fireballs, earthquakes, volcanos and tsunamis, the human death toll was already in the hundreds of millions and climbing rapidly.

It had taken centuries for Europe to become the wondrous continent of culture, art and architecture, and now it was lost forever. Likewise, the great cities of the rest of the World were going up in smoke as well.

God and *Pi* redirected the means of destruction towards locations where they anticipated Phillip might be or arriving at. Due to Phillip, Italy was now a smoldering wasteland with Rome as its epicenter.

There wasn't any hope of survival for anyone. The helicopter the Pope and his ministers boarded was destroyed in the ensuing bombardment of Rome by God's and *Pi's* redirected nuclear assault. Their last thoughts were those of resentment, disbelief and regret; *if only they hadn't called the IAT.*

Just as God and *Pi* wished, WWIII was in progress and a major cull of the human race was in full flight. Even though many missiles didn't find their targets, and many bombs failed to go nuclear, a quarter of the arsenals did. Not a single country had escaped numerous nuclear explosions and millions upon millions of people, all innocent of any connection to Phillip, had perished.

Phillip and his solemn passengers, descended down to kite height over the Sahara. Phillip had taken them to a tiny oasis called the Yellow River, where a handful of small crocodiles and other exotic creatures waited for extinction at the hands of man. A wait that now had a chance of being substantially longer than expected only a month ago.

With eyes wide open, Phillip performed a perfect gentle landing and let the windswept passengers disembark as if they were just exiting a cruise ship. He didn't even have to think about making his cape vanish; it just did.

It was blistering hot and humid in the tiny canyon where the stream rose up from years of hiding underground. For the mortals, the warmth was initially welcomed as it was in complete contrast to the frigid high-altitude air of their maiden flight.

Phillip hadn't been inconsiderate though. He remembered that he was once human like his cargo of mortals and they would feel bone chilling cold and dizziness should he fly too high. Boleyn thought Kelly would produce some sort of derogatory remark on Phillip's choice of hiding. To her dismay, none came.

She couldn't help thinking,"Was it true, did she really love him?"

Kelly appeared happy with Phillip's selection as she patted her hair back into place and embraced the warmth by tilting her fine-featured face backwards like a movie star.

"God, she was gorgeous." thought the brewing Boleyn,"She has everything. Even when she's all disheveled. I hate her and God and everyone. Everything."

Once a debonair statesman, Ross made little effort to reclaim his old station, choosing instead to remain looking rough and windswept.

Phillip didn't need to shake himself down, not that he cared anyway. Instead, he was perplexed, because Kelly was looking at him in an unusual way, one of respect and of love. He wasn't used to having this attention from anyone, let alone from a beautiful girl. All he knew was that he was really short. He didn't know that his plain looks now possessed that undefinable quality, confidence.

Strangely, Phillip was further than ever before from being human, yet his thoughts were the closest he'd ever had to being just that. Quite in contrast to the super mortals, they rarely felt anything akin to humility. WWIII was proof. He'd just witnessed the terrible length God would go to kill him. (Maybe though this was human like... self-preservation, (self-centered, self-absorbed, selfish, self-...)).

His friends were now true believers of Phillip and staunch disbelievers of God, of her ethics not her being.

"Ok." he said breaking the ice and commanding their attention. "We don't have a plan, and we don't have a plan because we don't know what we're doing. Are we just trying to survive, or are we going to... fight?

And when I say we, I mean me. Am I going to fight? And if so, how?

Or if we're going to flee. If so, where?"

"Can you fight God, Phillip?" asked Kelly, excited by the possibility of proving God's inferiority to man. Everyone waited for an answer.

"I don't know." was his disappointing answer.

But Kelly expected nothing less. It was Phillip with an honest answer, as always. There was no wild gun wielding charge, no "Let's do this", no reckless and insulting banter, just plain forthrightness.

"Before I jump to conclusions, forget everything I just said.
Does anyone have any ideas? Kelly, Boleyn, Ross."

It was the first time Phillip had used Kelly's name with a tone of affection. She cooed and replayed it over in her mind, forgetting he was asking for serious responses. This might as well have applied to all of them however.

No one said anything, leaving an unusually quiet moment that allowed them to contemplate that millions were already dead, and that they died as collateral damage in God's effort to kill Phillip.

He was the one they were conspiring with, the one whose side they had taken. Had he done the decent thing and turned himself in, then it was entirely possible that all those deaths could have been avoided. Kelly knew Phillip better than he knew himself, and she knew with one hundred percent certainty, that he was having the same thought.

"PHILLIP!" she yelled and grabbed hold of him in case he jetted off as he had done that time when they were on their way to Salem. Surprising her, he looked straight into her eyes and said, "It's not my fault. I have a right to live, and it's not me that's killing them, its God and *Pi*. I..."

She grabbed him and kissed him in front of everyone and he kissed her back. Kissing Kelly was love and he was experiencing it truly for the first time. When they separated, Ross smiled.

Boleyn was fuming, because she'd developed a crush for Phillip after he'd survived her last attempt on his life. She hadn't realized it, but it had taken hold of her the moment she tried to leave with the disgruntled Pope. It was the reason she deserted him and rejoined Phillip and his heretics on that windswept rooftop. Now however, she felt she had good reason to hate Phil, and even more reason to hate Kelly.

"It's just my fucking luck and sodding doomed life." she admonished herself, "just when I was having hope. And of all people, her. She could have anyone; Phillip is more my size than hers. It's not fucking fair."

Boleyn descended deep into herself, hoping that God would find them and nuke them, not caring that Hell was her next port of call.

It was time for Ross to take the lead.

"It's hot, and we've got to make a plan, sorry. Phillip? Kelly? Boleyn?" said Ross as he took a step closer to the creek.

Boleyn was so pissed off she could have spit. She was last in line again.

"Well." said Phillip reacquiring control and making Kelly proud.

"It is hot and STOP" screamed Phillip. He saw streams of numbers suddenly wrap around Ross's left arm, with a negative sign at its fore. Ross slowly retraced his steps backwards, deliberately and restrained, like stepping backwards through a minefield.

He had heeded Phillip's cry of alarm, and wondered why he'd shouted. The numbers on Ross vanished. Obviously to Phillip, something dangerous was near or in the river.

"There." said Phillip, pointing to a tiny ripple.

"What?" said Ross, and then he saw the head of a small snake floating on the surface, waiting deathly still for any unsuspecting animal, or human, to venture that shade too close to him.

"God, I mean hell. That was close." exclaimed Ross, hastily backing away to a safer, much safer distance. "Thanks Phillip, you s…, how did you know, I mean, it was basically invisible."

"It was *Pi*, I saw negative numbers on you, the numbers are always PI, 3.14…, so it's a sign that *Pi* is giving you bad luck. For you. It's also bad luck for us, 'cause that means she'll be tipping off God and they'll be trying to kill us ASAP. How long have we been here?"

"'bout half an hour." smiled Kelly warmly. "Time flies…" joked Ross.

It seemed completely natural now when Phillip made these incredible statements, and unquestioningly, they took what he said for gospel. Ross, who felt most relieved that Phillip could see bad luck coming, asked a question.

"So, if *Pi* took thirty minutes to find us, if we were to hide, where could we? Because *Pi* has found us here in a jiffy. So we'll have to move on soon. And then again, and again, and again."

"Well Ross, even if I left you, they would incidentally kill you thinking that I was with you, and" said Phillip without any drama, "it also means another thing, God will know where we are in about ten, fifteen minutes time and after Pi finds us… Wait. Ross. I think you said it. There is a hiding place that no one can find us. Although no one's going to like it."

"I did? When?" he queried. "Just then." replied Phillip. "Forget all that." interrupted Kelly, "Where?"

"*Hell.*"

CHAPTER 51

GO TO HELL

Their reaction was hardly surprising, at first it was utter silence and then it became shock.

"Hell! Are you crazy?" But the reaction wasn't unanimous.
Boleyn, who was already destined there, actually liked the idea.

And after thinking about it, she saw the beauty of it too.

"Who would think of looking there? Well, maybe God, but God doesn't live there. I guess, I mean, that's what we've been led to believe. As for me. I'm going there already, so what do I care. Wow. I wonder if Kelly would go, if she doesn't, I'll be alone with Phillip."

"OK." said Boleyn, snapping out of her self-imposed exile. "It sounds like a great idea." And with this sudden vocal support for Phillip, everyone turned and looked at Boleyn wondering what was going on.

She wanted to say 'What?', but she saw that that would reveal her inner thinking, so she quickly made a cover story.

"Maybe he can even defeat the Devil. Who knows? Imagine. Then… then Hell would be ours, I don't know, but we can't go on running forever. So, so, I'm in." said Boleyn, raising the bar, and hoping, expecting, the other two to duck.

"Where ever you go Phillip, I'll go too." said Kelly.

Boleyn hardly recognized her voice let alone the person speaking. "Where was me, me, me? What happened to her? Who is she?" thought Boleyn perplexed and ready to hate her further.

Phillip, too, was dumbfounded,

"She was ready to go to Hell with him?" he had no idea how she even liked him let alone loved him. He was so small, how could she? Yet somehow, from the moment he decided to put her behind him and not give up an inch of himself for her, after he'd yelled in anger at her and that he'd confessed he'd slept with an angel, she wanted him.

He didn't have a chance in understanding her. He had no experience with women.

Ross, however, was thinking.

"Phillip, are you sure? I mean... err..." mumbled Ross, voicing his opinion "Phillip, you want us to go to Hell? I mean, don't we have to be dead?"

"No." replied Phillip.

"Boleyn can get us in."

"What?" cried out Boleyn,

"What?
HOW?"

Suddenly, she couldn't make eye contact with anyone. "Could it be that Phillip knew what was going on? What she had done?"

"Boleyn. Did you sell your soul to the Devil?" "Yes." she said quietly.

"Yes, but ..." objected Ross and Kelly together before Phillip quickly raised his hand asking them to hush.

"Boleyn?" repeated Phillip with the utmost compassion. His voice was like truth serum.

The tears came so quickly it took them off guard. Unable to hold it in anymore, she blurted out how she had once again summoned the Devil, and how once again, he'd betrayed her.

"Frank the Lip? The man who raped you, all those years ago?" repeated Ross, speaking with obvious deep remorse.

"Yes." she sobbed.

Ross wanted to say "Now, now." but thought better of it as he saw how demeaning it would surely sound, so he said nothing and left it to Phillip.

"Boleyn. Sorry to ask, but you know something. You've met someone no one else, other than myself, has ever met. You've met Lady Luck."

Bending down to her size, which wasn't too much, he persisted. "Can you tell us about your encounter. Your... your meeting with 'Luck'the Queen of Spades. Back there in ClearStream. Please."

Between gulps and sobs, Boleyn started her embarrassing story of deception. Hers upon Phillip and *Pi's* upon her. It was a long story, but everyone insisted that she not skip or gloss over any part of it, and when she finished, she had the full sympathy of everyone.

She had stopped her crying, but at any moment, with the slightest provocation it was quite likely to start up again. A silence, interrupted only by the sounds of the insect wildlife, surrounded them and the longer it went on, the worse it got.

Suddenly, Boleyn burst into a torrent of soul crushing sobbing, enough to melt anyone's heart.

"I'm sorry Phillip. I'm sorry I tried to kill you. I'm sorry I sold my soul to the Devil. I just wanted to be a witch again. I just wanted to be a person again. Someone real, someone feared. Someone loved." It was a most heart wrenching confession.

For the first time since Ross, Kelly and Phillip had known Boleyn they saw the true childlike nature of Boleyn; the Boleyn who existed before her parents died, before they were killed. They saw the girl before the Devil, before Frank the Lip, the girl that existed when her father and mother were cobblers, innocent and hopeful.

They all crouched down and hugged her, although due to their size differences it was awkward for everyone, even for Phillip. Nonetheless, his new shortness made his hug the most enduring and consoling.

"I wish I...." started Boleyn.

"Remember the "O"s in the Entanglement Passage Boleyn." said Phillip.

"Yes..."

"Well... There was a secret passage in that secret passage."

"Ooooooo
Ooooo, ooo ooooo ooo oooo,
oooo ooooo o ooooo oooo oo.
O
oooo ooo oooo, ooo
O'o
oooooo, ooo ooooo, ooo
O ooo."

Boleyn went into convulsions. Her body jerked and buckled, but Phillip held fast and refused to let her go even after she started to thrash so badly that he was scared she would harm herself. She squirmed and writhed for almost a minute, until he saw that she was approaching a climax.

Like a rabid dog, foam started to collect around the corners of her mouth, then, finally, it happened. Her mouth stretched wide open and a person oozed out of it like a snake eating a huge meal only in reverse.

Ross and Kelly stood back in disgust as Frank the Lip materialized not quite out of thin air. In rags for clothes, Frank laid prostate on the warm Saharan sand like a new born piglet.

Too shocked to say anything, Ross and Kelly stood with their mouths wide open. Kelly had complete confidence in Phillip, who in her mind could do anything now, and she was exceedingly happy that she'd made the right choice.

The exorcism of Frank the Lip was only a steppingstone for Phillip; it was what he carried that interested Phillip, something dark, black and evil.

At that moment, an unnaturally searing hot wind gusted, and with a quick look to the horizon, they saw a massive sand storm about to bear down on them. Instantly, everyone knew they were under attack.

Phillip collected his partners into separate pockets of his flowing cloak, and ensured that the exhausted and faint Boleyn was wrapped caringly and snuggly in with the nursing Ross. The comatose Frank the Lip was in a tight and secure encasing. As for Kelly, he placed her close to his ear, close enough to touch, close enough to kiss.

The tornado strength winds tore into them as they rose up through the epicenter, but Phillip was undaunted as he ploughed through the buffeting wind, hardly noticing them as he had other things on his mind.

They kissed and caressed, and she couldn't believe it, but his body felt like the most muscle-bound man she'd ever seen and imagined touching. Raising to a high enough altitude above the storm, they made love under the Blue Green Sun, and they entered the mile high club as its last inductees.

S

Rhom

n

g

Up until this moment, inside his skull, a fragment of Joan's cross had floated aimlessly between the two halves of his brain. As his SongRhom erupted, the tiny splinter's orientation changed and lodged in a single pivotal position connecting and providing a new path between the two hemispheres.

Phillip suddenly felt more complete than at any time in his life. His body didn't change, nor his soul, but his mind did. His fragile constitution was tempered with inner confidence and its source was the total submission of the woman of his dreams.

Flying high above the tempest, he flew off in the opposite direction to the storm. Minutes later he changed course to what he hoped was a random bearing, fearing that his original direction was too predictable.

Kelly, however, cared for nothing anymore. She was ready to die.
Phillip was all she would ever want from this moment on.

They hadn't decided where they should head with their sudden escape. But Phillip wanted to go somewhere away from water as *Pi's* attacks always seemed to stem from there.

Also they needed to be somewhere outside of Europe, as Man's WMDs were heavily trained upon it.The Sahara Desert still seemed the best option, so he backtracked across the vast wasteland and landed in the outskirts of the Atlas Mountains in North Eastern Africa.

This time when he landed, it was as if he'd been flying all his life. It was smooth and effortless, and the passengers felt the mastery of it too. Even whilst making love, or maybe because of it, Phillip had guided their flight through the mini-typhoon in an assured and instinctive manner.

Now, however, it was time for serious thoughtful deliberation. "Ok, Kelly, Boleyn, Ross." said Phillip. He didn't dare preamble,

so he spoke quickly so he wouldn't lose track. Kelly struggled to maintain an even equilibrium and not burst into uncontrollable laughter.

"In our flight here, I felt something." The loving glances exchanged by the couple caused Ross and Boleyn to hold back their gag reflex. It was obvious that something had happened up there in the heavens.

Ross didn't take it personally however, whereas Boleyn was trying to fend off the jealousy she felt. It had the effect of giving her a full recovery from the exorcism, but it wasn't particularly what she wanted. Then it got worse. Phillip unraveled the tail of his cape and Frank the Lip tumbled out onto the gray slabs of Saharan rock.

He came round.

With a splutter and a cough, Frank the Lip opened his eyes expecting to see the plane of Hell, and couldn't believe that he saw the World and its amazing Blue Sky.

His eyes grew wider and wider as disbelief rocked his very being, daring not to think the unthinkable. He dared himself and took his first inhalation with the caution of a man returning from space. Soon he was gasping and not because he was short of breath, but to confirm that he was truly Topside.

"MY GODs. I'mth... I'mth...on Earth. I'mth... not in Hell. My GOD. I'mth..."

He had sat up and was beginning to take in the enormity of this miracle, when reality bit him. Unknown to Frank, his host had heard his cries of glee and the sound of his lisp energized her into action. The others'eyes were fixated on Frank the Lip and didn't notice that Boleyn was making a beeline for him.

He didn't get to finish his final inhalation before Boleyn began kicking and punching the cowering Frank who curled up tighter than a hedgehog. She fulfilled her prophesy, "Just when you think you're free of me..." when she had spared his life on becoming a witch. With his eyes squeezed shut, Boleyn pummeled him with every ounce of energy. There were many past reasons to hate him and now there was a new but obscure one. He was the catalyst that forced Phillip and Kelly together.

Being fresh out of Hell, Frank didn't know whom or what was assaulting him. There were so many to choose from, on Earth and Hell. Curled up and with eyes tightly closed, he took the battering until Phillip intervened and gently pulled Boleyn away.

He was not trying to save Frank, but to stop Boleyn from hurting herself. He consoled her saying that he understood, and that he'd let her continue if it wasn't out of his concern for her. He was the only one there who could have done what he did.

Had Ross or Kelly attempted it, she would have exploded. But Boleyn knew that Phillip too had suffered and endured torment, some of it at her own hands. It didn't do anything to stop her falling even harder for him as his touch was so compassionate, firm and yet gentle.

While Phillip calmed Boleyn down, Ross and Kelly watched over Frank as he gradually unrolled himself and joined life on Earth. He was wiping his face when he saw the source of his beating, he saw Boleyn.

There wasn't a second wasted in recognition. He knew who she was instantly. He quickly regained his feet and then he burst into a torrent of abuse in voice and gesture.

Even after the towering Ross spoke firmly to him, Frank continued shouting and shaking his clenched fists in her direction. Only when Kelly blindsided him with a vicious slap across his face did he stop.

Then Kelly's eyes focused back on Phillip.

Trusting Boleyn not to attack Frank again, Phillip let her go and he approached Frank who was looking down at him with contempt because of his size.

"My name is Phillip, and I presume yours is Frank the Lip." and he extended his hand. Frank refused to take it, but Phillip didn't take any offence. He'd only offered it as a peace offering, not in friendship.

Unfortunately, and with all pleasantries aside, time was ticking, so he continued.

"This is Kelly and Ross."He gave a stupid facial expression at Ross's introduction and Kelly wanted to slap him again as he stared at her.

He was a man who'd escaped Hell. His behavior and demeanor made it easy to see why he was there. Phillip could completely understand Boleyn's reaction. He was so crude, ignorant and boorish, that Phillip regretted pulling Boleyn off.

Kelly gave Phillip's arm a little tug and he looked upwards.The Sun blazed a brilliant bright white with massive black spots that merged, separated and rejoined. They moved back and forth over the Sun's surface like bacteria in an immense petri dish.It was time to get moving.

A gentle gust of wind from the north told them things were already in motion, hundreds of miles away. The burning acid from the two erupting volcanos would be falling their way in due course, which would be the least of their worries as any missiles, nuclear or otherwise would all be turned in their direction.

Knowing all of this didn't deter Phillip. He needed input from the others and specific direction and advice from Ross. He placed Boleyn diametrically opposite to Frank with themselves in between them to act like a wall.

Only after he ordered them to be silent did their taunting stop. Frank was oblivious to what was going on, but didn't dare ask as the little man's orders had hurt his ears and left them ringing.

"Ross." Phillip asked, knowing he'd spent his life studying ancient history, "Ross, is there anywhere… is there an entrance to Hell. Anywhere? Here on Earth."

Ross meditated on this critical question. Frank's face showed shock and a fear of impending doom, as he couldn't understand who would want to know such a thing.

"Take your time Ross." said Phillip trying to lessen the pressure of time passing, and only a few seconds later, he rattled off a list of places.

"Hell's Gate. BC, Canada; Hell's Door, Belgium; The Nine Gates, Spain; the Step Pyramid, Egypt; The Blackened Hole, Paraguay; and the Hole of Death, Russia."

"OK. Ross. Which do you think?"

"None of them." replied Ross, dashing the hope in Phillip's voice. "None?"

"None.

They're too popular, too blatant, we've met the Devil, Phillip, and you know he'd never be so crass. If it's going to be anywhere, it's going to be somewhere with… with taste, but not some obtuse place either, but somewhere that he'd consider clever, a little smug.

I don't know, somewhere, not ostentatious, but somewhere, that if you looked closely, you'd realize that it's very, very suave. Like one of those beautiful buildings in Rome, but not one that tourists go too, but one that's nestled in-between others and easily overlooked by the non-sophisticated eye."

"Wow." said Phillip,"You're absolutely right, Ross? Anyone? Ideas?"

"But." said Ross, "The building has to have been built around the fourth century."

"What, why?" blurted out Kelly.

"Because, that was when Hell was made, before that, it didn't exist."

"Really." said Boleyn, who became suddenly keenly interested, thinking, if it had a creation date, maybe there was an expiration date too. Frank's ears perked up too, this *was* interesting.

"Yes, other religions didn't have a Hell. So when Christianity became more organized, Hell, and probably Heaven came into existence. That's why I think we should be looking for a building from around that time."

"Well." said Phillip, "Most of those were in Italy and that's basically gone now. So, where else can we look?"

A sad silence ensued as Ross was thinking, and no one else had any ideas at all. With all eyes on him, he looked down at Phillip, and said, "Greece?"

"OK, then." said Phillip, "Let's go. We've been here long enough."

Endeavoring to minimize the amount of time over water, Phillip decided to get to Greece via the Straits of Gibraltar. This was a path where he could hop over the narrow ribbon of ocean when crossing from Africa to Europe.

Flying at an altitude that wouldn't harm his friends, he looked left then right, then left again and then made his mad dash when he thought that the Queen of Spades wasn't looking. Only by enveloping his passengers and himself in a ball of his Shoes' suede did they escape the glare of *Pi's* eyes.

Safely in Europe, he looked back at Africa and was spellbound to see that the whole continent was slowly shifting away from Europe and towards India.

"Maybe" he thought, "the two hunters anticipated an escape back through Europe and they were broadening the Straits of Gibraltar. He could see it was already over fifty yards wider than it was before they crossed. Clearly *Pi* would have a better chance of spotting a leap over the gulf now than just moments ago. They'd crossed just in time. As he turned his head back to resume their journey and incidentally looked over the township below. Old and weathered buildings filled his sight and amongst them something spiked his curiosity. It deserved closer investigation. Without notifying or asking permission of anyone, unlike Phil of old, he changed course and landed close to the structure. Only then did he answer the question everyone was silently asking,

"Why are you stopping here?"

"Look." And they looked, but did not see. "God likes circles. I've read her writings; I've sang a song of circles to rid Boleyn of Frank, but the thing is, when the Devil attacked me, I felt squares.

And when I passed through the Entanglement War, the one up there, God's Entanglement verses the Devil's Entanglement, again his felt of squares. That's why I've stopped."

Now they saw it, a square building,

The Square Building.

It seemed to be hidden, but not cowering, at the furthest edge of a cluster of old baroque church buildings. It stood out to Phillip because there was nothing baroque about it. Ornate and highly adorned with statues and carvings were its neighboring ecclesiastical erections. They boasted and fought each other for attention, but were pompous and pretentious. This small undecorated cubic edifice located on the periphery, held its own countenance without aid of embellishment.

Built from blocks of yellow and tan stone, honed straight smooth and square it stood alone at the back like a boss watching over his staff. It backed into the sheer rock cliff of the famous Rock behind it, not needing the attentions of meaningless humans. In plain sight, strong, stout and secret, it remained resolute against its only enemy, time.

Four windows, two on the ground floor and two on the upper were bricked over with the same clean stone. It seemed to have been built that way from the beginning. Perfectly centered was a single large gleaming black lacquered double door that announced its address, 416.

"What if Ross." said Phillip,"What if that isn't the address, but the date it was built?"

Ross wasn't listening though. He knew this number all too well, as its inception went all the way back to his distant relative, Curator Allan, and back further to the Devil himself. It was the Devil's number, not 666, but 614.

Ross was the least enthusiastic about venturing into Hell, but he'd agreed to it as a deep-down belief told him that an entrance to Hell couldn't be found. It was all the more poignant that it was he who'd described the features that a building should have in order to meet the Devil's exacting requirements.

"Ross, Ross?" asked Phillip, as all the color had drained out of his face and it looked like he was going to faint.

"This is it." he said gravely, "It's his building, because that's his number, look, 6, 1, 4. Phillip, you've found it… unfortunately…

Look at the building, could there be a better match? And its location, the place the Neanderthals went extinct. Wonder if he had something to do with that?"

As it turned out, no one believed in Phillip's idea, not even he. Now, as he looked at the others faces, he could see they all knew it too. They stood in front of the building's front door that would lead them into Hell. Everyone couldn't help but find it terrifying.

For the first time since the desert, Frank, was getting the meaning of their quest.

"Wass theyth crazy, they want to go to Hell."

"Ok Frank." said Phillip, "Give it to me."

"What. Give you what?"

"The key that's in your pocket."

After his last attack, Phillip was able to see more clearly into Boleyn's infection than ever before, and he'd seen something dark inside the entity lurking inside Boleyn's soul.

The Black that once polluted Boleyn, wasn't Frank the Lip, it was what he carried. He knew that the evil he'd seen in Boleyn's body was now in the pocket of her nemesis. He knew it was a key. The key, Phillip thought, would open this door in front of them and would gain their entry to Hell.

"What key? What you talking about?"

Phillip knew the longer they stood at this spot, the sooner God and *Pi* would discover their location and then the ruse would be up. Frank was playing the innocent and Phillip didn't have time for it.

He grabbed Frank's arm with more strength than he would have dreamed possible from such a slight looking frame, and pulled the key out of his pocket. Frank threw a hail of fists into Phillip's face not knowing the Pope and Crow had done very much the same and ended up with similar outcomes.

"Come on let's go." shouted Phillip. He put the key into the keyhole, and bumped his head onto the shut door. The door hadn't opened.

"What? Oh No. The key's not working."

"Hah Haaath." squealed Frank the Lip as he taunted and teased like an infant, *"Turn the key clockwise, one complete turn, no more, no less.* Turn the…"

"What?" said Phillip turning to look at the giddy Frank, "I turned…"

"Maybe it's not the right key. Maybe this one is?" said Ross,
holding up a key of his own.

"What?" said Phillip in wonder recognizing the key that Joan had around her waist. "Where did you get that from?"

"The Pope." he replied, with a broad smile.

"I… relieved him of it when Paul was shot." beamed Ross.

Letting Ross have the honor, Phillip watched the key fit smoothly into the lock and it turned effortlessly. They'd filed through the open half of the double door in a second, a little longer for one particular man.

Phillip was never a mean person, but although he'd only known Frank for minutes, he'd developed an intense dislike for him. All his life Phillip had been a good judge of character; however, he'd never had the confidence to trust it and had always let the opinions of others override his own.

Now, however, it was a different matter and from Frank the Lip's behavior alone, Phillip could see he was a complete reprobate with no redeeming qualities.

"Besides that, he'd raped a tiny innocent girl and ruined her life (and possibly death) forever. If God couldn't have mercy on Boleyn and stop her going to Hell, then well, God can stick it too." thought Phillip. "We'll hide in Hell, and somehow, I'll figure how to get us out of this mess if it's the last thing I do. So help me G... so help me ME."

So when Phillip gave the order to get inside, he'd also grabbed hold of Frank's hair, knowing that if he was going to make a run for it, then it would be now.

It came as a surprise to Phillip how much joy he derived from returning him to his rightful place, kicking and screaming.

With all present and correct, Phillip pushed the door closed and sealed their fate. It wasn't a moment too soon as the headwaters of the resulting tsunami from Africa's movement washed up against it. In that water, a searching *Pi* was looking. An earthly Hell was lapping up against the outside of the building, and inside, the official Hell beckoned. The definition of 'Between a rock and a hard place.'

If there was a way to turn back, they couldn't see it.

CHAPTER 52

UTTER DESTRUCTION

God checked the logs with every influx of new arrivals in Heaven, and there were a lot. The death toll across the World was mounting, and it would continue to increase for a long time to come. Even with less than five percent of the atom bombs detonating at their targets designated by man, millions of people had died.

Even with Rome being nothing more than a steaming pile of rubble, Heaven remained depressingly Phillip free. Nothing stood complete anymore, not only in Italy, but also for most of Europe.

The rest of the World was close behind. The chemical and biological weapons of mass destruction complemented the nuclear holocaust.They too were also only about five percent effective as for the most part, their new atomic structures rendered the manmade poisons and diseases impotent.

Again, however, the law of large numbers won out. With millions of tons of each type released, the net effect was still deadly. Populations were decimated across the Modern World with only remote and low-density areas of Earth remaining relatively unscathed. God recognized this, so *she* accelerated tectonic plate movements.

Australia's collision with China would have taken millions of years. Now its impact would take a meager couple of thousand, and its journey there would tear the island continent apart decimating life on its liquefying hinterlands. The Asian and African plates too where lubricated. Their titanic forces would ignite long dormant volcano chains, as Earth became hell-bound with an awakened desire to return to the one gigantic Super Continent as it had once been in the long ago past. Only because these things were destined for in a distant future, could *she* set in motion now.

God knew Phillip's soul was unique, and that *Pi*, along with the Devil, were most interested in laying their hands on it,

"The stupid Devil believes he actually has it already." *she* sneered. Nonetheless, *she* still hoped her assumption that *Pi* had just as much trouble as her in locating his soul was right, and that the normal course of events would carry it to Heaven for her sole *imprisonment. (Not something normally associated with Heaven)*.

On high alert, God investigated everyone with any derivation or phonetic likeness of his name and dismissed all other guests as nuisances. *She* hoped her hypothesis was correct and that *Pi* hadn't snapped up Phillip. It still appeared that he wasn't dead yet, as no one of his description had entered the Kingdom of Heaven.

As a precaution, *she* double and treble checked all the new inductees hoping against hope that he had been admitted but just hadn't been recognized upon entry. *She* had some reason to believe that this was possible, as *she'd* seen pricks of light of Kelly and Ross flitter over two different and distant parts of the Sahara Desert, but now, nothing.

If they were dead then Phillip would be dead too. So *she* started to go over the logs, examining the names of Kelly and Ross as well. Harry was already in Heaven, but he already thought Phillip was there and was expecting to join him.

No help there.

God wasn't panicking, well, that's what *she* said.

The Devil's Entanglement barrier caused a round trip delay of twenty minutes, ten minutes for her desired actions to get to Earth and ten minutes to see their result. Earth, not the Sun, was the center of the Entanglement War. This meant the Sun was like a satellite of Earth as people once believed. However, this didn't change the fact that it takes eight minutes for light to travel from the Sun to Earth.

It did, however, mean that Mercury's orbit would take it outside of the ten-minute Entanglement boundary in due course.

God was most interested in Mercury.

She believed Hell was located there. As luck would have it, Mercury's ascendency was due in less than a day. *She* had *Pi* to thank for that.

Putting Mercury aside, God was regretful that the ten minutes couldn't be less, because its resulting delay still caused considerable obfuscation. Although *she* was in constant communication with *Pi,* synchronizing the war still led to some confusion. It did however give God some insight into *Pi's* wellbeing.

She got the impression that *Pi* was just as perplexed with Phillip as *she* was. *She* could see *Pi's* atoms were dysfunctional at least half of the time, but *she* also wondered if there was something else alarming about Phillip from *Pi's* point of view. "Why else is *Dia* being so cooperative?"

Never in their long history had their collaboration been so aligned and so freely offered. Nevertheless, both weren't being completely honest with each other, not wanting to be perceived as weak or vulnerable. And both were feeling the same thing.

For the first time, they were experiencing the same doubts as man, the unknown and the future. Unlike humans who never knew where or when death would arrive, these two even never considered that their end was conceivable until as of late.

Worried, God's lengthening list of concerns didn't stop there. The transformation of peoples' fantasies into reality, such as vampires, dragons and the occasional ogre, was troubling, especially because *she* didn't have any part of their inception and so *she* couldn't keep track of them easily.

They appeared like an image in a strobe light, but a very slow one. Nor did *she* understand how any of it happened, but neither did *she* care. *She* only contemplated what *she* believed was the root cause.

Phillip was proving more than a handful and he was deserving of her hatred.

~~~

Kelly handed her key ring torch to Phillip without him even asking. Their hands touched in the exchange, sending chills down each other's spines. Kelly was stunned. She had had many lovers, but none had elicited such feelings.

He flicked it on and confirmed what they'd seen when the door was open, nothing. He scanned the unfurnished room and saw five sconces, one each side of the door and one in the middle of the other walls.

Everyone saw the large black lever next to the entrance door and was terrified at what Phillip would do next.

"Well, either it opens the door back to Earth, or it opens the door to Hell. Here goes." He grabbed hold of it before anyone had time to object.

Above the unified screams of "No." Phillip wrenched it downwards.

The sconces burst into flame casting shadows of themselves over the walls and ceiling. Other than highlighting the fact that the room was a featureless, empty space, nothing else happened. There was nothing in there and although it wasn't what they wanted; their sighs of relief were plainly audible.

"Are your sure this is it?" asked Ross.

"Err…" started Phillip, "it err…" he was going to say he heard a click noise from the center of room. But Kelly had already come to his defense.

"The key worked so it must be."

Frank had stopped swearing, and smiled in defiance when Phillip looked at him for conformation. He didn't know anything. His shrugged shoulders were one of the few honest things he'd ever done.

Ross now asked Phillip the question that perhaps he should have asked on the other side of that door. "Now what?"

It wasn't an accusation, but it did suggest that Phillip could be wrong. However, Phillip knew he was right.

He *couldn't* feel God's, *Pi's* and even the Devil's eyes sweeping from side to side looking for them. It was only the absence of the noise that made him realize that he could feel it in the first place.

He knew he was right; he knew what had to be done, he knew it all along. *From the momenthefound out that Frank the Lip was inside Boleyn, from the time he spied The Key's Black, and from the instant he realized that God wouldn't be able to see them in Hell.*

Now the three things became clear to him, they said to him that this was the right course, that there might possibly be a destiny that no one could foretell - not God, not *Pi,* not the Devil. And certainly not him. Most definitely not him. Phillip was not a prophet, he couldn't foresee the future, and believed that actually no one could.

Another opinion took form.

He dearly hoped that destiny and freewill would share the same properties of the quantum, where all outcomes exist until a resolution is fulfilled. He hoped they were choosing the right one, the only one in which they'd survive,

They weren't in Hell yet, but the lever had confirmed this was the starting place of somewhere. Following his gut feeling, he felt without a shadow of a doubt this was the only course of action available.

He spoke with utmost conviction, without his magic voice

"We're going to the deepest, darkest, dreaded place in the Universe. Where is that Frank?"

"It'sth the the Ninths Level,The The Devil'sth Jail."stuttered Frank.

"We're going, Kelly, Boleyn and Ross.We're going to The Devil's Jail. Oh, and by the way, Frank, you're taking us there."

It was their bravest hour. They all rallied to Phillip's stirring speech, except for Frank. To him the difference between heroism and foolishness was only a matter of opinion. He believed that they were being beyond stupid, and with Hell, there was no look before you leap.

As it was his idea to go to Hell, he felt obliged to lead the way, so Phillip boldly took the initiative. He took a step forward towards the middle of the room without waiting for encouragement or moral support; it was his to set the example.

He was also sure that the little square inch wide hole in the middle of the floor wasn't there when they entered. Just as he stepped forward, Frank realized this was his last chance to escape, because he felt a familiar prickliness that he recognized. He felt it only in one particular place, Hell.

He turned round and pulled frantically at the door in a vain attempt to escape. Using his feet against the doors, he yanked at the two large door handles. They pulled right off. He crashed to the floor and not one person bothered to suppress their laughter as it was so incredibly funny, except for Frank who looked inexplicitly terrified.

Their joviality suddenly stopped dead in its tracks as they saw something horrific. Now they understood Frank's panic.

Black sludgy water started to burble up from the hole in the middle of the room. He dropped the two handles to the floor. He was seeing the last thing in the World he wanted to see.

"Itsth the Styx."

It touched Phillip first.

CHAPTER 53

INNOCENCE

"My G.." Ross found himself rugby tackled to the ground by Frank.

"Yer can't say that downs 'ere." And he'd forced his hand over Ross's mouth.

It didn't go unnoticed how fearful Frank must have been to knock a man of Ross's size down just to stop him saying the forbidden word.

Likewise, it didn't go unnoticed that everyone was now whispering in the lowest whispers ever.

"DOWNth" and Frank grabbed Kelly and pulled her down to the ground saving her from being spotted by a roaming demon.

He yelled, "Crawl" and they did.

On their hands and knees, they scuttled after Frank until he gave them the all-clear signal.

"What are yer, children? Yer in 'ELL. Yer gotta be careful. Yer can be... 'urt."

Suddenly, there was no doubt now that they were in Hell as fear shone out of Frank's eyes like beacons.

Breathing hard, he dared to raise his head and spied the demon walking away from them in the opposite direction. The beads of sweat on Frank's forehead brought home the danger they were in. Frank already knew this. Now they all realized they were in over their heads.

Finally their panting was over and Frank whispered to them angrily. "Keep your 'eads down. Look, the sky's green that means it's one of the top levels of 'ell. This is Green'ell, this is one of the easiest levelsth. It'sth my level, it'sth the Forth, itsth only bad. The lower levelsth, thatsth where itsth really bad."

Rank, as he'd insisted was now his name, had kept them from being discovered in the first second of their venture into Hell, revealing their presence and probably signing their death warrants. But now, with the panic over and the monster lashing someone in the distance, Kelly, Boleyn and Ross suddenly realized that Phillip wasn't with them.

"My Go..." and a vicious whack across the face stunned Kelly into silence.

"I told yers can't say that's 'ere." said Rank with glee.

He'd managed to find a way to justify slapping Kelly. Kelly looked daggers at him knowing exactly what he'd been thinking, and although she was a pampered spoiled brat, there wasn't a tear in her eye.

"I was going to say, what's happened to Phillip?" she continued coolly, determined not to show pain or appear meek.

Inside, she wanted to cry, not from the shock of Rank's smack, but from a terrible thought that they had decided to go to Hell, and now the mastermind with them and might not even be in Hell at all.

Kelly hoped that Boleyn and Ross weren't thinking the same, but one look at their faces told her that they were. In following Phillip, they had most probably made the worst possible mistake anyone was capable of making.

Incredibly, she recognized the color. It was the same as Hecate's blood. Rank motioned to them and they all cowered behind a mound of rubble for cover in keeping with one of the realities of Hell, trying to avoid demons.

"OK, Rank, now what?" asked Boleyn who was in a terrible situation because although she loathed Rank from the bottom of her heart, they and she especially, now needed his help, and there was no Phillip to protect her.

"Well you two isn't going anywhere like that." he said referring to Kelly and Boleyn with a sideways glance of his beady eyes.

"Like what." retaliated the both of them equally affronted, and strangely enough, making the thought of descending to the nadir of time in memorial seem like an equal opportunity thing.

"Like WOMEN, there's no WeMONs down 'ear don't yer know." said Rank in a superior sounding voice, for him that is.

"Wellsth."started Kelly exaggerating an imitation of his slur,"thenth we'sth better startsth dresssingsth upsth asth menesth thenthth."

It momentarily put Rank in his place, although biting the hand that was keeping them alive was probably a foolish thing to do, but his slap still stung and any retaliation was better than none.

With her morale boosted, she set about a makeshift make-under. Clothes and faces were dirtied and ripped. In less than a minute, the band of intruders looked the part, hell-mates anonymous.

"OK,Rank, which way?"Ross asked without trying to pressure him. "Errss, I don't knows, it'th big down 'ere you know, I've gotta get me bearingsth. We needs usth to find usth the Styx."

"Ok, how do we get our bearing and go about finding it?"

"Well, before I'vesth got to be put inside Boleyn, I'sth used to be a Warden." Boasted Rank, "It'sh because we'th, I mean I'th did such a good job in locking up this guy called Phil.

You know, asth a reward. And I think…" everyone's ears perked up and suddenly he had their full attention.

"A guy called Phil?" asked Kelly, the most interested, trying to make nice and not imitate him again.

"Yess, Phil, Me crew, Ego and Vin's, they knew him Topside, on Earth. They 'ated 'im they did. Something about, I don't know, he caused their death they said, Ego said heth even met the d…, you know who, up there on Earth, cut his face up good, The, you know who, did, up good."

"Err… Rank." asked Ross "When you were on Earth, you were Frank the Lip, but here in Hell, you're called Rank. Is that true for Ego and Vin, in other words, did they have different names on Earth too?"

"Yes." Replied Rank.

"Well?" said Kelly getting a little impatient with the man, no matter how much they needed him.

"Yesth, Egoth was… I can't remember…An.." "Andy?"

"Andy? No one ever called Andy ever go to Hell, not like Johnnies, theys a ton of 'ems."

Kelly in a slightly raised voice, still wanting to slap him and get revenge, "So… An… geeze?"

Boleyn could see her ire, and was hoping she'd do just that. "Yeah, yer right, could have been… Angel…"

"Angelo Diablo." blurted out Kelly, a little too loudly, causing everyone to duck.They finally understood where they were. Flushed with embarrassment, Kelly asked again quieter, "Angelo Diablo?"

"Yess, thatss it."

"Was Vin, GaVIN?" continued Kelly. "Yess, yer right again. Gavin, ugly geezer."

"So you three did what?" It was Ross's turn to question Rank. "Eh, what is this? Yer ganging up on me?"

"No!" said Kelly, in a whispered shout."No, we just are, you know, interested, you were after all the only person to ever escape Hell."

And before Rank could moan about being tricked back there, she whispered, "You did something special, you…escaped…H e l

l. I bet no one's ever done that, eh Rank. No one. That's amazing." not waiting for a reply,

"Amazing." concurred Ross, "But how? You locked up this guy called 'Phil' right?"

"Yesth?"

"So, what did he look like?" asked Boleyn. They were all taking turns to interrogate him, causing him to turn round each time they asked a question. It was the critical question.

"OH. Oh. Oh. Well… He was, was, err… tall?" subtle nods from Ross concurred, "Yessth… Big man, err, yeah, big man, black 'airs and err… big."

"Yeah. That's Phil alright." sighed Ross convincingly, "Yep, we knew him too." Everyone nodded in agreement. Seeing the palatable relief on Rank's face, Ross continued.

"Angelo and Phil did some, err, nasty things, well, not to beat around the bush, they got into black magic and summoned the Devil. It was a huge mistake."

Rank smiled at that, "Theses foolsth had voted with Phillip to go to Hell. *That* wasth a huge mistake."

Ross continued "And the next thing we knew, Ego and Phil had their faces cut up and Ego was dead, soon to be followed by Phil."

"Yeah, terrible." said Rank. He'd seen Ego's face and heard it firsthand from Ego that the Devil was responsible, so Ross's account seemed quite plausible. It also told him why the Devil hated him so much.

"Messed up his face bad." said Kelly bolstering Ross' report. "Yess, wess, I mean Ego and Vin hardly recognized him." "Terrible." said Ross,"So where did you take him? Dumped him

in the river, no, you said you locked him up in..." "The Devil'ssth Jail" completed Rank.

"Thanks Rank." continued Kelly,"And that's where we're going. I wonder if Phillip knew this? And that's why he wants to go there? Because that's where that key's from right? RIGHT?"

"yesth" whispered Rank.

"So you stole The Devil's Jail's Key." said Ross. "No, No. That was Ego."

Kelly knew Angelo all too well. It sounded just like the sort of thing he would do, but he wasn't the kind of person to give up something either. (He was so much like Bill).

"So, how did you get it?" inquired Kelly. "Well...'"

"Com'on Rank, spill it." said Kelly not given to suffer fools gladly.

"Well we pretend to lock up Phil in the jail, bitter cold it was too, then…"

"What?" said Ross, "You pretend? What do you mean? Pretend?" "Errr, I meant, we loc…" retreated Rank, but it was too late.

Kelly pounced, "You didn't lock anyone up right, Phil never appeared, did he? You pretended. You pretended to lock him up and you lied to the Devil."

"NO, NO, ITth WAS VIN."

"Gavin? Gavin lied to the Devil." said Kelly nodding. She knew this was just the sort of thing to expect from him after his antics in the caves at Witchiton. So it wasn't too much of a surprise. But getting away with it most certainly was.

"Yess. It was Vin's, he's, ugly."

"And the key." shouted Kelly at the top of her whisper. "OK, 'K. Well, Ego goesth and throws the key into the fire,

but he faked it yer see.

He thinks I'm not looking, he forgets I'm a thief… I'm a… So I see it, he don't throw it at all, instead of throwing, he doesn't.

He didn't tell us nothing either. Thinks I'm stupid! He did the throwing arm to deceive me, and Vin too. But he keeps it, yer see. Feignesth it.

"OK. We get it. How did you get it? And why did he kee…"

"'dunno. That'sth Ego I guess."

"And…"

"I stoles it from him, 'Cos he stole it from the Devil. That'sth why I did it. Him, I Donno."

Nor did Ego, he didn't have a clue why he'd done it either. He had plans. He just didn't know what they were, but that had never stopped him before. If he was asked why he'd done it, he wouldn't have been able to answer. It was just his ambition coming through in another of its attempts to elevate him to the position he deemed rightfully his. (President).

Luck was on his side that day, because he didn't have a clue where it'd gone, but he was thankful that it had. Had the Devil discovered it in his strip search, then he, and of course Vin and Rank, would have been found out, and the Devil would have sentenced them to The Devil's Jail to replace its missing occupant.

Kelly, Boleyn and Ross all nodded again at Rank's answer. It was typical of Angelo D and Rank and Gavin. Everything made sense, especially to Boleyn, who saw another injustice in him.

"And you, you little bastard, you." she said barely containing her rage. "You took all the credit for locking up Phil and the Devil put you inside of me as a reward." said Boleyn with loathing.

"And you ended up escaping Hell. Well I'm glad we're back here now you, you…"

"Shhh." said someone, but it was too late. A demon was making its way towards them in a menacing fashion with its arm raised and whip at the ready. Ignoring some other souls along the way, it didn't deviate from its course one iota.

"SHITE" said Rank.

"You're a warden, do something." said Boleyn bitterly.

Rank stood up from his crouching position and took a step towards the demon.

"I'mth Rank. Warden. I'veth just captured these inmates, they belongs in the Seventh Level, the Red-Hell."

CHAPTER 54

EGO LAUGHS

"You bugg..."

The crack of the demon's whip cut off Kelly's insult. Luckily for her the whip just missed, nonetheless, its thwack was so close it made her jump. The demon herded Kelly, roughly and with unsparing warning cracks, then pushed Boleyn and Ross in front of her, and Rank followed up in the rear, smiling from ear to ear.

"They wanted to comes to Hell. Now they know how stupid they are."

"But in a way." whispered Kelly to Ross,"Rank has sped up our mission as we've got a police escort to the lower levels."

"Yea, but will we survive it?" Another crack from the whip erupted over their heads.

They walked across a wasted landscape until they reached a cobbled path next to a dark body of water.They didn't speak to avoid provoking any further lashings, and within hours, they approached the gates that led to and would secure them entry into Yellow-Hell.

As always, at the juncture between the levels of Hell, the river left the road's side and chose its own mysterious course into the gloomier circles. In all the centuries Rank had lived in Hell, he'd never wondered where it went at these crossroads. Only within a few days of his arrival however, Ego had posed the question. It was never answered. Just like the river at the Landing Dock,the head or mouth because no one knew which it was, everything about the Styx was shrouded in mystery.

Even the Devil wasn't sure of its source but that was something he'd admit to no one. Nor was anyone (again he'd never admit it) certain of the direction of its flow, appearing to go in different directions according to the observer, but one thing was known, it wasn't anything anyone wanted to touch.

The demon opened the gates, and there on the lower side, another demon, larger and yellow eyed waited for them. With another lash, the green-eyed monster shepherded the group through the open twin gates and ushered the prisoners into Yellow-Hell.

"NO, NO." shrieked Rank,"I'm not with THEM." but neither brute listened. Suddenly the number of prisoners became four again. Before Rank could muster any last retort, Kelly yanked him aside and whispered nastily into his ear.

"Betray us again, and we'll tell the Devil that you lied to him about Phil. Get it?"The look on his face was all the reply she needed.

"HAH!" screeched Boleyn. She'd never thought she'd have to come to Hell to see justice, or that she could feel happiness there.

The chastisement and demotion of Rank gave Boleyn a feeling of exhilaration and vindication. She was the one who supported Phillip the most in his idea. Now all she had to do was dodge the Devil and all would be well. She was being a little short sighted, but it was a victory and she hadn't had many of them recently, or ever.

Witnessing the crushing humiliation and suffering of a man who was the cause of most of her misery left Boleyn feeling elated. Here and now, Rank was no one. Maybe it wasn't so wise for Boleyn to tell him so, but she was going to one way or another, indifferent to any future reprisal.

CHAPTER 55

THE DEVIL CRIES

The Devil fought off despair. Earlier, he'd had spurned the chance to escape the millions of years of incarceration in his Entanglement Prison, his own Devil's Jail. Now God had released such wrath upon him that his two-hour cushion was down to less than fifteen minutes.

God's anger didn't stop with the Devil. It extended to Earth as *she* laid waste to it, and her instrument was Man. The ease with which God and *Pi* started WWIII was frightening.

In the past, the Devil had conspired to bring Earth to its knees via war and famine. Now, he stood on the other side of the equation, his initial glee gone. If it wasn't his war then there should be no war at all. It was too late, though, God and *Pi* had done it, from afar, with consummate ease.

Catastrophic decompression.The type a bursting balloon suffers. That was the Armageddon that he was witnessing now. All the pent-up stresses of unresolved territorial claims were being settled today.

Hoping to salvage the deteriorating situation, he frantically rushed and tried to arrange coups and assassinations in an attempt to stop the World Leaders. But nothing could sway them from pursuing this hell-bent course of annihilation. Unfortunately for him although he knew this, the lowest common denominator always won.The worst and deadliest options always ended up being the de facto avenue of choice.

Even though he knew the incredible lengths Man had gone to in preparation for this day, it still gave him, God and *Pi,* cause to wonder. Nuclear arsenals, large enough to destroy the World a thousand times over, chemical, conventional, technical and biological weapons of similar capability, and it seemed no holds were barred.

When push came to shove, The Geneva Convention meant nothing. Nothing on Earth could stop Man from pushing every dreaded red button at the first opportunity, as if they'd wanted this all their lives. Even with only five percent of weapons finding their targets, the law of big numbers doomed the World many times over.

The Devil's once ancient desire to fill Hell was coming true.

At first, he had rubbed his hands together with joy. He employed bagpipes and drums, to play the music of war and remembrance, a fitting welcome to the men landing at the Landing Dock. Overwhelmed, his monitoring of Hell became erratic, as he preferred to spend time seeking the reasoning behind God and *Pi's* actions.

"It must have had something to do with Phil, yet he's in my Jail and they must know this because there's no sign of him on Earth. Ergo, he's in Hell with me. Wish Ego hadn't thrown away that key though. Trust him to end up doing exactly what I didn't want. Then there's Basher and Smasher, maybe God has a similar pair of twins? It's like seven and seven not adding up to fourteen anymore.

But to start WWIII, that's a bit extreme, there has to be another reason, but damned if I'm going to ask and look stupid. I'll find out some other way."

～～～

Unwittingly, the Devil was right. God, in Heaven, was running round trying to solve the unthinkable, a murder.

At first, when Angel Petra told God of the homicide, *she* didn't believe her. It was a natural reaction to the unprecedented news. This was the last thing *she* needed what with everything else that was going on. But *she* didn't have a choice. This had to be solved and the sooner the better.

The first thing *she* did was go over the new arrivals since Phil had disappeared from sight. Then *she* eliminated all the women, which was eighty percent. Next, *she* checked all the English-speaking people, because those were the people who Phillip might have had contact with.

Removing all people who hadn't resided in any place where Phillip had visited, and in less than five minutes, *she* had a short list. Only then did *she* look at the souls, and instantly, two souls stood out. A pair of twins called Basher and Smasher; their names were a dead giveaway if nothing else. God didn't know that the Devil had the exact pair of twins in Hell.

Somehow, Phillip's RhomSong's defense had split the pair into two, and muddled everything up. When Basher and Smasher arrived in Heaven, they couldn't believe their eyes, or their bodies. As they looked at each other, it was like looking into mirrors. Basher's looked at Smasher and saw himself and Smasher likewise. When either spoke, the others body mouthed the words, when either moved, the others body stirred. Just as the pair of Basher and Smasher twins in Hell, whatever they attempted, it was exactly like their last moments on Earth; disjointed, uncoordinated and fragmented. Murder was bound to follow as their frustration at their disabilities mounted. In the past, killing something had always been their outlet for anger, just because they were in Heaven hadn't changed that.

One look in their eyes told God that there was no way that they should be in Heaven, yet here they were. Petra looked at God and pleaded for forgiveness. In her hand, she held out a key, *the key* that opened the Pearly Gates, and the gates through which the two murderers had entered.

She offered her resignation; however God waved her hand in dismissal. Petra's error was immaterial and trivial at worst. She was just another victim of PhilLIP's.

And besides, the two brothers may even aid God, if *she* studied them. So *she* took a long gander at the two misfits, and what *she* saw scared her. *She* looked deep into their hearts. It wasn't the fact that they were killers that took her back; it was what was in their souls.

She made a terrifying conclusion. *She* discovered that they only had half a soul each and they were in the wrong bodies. Whether this manifested itself in their strange gaucheness, their chaotic and tangled speech, and their bodily maladroitness, she couldn't work out. Then *she* thought.

"Where were the other halves?"

She was worried. More than troubled, because *she*, and *she* had kept this secret from the Devil and especially *Pi,* had exhibited a minuscule but similar frailty within herself.

Buried deep inside her Entanglement attacks, *she'd* noticed that LIGHT and LOSS sometimes became malformed resulting in a slight but fundamental weakening. It wasn't just another thing for her to worry about; it was her immortality that was questionable. *She* was looking mortality in the face.

Her Entanglement was compromised, but how bad it was, and what the prognosis was, *she* couldn't tell. As for the cause, *she* wasn't looking any further than Phillip. *She* didn't know for a fact that it was he, but *she* wasn't interested in evidence anymore.

He was a WMD, and there was nothing that could convince her otherwise. If it wasn't personal before, it was now. God would find a way to rid the Universe of him.

~~~

While the Devil was preoccupied on Earth, trying to patch up every ripping seam in the fabric of peace, the green and yellow eyed demons marched the intruders further into the depths of Hell. Kelly, Ross and Boleyn stuck together, whilst Rank tagged behind as they wouldn't let him walk with them. And with every step he took, he grew more and more bitter.

They only let him join them when they became too scared to continue without him. Amazingly the hardened Boleyn actually chose to lead the way, preferring the fear of Hell rather than his company. She made it plain for all to see to boot.

Rank was livid, being humiliated like this, and it caused Kelly to whisper a reminder to him that she could easily let his secret out. The threat wasn't lost as he just kept his stare fixed ahead and said nothing. "I managed to escape the wrath of the Devil. Then I steal the key. The Devil rewards, me, Rank, both putting me in Boleyn on Earth. Phillip exorcised me out of her and I was free on Earth.

Then, as soon as It's nice with them, this idiot Phillips persuades his idiot friend to go to Hell, and they abduct me, here too, it's not fair. Steals me key too, me key.

Then, I help them in 'ell, tell them to get disguises, saves they lives, then I shows them the way to gets to 'ell bottom fast, and they blameth ME? And want to take meth with 'em. I'll gets 'em, I will, and that Boleyn making meth looks bad, I'll gets 'er. I will. Make me walk behind 'er."

Not deaf to Rank's mutterings, Boleyn straightened her back and became the tallest she'd ever been. Prouder than she'd ever imagined she could be. Hell wasn't Hell for her at all, yet. Not being stupid either, she knew he was plotting against her, and she didn't care.

She was Boleyn and she was fearless. She was as hard as nails and tougher than leather. Let him.

Losing track of time, they came to the spot where the Dark River left the side of the road, indicating that the gate separating the second level of Yellow-Hell and Red-Hell was close. It was here that Rank commented on the fact that the green-eyed demon was still escorting them. Ross, pondering Rank's observation, whispered across to him, "So the green-eyed demon doesn't normally come down this far? It's not normal?"

Rank was still in a snot and he thought about not answering. "Rank?" reiterated Ross "Rank?"

"Noosth." whispered Rank through his gritted teeth, "Itth ain't."

And no sooner had it been spoken, the ogre turned round and left, leaving them alone. It was almost as if Rank's remark had found the demon guilty of breaking some unknown demon rule of Hell.

It was most puzzling, especially for Kelly who ducked in panic as she'd accidently locked eyes with it and expected the whip to lace her back. It didn't.

"Puzzle one." she thought.

She felt more afraid, alone and exposed more than ever without the escort which made puzzle two. Puzzle three was that never once had its whip actually made contact. Puzzle four, was that in the company of the green-eyed demon, the feeling she felt was familiar. A fear she first experienced with a stranger called Phil in a town called Hecate.

~~~

"WHAT THE..." Charonne, the boatwoman, suddenly found herself in a fight to keep her craft afloat. After a brief but intense struggle with the pole, frantically poking the bottom left and right, she managed to stabilize and gain control of the pitching and wildly rocking rowboat.

She'd taken on some water but the boat was supposed to be unsinkable even though it just floated above its rim.

She looked back at her cargo and her eyes almost popped out of her head. The rule was, one man, one boat, one Charonne. She was completely astonished when she saw that she had two fares. The large man's name was Glenn. How she knew his name she didn't know, and like most of the clients of late, he didn't have tuppence.

"Cheapskates. Another one, a lower level of Hell for him." had been her automatic response, but now she was staring at the second passenger.

"Such a small man, Errr..." and she searched for his name, and couldn't find it.

"Err..." and it still wasn't forthcoming, "Err... Err..." "YOU. Who are you?" she asked the little man nastily. "Glenn." replied the big man.

"Not you, YOU." this time pointing her finger at the small man. "Phillip."

It took some time, but finally Glenn and Phillip figured out where to sit in the boat without causing it to capsize. Phillip sat in the middle with Glenn almost on his lap. Glenn had also figured out

375

that Phillip wasn't too concerned with threats like clenched fists an inch from his face. He found out after he launched a surprise head butt and knocked himself out on Phillip's unscathed nose.

Phillip was doing his best to ignore the big man for all his efforts to intimidate and bully, as he was more interested in the approach the boat was making at a harbor, the Landing Dock. When they made port, the waiting demon exchanged shrugged shoulders with Charonne. *"Two?"*

She shoved them both forwards down the oil-planked promenade and into Green-Hell II, destined for Level III. Along the way, they received several lashings but only Glenn's screams were genuine. Phillip yelped but only not to look out of place. Their escort dumped them off once in Level III. They were oficially, hell-mates.

Glenn looked about as if looking for a friend or someone he could hang around with. Although 'shorty' was small, he was tough, and he was the only person he knew down here, so…

"Hey Shorty… What the…" Phillip had gone.

Phillip was probably the only man ever to be happy to find himself in Hell. It was a terrible worry however that his friends, especially Kelly, weren't with him.

"Did everyone get split up? Are they together?

Are they even in Hell? Is Kelly OK?

I just hope she doesn't die for me, no one, should do that."

For Phillip, the lashings of the demon's whip were immaterial, but he'd seen their impact on Glenn, who was a big guy, and yet they hurt him.

"So how would Kelly survive?" nevertheless, if had they stayed on Earth, they'd probably be dead by now. The Tsunami that was surging towards the Devil's building bore the Red Queen of Spades, and had it touched any one of them; then *Pi* would have unleashed crushing attacks against them all. And God's would surely have followed.

Maybe Phillip would have survived, but not his companions. So he hoped they were in Hell, and he laughed that a month earlier that would have had a different connotation.

The demon had delivered Glenn and himself to this the Third Level of Hell, their new home, but for Phillip, this was just the beginning of his journey. So far, other than not knowing the fate of Kelly, he was pleased. He just wished he knew what had happened to his friends, and he also hoped that if they were in Hell, that they would be heading down to Level IX. As for him, he ploughed ahead with his plan.

Being small gave him an advantage, it allowed him to hide. He dodged and weaved as he scurried after a beast heading downwards. He darted behind rubble and other cover, until in the distance he saw a dark line running though the waste-scape. He'd spied the Dark River, and instantly knew this was where he should be heading. He abandoned the demon not having any need to follow it anymore, and made a beeline for it.

Looking for cover, Phillip squatted down beside the raised levee that carried the road, but it was scant at best. In fact, his location on the landside meant he was exposed to all onlookers. Luckily, and nothing to do with *Pi*, he'd noticed that the hell-mates avoided looking in the river's direction.

He didn't know why, but it wasn't them he was worried about anyway. He greatly feared being discovered and caught by a demon and by extension, being turned over to the Devil. Where he was crouching, any demon that was walking down the road could probably see him. They too, seemed to avoid looking directly at the river, which must have been the only reason he hadn't been spotted already.

He noticed that even though they appeared to be the sole custodians of the riverside road, when they stopped for conversation in whatever strange language they used, they always presented their backs to it. This meant that in his current position he was particularly exposed. Obviously he needed to be on the other side of the road, right next to the river and away from any stray glance.

A couple of demons were about a hundred yards away. At any moment they could turn and walk his way so he had to move immediately. Phillip watched their body language closely and prepared himself for a quick sprint. When they seemed particularly distracted, he made his mad dash.

He slipped off the far edge of the road onto a steep slope that led straight towards the gloomy waters. Turning from his side to his stomach, his hands reached out and grabbed a crumbling stonewall that stopped his momentum from delivering him into the river. As he twisted round, he slipped into a small bunker and woke someone up.

"I wasn't sleepi... what? fuck! PHIL?" whispered the person who was already occupying the tiny shelter.

"Gavin? GAVIN? GAVIN! Quick, move over, and he pushed Gavin over and hunkered down beside him.The two demons started to head their way, but Gavin hadn't noticed. His eyes were wide open and he was staring wildly at the apparition that had just discovered one of his secret spots, and was actually shoving him around in it with impunity.

"Phi... PHIL! Hey you, demo..."

Phillip saw what he was trying to do so he clamped his hand over Gavin's mouth and held it firm. Gavin's eyes were so wide, that Phillip was scared they might pop out of his head, but he couldn't do anything other than keep his grip and wait until the demons strutted off.

"I see you remember me." said Phillip. Even though Gavin was much taller than Phillip, he trembling as if scared. He'd just survived five minutes with the Devil, so it was understandable. And besides that, the weight of Phillip's hand and body reeked of power and strength.

"So I don't need to introduce myself, except that my name is now Phillip, not Phil."

"Yea, well I'm now called Vin, so fuck you."

"10-4" replied Phillip, "but, oh, sorry about that, you know, stopping you ratting me out to a demon."

"You're welcome."

A distrustful pause of eyeing each other continued until Phillip broke the ice. "Ga... Vin, I don't know how to put this, but, well, I need your help G.. I mean... Vin. I need your help."

"Help, why should I help you?"

The question stumped Phillip. Help for Gavin meant effort; industry wasn't his greatest quality. Slothful was. Phillip also knew in the brief time he'd known Gavin, that he wasn't one to volunteer his assistance on anything. So if he was going to get his help, he needed to offer him something.

There was another issue Phillip feared. At the first chance Vin would get, he'd grass on Phillip. "Well. Vin. I can't think of anything."

"Then you can kiss my ass."

"Except, that maybe, I can get us out of here." said Phillip, thinking, who's going to buy that.

"HAH. YOU. You... get us out of here? Where's that demon?" "NO, Really. I'm going to... err, kill the Devil."

"HA HA!" snorted Vin, not making any attempt to conceal his contempt or equally and more importantly, remain hidden. Phillip had no choice.

"Get down and shut up Gavin."

And Vin was back in his hiding place - something in Phil's voice compelled him to do so.

"Listen gaVIN, I've tried to be reasonable with you, but you've forced me. I need your help, and I'm not asking.

I can't. Actually... I can... make you, I just don't want to. I know how you died, I know what happened, and I know at the time it was happening you hardly believed it.

You know, the Yellow Witch, Ruebella wasn't the only witch. There were three, a green witch called Hecate, she was the weakest, and a red witch, Boleyn, and she was the strongest. Now there's me, Phillip. They've all gone, but I'm still here.

You felt how heavy my hand was, well, I can sit on you, if you want some convincing that I'm, err, that I'm, err, different, special."

"You want to sit on me?"Vin said in a feminine tone and manner. "NO, not like that you idiot."

Phillip would have said God in the old days, and Vin was expecting him to do so. That would have ended his problem of dealing with the man. The Devil would have descended into Hell and captured him. He was so short sighted, he didn't appreciate that should Phil be caught, that his lie would also be exposed.

"I'm trying to tell you that I need your help, and if you were scared of the witches, and I know you were, well you should be really scared of me." continued Phillip.

"Sure…" said Vin boldly.

"But I don't want you to be scared. I want you to help me voluntarily." he responded.

"As if that's going to happen." said Vin sarcastically seeing how small he was.

"I must have been in shock from his surprise attack and that's was why his hand felt so heavy.'Cos, look at him, he's a midget." Vin thought, feeling much more confident.

"OK sit on me if you feel like it Phil, Com'on, little man, sity, sit sit." said Vin feeling quite cocky now and slapping his thighs.

So Phillip did.

"AWL. Get off, Get off, GET OFF."

But Phillip wouldn't, not until gaVIN screamed loud enough that he would have drawn attention to them. When he got off, he rose in the air and hovered above Vin's lap like a humming bird.

"You'll help me now? Yes?" "Yes. YES."

"You did that?" Said Phillip as he floated.

"What? No. It was here when I discovered this place."Referring to a little doodle akin to a rough coat of arms inscribed in the rubble behind them.

"Thought not." reflected Phillip to himself. "Looks old. Looks good."

As for gaVIN's response, Phillip wasn't sure if he lied or not. It didn't matter though, as long as he had him, he didn't care. Neither was he going to let him out of his sight.

It was much slower walking along the edge of the river, but if they were perfectly quiet, as Phillip demanded of him, it provided them with ample cover. If stealth wasn't the first priority, Phillip would have just flown through Hell.

When they reached the junction where the river and road went their separate ways, Phillip asked Vin, "What happens next?"

"There'll be a gate soon, and as we're in Green-Hell Level III. The next level is still green, but to get there, you have to get through the gate, and it's got a Gate-Demon Demon guarding it.

If you're stupid enough to actually want to go further than that, the next is Yellow-Hell, Level V. But you'll never get that far, there's a Gate-Demon demon on every gate."

Phillip listened carefully as he believed gaVIN was holding something back. But not knowing anything about Hell, he didn't know the right questions to ask.

And now he had a problem - *how could he get pass the Gate-Demon and what was he going to do with gaVIN? He knew the moment he let him out of his sight he'd snitch.*

They were questions that never saw the light of day.

A demon had secretly crept up on them, snatched them off the ground and held each one in its grasp. Vin wriggled and squirmed to get free but he was overpowered.

Phillip stood still, turned his head towards the monstrosity and said, "Hello Hecate."

CHAPTER 56

RAT

Vin stopped twisting and looked at Phillip, who stared directly into the demon's eyes. In his panic, he hadn't heard Phillip address her by name and instead charged into his default action. He started to rat him out.

While still blabbering on, Hecate's tail expertly wound around his neck and with a single flick choked him into silence. The more he resisted and fought the stronger its grasp tightened and soon he passed out.

She looked deep into Phillip's eyes, in a surreal moment. It was Hecate remembering her attack. It was her Entanglement that started Phil's transformation. It was she who transformed into the Angel of Death in the Chamber of the Cross. Most importantly, it was she who had deflowered Phillip in God's and *Pi's* bid to kill him. Of all the witches, Hecate was the weakest, and yet she had changed the course of history the most.

Unlike the bond between Hecate and Kelly that was personal, there was no bond between Hecate and Phil or Phillip. Now, through his gaze, he connected. In an unspoken appeal, he asked for her aid. Her green eyes were hard and glaring. Phillip saw through them to her inner being, and although condemned to Hell, he believed her to be good. His request was heartfelt and sincere. Her eyes acknowledged his plea.

With a nod and a tilt of his head, Phillip signaled it was time to get moving. She led him off to the lower Gates of Hell as if reading his mind. She roughly pushed Phillip ahead of her as she crossed the entryway into the last level of Green-Hell to mimic what any demon would have done, and Phillip played along, crying and whimpering.

With the unconscious Vin wrapped in her tail, Hecate silently ushered Phillip deeper into Hell's depths, beating him whenever she came close to any other of like kind. They passed into Yellow-Hell without incident and walked with determination and purpose when not being observed.

When challenged by other demons, Hecate sat down, feigned exhaustion, and allowed the other demon to lash her prisoner. Phillip assumed that she'd figured out that the thrashing didn't hurt.

The hardest thing about the beatings were to make them appear genuine, and more than once he mistimed his screams causing quizzical looks from his tormenters. It was always at these times that Hecate would step in and resume their passage.

Soon they were halfway through the second and last level of Yellow-Hell.

Hecate unexpectedly stopped. She put Vin down on the path's cobbled stones and released him from her tail's grip. He came round coughing and sputtering about a minute later. Always the opportunist, he instantly thought about bolting as Phillip was cowering at the demon's feet. Unknown to Vin, he was pretending to be under arrest. Vin decided this was his chance. He picked himself up and attempted to run off. But Phillip knew the stakes were so high that he couldn't allow it. He didn't want to kill Vin, but his options were limited.

And then he thought of something.

"Vin, get me some freshwater, and don't say anything until you do." Phillip's voice of command had to be obeyed.

Vin was doomed to aimlessly search Hell knowing no such water existed. Resentful and without a motive all of this time, he finally had an actual reason to hate Phil.

It was time to move on, so Phillip looked again into Hecate's eyes and they exchanged a long, silent but warm goodbye. There was so much that could have been said, but nothing needed to be. With a sadness in both their eyes, they parted ways for what both believed was the last time.

Phillip turned and resumed his descent on the river side of

the path where there was plenty of cover from the patrolling Hell guardians. Interestingly, another cubbyhole had another scratchy coat of arms, but he had no time to waste, so he moved on.

The only disadvantage was that it was slow and all the time Hecate had made up for him gradually whittled away. Nevertheless, it was better to remain undetected then rush ahead and get caught for real.

He would have continued his clandestine journey under cover had he not heard a cry that didn't fit, even here in Hell. It could have been one or a million miles away. He heard it and he knew to whom it belonged.

CHAPTER 57

THE RAPIST

Kelly, Boleyn, Ross and Rank suddenly felt quite exposed with their escort now gone. This left them at the mercy of any other malevolent demon. In fairness and truth the green-eyed tyrant had in fact been somewhat benevolent. She had spared her lashes to occasions when other demons were present, and even then, astonishingly missed.

The demons in Yellow-Hell had yellow eyes and their whips were much more painful, something Rank went to great lengths to explain. He emphasized this as he had a deceitful motive. He had a plan. He was going to get Boleyn, and this time, rape was going to be the last thing she was going to have to worry about.

As for Kelly, well, that was a different matter. Kelly had noticed that the last time they were on the road he appeared to be in some discomfort, and more often than not kept his back to the river as if avoiding it. When he did have to look in its direction, he shielded his eyes.

After an hour or so walking on the road, with intermittent departures onto the wasteland to avoid any demons coming their way, Rank changed their tactics and decided to stay on the plains. As conversation wasn't that easy with their preoccupied leader, nobody questioned him about it.

However Boleyn and Kelly didn't like it. They were in Hell and their guide wasn't someone to be trusted. He'd already betrayed them once, and Kelly too had already reminded him again, that she knew his secret. "Odds were, he'd squeal on us again." she thought.

"EGO!" shrieked Rank at his unbelievable good fortune in stumbling upon his subordinate. But his joy was short lived.

"RANK?" and suddenly the big man had Rank's throat in his hand as he swore up and down at him.

"We heard that the Devil sent you Topside."

"Ego." said Rank between coughs,"Yeas." some more coughing, "He didn't, but I'm back, and I's not alone" and he pointed behind to Boleyn, Ross and...

"Kelly!" cried Ego instantly forgetting Rank's transgression. Even though she was dressed to look like a tattered young boy from the Victorian age, she was a gorgeous woman in Hell.

With all inhibitions gone, with all moral standards meaningless, Ego raced forward and attacked her with only one thing on his mind. Ross jumped in front to protect her as he too was a big man. But Ego didn't worry because he had a backup gang. Out of nowhere, Basher, Smasher and Buster appeared and tackled Ross to the ground leaving Ego free to attack Kelly.

Ambivalent to her screams, he overpowered her instantly. He'd lusted after her on Earth and mocked her ridiculous obsession with the idiot Phil. Not untypically, he'd laughed to hide his jealousy that she was falling for the loser when he, her match, was right there.

Hell now was a blessing; the action he was contemplating couldn't condemn him. His trousers were off in a flash and he started to tear off Kelly's. Things all around were happening fast. Ignoring her slaps and kicks, Ego pinned her down as he savored his next deed. And Rank had grabbed hold of Boleyn with a similar intent in mind as he proceeded to grope her and loosen his own pants.

"I'th do her first and pick up the pieces of Kelly after Ego and the other three have finished." Rank thought.

"This was going to be one good day in Hell." For the first time, Rank and Ego had had the same thought.

It was one of their last thoughts as a surprise outside the realm of Hell or fate felled them like a cannon ball. Cued by the cries of his loved one, Phillip resorted to flying, albeit only a foot above the ground. He sped over the wasteland and smashed into Ego and his gang with the kinetic energy of a truck. The bodies of the would-be rapists were strewn over the ground like chicken innards.

Phillip stood up, dusted himself off, and Kelly's arms embraced him. Her knight in shining armor. He'd saved her life when he jumped out of the plane, and again now in Hell. He held her tight and kissed her.

Ross brushed himself down and waited for their loving embrace to finish before saying, "Phillip, we're so glad to see you, aren't we Kelly." She grinned manically.

"And Boleyn. Boleyn. Boleyn? Where's Boleyn? Where's Rank, that's Frank the Lip, Phillip."

In the confusion, Rank had dragged Boleyn away by her hair to one of the many ruins that littered Hell. He mounted his body on top of hers, grinned and said, "That pig-head Ego pulledth the short straw and got away with it, now, HAH Now that Phillip'sth flatten him, he aint getting none. But me, HAHth, I'mth gonno getss some, 'cos I've got you."

He ripped her clothes off until there was only her underwear left. Rank was more than twice her size and three times her weight, so all he had to do was lie on top to subdue her. Her flailing arms tried and failed, and just like before, over two hundred years ago, he raped her. And this time, there would be no second chance. This time he was going to kill her. He put his hands around her neck and just leant on them. She was small, he strangled her in seconds. But she didn't give in, not once.

Even though she had no strength to fight off Rank physically, she didn't let him defile her emotionally. Even as her life waned, her stare never once deviated. Rank twisted and turned his head to avoid her glower but he couldn't escape it, nor could he close his eyes. They stung as if there was salt in them, and even after he pulled his hands away, Boleyn's penetrating gape, even when dead, petrified him like a stone.

Phillip saw him and shot across the hundred yards that separated them and flattened him. Frank the Lip, Rank, may not have been most remarkable rogue to ever live, but he may have been the most world-altering criminal.

If he hadn't raped the innocent child Boleyn, would the World be as it was now? With this reflection in his mind, Phillip picked up his body and crushed it into dust with his bare hands. He brought his open palms up to his lips and blew the dust into the wind.

Satisfied, Phillip knelt by the body of Boleyn and held back the prayer that was crying out to be said. He cradled her in his arms and rocked her small body hoping it would materialize. Kelly stood strong and pulled him back to his feet.

"Phillip. You are a good man. I've been meaning to tell you this for some time."

"Thank you, Kelly." said Phillip. He smiled, and a tear or two escaped.

Hell was hell, but they felt like they were in Heaven.

"There was nothing you could have done Phillip." consoled Kelly. But he did have an idea that he could do something.

He collected Boleyn into his arms again and held her as gently as possible.

He didn't expect anything to happen, because he knew her soul wasn't hers to recall, but he tried anyway.

S

Rhom

n

g

But something did. Without warning, her body started to throw up and wrench violently just as it did the time when Rank was exorcised. The gigantic heaves caused Phillip to let go.

Even though Boleyn was dead, they were scared. He suddenly wished he hadn't attempted to resurrect her as they could hear her bones cracking and braking. As such it wouldn't be much of a homecoming now if Boleyn did reenter her body.

Ten seconds passed and then a small man, a shade taller than Phillip's size, was ejected from her stretched and contorted mouth.

Phillip and Kelly took a step back unable to tear their eyes away. Then they saw that the first regurgitation wasn't the last. Using its hands to pry Boleyn's jaws wide enough to climb out, another form appeared, an ugly, ugly woman dressed as a witch.

Out had come John Abbott the XXVIIth and Ruebella, the Yellow Witch. It was a complete shock, for everyone, including Phillip.

Both were last seen in ClearStream, alive or dead.

Phillip deeply suspected that *Pi* took them, and then put them in Boleyn as penalty for not slaying Phil in the cow drink.

"*Pi*," he was beginning to realize, "does a lot more than I'd ever dreamed of." The appearance of Ruebella explained how Boleyn was able to navigate the Chamber of the Cross's Passage. Ruebella still a witch, possessed Entanglement, the only qualification required for the crossing.

Had the IAT still existed, there would have been two new partners. As it was, there were two new lives amongst the deceased of Hell, two who would be free to do as they wished. Phillip gazed at them as they lay on the ground exhausted, choking in fits and coughs.

They quickly gained consciousness but carried a look of disorientation and bewilderment. With wide open eyes they took in their first sights of their hellish location. Rather than shriek or question where they were, they just stood up and hugged each other.

At first, it seemed natural that they should seek solace in each other's company given whatever it was they'd endured, but Kelly thought there maybe something more to it. Her suspicion was confirmed when, after releasing each other from their embrace, they linked fingers.

Phillip was agog, and looked back at Boleyn's tiny shell, only to see it dissolve and disappear. The Devil's claim upon her became her reality. Somewhere in Hell, a new demon was born. She had sold her soul and Hell had readily accepted it without due process.

Before he knew it, he was kissing Kelly as they comforted themselves. Only after gently pulling apart, did Phillip and Kelly see John Abbott and Ruebella separate from a loving embrace of their own. The World, Heaven and Hell were now officially places beyond recognition.

"Ok, Phillip, lead the way." said John Abbott, surprising the dickens out of him and Kelly.

"Err. OK. Don't you err, want to know what's err, happening or where we are?" asked Phillip inquisitively.

"Oh. We already know, we've watched everything, felt everything, through Boleyn. G.. bless her sou... bless her." replied John.

Ruebella nodded in agreement. As Phillip, did his best to retain his eye contact, somehow her looks now held no repulsion. This was true also for Kelly although her eyes were more focused on Phillip rather than the new couple.

Just then, Ross caught up with them but instead of asking questions or looking bewildered, he just looked at Phillip and almost repeated John Abbott's question verbatim. He'd seen everything now, and nothing could shock him anymore. Phillip looked back towards the path next to the river and they all followed him, the shortest man.

The route back took them past the bodies of the attackers. He kicked each one with hatred. Not just because they'd attempted to rape his love, but also because their actions had caused Phillip to take their lives. Even though a billion lives had been lost in the past day, their blood wasn't on Phillip's hands. Not like these. However, he felt justified and defiantly unremorseful.

"These were bad people Phillip," said Kelly, "and those above, those killed by God and company. That's on them."

"Thank you, Kelly." replied Phillip breathing again, "Thank you. I know that, but it's nice to be reminded. Thanks." and they made their way back to the path, and the foreboding Dark River that it accompanied.

Now a group of five, they descended. Scurrying on and off the road and ducking in and out of cover whenever a demon came within earshot, they went ever downwards. As they did, Ross looked at the millions of hell-mates in the far distance suffering eternal damnation.

"Forever? It's a bit extreme don't you think?" he asked himself.

Time passed until they were soon upon the gate that would take them from Yellow to Red-Hell. At first, they were excited because there wasn't a demon guarding it. How easy to quickly open the gate and sneak into Red-Hell without detection. However, it wasn't until someone asked who's going to open it, did they realize there was only one person amongst them with the necessary credentials, Ruebella.

She looked at everyone looking at her and let go of John Abbott's hand. Then she ordered the unyielding door to open. But it didn't and now they were stuck.

No one said anything, not even Kelly who would have made some comment a month or two earlier. Now she bowed her head knowing what sacrifice was required.

Many demons came and went, but not one with the right qualifications was found. Every time they were disappointed, they went quiet and avoided eye contact with Ruebella. Phillip specially made pains to not look in her direction as it was his quest and she was the figure holding it up. But finally after another disappointment, he spoke to Kelly.

"Asking anyone to take their own life to further this mission is not why I'm doing this. I'm going to find another way, without Ruebella making the ultimate sacrifice."

Kelly squeezed his arm reinforcing his commitment of righteousness, but he didn't know that Kelly had made up her mind. She was holding a sharp piece of flint in her hand. She stealthily slid over the distance between her and Ruebella and crashed it down on her head with a force she didn't know she possessed.

The strange thing was, Ruebella seemed to make some movement, a small indiscernible twitch that betrayed that she knew someone was behind her, yet she had done nothing. She had allowed Kelly to take her life.

John Abbott screamed and flew forward to attack Kelly. Phillip intercepted John Abbott's beeline and placed him in a gentle but firm bear hug as he struggled to lay his hands around Kelly's neck. John had never loved before and that was all he ever wanted. He had ironically found it in the witch of most people's nightmares. And in Hell of all places.

Even though Phillip had declared that his quest wasn't worth a willing sacrifice, and hadn't wished for Kelly to do his bidding. Yet, as he replayed his words in his mind, it was clear that that it was his request. He had indeed asked her to do what she had done.

Her understanding of him went beyond his own. He mouthed the words, *"thank you"* to the sheepish Kelly, who responded in kind.

"Let's finish this." And as if on cue, the demon Ruebella with bright yellow eyes materialized in front of the Gate. The sight of Ruebella returning as the demon reduced John Abbott to tears. He'd lost his love and there wasn't any way that he could turn back the clock. Although together in *Pi's* prison, and then imprisoned in Boleyn, they were never able to consummate their love. She had died clean and tidy.

Avoiding rape, from fiend or friend, was the difference between Ruebella and the other two witches and was the reason that she remained a witch Topside, but John Abbott only cared that he'd lost his chance at love.

As he passed through the gate into Red-Hell, he pleaded to her to take his life, wishing only for his own death. She looked away, shameful that she couldn't do his bidding, and allowed him to walk away from her and continue in Phillip's quest.

Ross was suffering with sadness and loss to his core as images of Harry popped into his head, and he felt alone and lost, just like John. So he stopped and waited for the small man, who was dragging his feet, to catch up to him. As he looked back, he thought he saw something over John's shoulder. For a moment, he thought they were being followed, but it was only his conscience trying to catch up.

Phillip and Kelly trudged ahead with heavy hearts as Ross put his arm around John's shoulder and picked up the pace. They were in Hell, letting the two in front get too far ahead increased the risk of becoming separated. That was the last thing Ross wanted. Actually, going to the bottom of bottoms was the last thing, yet they were on their way to that very place.

Little was said between Phillip and Kelly, they were in love and that's all they needed. Ross kept a respectful distance between the solemn couple, and found he also needed consoling as well. He sought to comfort John; maybe they could help each other.

The death of Ruebella was a trigger for Ross for it allowed him to experience for the first time, the deep loss of his best friend in Harry. As he talked to John, he felt better, but whether he was helping John was another matter.

"There it was again." Ross's sixth sense caused him to look back over his and John's shoulders, but nothing was there. And so, putting it down to being an imposter in Hell, he closed the gap between them and the couple ahead, and joined them in their remorse.

They approached the Gray Gate, and as expected the red eyed demon, Boleyn, was standing guard. She granted passage forthwith without hesitation. If she'd been able to wish them luck, she would have, as she was experiencing the feeling that something profound and possibly pivotal was bound up with the non-*Pi* fate of Phillip.

She wasn't the only one either; Kelly and Ross felt it deep in their guts too. After honing in on their thoughts, they believed that they were in the process of ending history.

The four carried on with their heads down, and trudged through the final level towards their destination hoping the quicker they were through it the better.

Although Phillip had no basis for his belief, he had a terrible feeling that their ruse was soon to be discovered. Then God, *Pi* and eventually the Devil would suddenly be forced into an alliance or at least a truce and that Hell would be the object of the scrutiny. He didn't tell his companions of his concern.

Meanwhile they thought the reason he was quiet was either because he was mourning the loss of Ruebella and Boleyn, or that he didn't know how the last gate could be opened. In an attempt to draw Phillip out of his shell, Ross broached the issue, as it was his genuine concern and he didn't want to see another murder. Phillip realized the diplomatic and clever opening and accepted it naturally and with ease. Kelly was most impressed, because she easily recognized the gambit, and the Phil of the past wouldn't. She clutched onto Phillip, he was hers now, and she was ready to kill for him. She'd done so once already. She could recognize herself either, she used to be weak and frail. Now she was an Amazon.

"Ross," replied Phillip, "and you Kelly, as I believe you may have met her, I'm hoping G.. has betrayed the Silver Witch, or as I know her, Saint Joan. Yes, Kelly and Ross, Saint Joan.

It was her death that aided me in locating the Chamber of the Cross. She made attempts on my life... yes, she... in obeying G..., had tried to kill me twice. In my head is still a piece of her G..'s cross

One of the men I killed, one of Angelo D.'s cohorts, accidently killed her when trying to kill me."

They all listened, yet nothing he could say anymore could shock them. Kelly's radar was on high alert as she wondered, "Was there something else between them?"

Phillip squeezed her hand, but she interpreted it as a guilty conscience and she let go. He did nothing to chase after it or her, and suddenly, she realized that she and he were nothing to each other at that time. In fact, she had actively distanced herself from him and had almost allowed herself to be seduced by his brother.

She suddenly realized, "My God." she thought, "He's such a different man than Phil, or even the Phillip of before, he's... he's... a real man. Confident and... and... strong." and clasped his hand tightly.

Even in Hell, time can fly when a mind is elsewhere, and soon they were standing in front of its Last Gate. The demon, the incarnation of Joan, opened the gate and stood back.

Phillip led the way, as was his obligation, and entered the lava lake cavern first. It was a shocking sight for all of them, as it was the depiction of Hell they'd seen in films time after time.

As the first eight levels didn't conform to that image, they were surprised to see it now. Slowly, he surveyed the landscape, and saw unmistakenly the way ahead. The charred wooden bridge that traversed the molten lake. Not wasting any time, he headed straight for it and started to walk across it before he gave anyone a chance to back down, not that anyone would.

Phillip didn't want a futile debate. He had a feeling that time was running out, and if he didn't do what needed to be done, whatever it was - then it would all be for naught.

"We're here. Now what?" said Kelly.

All eyes were on the black cube obelisk in front of them, and then upon Phillip. Like them, he didn't know what it was, or what to expect, but whatever his course of action was to be now, opening its door was going to be the beginning. He realized that not trying was the only failure. Failing wasn't - not trying was, so he approached The Devil's Jail Door.

He took Rank's key and inserted it in the keyhole. It fit perfectly. "Turn the key clockwise,one complete turn,no more,no less.That's what Frank had said back at Gibraltar, that's what I'll do here."

Phillip turned the key, one complete turn, counterclockwise. Taking hold of the two handles used for opening and closing the massive door, he pulled.

It glided out smoother than a well-oiled engine piston in its chamber. Then, as it reached its hinge, it swung out triumphantly, begging anyone, only one, to enter. Instantly, Phillip knew what he had to do.

"Kelly. Do you love me?"

"Yes Phillip." She'd never said it before, she'd never thought about it before. But here in Hell, it was called out of her and it came easily.

"I'm sorry to ask this of you, but because I love you, and I do, and you love me, I can ask you, and only you. I can't ask Ross or John, because it's not their responsibility, it is yours, and this is something you cannot refuse. I don't ask you out of anything other than love, I can make you, but I wouldn't. Please Kelly, you have to do this for me, for us. You have to lock me in The Devil's Jail. And you must turn the key. Turn the key clockwise, one complete turn, no more, no less. You know it has to be, that's why we're here."

With tears running down her cheeks, she nodded. She knew it was her job. Although she didn't know why, she knew this was the path they had chosen and it was the only logical conclusion to their journey; for Phillip to sacrifice himself in this inescapable jail.

If Phillip knew what he was going to do in there then he wasn't saying. The problem for Phillip was that no one knew what his plan was, including him. Just that it had to be done.

Now it was time. Phillip was proud of Kelly, because even as she sobbed, she pushed him away from their last embrace, and forced him to contemplate the interior that was soon to be his home. He looked at the inside of the door and wiped the mud off the spyglass, and instantly recognized the jewel.

It was a sister of the Vatican's Opal. He touched it gently, lovingly, not even thinking that anything could happen, but something did.

NULL

NULL NULL

NULL NULL NULL NULL NULL NULL NULL NULL

NULL

NULL NULL

NULL

Kelly, Ross and John stood only yards away, yet they saw, felt, and heard nothing. But something fundamental had occurred. It wasn't an attack, but an embrace, and Phillip's acceptance was unconditional.

In the Entanglement Tunnel, Phillip, being the only living person able to decipher the "O"s, had read about the two stones and what they really were, the two halves of a single mammoth tear God shed many years earlier. Now, they were both Phillip's.

When his two Shoes recognized each other in Salem, nothing could keep them apart. And this was true for the Opals. Now, in the embodiment of Phillip, they became one in spirit. The two connected with its sister counterpart on a wavelength outside of any known spectrum. Phillip felt the unification of the two separate and distinct gems become RhomSong, and it rumbled and thundered throughout his body.

Likewise his *Shoes of the Devil* and *Tears of God* joined in unison, invisible to the God's above. It was only the fact that Phillip was undetectable that spared them from feeling a terrifying shiver.

Acting like an emulsifier, the union of the *Tears of God* cemented the indivisible bonds between all aspects of Phillip's being, and affirmed the existence of the new God. He knew now he had the power to fulfill the promise made when they'd entered the Devil's building in Gibraltar.

Here and now, this was the moment; the risk had to be taken. He felt it as did everyone, including those who were alive and not. This was that moment; it would never happen again.

His last embrace, NULL, the Entanglement Signature, gave him the answer he needed.

He knew what to do.

This was the time and the place. This was it, here and now.

HERE. NOW.

Phillip looked back at Kelly and when their eyes locked, she almost died. Her experience was akin to the time Phillip first spied God from the edge of the Universe. Suddenly she was utterly breathless.

Phillip had magically grown six inches and his body was ripped like a body builder. This would even have been apparent if he were clothed normally, but now, as his last gift for Kelly, he willed his clothes to be the epitome of chic and masculinity. It was hypnotic for Kelly. His eyes radiated compassion, empathy, LOVE.

Only Ross's shoulder stopped her from collapsing.

Ross too could see in Phillip's blue gray eyes that hope and purpose resided there.

Despite weighing over two tons his steps were light and elegant, not breaking the connection between their eyes, Phillip backed up into the cell until the *Diamond* halted his retreat. The miraculous balancing gem drew little attention from the imposters. They'd seen so many miracles that this one was hardly worth mentioning.

Living in the here and now, Phillip was truly superior, matching the women of Earth with a super conscience equal to theirs. Even with the unknown waiting just seconds away, he was enthralled at the thought of what he proposed to do next rather than being scared.

He was going to do it.

Not breaking his gaze with Kelly, with a loud crash he pulled the redundant empty coffin off the massive gem and pushed it with his foot towards the door opening. Ross bent down and dragged the coffin out of the way being more than careful not to break the look between the two. He acted not only out of courtesy, but also because he was scared that it might have the power of a laser beam and burn a hole right through him. He shoved it over the edge and into the lava lake where it was greedily devoured.

Then slowly, and with the greatest respect, he swung the door round ready to be closed.

With one last, "I love you." Phillip broke his gaze with Kelly, reclined onto the *Diamond* and relaxed, adjusting his arms and legs to dangle over its edges. Kelly slowly pushed the vault door towards its final resting place, hereby fulfilling her pledge. She didn't know whether she would ever see her love again. The stage was set and there was no turning back or backing out.

He was alone, lost to the World, Heaven and Hell. The beginning.

The end.

The beginning of the end.

The World, Heaven and Hell would never be the same.

Tears cascaded down her cheekbones as she took hold of the key, and turned it.

CHAPTER 58

THE SPITE-FILLED MAN

The memories of his adoption were almost non-existent, more akin to a shadow of a distant and long forgotten dream than the reality of his past. It only took a day after being given his beautiful blue room to feel like he'd lived here all his life.

This was Bill's new home and these were his loving parents.

He gaily rejoiced his third birthday even as he heard his mother say "I guess we have to paint it blue. Just blue. Any blue." she sighed whilst looking at the plain small undecorated spare room.

"Sky blue." the young Bill chuckled not understanding or detecting the utter dismay in his mother's voice. Nor did he register the consternation in his father's heavy groans after the miraculous arrival of Bill's baby brother, Phil, as Bill named him.

"Typical." He'd heard but didn't understand his parent's mutterings."We fought and fought for the adoption, and found the perfect smart and handsome boy in Bill, and then we get pregnant just after we'd given up trying. Why couldn't he have come only a year earlier? Why did he come now? Just when we've got what we wanted. We wouldn't have to have paid at all. Just typical."

This was the welcoming party that greeted Phil to the World.
Decades later, Phil still bore deep scars in his psyche.

His personality evaporated away until there was nothing left other than conformity and submission. A constant onslaught of parental disappointment and negligence does that.

His family's passive aggressive behavior and utter indifference permeated his mind, body and soul. Phillip's life was miserable and yet he would vehemently deny it to anyone who suggested the truth.

Over forty years later, his elder brother Bill had sent him away to investigate a double murder in a hamlet called Hecate. His logic was sound, but the underlying reason was less obvious. It was his means to escort his elicit lover, Kelly, out of harm's way - *his wife*.

Only a fortnight later Bill was visiting his brother in the Evelyn Mills hospital where he lay in a coma of mysterious origin. Also a strange coincidence was that Kelly, now his ex-lover was also in a similar state.

Before Kelly succumbed to the Devil, she spurned Bill and so he deemed it just that she had succumbed to a mysterious ailment. Things were going so well now that he surveyed the path before him. Gone were the possibilities of malicious gossip or even blackmail in the comatose beings of Phil and Kelly.

To Bill it just couldn't get better. The stars were aligned in his favor, so why not. Only a couple of days later, a callous, calculating, and charming man called Bill put a plan into action. Phil? Who was he anyway?

Secretly Bill had sought out the down and outs under the railroad arches and filthy alleyways. He had a proposition for someone willing and able. When Bill's chauffeur driven car stopped at the red light at Fifteenth and Eighth, Bill lowered his car window and generously offered a vagrant spare change. Instead of a dollar or two, Bill gave him a hundred dollars to impress his date.

Street people have certain skills needed for survival. They can be mean and untrustworthy. But they're always tough and savvy. But they'd never met the likes of Bill - rich, smart and devious. It was easy to underestimate him, a wealthy polished man wearing a business suit and looking the model of sophistication.

So the homeless man eagerly agreed to the strange rich man's request."If he had to go that far to get laid, then it might as well be me who is going to profit." he thought.

The moment the vagabond extended his hand through the open window of the limousine's backseat, Bill discharged his concealed weapon. The drifter had to be killed first, to dispose of the witness and create the perpetrator at the same time.

Then he shot his stunned stepfather, mother and dumb-ugly wife. As a tour de force, he then shot himself in the shoulder. Next, he placed the gun in the tramp's hand and fired the remaining rounds from his dying hand.

According to the police report,"This upstanding businessman and his dear family were the tragic victims of a carjacking gone wrong, and Bill had only acted in self-defense, only sadly, too little too late."

In one fell swoop, Bill became the sole heir to the family fortune, businesses and all their holdings. Not bad for ten minutes of work and a bit of pain. But even that was a win because he could play the wounded soldier routine to the beautiful Kelly who'd miraculously appeared at the funeral.

All his life, he got anything he wanted; his greed and luck were not unexpected, in fact, they were natural. Having Kelly and inheriting a massive fortune was just a day's work. Everything had gone so smoothly until Kelly suddenly baulked at his lie. Her reaction should have been a harbinger for Bill to quit while he was ahead. However, it was his constant yearning to twist the knife that ultimately brought death to his door.

Bill had been driven his whole life to suppress or stifle every initiative that Phil created or developed. When Phil faxed a superior piece of journalism to Bill reporting a double murder, Bill was tempted to falsify the identity of its originator, and only because it was Phil.

From the moment Kelly rejected Bill, not one thing went his way. Eventually he was denied the opportunity to ask for forgiveness from God, and ultimately arrived in the lowest level of Green-Hell.

~~~

Ego and Bill were so much alike that had met on Earth there would have been instant loathing. It was no different in Hell. With his cohort, Vin, walking by his side, Ego and Bill literally bumped into each other. Ego had no choice other than to utter some threat unless he wanted to look weak in front of Vin. That wasn't an option, so he dispensed a few choice words in Bill's direction and continued on his way.

It didn't scare Bill one bit. He instantly recognized that Ego was once a leader of men Topside and probably held a position of authority. He found it interesting that such a man would share his company with a so obviously inferior and worthless person as Vin.

Of course it was natural for Vin to seek the company of an alpha male, but Vin didn't seem too awestruck by Ego. The two of them were worth more than a casual glance, and the opportunity to pay Ego back might arise. So Bill followed them. When they parted ways, he had to make a choice, to follow one or the other. He chose Ego of course.

He saw Ego hook up with two strange deranged men who looked like twins, and who obviously shared the same condition. Their speech and motor functions were grossly maladjusted and dysfunctional. A third man accompanied them. With Ego as their leader, they formed a troop to avoid at all costs.

Bill hadn't been long in Hell, but like Angelo D. he figured out the place in a second and easily slipped the detection of a demon at the first opportunity. He preferred to strike out on his own knowing he could outwit, survive even flourish if he played his cards right. He tracked the strange fellowship for a day or two as there didn't appear to be anything better to do. Besides, the two imbeciles provided ample entertainment. Bill's hardest task was to stay undetected, as he had to suppress fits of laughter from spontaneously erupting out of his mouth as they constantly fumbled, fell and flopped over each other and anything else in the way. Bill saw that Ego routinely threatened to beat either one of them for their stupid antics. Save for the intervention of the other brother, he surely would have.

Then something amazing happened. The little gang of four as he called them; landed themselves a truly amazing catch, Kelly. In her group there were two other unimportant men, one short with a cleft lip, and the other tall, and definitely not Hell material. There was also an extremely short and malevolent looking woman who looked like a toy witch.

Upon seeing Kelly, the men reacted like a lawless indecent mob, which was what they were. Bill was torn between two choices; should he help her, or join in? But it was a moot point.

Out of nowhere, a missile smashed into the cluster of the four men literally catching them with their pants down. Angelo D, Smasher, Basher and Buster were scattered like bowling pins. Bill ducked at the moment of impact for fear of the spraying blood.

Moments later, he peered back over his cover to see, to his horror, that the projectile was his brother. He had single handedly killed four men.

Much to his fury, he watched Phil and Kelly embrace intimately and passionately. She reciprocated all of Phil's affection. He thought she was his Kelly! That was it. Bill had reaffirmed his purpose in life albeit in Hell.

Whether it was divine, fate or Devil spawned, he resumed his 'practice' to thwart anything his brother did.

"Be it good, bad, or whatever, I know, me, I, myself, BILL, I'm going to rid myself of that infernal brother once and for all. AND I WILL NOT CALL HIM PHILLIP."

Vows of hatred went unpunished in Hell as they were the rule not the exception. Hell was full of men who'd vowed evil intent. Once made, the vow meant that from that point on, Bill would have to follow Phillip wherever he went, sabotage whatever he did, and meddle with every plan. Not until his pledge was satisfied could he rest.

He watched Phillip and Kelly, hand in hand, sneaking their way through Hell, towards the lower gate. He followed them with utter conviction. Having a purpose filled him with life and energy. He would shrug off the pain of the demons' lashings without thought.

Wherever Phillip and Kelly would go, he would go too, because he only had one choice, and he didn't want another. Evading the same demons they dodged, he approached the Gate they'd just scurried through. Bill didn't know what the rules were to gain entry to the lower levels of Hell, but there was little choice as the only path to take was the one blocked by the Gate and the Gatekeeper.

"Good evening." It sounded so lame to address a fearsome, loathsome demon in such a manner, but he had to start somewhere. He decided he was going to have to talk his way in. And if anyone could do that, Bill could.

"Have you seen, no, I didn't... oh..." the demon made a motion, and the Gate opened before him. It took a couple of seconds to register that it was open. He quickly came to his senses and scampered through without delay barely concealing his smirk of superiority.

He surmised that the vow he'd taken was somehow made known to the Gatekeepers and they would grant him free passage. While descending to the lower level the thought crossed his mind, that maybe it wouldn't be so easy to go back up.

It was the first doubt of his quest, and Bill being Bill decided it was worth it. Taking his eyes off the direction his targets were going, he looked back towards the Gate and thought that indeed the Gatekeepers wouldn't be so accommodating upon ascension. Immediately he paid for it.

"OUCH." A jab of pain struck the back of his roaming eyes. "Ouch, what was that?" he mumbled as he reached up to his face to rub his eye socket. He felt wetness under it and discovered that it wasn't a tear but a drop of red blood. He was crying blood.

"Ooouch." The pain shot through him again. It was clear there were consequences to his vow.

"Phil it is, all or nothing." he said aloud, and he didn't look back again.

Phillip and Kelly ducked and hid as the demons wandered close by, so Bill did the same. He had to do it more often. He was hiding from not just any demon who passed, but also those in the group up front. Maybe even twice the tall gentleman may have seen him, but he was sure that he never got more than the briefest of glimpses.

It didn't deter him in the slightest in any event, not that he had much choice.

"Thank you, Ross, you're a life…"

"Taker." said Ross finishing her sentence. He'd felt like dead wood for a long time, always feeling that people were acting heroically when he wasn't. He'd seen Phillip, Kelly, Ruebella and Boleyn all do it, now he had finally contributed on the hard stuff.

"What do we do now Kelly?"

"*Wait*" she whispered and sat down in the Ninth Level of Hell as if in her living room.

~~~

When Phillip closed the door in the Square Building in Gibraltar, he felt the presence of Eternal Mortal beings flicker like old light bulbs. Like everyone across the Universe, he was unaware that there was this background drone on the edge of quietness, and he only noticed it because of its drop in volume.

At first, he didn't know what it was and wrote it off as inconsequential, which was until he experienced the sensation again when the gates of Hell between Level II and III closed behind him.

So when the gate between Level III and IV shut, he focused intently for a possible dip in the vibration, listening for it like an owl hunting a mouse. Unfortunately, although he felt the experience, it got away from him before he had a chance to grasp it.

However, when he traversed the boundary between Green-Hell and Yellow-Hell, he felt a bump in the silent whine. It was large enough to dispel any nagging doubt that it was a hallucination, but didn't help other than that. It wasn't until crossing of Yellow-Hell to Red-Hell that he made a breakthrough.

The imperceptible buzz had three frequencies, and two of them were much weaker than the dominant one. Instantly, he knew what and why. He was feeling the presence of the Devil, *Pi* and God's souls, and he could differentiate between them. The Devil's was the most prominent as they were in Hell.

What he once considered immaterial and had dismissed, now,

he believed, was important. Only knowing that there was The Devil's Jail at the end of the road, but not knowing the nature of the torment, caused Phillip to think about what he was going to do when he got there.

He toyed with many ideas, but none of them matured to become anything close to a plan. He recalled that only two months ago, the World was round, Armageddon wasn't even loose talk let alone a reality, and Phil was Phil, not Phillip. His lost innocence was the World's loss too.

The toll of the above WWIII continued to mount, not just on humans, but upon the planet, while the physics of the Universe foiled the best scientists of the day.

After he crossed the threshold into Gray-Hell, manic ideas leapt into and swirled around in his head as the clarity of the Eternal Mortals' insignia crystalized, and so too did a plan. Then he felt the jolt of the Devil's presence. It could only have meant one thing.The Dark Lord had reentered Hell on the Green Level.

Now, inside The Devil's Jail, he breathed hard because of the insanity of his plan, and that he was actually going to go through with it. Kelly had been brave, accepting his decision and not attempting to stop him. She had pushed the door shut and confirmed that she trusted him to do what he was going to do.

Everyone had stepped up to the plate. Now all they could do was wait, since everything, was up to him.

Getting snug on the diamond's tabletop, if it were possible to be comfortable lying on the hardest natural material, Phillip set his absurd idea into motion. And strangely, his plan was to do nothing. It was nothing. If doing nothing was nothing. It wasn't.

Only in the fatal seconds after the door was shut, did he know. The answer came.The answer WAS Null, the second Opal told him so. Most importantly, he had confirmation.The silent whine of the three gods was gone. He searched for it, but couldn't feel it.

It was Null. It was the start. It was the start of nothing.

Contrary to being the Devil's worst punishment, here in the cell he wasn't in any distress. The cell was the center of the Ninth Level of Hell the furthest place in the Universe from God's love, but for Phillip, this was no torture, it was what he wanted.

The seal between the door and the cell walls was perfect. No air could enter or exit. He was at peace and had to be for this to work. He closed his eyes and focused.

With the power of thought, he lowered the light emitting from the diamond, thinking things through would be better when not in a glaring light. It had truly begun.

CHAPTER 60

THIS IS HOW MANY PEOPLE WILL REALLY DIE IF THERE WAS A WWIII

"I've lost sight of her." said God to herself."Something's happened and I'm twenty or so minutes behind the action. I wonder if *Pi* is having better luck, and that would be funny if this wasn't so important."

Twenty minutes passed before the negative response told her that there was nothing remotely amusing about this new development. As the last of the warheads stuttered or roared, *Pi* looked over what remained of the Earth and scoured all living beings.

The death toll was staggering. Three billion were dead and the remaining population was destined to half and half again. Ebolux, a natural amalgamation of the three deadliest diseases and radiation sickness would rage on well past the last bomb's detonation.

Like a cleaner sweeping away dirt, *Pi*, God's proxy, scoured the Earth for any sign of Kelly, and hence, PhilLIP. If he wasn't found soon, then the accusations would start amongst the partners as they faced their failures.

Deaf to the prayers of the suffering, the two Gods combed Earth until they were left with only one conclusion, given that neither had captured him without the others' knowledge.

The Devil had found and hidden Kelly and PhilLIP in Hell.

If this was true,then they had no choice other than to negotiate and cajole him into a joint venture. Putting their pride aside, God reached out to the Devil. Though he and *Pi* never exchanged anything other than insults and barbs,*she* could talk with him. However, as always when dealing with the Devil,there was a problem.

411

This time he didn't want to talk as he was in a snot due to his humiliation in the Entanglement War. Under different circumstances, *she* might have a small crumb of sympathy for him, but not now. Her back was up against the wall and time was of the essence. So instead of leaving him to his own devices for a century or so to fester, God was going to have to suck it up and apologize, and do it now.

"Well, you know I'm busy dealing with all these new hell-mates which you've caused."He finally replied after what seemed like an eon.

God winced. He was behaving like a petulant child and when he was in that mood, nothing would work. If she told him this however, she might as well kiss negotiation goodbye. So *she* did what *she* didn't want to do - but had to. *She* asked for help, heaped with pleading and groveling.

"So, now that you need me, now you're making nice?"He hung up.

God didn't expect anything less. *She* was going to have to lose a few battles if *she* was going to win this war. Hence, *she* waited and suffered a humiliation of her own knowing he knew *she* was steaming with anger. It was too bad, but *she* faced a delicate situation and based on her long experience, *she* knew that this was the quickest way. *She* was going to have to gauge how long *she* should wait, compared with how long *she* could.

To distract herself, *she* halfheartedly searched the World trying to keep busy while *she* considered the appropriate time to call again. *She* waited only an hour knowing that the Devil would hang up immediately as a matter of principle. True to her belief, he did.

In the meantime, *Pi* continued to confirm there wasn't any trace of Kelly whatsoever. It only bolstered her belief that PhilLIP had descended into Hell which made her handling of the Devil all the more critical. *She* waited another hour and wasn't too surprised that he rejected her again.

On the sixth time, he replied with, "What?"

It may have been six wasted hours, but was better than a couple of years.

"Devil, you realize what's going on, don't you?" "No." and he hung up again.

She called back immediately and before he had time to reject her,

she told him, that *she* was sorry, and that maybe he should check the Sun, just to humor her, if he so pleased. As a testament to the pickle *she* was in, the Sun had just turned back to its former yellow self.

Ever suspicious, he thought, "God and *Pi* are pulling a fast one. Just as I was beginning to believe her. That was close."

The Devil scoffed and hung up, but not before he unleashed a torrent of abuse. God was patient though. *She* knew he'd check the Sun periodically out of pure curiosity, and after it changed, he would begrudgingly accept her next call.

And he did.

And it was a good thing he did as there was still no sign of Kelly, and still the death toll rose, if anyone cared.

The Devil listened to God before hanging up again *when he heard her suggestion that Phil wasn't on Earth anymore but was hiding in Hell.*

This time, *she* knew *she'd* have to wait.

She knew her proposal was paramount to accusing the Devil of doing something wrong or making a mistake.

Biting her nails in frustration, *she* waited two hours before calling back. Although he still wouldn't be open to the idea, *she* would be able to plant another seed of doubt in his mind. After several additional calls, the Devil was finally ready to listen and be receptive.

God divulged all her theories upon him, and finally there was a moment when a light went on in the Devil's head. He went quiet before hanging up.

She was in. *She'd* call the Devil back in a minute to reiterate that this was in everyone's interest and that no one was culpable.

She made the call.

When he answered this time, *she* took his side saying that,

"He was probably right in doubting her theory." It was a necessary self-depreciation to give the Devil's ego the recognition that he was the smartest one there.

"But they needed to be sure." he listened and reluctantly started to acknowledge that there might be some merit to God's arguments. As he started to consider the unthinkable, *that he could be wrong,* he noticed something that terrified him. Worse still was that it could possibly be her proof.

He couldn't share this - especially with God, so he hung up.

The Styx had gone down about a millimeter.

For any normal river, a millimeter was utterly insignificant, but for the Styx, this was unprecedented and could be a foreshadowing of darker things to come.

Exposing pure white bleached rock as its witness, the Devil fretted in disbelief. He'd never seen or even heard of the river's height fluctuating before. It was as it was and always had been, even in Level IX. Now a drop in its level was easily visible and the Devil was amiss for its cause.

Its folklore gained such purchase in Man's psyche that the Devil was happy to oblige in the recognition of the river's existence. Seeing the Styx for what it was it heightened the mystic of Hell, and crazily, making the journey there an appealing prospect. He created and named ferrywomen (failed witches) and imagined the existence of dark, evil rites of passage.

" Why stop there?" He dismissed that Hell's landscape and realms were the product of Man's imagination. He proclaimed himself as Hell's great architect and before too long, he believed he was. Hell was not the boiling brimstone of Man's sadism, but a cold and frigid place due to one thing, the absence of God's love.

He decided to investigate by following the river along its course down through Hell and 'be damned' with God and *Pi's* whining. At first, he was mildly concerned, but by the time he was halfway through the second level of Yellow-Hell, he broke out into a run.

He'd confirmed to himself that the Styx was actually draining, and rapidly. It wasn't down by a millimeter anymore; it had lost about that much per level of Hell and was now down at least five or six where he stood.

It was causing widespread consternation and optimism throughout the hell-mate populous. To dispel any of their foolish thoughts, the order for extra lashings was quickly dispatched. Little did he know that three demons, risking all, had furtively lowered themselves into the waters of the Landing Dock and let the current take them away.

By the time the Devil had arrived in Level IX things went from bad to worse. From a vantage point on the wooden bridge, the Devil was stunned to see that the waterfalls of the Styx had split into two upon entering the lava lake. The splintered falls gave the Devil a real jolt of reality.

"Shit!" barked the Devil. When the Devil shouted, Hell shuddered. His thunderous shout caused reverberations that took many seconds to stop.

For the first time in history, it was possible to determine which way the river flowed and it wasn't from Level I to Level IX, but instead it travelled the other way. When the Devil looked back towards the jail, he saw that the trickle of the Styx that used to reach right up to the jail's door had gone.

Although this wasn't unexpected and certainly not the best news, it meant that the Devil was at the wrong end of Hell. "OK, The Landing Dock."

He swore. He could easily retrace his steps back to the Landing Dock to see where it was going. It was something he was just about to do. Until he was hit by another profound shock. Although the river was water, it consisted of something else, something the Devil had lost plenty of, Entanglement.

His Entanglement.

He'd never detected it because it was neutralized with something.

Ironically, he would call it something evil. *Pi's* numbers.

He stood aghast, completely dumfounded that his missing Entanglement was in Hell all this time, and that *Pi* was responsible for its theft. He was about to project himself off to Hell Level I, to the Landing Dock, when another impossibility stunned him.

Kelly! In of all places The Ninth Level of Hell. At The Devil's Jail.

At Phil's Cell.

Half of him was already in the process of materializing and he almost tore himself into two when he changed his mind to stay put.

" Why and what was Kelly doing in Hell Level IX? And, whatever… I'll be doing her in a quarter of an hour… whether I find out or not… Landing Dock. Sure."

Maybe raping Kelly would temporarily alleviate his feeling of ignorance and maybe it would even inspire him. He'd justify his action any way he could; not that he must to Man, but to God, yes, he would have to explain his delinquency to her.

He didn't know how long he had before the river Styx ran dry and what that would mean. Nor did he even know how deep it was. He just assumed it was deep but he'd had no reason in the past to think about such a mundane thing. Now the question wracked his brain. Although the hell-mates had said it was bottomless, they were not really a reliable source. Even when it was draining, its sinister waters revealed nothing.

The presence of Kelly as always made it hard for the Devil to think clearly."Christ, and there's so much going on,The Styx, God, *Pi*, WWIII, and whatever else is happening. Kelly…"

He planned to drop in on Kelly in the form of the flying gargoyle, to strike fear and horror into her.

"Ouch. What? I can't transform out of human form? Shit. See. Yet another thing. God's right. Probably, bitch, as normal. I'll make her wait out of Kar... I mean spite." she was in his head, and he wanted to be in hers.

"Hello Kelly." He materialized in front of her in human form. "Oh and yes, Ross. Pardon me, I almost forgot." He endeavored to be his ever-charming self.

"Hello err... Mr. Devil." replied Kelly, obviously afraid but not half as much as she should have been, and neither was she in the least bit shocked by his sudden appearance.

Ross nodded in his continually polite manner.

"Well Kelly..." but he didn't get to finish his sentence.

~~~

The Devil wanted Hell to be a God free plane of existence, "Because it's Hell, that's why." he laughed loudly to himself. "Not only have I done Man a great service, but also *you*." He pointed upwards to where he thought Heaven was.

Out of all the insults the Devil had levelled against God, this one was the worst. *She* had viewed him in many ways as an innocent bystander, who weathered a constant storm of human sin and desire. However, when *she* heard his latest slander, *she* felt betrayed. *She* had endeavored to give him the benefit of the doubt and all *she* got in return was lies. It stung all the more because of this, and *she* was forced to wipe away a tear that leaked out of the corner of her eye,

The Tear of God.

Never had *she* been so affronted, and that was saying something with the things the Devil had done in the past. Carrying eons of suppressed emotions, the Tear was so large and heavy that as it traveled through the Entanglement War, it acted as a magnet for God's Entanglement.

It absorbed and condensed so much that it solidified into the form of an opal, and fell towards Earth. Months later, the Chinese conceived the Fire Dragon to explain the bright path it made through the atmosphere.

The Devil, who acted with the wisdom of three men, was there to snafu it up tout suite. He had a very special use for it. It was exactly what his Jail needed, a spyhole.

In his hurry, however, he missed the fact that the Tear broke into two uneven halves. The smaller piece strayed off course and crashed in the hinterland of Australia rather than the orient, a place that would be known as Coober Pedy, the Opal Capital of the World.

The unearthing of an enormous and glorious opal didn't turn the Devil's head, but Pope Raul's was.

Relieved, God smiled when the Devil failed to rummage through the Australian Outback. *She* was left to surmise that he didn't know of its existence. Even from her distant outpost on the far side of the Entanglement War, *she* never lost track of it. That was until the advent of PhilLIP, and the demise of Godiva.

As for the principal shard, *she'd* lost sight of it the moment the Devil placed his hands upon it. *She* didn't wonder where he'd hidden it. There was only one possible place it'd gone; *she* knew it was somewhere in Hell.

With the larger Tear of God in his clutches, he beamed in pure delight as he cruelly rolled it into an elongated shape like a thin baguette. His purpose for it was to make it suitable for its new function, as his Jail's Peephole.

He knew the prize that it was, a little piece of God. Thus he intentionally enslaved it with maximum malice and minimum chance of rescue. It was in prison itself, and although part of God, he knew it wasn't really her in persona, just like a lock of hair.

CHAPTER 61

DOWN TO BRASS TACKS

God had had it with the Devil. The World, their World, was falling apart and all he wanted was to play the injured party game. Things were too important to "Fuck around anymore."*she* expressed to *Pi* furiously. Even *Pi* feared God's wrath when *she* was like this.

God had good reason to be so, because if things were bad before, they had just become much worse. The only consolation was that it was *Pi* who was the victim. Other than that, it was another evil manifestation of Phillip's existence.

The Dead Sea was spitting out Entanglement like a frying pan full of sizzling hot oil.This wouldn't have been a problem in the past, but that was before Phillip.

Now,as it spewed out into the expansive Universe, instead of uniting with its Entanglement complement, something else was occurring. Worse still, it depended on the Phase of the Sun. Counterparts were resolving,but with the new laws of physics,they didn't just resolve their spin, orientation and balance,there was an additional reaction.

They left behind a negative and a positive *Pi* remainder. Those residuals were binding with the probabilities of her stream of luck, corrupting, inflating or neutralizing them. And the Sun's Phases dictated the polarity and severity.

The Red Queen of Spades was under attack, giving *Pi* another reason (not that she needed one) to seek Phillip's speedy demise.

As a testament to the immensity of the Eternal Mortals minds, God saw that Mercury was approaching its furthest distance from the Earth. The Blue Planet was the epicenter of the Entanglement War and in the aftermath of God's latest attack, the Entanglement boundary only had a radius of ten light minutes.

That meant that, very shortly, Mercury's orbit would pass through the Entanglement frontier and soon would be on its outer side.

"Whichs means God..." *Pi* said to the 'dearest' ally.

"That I can... get to Mercury, which is where we think Hell is" cried out God in delight.

"Great work *Pi*." For the first time in eons, *she* meant it. And for the first time in eons, *Pi* needed God as much as God needed *Pi*. Finally, both were willingly working together.

Unhindered, they could deal with Phillip whether the Devil was on side or not. He was hardly relevant anymore, so they thought.

~~~

A blinding light filled Hell Level IX. It was bright enough for Ross to see Kelly's skeleton through her body. Using their hands, the mortals shielded their eyes from God's sudden arrival, but still they fell to the floor.

With her regal arrival announced to all, God lowered her brightness (and her beauty) to provide the Devil's lair some modesty, but not enough to keep his barefaced intentions obscured.

"I should have known it Devil. Kelly? Com'on.

While Earth and the frigging Universe are teetering on the brink of destruction, here you are trying to chat up a woman, Kelly no less. Again. You're such an asshole." riled God upon her materialization in the nadir of space and time.

Luckily, for Kelly, she was already in a partial fetal position, which saved her from the deafening words. Ross and John XXVIIth too had fallen to the floor with their hands pressed hard against their ears. Still, blood started to seep between their fingers and they fought unconsciousness.

The Devil just looked away from Kelly unfazed by the harm the immortals were causing. Then he spoke to God trying to portray superiority.

"What? And you too *Pi*, I see you in the Styx. Your stupid river of possibilities and my stolen Entanglement. I should have known, so... where's it going now Eh? Where's my Entanglement ending up? Heaven? No, I don't think so." he continued glaring at God. But he couldn't think of anywhere, and his emotions were clouding any invention, so he gave up, and instead said,

"What the fuck do you two want anyway?"

Not mincing any words, God bluntly said, "We want Phillip. He's here in Hell, so that's why we're here. You wouldn't catch me dead down here otherwise."

"I wish, and I've told you before, I have no Phillip. Phil, the guy you idiots think is Phillip is in there." He tipped his head to point towards the jail behind him.

"No he isn't, he's in Hell, somewhere." insisted God with as much patience as *she* could unearth.

"YES HE IS." reafirmed The Devil. "He's in MY JAIL CELL." He was unable to conceal that he was enjoying this. He couldn't remember the last time, or even if there was such a time, that he had the pleasure to watch God squirm and *Pi* fidget.

The Queen of Spades rose up from the receding Styx and took up a position behind God. Although this was a joint venture, it was God's show. However, there may have been another reason, embarrassment. She looked unusually worried for the normally indifferent and expressionless card. Even though *Dia* stood behind God, God was keenly aware that something was wrong with her.

Like the Devil, an anxious *Pi* was something *she'd* never sensed before. The reason would have to wait; dealing with the Devil took center stage.

"NO HE'S NOT." shouted God.

"YES HE IS." The Devil shouted back and rendered the three mortals' unconscious.

God incidentally noticed the injuries they had caused; but only because *she* wanted something from them.

"Well done, Devil." said God sarcastically, intending to humiliate and shame him.

"Screw you." he squabbled back."Anyway, you're wrong, but it's immaterial anyway. Phil is in the jail."

"Nooo. And it is important, because, we can't see him. So you'll, have to find him for us, because, you idiot, you've just knocked out the people that know where he is."

"Well. You're so clever, you are *God*, bring them round why don't you?" retorted the Devil.

God couldn't deny he was right on that fact. So with a humph, *she* knelt down next to Ross and put her mouth close enough to kiss him. *She* breathed into his mouth.

Then *she* turned her attention to Kelly and repeated. Like Ross, Kelly also came round and bravely managed to keep her sanity and sight. Even after looking into God's face, albeit with a sideways glance.

As Phillip's woman she had willed herself to live and to fight to prove her worth. This was a complete turnaround of the Kelly of the previous month. Neither was she stupid, she knew she was in mortal danger. So she kept her gaze lowered and avoided looking at anything other than God's feet.

A moment later she heard a cough, as the overflow of God's breath brought John back. It was doubtful he would have survived a close personal encounter.

"Ok, Devil, ask them." And even though the Devil hated taking orders, and secretly thought about ignoring the request out of recalcitrance, he obeyed.

"Kelly. Do you know where Phil is?" he said in his smoothest of tongues.

She complied and answered him. She knew the presence of God and the other entity who she presumed was *Pi* meant Phillip had caused something to happen in the Universe.

This was critical, because she knew neither she nor Ross could withstand the Devil, or any of the others. So because of the probability that Phillip was working his magic, she wasn't afraid to spill the beans.

"Bless him." she thought, not "God bless him. Phillip's fighting back, I can feel it, and it must be significant, as God isn't taking any prisoners by the sounds of it.

Listen to the way *she's* talking with the Devil. And Phillip was right when he told the Pope, God is a Woman. Wish He and the cardinals were here so I could rub their noses in it.

'God IS a Woman, not a Man, Pope!'

Anyhow, now it's my turn. My turn to face them. My turn." So Kelly addressed the Devil without evasion or hesitation.

"He's in there." Nodding her head towards the jail. "HAH!!!" boomed the Devil gleefully.

Kelly's answer had put a wide smirk on the Devil's face, but although that wasn't what God wanted, the news in itself wasn't that bad. The dificult task of finding an invisible man in Hell wasn't required now.

Happily all the hypotheticals envisioned by God fell by the wayside with Kelly's admission. For instance God wouldn't have been troubled in the least if *she'd* taken Kelly hostage and threatened her imminent torture if Phillip didn't give himself up.

Kelly had said Phillip was in The Devil's Jail and all God had to do now was decide if *she* was going to go to the trouble of trying to figure out how. *She* hated mysteries, and this was another one to chalk up.

Keeping her own council for the moment, *she* motioned to the Devil, granting him the honor of opening it and ushering them inside.

"Devil… if you please…" said God with a sideways glance at the door. *She* also knew the Devil and expected that he'd make a meal out of it.

"But let him have his moment. Who gives a shit who opens it."
It was obvious God knew the Devil all too well…

"God and *Pi,* it is my pleasure, but also my duty to u…"

"Ok… Ok… That's enough." Changing her mind. "Forget the frigging speech. Just materialize inside, grab the SOB and get him out here. AND let us deal with him."

"Because it's obvious he's out of your league." She silently added.

"Actually God." said the Devil smugly, "You can't materialize
inside, there's… you know, a curse to stop anyone from doing so."

"Sure."retorted God trying not to smoke the Devil out of existence for his antics."A curse? OK. Fine. Have it your way…just get on with it."

"Right then." said the Devil resuming his grandstanding,"God and *Pi,* it is my pleasure, but also my duty to unlock The Devil's Jail Door and escort the deadly Phil into your awaiting arms. With a single turn of the key, the key you see in the lock will…"

And for long moment the Devil just paused and wondered to himself.

"Where did the key come from? I remember that it wasn't in the lock when I visited it… when I wanted to check if Phil was in the Jail myself. Then I searched Ego, he didn't have it, although I was certain he was lying. Come to think of it, he looked a little too relieved after I finished interrogating him.

I thought it was because I didn't find the key. But maybe, he was relieved, that I didn't find him with the key. Or maybe he was wondering, if… if… I donno.

If…if he'd lost the key? Got it.I bet Vin had it all along, and they… What's Kelly doing here in Hell anyway?"

To the frustration of God and *Pi*, the Devil had stopped what he was supposed to be doing, and turned his attention to God.

"You… You… You said, God, that his guy called Phillip was alive on Earth. That was, up until yesterday." Deflecting attention away from himself like a seasoned politician, he focused on Kelly next.

"Kelly, how did you get here?"

God had thought that the quickest way to get that Jail Door open was to appease the Devil and let him have his way. "Well that idea failed miserably." So to speed it along, *she* took over the questioning of the mortals.

"So Kelly and Ross and John. You know who I am, right?" *She* spoke quietly and in comforting, kind tones.

They all nodded.

"So you wouldn't lie to me, right?" More nodding occurred.

"Tell me, how did you get here, who brought you here, and when?"

"Well." said Kelly, deeming it her responsibility to reply as Phillip was her charge, "We got into Hell through a Cubic building, similar to this one actually, in Gibraltar."

"It was Phillip."

"About a day ago."

"Yes."

"That's about it."

God was stunned. Kelly had answered every question without contempt, hesitation or quibble. *She'd* seen this, from afar, on Earth from other people, but the only time they answered like that was when they were confident that they were winning, or were going to win.

God questioned Kelly further. "You think Phillip's winning? That he's going to beat *us*?"

"You're here, aren't you?" Kelly replied with her diva tone.

Ego had felt the wrath of Kelly's tongue and now God was receiving it. The Devil was enjoying every moment.

"Oh." said God, trying not to be bettered by a mere mortal, "So Phillip brought you here, yes? Then you... what? Locked him in there?"

"Yes." said Kelly, almost chirpily.

God turned and looked triumphantly at the Devil. *She* quelled her growing suspicion that Kelly had something up her sleeve, and summarized Kelly's answer, "So it was you that locked Phil in the Jail."

"Phillip." She retorted. Kelly had conveniently forgotten that it was she who originally refused to call him by his new chosen name.

"PhilLIP. In there. You did that. Yesterday." said God for confirmation.

"No." interrupted Kelly, "No, not yesterday, we got into Hell yesterday. I locked Phillip in the jail about an hour ago. It took us a day, to get here, 'cos we arrived in 'Green-Hell' and we had a few detours, as you might say, getting here."

All this time, God was looking at the Devil, not Kelly. It was her time to smile. While all this was going on, *Pi* just watched them.

She suddenly interrupted them to say, "You's betters get on withs it, me's river." admitting that the Styx was indeed of her making. "Has gone downs some more's. Looks."

Everyone looked at the falls on the distant shore. It had split apart again and now there were three smaller falls streaming up the cliff face.

"Not so fast." said the Devil. He was both questioning and angry to be proven a fool. "So, if what you say is true. Where did you get the key from?"

Kelly suppressed her immediate response, "Don't you know anything?" Instead she replied, "From Rank, Frank the Lip, when Phillip exorcised him from Boleyn's body."

"He can do that too?" thought God.

"He said that he stole it from Ego who stole it from the lock, that keyhole lock there." pointing at the door.

"OK Devil. There you have it." interrupted God, eager to get moving. In doing so *she* inadvertently thwarted the Devil's desired retribution upon Kelly.

"It was Kelly not Ego, Vin or Rank that locked PhilLIP in there, now it's up to you to get him out."

"OK, OK." but the Devil was deeply embarrassed. He couldn't believe he'd been duped by the three hell-mates.

"Are you sure PhilLIP is Phil?" He hoped for possibility that they were wrong.

"YYEESS." said God and Kelly together.

Kelly was being so cooperative that God was really worried. "Who knows how these mortal Earth human women think. I never could figure them out. But she has a plan, they always do." fretted God. "Christ, she's even looking at me now. Shouldn't she be dead? Have I been wrong all this time?"

God didn't know that Kelly was burning up inside. However, she wasn't about to drop eye contact now, not if she could help it. She also knew exactly what to do. *Buy Phillip as much time as possible.* Her only choice was to cooperate, least God turn her attention to Ross or John who were more tender-hearted.

Kelly thought they wouldn't last a minute under God's scrutiny, but if God kept her focus on her, she could control the conversation. God had no idea how good Kelly was, because she had had the best of teachers, Bill.

"Yes." reiterated God, not to be trumped by Kelly. "Yes. Phil IS PhilLIP. AND HE'S IN YOUR STUPID JAIL."

The Devil simmered in anger at everyone in attendance. He was more furious with Kelly because of the lies she'd told the others, and her beauty. Now worse still, due to God's presence, she was safe from his clutches.

The Devil hastily reached over and grabbed the key, and turned it with every ounce of malice in his soul.

CHAPTER 62

NULLIFY

Phillip laid on the Diamond Table, and although he'd done everything he thought he could do, he knew there was more. If only he knew what it was? The door's Opal Spyhole was now part of his being and a welcome surprise it was, and now, with its addition, it just may supply the tipping point if he could do the rest right, whatever it was he was to do.

"What was he missing?" he wondered, "It just didn't feel right."

He fidgeted on the tabletop, getting more and more uncomfortable, until he realized that that was the problem.

"I'm trying to get comfortable. Instead, I have to find the most uncomfortable position possible. I have to nullify myself. Become as small as possible, as unsymbolic as possible. A NULL position."

He knew he was on the right track. He had to invent the most extreme and inhuman posture conceivable. He started to maneuver and twist his body, getting himself into a more and more contorted position.

Never a flexible man, he did something unimaginable. Almost breaking the bones in his hips in a herculean effort, he did the perfect horizontal splits. This was just the beginning. He continued their lateral movement, until they were crossed in a double lotus position behind his head. Similarly, he did the same with his arms, going backwards behind his back until the right hand was in the left-hand spot and vise-versa. With supreme effort, he threaded them through the tiny gaps at his knees, focusing his mind on the outcome rather than the pain. Now, all he had to do was buckle his body and head backwards, and with a final push, he was finished.

He'd folded his entire body into the minimum space possible. He took less space than that of an aluminum deck chair and was more tangled up than a knot in a piece of string. He didn't wonder if he could get out of it; there was only room in his mind for the quest and nothing else.

Lying on his stomach on the slick diamond surface felt genuine
- it was perfect. Now that that was done, it was time to get down to business. He slowed his shallow, rapid breathing and gained control and composure. Considering the knot he was in; it was this or his own death by lactic acid poisoning. Once calm, he pushed the claustrophobic discomfort out of his head. He had achieved and surpassed the greatest of mind control of any age or faith.

He was ready to do the insane, something that had never been thought of as possible. As his lungs were already half empty, it seemed a logical place to start. Vowing to keep his eyes open, he exhaled, and watched his breath slowly leave his body. An ordinary winding, one from being punched in the chest, was only a steppingstone on this journey. He needed to be completely exhausted, so he wrenched and screamed a silent curse, and forced the last breath out of him, ninety-nine percent, ninety-nine point nine, one hundred, he was officially out of breath.

Normal people wouldn't have been able to even get close to this, even the drowned or suffocated still have some air inside of them, but not Phillip.

And this was just the start.

Normal people too would also be dead. He was alive and unconcerned.

He would be testing the limits of life and indeed existence by the end.

Still functioning as if everything was normal, he considered what to do next. Now that his lungs were empty, it was time to empty the room of its air as well. He might have smiled at the coincidences that were going his way, because even though the door was sealed airtight shut, there was a place to express the air, and that was through the Opal Spyhole.

Although not physically connected to his body, it was connected to him *psychically*, and was part of him like any other limb. Identical to a muscle in his arm, he could flex it, and just because it was set in the Jail's Door, made no difference to the way Phillip thought of it. He could ask, and it would do it just as his eyelids open to see. Now he needed it to be the portal of the room, not just an opal spyhole but also a valve of his bidding.

He could feel its excitement and readiness for action. Minutes earlier, it was a lonely abandoned tear from God's eye, now it was united with its sister in his throat. Now it shared a purpose, to be exerted. Just as the Opal in his throat was an integral part of him, so was the Opal of the door. They were both part of Phillip. He willed its atoms to align in a one-way porous configuration, and the Opal willingly complied without asking why, but Phillip told it anyway.

"I have to stop anything and everything from entering. And I need anything and everything to exit.

What I desire is the perfect vacuum.

First, I'll remove the air, but there will be more. This is just the beginning."

He felt the Opal's atoms lattice reconfigure. No sooner was it done did he slowly expand his clothes outwards from his body. He pressed them into the farthest corners of the room and drove the air along exit channels that led to the spyhole, the only escape route. Slowly, methodically, his apparel expanded like a thick-skinned malleable balloon, filling every crevice and corner, forcing all the air out of the cubic through the rooms exit valve.

"Luckily," he thought again, "and nothing to do with *Pi*, the length of time this process is taking is letting me acclimatize to the growing vacuum. I'm not holding any breath but I am suppressing the pain. Shit, it hurts, but I've got to experience it, else it'll be too easy. When the air's all gone, then the pain will be too. Luckily, the room isn't too big. I think, yes, almost all the air's gone now."

Upon completion, he squeezed his outfit as hard as he could to ensure that every single atom had been expelled, and once satisfied, he sealed his Opal Peephole shut fast.

"That was the easy bit, now for the tough stuff, quantum fluctuations." So he deliberately and forcibly focused his entire being on the extraction of the phenomena. It was going to be a tricky process as he knew that it was in vacuums that they came into and went out of existence. Phillip recalled a science show where it was postulated that Black Holes could, over immense periods of time, disappear if two physically entangled particles on the opposing sides of its event horizon annihilated each other.

Phillip summoned a variation of this process in his cell with his external Opal defining it as an event horizon. "Then when the mutual destructions took place, it would consume the space-time fabric it once occupied and instead leave a void not a vacuum; and with no space, no new quantum fluctuations could occur.

He strained and heaved. He couldn't find any.

"Doesn't make sense?" He tried again. Just as he was about to give up, he found one, and only one."What? OMG.This is the secret of The Devil's Jail. There's only one Quantum Fluctuation. *That's why there's a key.* The Devil, and presumably God and *Pi,* can't get in without it.There's not enough Quantum for them to materialize in here. Like a curse, only now it's a blessing. I'm safe. In a way, if you call being locked up for possibly ever. I'll persuade this little guy to leave. He maneuvered the Quantum towards the Opal valve and ushered it out.

Imprisoned in his cell, it was impossible to know the profound effect his actions were having on Hell and the Universe outside. Like a string of dominos, this one Quantum started the rest to tumble.

As they fell, they took the most direct route to space and that was the river Styx,*Pi's* creation. For the first time in history, the Styx showed signs of a discernable current due to the friction from the fleeing fluctuations. It was draining in the direction of the Landing Dock and the sea beyond.

The river that the hell-mates took pains to avoid looking at; suddenly had their full attention. The hell-mates chose to suffer in pain as they watched and wondered where the Styx was going. Until only recently, Rank was the sole escapee from Hell, but now, the hell-mates risked all, and plunged into the foreboding waters to be carried away to an unknown end. They were already destined to Hell forever so what was there to lose? It wasn't just the male hell-mates that saw an opportunity. The Styx's new behavior wasn't lost on the Demons either.

CHAPTER 63

FLOOD, OF WHAT?

Noah relaxed. He'd lived his life without compromise and without care. He'd never kept his word, but he'd never stolen either, other than the hearts of women. His charm and past performances endeared him in their memories and so, despite their sorrow, they always understood. Many sent him money years later and just like the charmer they remembered, he'd always replied and wished them love and luck. They loved him, knowing they could never have him, and in some strange twist, many credited him for saving their marriages. He enjoyed life like a small boy. No wonder the elder women loved him.

The guests panicked and worried themselves sick as they talked about the dire events enveloping the World. There was the real possibility of all-out war, and worst of all, the loss of cellphone service. No one cared that the Spa's cold tub was close to overflowing, no one except for Noah. He was intrigued, caring little for worldly events. There was nothing he could do about them, and nothing he would have done if he could, he just wasn't that kind of guy. However, the overflowing cold tub, that was fascinating. The rock that was its source was bursting with clear blue tinged water forcing its way into the World, and in this year of so little rain.

" With all the talk of war, why has it chosen now to spring forth? Was it in any way related?" Noah couldn't help asking these questions. He believed that Man's sudden rush to destruction was rather leery and even suspicious, not really of Man's making at all. It was too contrived and smooth, just not something Man was capable of, not even when going to war. If it were Man's doing, it would be longwinded, fragmented, and defective. Noah felt it was the work of destiny, and so he thought in his true spirit, "Why not enjoy it?"

And with that, he decided it was time to take his customary stroll down the Dead Sea's shore, to his favorite secret spot. "Why not? I wonder if there's something afoot there."

This time, he walked with rare purpose and determination, because, despite the year's dryness, the level of The Dead Sea too had risen without due cause.

He wasn't surprised.

The cold tub was a harbinger that only he saw, and he was excited to feel part of it. If death was coming his way, then so be it. He was living his life as he wanted, and he wasn't going to stop or change now. Besides, it would be almost impossible. It was his nature, happy go lucky Noah.

He wasn't in the least disappointed. He'd never been able to find the location of the 'returning spring', but now it was obvious. The surface of the sea was roiling as dark evil looking water broke its smooth surface, spilling over the top of the salty sea like a black oil slick.

Transfixed at the sight, he shrieked when a body suddenly popped out of the water like a fisherman's float. He was already in the water swimming out to save the person, a woman, an old weathered woman, when another woman surfaced, and then another. He pulled all three of them over to the shore easily as it was impossible to sink, and there, they uncaringly basked naked in the hot sun.

He didn't know who they were, and more importantly, where they'd just come from. But before he could wonder about it, the roiling water bore more fruit. Men and the occasional woman thrashed on the surface at the spot where the first women appeared. At first there were ten, then twenty, then fifty, then a hundred, then hundreds before soon there was a thousand. Shoving and piling up on top of each other they surfaced in a seemingly endless stream. A thousand turned into two in a blink of an eye, and that too doubled. Soon there were over five thousand and then ten.

Noah had forgotten all about the women he'd rescued as shock, swiftly turning to horror, swept over him. For the first time in his life he wasn't the confident casual cocky kid. Now he was running for his life with his arms fraying in wide circles as he sought any direction as long as it was away from the not so Dead Sea.

He was last seen climbing and stumbling on all fours frantically making for higher ground. Once he'd attained the vantage point of the top of a dry desert hill, he saw a distant mushroom cloud of a nuclear detonation on the other side of the horizon. He was caught between a rock and a hard place as he turned round and saw a heap of writhing men spew out of the Dead Sea and spill out to the edges. Ten thousand was a low estimate; a football stadium could be filled with the number of bodies he now saw.

"If there wasn't an end to the gushing river of people soon, then it wouldn't be long before they filled up the whole lake." He had no idea that this was just the beginning. Ten billion hell-mates were about to be let loose on Earth, and all hell would follow.

~~~

Unaware of the consequences of his actions, Phillip moved on to the next step in the creation of the perfect vacuum. Now he was going to remove gravity. He knew that scientists have long speculated on the existence of gravitons, but Phillip didn't need scientists to tell him; he could feel their presence, pulling at him, holding him in place. Phillip saw how to remove them from the cell. He concentrated the atoms on the Hell side of the Door's Opal, making it extremely heavy at its extreme outside edge. Sure enough, the gravitons were sucked out of his cell like sand up a vacuum cleaner.

Although it was silent, it seemed to get more so. That's when he heard it for the first time. "Boom. Boom. Boom." His heart reverberated through his body. If he was going to fulfill his quest; Phillip knew that it was time for it to stop. Slowly, so as not to shock his body any further, if that was possible, he brought his heart rate down, thirty, twenty, ten beats per minute. Three, two, one then zero, he stopped his heart and he listened inside his body for any sign of life. Not just his, but any and all life.

It was quiet. He listened for anything. Nada.

He waited a bit more. Still nothing. Real nothing.

There was no God, *Pi* or The Devil's presence in the room. It was empty.

Through force of will power, he suppressed panic. He was alone.

For the first time, the first of anyone, ALONE.

A mortal would die through loneliness without knowing why. It was only natural that concern was growing in his still heart,

because he thought that something should be happening by now. Yet nothing was. He couldn't sigh, as he had no breath.

His heart couldn't race, as he had stilled it.

It was only for these reasons that he didn't panic; he just couldn't. Yet the niggling feeling of concern crept up sneakily anyway. Nothing was happening.

Not praying, but only because he reminded himself of its futility, he was beginning to think, this was a bad, "REALLY, REALLY BAD IDEA."

There was a perfect vacuum in the room, no air, no atoms, no quantum fluctuations, no space and no gravity,

"Something should be happening by now, but I can't see anything left to do. I've got rid of everything. We should be at NULL." he thought. But then he realized that he'd spoken the answer, he could see. After another retransformation of the Opal's atoms, the Opal began to behave like a one-way mirror - light photons streamed out through it and were unable to reenter. Gradually, all light from The Devil's Jail drained away. Resting gently belly down, but still in contact with the gem, Phillip watched the last store of light, the Diamond's, fade away.

He watched and waited.

Not technically alive, he knew he could move if he wished it.

He sensed, without knowing that it was imperative, that he stay in contact with the Diamond. So he tried his best to stay as still as the dead. Scared even to think as the slightest move might send him floating randomly around the room, he sought to maintain his faint contact with what he hoped would not be his final resting place.

Cajoled into releasing its own light, the Diamond's radiance first began to fade from its extreme corners. Flashes of brilliance paled, and slowly a darkening patch consumed the gem's last life. As time passed, the glow of the great crystal grew weaker like a piece of red-hot metal cooling down, and all that was left for Phillip was to be patient and hope that something would come of it.

Slowly, the Diamond descended deeper inside itself until only at its very center did any light shine at all.There it paused for longer than expected, almost fighting to stay alive, before going out. Phillip had succeeded in plunging the jail cell into complete blackness akin to that of a deep cave.

Not breathing and heart not pumping and yet still living, Phillip relaxed and contemplated the uniqueness of what he'd created. Lying face down in absolute darkness on a gigantic diamond in a place where gravity and space didn't exist, he thought he was close to perfection until he looked through the blackness and into the heart of the Diamond itself.

It was flawless but it wasn't without flaws.

Lines of gravity slightly distorted its formation tarnishing its perfection. Here, he could remove them and make the gem the purest and the hardest solid in the Universe. Phillip was grateful that he had something to do while he waited for an outcome, any outcome. Surprisingly easily, he straightened out the fractionally curved gravitational lines and made them as straight as a mathematician could theorize, until, every erroneous contour suddenly vanished.

Dot Dot Dot Dot Dot Dot Dot
Dot Dot Dot Dot Dot Dot
Dot Dot Dot Dot Dot
Dot Dot Dot Dot
Dot Dot Dot
Dot Dot
Dot
Dot Dot
Dot Dot Dot
Dot Dot Dot Dot
Dot Dot Dot Dot Dot
Dot Dot Dot Dot Dot Dot
Dot Dot Dot Dot Dot Dot Dot

A brief intense flash of pure purple light blinded him and lit the entire room for a second as the Dot Entanglement revealed itself. He almost died from shock.

He thought he had eliminated literally everything from the room, but now there was another sudden and astonishing discovery. An undetected entity lurked right under his nose and had he not decided to perfect perfection he would never have discovered it. Thinking back, he recalled how his super awareness had detected a minuscule last glimmer of light just before the Diamond went out.

Without hesitation or fear, he let his awareness flow into the crystal's lattice of atoms again and dove right to the origin of the new Sun. It wasn't long before his consciousness was only a single layer of atoms away from the absolute middle of the Diamond, a spot that looked like a tiny single lone, lost electron, a single dot. Fearful that it might disappear if he startled it, he gingerly moved the encircling atoms aside and reached out with an open hand.

"Join me." said Phillip with the utmost sincerity.

Cut off from the Universe, this Entanglement had laid buried deep in the Diamond for more than a thousand years. And it wasn't just anyone's Entanglement, it was Pi's.

~~~

The Devil had shamelessly encouraged the mythology around the Styx. He conjured up a magical ferryman and concocted endless folklore around him. For centuries, people placed a penny over each of the deceased eyes to pay for the crossing into Hell. Writers and great storytellers named Hell's planes and artists painted gory scenes of torture and debauchery. The Devil was nothing but pleased.

The hullabaloo incited him to conceive his crowning glory, his impregnable jail, The Devil's Jail. He forged it from solid mercury and cut its lines with the precision of a surgeon before standing back and gazing at a creation of rare, simple elegance. So besotted with it, he decided not to boast and instead vowed to keep it secret for his own means and pleasure.

But despite all his best efforts, *Pi* had her methods and sources and once she found out about his cherished vault, she too, found a new purpose in life. She decided she was going to use his most secure and protected crypt for her own ends. If she succeeded, she would laugh in his face at his ignorance and abject stupidity.

The instrument for this deception was the use of an obscenely large *diamond*. Hardly able to suppress her mirth, she cackled at the guile she'd used into tricking him. She had craftily ensured the ultimate safekeeping of her most precious artifact, not the Diamond, but what lay inside it. It would act as an anchor, a power station, a conveyer. It was to be a piece of her. The presence of her treasure would be an underhanded corruption of Hell. It would weaken him whilst all the time he'd be blind to it.

Pi knew if the Devil discovered this flawless Diamond, he would want it for himself. She also knew she would have to be clever, for he would be suspicious of such a trophy if he were to come into its possession too easily. He would have to learn of its existence from his own sources and in his own time, otherwise he wouldn't take the bait. If *Pi* could do this, then she was sure he'd steal it away to his not-so-secret jail. He'd do it, if for no other reason, than to make sure nobody else could have it.

When on Earth, he often posed as a private art collector, miserly amassing masterpieces for his own and sole purview. Therefore, she hid the rough unpolished stone deep inside the Great Pyramid of Giza, in a secret treasury with only a four-inch square shaft connecting it to the burial chamber.

The Pharaoh had granted eternal afterlife to a condemned team of gem polishers for completing the final honing of the diamond. They thanked the Sun God not knowing the *Dot* hidden in that massive stone was the patron of their good fortune. *Pi* laid in waiting for the Devil to take the lure.

It took a decade for the discovery of the main passageway to the primary burial chamber. Grave robbers stripped naked the dead King's final resting place, leaving only a worthless mountain sized pyramid of stone in their wake. None knew, however, that a priceless jewel lay buried deep and hidden inside, out of reach of human hands and imagination.

Centuries passed before a rumor circulated of a chance discovery in the pyramid. It was told, in dark narrow alleyways of Thebes, that a child's pet monkey had crawled up a small square 'drainage' channel. The hushed whispers said it had returned covered in dust, but not just any dust, diamond dust. Parents returned armed with picks and greed.

Vague reports, full of falsehoods proliferated like wild fire in houses of ill repute, and he would have ignored them all, had it not been for the spike in the number of murders.

"And that" he said to himself full of self-congratulations at his shrewdness, "is a sure sign that something valuable, something worth dying for, something worth killing for has been found."

The murders became more frequent, numerous and gruesome. The Devil followed them until he made the obscene discovery. Once seen, the gem was his in all but name.

People said it came from Heaven. The Devil knew first hand that the strangest things could fall out of the sky. The Devil was consumed by its flawless beauty and was instantly infatuated with it. He claimed it as his own and knew that his Jail was the perfect vault.

Using the obligatory pyramid curse as cover, local grave-robbers met mysterious and timely deaths. The Devil was finally free to acquire the Diamond without too much ado. Like the thief he was, he hauled his bag of swag away without any further thought of the stone's origin or creation, and when *Pi* no longer felt the stone's presence, she knew then that the Devil had hoarded it away in his treasure chest.

Using the Diamond as her foil, Pi had successfully implanted a Trojan Horse into the Devil's fortress. And with it, she would steal back what was originally hers.

The Dot in the Diamond acted like our Sun in our Solar System. It anchored and energized the river Styx. It caused the watercourse to have an *alternating current* making it impossible to determine which way it flowed, right down to the quarter inch grout-less gaps in the Ninth's Plateau.

The Devil pondered the direction of the solitary river many times, until humanity discovered alternating current (AC) electricity. Then the Styx lost its curiousness. Nature was generally weird it seemed and besides, "It was, remember," he'd say to himself, "the most well-known thing about Hell. Anyway, I hear that Heaven's got a river too. Not as famous as mine, actually, HER's is basically anonymous, more like a frigging stream too from all accounts."

Eventually bored and distracted with other things, (tormenting Man), The Devil put aside all thoughts of the Styx. Apathetic to its murky depths, he didn't know there was a current at the bottom. It wasn't, however, an undercurrent of a watery origin. Coursing through the river faster than electricity and at the speed of Entanglement, Dots generated from within the Diamond shot out of Hell.

The abstract particles streamed through the Jail's Peephole and found their way to the Landing Dock and beyond. Then they were dispersed into the wide wild Universe where they hitched and fused with the equations of *Pi's* probabilities, long and short, negative and positive.

The passage of the Dots through the Styx caused a static charge similar to the one used in the process of electromagnetism of surfaces. Consequently, the Styx easily bound with the hell-mates' evil, darkening and blackening its extreme alkaline and acidic waters.

It was not surprising that the river turned on Hell's populace so readily.

The Devil's evil also polluted it, and it was this that satisfied *Pi* the most. By way of this process, she reclaimed his ill-gotten colored Entanglement. And its black waters provided perfect camouflage with which to conceal the theft. *Pi* was immensely proud of herself, and scoffed at the Devil from her cow drink. The Devil's malice in the creation of Hell and imprisonment of hell-mates provided the perfect means with which she could steal back what was rightfully hers. Without Hell, there would be no Devil's Jail, no Diamond, no Styx and no way for her to right the wrong. The irony. No wonder the Devil hated Iron.

So successful was it that she couldn't pass over the chance to repeat it in Heaven just in case God slipped up. The Chamber of Snakes was its Landing Dock, and the ClearestRiver was the infliction in Heaven. God was wiser though and saw through the subterfuge.

In Hell, the Diamond slowly sapped the Devil's Entanglement from inside out. By the time he would discern what had happened, *Pi* would have reclaimed back most her stolen property.

It was a bad day in Hell when he stumbled on to this fact. A most unwelcome surprise upon his escape from the shoe. The Devil had flown into a colossal rage that day and everyone paid in Hell's global currency, pain. He didn't know how it had been done and although there was no apparent culprit, it was obviously God or *Pi*.

How was he to know he had a collaborator in his midst? How was he to know that in the centuries that followed the acquirement of the stunning Diamond that, *Pi*, little by little, had syphoned off all but his Black Entanglement?

It seemed only fair. He was the one who had poached portions of her Entanglement eons ago. How she'd hated the Devil when she'd discovered what he had done. Tit for tat. *Pi's* revenge was sweet.

The anchor, *Pi's* Dot sought a new residence. Abandoned without reason, why wouldn't it? However, the Dot could only find a home in a Diamond, and luckily, Phillip had just such an abode. His RhomSong, symbolized by the diamond shape, the perfect Rhombus, offered safe haven, a new family.

R

h

Song

m

Lonesome, neglected, without hesitation, the Dot accepted the invitation. Not made of matter, existing only in the simplest of arithmetic as an abstract concept, the essence of Dot was its own reciprocal and consequentially it was immense. Phillip's consciousness swelled to the brink. If it wasn't for *Pi's* earlier attacks, Phillip's mind wouldn't have had the capacity to accommodate or absorb this new life force. But neither would Dot have responded positively to his invitation knowing that she was impossibly condensed. She knew only a super being could survive her assimilation; hence, she would not have revealed herself to Phillip and encouraged his solicitation. The Devil didn't have the necessary qualifications.

Phillip did.

The moment Phillip brushed away the atoms that concealed Dot, it recognized his power and accepted the summons made in their shared language. A second later, *a branded image of an inverted triangle* scorched his skin. If there had been any air in his lungs, he would have gasped in pain. Instead, he bore the smarting sting and felt the better of it.

The hardest natural substance in the Universe, the super flawless Diamond, crumbled away under his body. First, it broke down into its molecules. Then they in turn fragmented into their constituent atoms before Phillip shepherded them out of the room through the only exit. He did so with minimal thought.

Phillip reflected on what he'd now become - he knew he was still a man. He had evolved into a synthesis of the Devil, God and now *Pi*, all things Entangled and more. However, he was something they weren't; he was RhomSong. And still human.

And he was their foe. They would have to respect him and fear him too. The merciful and gullible Phil whom they thought they could routinely corner and murder, was that man no more.

"But was everything, absolutely everything gone from the room?" he wondered "The single Quantum Fluctuation, the Space Time Continuum, temperature. Temperature!"

There was one last thing that he needed to do. He was going to reduce the temperature of the cell, to the logical conclusion, to absolute zero. Using his willpower, he focused on eliminating any energy left in the room. He searched the room high and low, back and forth, front and back. And there it was, a single speck of heat, caused by the friction of the atoms forced to evacuate the room, a tiny dab of energy loitering on the surface of the spyglass.

He expelled it. His job was done.

He'd gone further than humanly possible.

He now existed in a vacuum within a vacuum.

Even the quanta of the subatomic world couldn't make their random appearances.

He'd eliminated the space-time fabric.

Just as, if not more importantly, he'd eliminated any doubt that he'd done the right thing. The lines on his triangular tattoo, scorched there by Dot, were made of letters.

They spelled the word, null.

Three nulls.

It was done. All that was left to do was wait.

Due to his complete isolation from the outside Universe, Phillip didn't know what form these potential consequences would take, or even if they had already started.The laws of the Universe, equal and opposite must be obeyed, he knew this. If nothing was inside the jail then there must be compensation outside.

This was his intuition and this was why he'd done everything he had. Unknown to him, but because of him, things were indeed happening.

The Styx was flowing in a definite and single direction for the first time since its inception. When the Dot chose Phillip, the river's last anchor and its connection to it ended. Completely untethered, the Dots accelerated the exit of the river. Despite it being uphill, it flowed out towards the Landing Dock and away from Hell's nadir. Between the plateau's tiles where grout should have been, the blackest acidic rivulets had already drained dry.

Although Phillip didn't know what was happening outside the cell's walls, the fusion with Dot gave him new heart and hope.

"Hope… that all this wasn't for naught. There it was again, nothing. I guess the story, then, of nothing, is the story of the Universe." And as soon as he thought this, a mental image narrating its history began.

"It must be the Dot." Phillip surmised.

Unobscured by the eternal mortal's background drone, the Dot's *tale* was clarity and succinctness. Without their bias to sway the chronicle, it was truthful.

Right away, Phillip saw that the Universe gave birth to the *Eternal Mortals au contraire* to God's insistence otherwise. It was understandable why the Gods believed differently as they came into existence moments after the start of time. Unfortunately for God however, it was undeniable.

The Dot exposed the awful truth that the Big Bang was not of their doing, and instead, it was in the eon of Universal Inflation that bore them. First *Pi* appeared, immersed in the primordial realm of quarks, and then God appeared intertwined in the space-time continuum. The Devil, like a baby brother was last.

There was infighting and rampant jealousy amongst the three, and the one to suffer the most marginalization was the newest member to the immortal family.The Devil's life wasn't unlike Phil's own story, and Phillip felt a wisp of kinship.

"Perhaps," Phillip thought, "after billions of years of psychological torment, I would have gained homicidal traits too." Horrified Phillip stopped before he did something stupid like feeling compassion for the immortal.

"Hey, what did they do when they had the chance to show benevolence towards me? They attacked me. God used Joan. *Pi* used Boleyn - and gave them little reward to boot."

The callous disregard shown towards their workers made Phillip's mind up, he wouldn't be extending any mercy to the eternal mortals if they asked for it,

"If their time has come to pass, then it is meant to be. They'd had no trouble in metering out punishment and death to others, and even when they had spared the rod, it was so little and so late that it was hardly worth the tallying. Besides, was showing mercy to the few enough to offset the lack of it for the many?"

With a hardened mindset, Phillip watched the many other stories flitter through his mind. He ignored many other tales until he refocused on a quaint one of more recent times. ClearStream, past and present. That was the last episode.

When the account ended, it left him with a feeling of anticlimax.

The room was truly empty other than his own being, until horror replaced his smugness and terror asunder any feeling of security. His soul, hiding in his Shoes, registered something scientists have speculated about, should a Super Vacuum occur. The Big Bang.

In his vacuum, a Big Bang began to emerge.

"It was all for nothing. Not only will the World End, so will the Whole Universe. The Big Bang will destroy it all, and there's nothing I can do to stop it." It raced towards its climax and he waited helplessly for the comprehensive annihilation that it would bring.

Then it completely vanished as suddenly as it appeared. Phillip didn't need to look far to see why.

The void had suffered a breach.

The Devil's Jail Door had emitted a sudden brief microscopic burst of Entanglement.

"BLACK"

The super vacuum a Big Bang required was broken. Regardless of how short a time the blemish lasted; the conditions would have to be recreated again from scratch for it to re-emerge.

The threat was over.

"Thank G.. Thank who, I don't know who to thank anymore, Thank… Thanks. Yes. Thanks. Thanks Quantum Universe. There, that's what I'll thank from now on."

"Something's happened. At last. Hooray." he thought with a twinge of relief.

"However, whatever it meant, it didn't necessarily mean anything good. But at least something has happened. That means that there must be something going on outside the door, and by one of the gods. Most probably the Devil as it was BLACK."

CHAPTER 65
LIKE A SAFETY DEPOSIT BOX

God had told the Devil to get on with it and open the Jail door. He wasn't obeying God. He was going to do it anyway. When the Devil turned the key, it jammed. It jammed for good. The Devil tried forcing it, although he knew that it should never require effort, but he was in front of God and *Pi*, and he had appearances to keep up. Inexplicably, it just wouldn't turn. Resisting the temptation to use both hands, he exerted as much torque as he could with the one hand, whilst trying to maintain the façade of confidence.

"Need a hand?" God suddenly said in a tone of superiority. "NO. no. Think I must have tweaked it or something. I'll get it

right this time." He attempted to turn it back to the original spot. It didn't budge, and before he could stop himself, he'd placed his free hand on the key to help.

"Just… err a little stuck here… But I'm ok, just a minute… It'll turn in a sec... Oh. OH. Can't… err seem to take my hand off… No… It's OK… Just. God. *Pi*. Yea. Why not? Give me that hand you just offered."

"I don't think so." said God flatly. "What?" said the Devil.

"No." replied God again.

"WHAT? Just give me a hand. WHAAAT?" screamed the Devil and for the first time, he saw the reason why God wouldn't help.

"AHHHH" he said. He writhed and wriggled like a dog desperate to pee.

But he couldn't let go. "GET ME OFF !!!"

But God and *Pi* weren't going to do anything as they were

scared to touch him, just in case what was happening to him; would happen to them.

"GET ME OFF" he screamed again.

But it was too late for help. He watched as if a scorpion was crawling up his arm.

His Entanglement was streaming out of him.

The BLACK, that was the core Entanglement of the Devil, was coiling up, over his body and down his arms, down to his hands, down the key and into the door. It reminded Kelly of how the Devil escaped the John Abbott Shoe.

She would have smiled at the irony, but was too stunned by what was happening to think about doing it. It wasn't just she who was unable to avert her eyes, no one could.

The Devil was screaming and yanking with all his might as he tried to let go of the key, but his clenched fists held him tight. Frantically, he twisted and turned. He tried to morph into something else. He couldn't. He hadn't forgotten, but he was going to try anything. Along with God and *Pi*, he was now convinced Phillip had removed that ability from him, but it mattered little as his remaining Entanglement and hence immortality was seeping away before his very eyes.

It wasn't too long before the last of his Entanglement left and his fingernails started to return to their original color.

His own Jail had taken his Entanglement. It had spared nothing. His fingernails went white.

The door flashed BLACK telling the World it was finished. The Devil had fallen prey to his own door.

Silently, like the sound of big snowflakes, the door's key released its hold on him.

He fell to the floor. The Devil was dead.

His body lay on the floor in a crumpled heap.

And no one said anything their shock was so complete.

God and *Pi* broke the deathly silence.They breathed a sigh of relief that they hadn't attempted to help him or maybe they'd be dead too.

Then an "Errrrr" emanated from the prostrate body. The Devil wasn't dead after all.

"Ouchhh. I'm… I'm not… I'm not dead, oh no." he moaned painfully rising up to his knees and then feet. It was worse - he was mortal.

Kelly could hear her heart thumping as she stood in disbelief that the Devil was alive and immortal no more. Unlike everyone who was rooted to the ground, Kelly saw her chance, strutted over to him and slapped him across the face as hard as she could.

"Take that."

Too stunned to respond, the Devil just rubbed his stinging cheek failing to hide his shame of feeling pain. He wasn't dead, but the whole meaning and purpose of Hell was, which was of great interest to ten billion lost souls.

"What…What happened…Why… Was…" stuttered the Devil, but no one was listening.

"The door's key must have been…" God failed to complete the thought as *she* didn't really know what or how this had happened. *She* was more concerned with losing her own immortality to worry about or console him.

"But, true, mortality was death for the Devil. But who cares now, Phillip is still in there, despite the Devil's remonstrations to the contrary, and while he's alive, I'm in real peril, so screw him, I came down here to do a job, and I'll do it, so help me myself." *she* thought before ordering,

"Devil. Get back to that door and open it."

"I… I can't" raising his red, bloated and swollen hands in surrender, "and…" gaining strength, "Fuck, FUCK YOU. Why would I? Do it yourself."

God saw in the Devil's eyes that he didn't give a shit what *she* wanted. So that left...

"Kelly, unlock that door." commanded God.

"What? NO!" said Kelly equally defiant. She'd stood up to the Devil in the past and she'd stand up to God now. She took orders from no one. So if God wanted the door open then *she'd* have to make her, and to prove the point, she looked directly into God's eyes, and *lived*.

"Yes you will, because I'm asking you to." God instructed Kelly in a voice impossible to deny. She'd heard Phillip use his magical voice on occasions and she'd learned to distinguish a polite request from an unwanted order.

This was a demand she couldn't refuse.

Kelly found her feet walking towards the door with her hand reaching out to grab the key. Even as her mind screeched at her body to halt, her hand had a will of another.

"Kelly, try the key." The soul crushing order had no antidote.

She went to grab hold of the key and prepared to turn it, until death took her, such was the potency of God's command. Suddenly, she just stopped. There could only be one reason why she had. God had stopped making her.

And she saw the reason why.

CHAPTER 66

NOTHING LEFT TO DO

"Something happened, I guess it's the sign that I've done all that I can. Time to get out of here."

Thoughtful of the shock his body might take when restarting his heart, Phillip decided to govern its rate to fifteen beats a minute. It was a shock when he felt three separate pulses from three distinct hearts. The beats were stronger than he could ever remember causing glorious surges of blood to gush through his beautiful pristine veins. Each beat was so strong and pure that at its onset it felt exhilarating and primal.

He couldn't help imagining how wonderful it would be when they were performing at full speed. Then he wickedly thought of how happy this would make Kelly. Those intimate moments were going to take on a whole new dimension. He also thankfully thought that despite all of his transformations he was still a man. He was still Phillip and human, and a man in love. It couldn't get any better.

It was time to untangle. First, he straightened his body, which felt noticeably bigger. Then he unlocked his arms, which also felt longer and more defined. When he straightened out his legs, they too felt longer, much longer. Still weightless, his exertions propelled him into the center of the room and he started to float aimlessly.

Due to the momentary flicker of the jail door, Phillip knew approximately where it was. He locked his eyes on that particular piece of darkness, and waited until his floating body bumped into one of the walls where he could then push off in its direction. Once he believed he was within reach, he stretched out his hand and touched it,

BLACK, BLACK, BLACK, BLACK
BLACK, BLACK, BLACK, BLACK
BLACK, BLACK, BLACK, BLACK
BLACK, BLACK, BLACK, BLACK

Phillip felt the Devil's Black enter his right hand where he had once been so relieved to feel it leave. Today, Phil was Phillip, and the reversal was true. Phillip accepted the BLACK into his body without prejudice. Weighed against the other eternal mortals' Entanglement, the Devil's Black was trifling, but Phillip wasn't playing favorites.

If he were going to survive his foes, then he'd need all the Entanglement he could get. He felt it sharpen his wits, but that wasn't all. It carved a small deep black sixteen square tattoo over Phillip's original heart. Then the Entanglement did one last thing to proclaim its new ownership. He couldn't see it, but Phillip felt the sudden presence of a halo spring into existence about a foot above his head.

It wasn't circular nor golden, but black, square and of utter masculinity. About an inch wide and thick, and nine inches square, it flew in the face of all traditional halos. Four countersunk square nuts with no apparent purpose other than ornamentation decorated each side. Ageless, simple, chic and tough, it was the epitome of modern engineering and design.

Phillip took in the Devil's Black Entanglement without question or recrimination, but he wondered why it was in the jailhouse door rather than in the Devil. As he thought about that, he realized that it wasn't the Devil's Black or even the Devil himself who was evil, but how the power was wielded.

So he then considered God. Was the converse true for God's Entanglement? Just because it was hers didn't mean that it was always good. But the overriding factor on what was good or evil was, as Phillip sighed, was which side you were on. The winning as opposed to losing. In wars, it is the winners that write the history.

Willingly, he'd accepted the BLACK believing that every ounce of Entanglement was going to count. He didn't know that God and *Pi* were preparing for the final battle outside his cell, but he'd be disappointed in them if they weren't.

He also didn't know if The Devil was dead or alive."But without his Entanglement, if he wasn't dead, then he might as well be." How right he was.

Hoping the door would turn to ashes, dust or anything in order for him to leave, he reached out for it and touched it again. Laying his palm flat against it he called upon his power.

R

h

Song

m

No crack of thunder and lightning, no blast of trumpets, no crumbling walls of Jericho filled his senses, nothing. So he waited. Still nothing happened.

At first, Phillip was dismayed, and felt around using both hands, but he had to be careful because if he pressed too hard, he would float away, and a second later, he did.

"Damn."

Just as he drifted away, he started to descend to Earth, meaning one thing, gravitons. Then, a glimmer of light trespassed into the room stealing its way in through the top of the door. Moments later enough light had seeped in for Phillip to see silver liquid, mercury, pooling on the floor. Shortly afterwards, there was enough gravity to force him to use effort to stand up.

Enjoying the presence of weight again, he watched the door melt around the long thin spyhole. Soon it was free enough to float slowly through the air to find its resting place in Phillip's open hand. The liquid mercury continued to run over the floor and accumulate around his feet, which might have held his attention as it was surprisingly beautiful. However, it was eclipsed by the beauty flooding into the room from an external entity. Phillip looked through the door at its source. At Kelly.

CHAPTER 67

TOUGH TO THE END

Kelly's eyes had never been wider nor had her heart ever soared so high. The door that had sealed her love away, possibly forever, was melting away like a black iceberg. God had stopped forcing her to turn the key as *she* too watched and waited, readying herself to meet the man whose existence was altering the Universe.

Dribs of Mercury streamed down the door's front like little driblets of condensation rolling down a steamed-up window. The door was going to open one way or another, with or without help from God, *Pi* or the key. Most importantly from Kelly's standpoint, it was opening without help from her, and therefore she hadn't betrayed Phillip.

She stood up straight and proud, glorious, triumphant, defiant. She had fought the Devil in ClearStream and lost.

Here, she had fought God and lost again, but not once had she given in.

She was full of pride.

Against all the odds without the aid of *Pi's* numbers, Kelly had bought enough time for Phillip to complete his quest. Whether he'd succeeded or not, she didn't know. Nor did she care; she was going to claim him as hers no matter what. When Kelly first met Phil, she knew he wasn't playing the same sport let alone being in her league, but since his amazing metamorphosis, she found herself afraid of losing him to another. The only other worthy of him was God.

Although Kelly was now his love, she wasn't his first. It was actually an aspect of God, Godiva. Despite it being the instrument of war against him, she knew how significant that act of sex was.

Now she was scared he would see the glorious God and the plain old her and that he'd remember all her long past slights.

"So what?" she said to herself, "He's mine, and I'll fight for him, even if I die. There's no one left anyway. And maybe God wouldn't like a short man either, I know I didn't."

The Devil was the only one watching who wasn't happy, instead, he cursed that the fruit of his artisanship was liquefying in front of his eyes. Nonetheless, he was amongst those marveling that this someone was able to liquefy the solid mercury door when no one else could.

Whoever was on the other side of it was someone equal to them and he could see in the eyes of God and *Pi* that they knew this too. They held their breaths waiting to see who (or what) would be revealed. It seemed to take forever for the door to dissolve, and when it had, the cell was too dark for anyone to see what was inside. Then something in the cell started to stir and as if to pave the way, God shone a shaft of her brilliance on the entrance floor.

They all jumped when a shoe broke the light. Then a second shoe filled the entrance. Phillip softly emerged from his self-imposed imprisonment with only one thing on his mind. Kelly.

She struggled hard not to faint as now he was six inches taller than she. He looked directly at her and ignored all the others, including God. Not a single feature in his face wasn't that of Phillip. His mousy colored hair was still simultaneously combed and unruly, but now it reeked of maturity and experience. His plain nose looked small in his face, yet now, it didn't look lost or stubby. While the shape of his eyes was still the same, the spark they bore made them hypnotic and seductive. There was not a hint of Entanglement to pollute them.

Individually, his features were average, but together they melded into a single expression of heterosexual masculinity. The kind, mild Phillip was still visible but not the gullible or insecure timid Phil. There wasn't a trace of that guy whatsoever.

Clutched in his hand was the saber like Tear of God, and if it weren't for it, he'd have never been able to do what he had done. Sadly, this larger section of God's Tear had been permanently contorted out of its original plump shape, into an unnaturally long, thin tapering cylinder. Its long use as the Devil's Jail Spyhole wasn't the only culprit, Phillip's strenuous demands left it close to exhaustion. Even so, Phillip cherished it. Just because it wasn't internal to his body didn't mean it still wasn't him.

Deep in his hearts, something told him there was yet another job that only this lost piece of God could perform. Honed upon the fulfillment of each of Phillip's requests, its end was needle sharp and he feared there was a reason for this.

He raised it up to his mouth and kissed it in thanks, and consummated their union.

Kelly, Ross and John Abbott the XXVIIth stood together seeking each other for safety and comfort. God and *Pi* gawked at the man they'd hunted and loathed.

They were seeing him for the first time. They were not disappointed. Phillip had a halo. They didn't. The most jealous was the Devil, who had lost everything and now stood humiliated by his own Entanglement.

Acknowledging the presence of the audience, Phillip, with his mouth still in contact with the Tear of God, tapped his halo with the blade. The Tear vibrated like a tuning fork in a tenor octave and the Halo sung like a deep bass. The heavenly harmony was like trumpets heralding a royal entrance. It brought Hell to a stand still.

Though in Hell, the hell-mates suddenly feared death. They knew the end was nigh seeing the sudden exiting of the Styx and now this iconic mesmerizing reverberation. The Styx beckoned.

Free and transformed, Phillip had something pressing to do. Only steps away from Kelly, he closed upon her, gathered her into his arms, and kissed her. She was enraptured.

Confident in her hero's arms, Kelly turned her neck and looked straight at God. A month ago she would have died and turned to salt, but now she could look at her directly announcing she was equal in brilliance her love was so strong.

Ross and John saw where she was looking and turned in God's direction. Even though they could only withstand the pain for a second, in their fleeting sideways glance they saw that *she* wasn't perfect. Soon everyone was looking at God, albeit the mortals focused only at her feet. For the first time, they saw that *she* wasn't quite flawless, and because *she* wasn't perfection, they didn't die. God was not amused. And when God is not amused, people die; one way or another.

With a generous and heart stopping smile, God looked at Kelly, and only Kelly.

light

Alone in a spotlight, before anyone could think, Kelly was gone. It was so easy, so simple, and so quiet that Phillip only realized it by her body suddenly falling through his arms. Desperately his hands grasped and waved around, but all he caught was thin air as he fumbled her. Before he knew it, she was lying dead on the floor.

He looked up from her body and straight into the eyes of God. *She* could see shock in his eyes. God was obviously more potent than he could ever imagine as her murder of Kelly was effortless. If it wasn't for Kelly's lifeless body as proof, no one would have ever known that an attack had even taken place.

"What could have happened?" he thought still reeling from the astonishment of God's logical killing, but not just that, the callousness. Before he could comprehend why *she*'ddone such a malicious act,he saw her eyes refocus on something behind him. Phillip turned and his eyes met another pair. They were Bill's eyes. It was Bill - still recognizable although his face was charred and burnt. Bill.

Hot vile spit hit Phillip square in his face before he could even think.

<div align="center">~~~</div>

Bill could not have chosen a worse thing to do. Spitting in Phillip's face was Bill's way of hurting his little brother the most. He had no idea it could kill him, had he known, he'd have done it twice.

460

Pi had planted her positives on Bill's mouth to release his watery venom and her negatives on his spit the moment it struck Phillip. This way, her numbers would stick. Otherwise, if she targeted the numbers for Phillip's body, they would just slide off.

Pi did it, for one reason. It was critical if she and God were going to launch an Entanglement attack, that it took some non-Entanglement form, physical or mental, or preferably both, to anchor it to Phillip's core. Otherwise, as Joan first witnessed, their attacks would go harmlessly right through him.

For God's Entanglement attack to prevail, *she* needed Phillip to experience some psychological burden. What better baggage was there in Phillip's psyche than that of the childhood recollection of his brother's sadistic act? Pinning him down and spitting in his face. The moment Bill's spit hit Phillip; he was transported back to that pivotal moment.

This was PhilLIP's only remaining psychological issue, his only weakness. It was his Achilles Heel. Bill's spittle also supplied the physical material required for *Pi's* Entanglement attack, that of water. In performing this single mortal and harmless attack, Bill had chosen the deadliest possible weapon.

God attacked. And so did *Pi*. Simultaneously.

WHITE
WHITE LIGHT WHITE
WHITE LIGHT LIGHT WHITE
WHITE LIGHT LIGHT LIGHT WHITE
WHITE LIGHT LIGHT LIGHT WHITE
WHITE LIGHT LIGHT LIGHT LIGHT WHITE
WHITE LIGHT LIGHT LIGHT LIGHT WHITE
WHITE LIGHT LIGHT LIGHT LIGHT WHITE
WHITE LIGHT LIGHT LIGHT LIGHT LIGHT
WHITE
WHITE LIGHT LIgHT LIGhT LIGHT WHITE
WHITE LiGHT LigHT LIghT Light WHiTE
WHITtE LIGHt LIGH LIHT LIGT HITE
White White bLIGHT BLIGHT kITE
WHITE LIGHT lIGHT ite Flight
WHITE Light whitE
WHITE
-3.141592653594658487621...
-3.141592653594658487621...
-3.14159265359(4)658487621...

God couldn't remember the time when *Pi* and *she* were so coordinated and s*he* turned to *Pi* to give her a smile of gratitude, and gave herself a shock. *Pi*, The Queen of Spades was three-dimensional. *Pi* was sick. It explained why she was so keen and invested in helping God with her mission.

"Finally" thought God,"she's as much a stakeholder as me. Now we can get the job done." and a twinge of optimism bolstered her spirit. God was tired of doing all the heavy lifting. *She'd* been the one who'd spent all the energy and effort to rally the troops, almost against their will. *She* especially despised the "idiot" Devil. *She* was sick of his pedantic games and petulance."Hah. I'm glad he's mortal now."

In the not so distant past, *she* had hoped this many times for the enigmatic, baffling and obstructive *Pi,* but not now that she was a willing ally. It would have been a different story had she hesitated. The combined attack of the two gods slammed into Phillip with the force of an atom bomb, and to boot they had the advantage of surprise.

Reeling, Phillip spun away from his brother and attempted to deflect their attack by raising his arm up across his face. It didn't even slow it down. It flooded over him like a tsunami. Ironically, in attempting to deflect the attack, he scratched himself in the face with the spyhole dagger Tear of God.

"ouch."

A tiny scratch was all that it was, but now the Entanglement attacks had two means of entering his being, and they did. Their voracity was dizzying and his head swam under its massive volume. He lost balance and lurched sideways.Twisting, turning, and failing to stay on his feet, he unfortunately fell and drove the knife deep and deadly into John Abbott's heart.

John's death was the fastest death ever. The Opal was the sharpest pointed blade ever honed, and John Abbott was dead before his knees knew they should be buckling.

~~~

All was quiet. Like a muffled snowy night, it was as if the surroundings were on mute. He could still hear everything perfectly well although it sounded miniaturized and shrunken. Even Phillip's loud breathing now seemed like it was coming from another planet. With absolute indifference, he watched his own body silently sag like a melting candle as it began its short but certain journey to the ground.

John Abbott the XXVIIth was silently dead. For the briefest of moments, he watched the battle royal of Gods verses Man before his soul soared out of Hell in a tunnel of invisible white light. John looked around wildly as he flew through a cloud of soft mist simultaneously knowing, but disbelieving, he was dead. Whether it was a second, minute or a day, or even a year, he didn't know, but suddenly his feet felt solid ground under them, and the mist around him evaporated.

The tunnel of light had placed him in front of a beautiful harmonious landscape of white paved roads, pale blue skies and golden turreted palaces. Other than a thin, colorless tiny stream winding not quite aimlessly through the panorama, everything was in accordance with Fengshui. When John focused hard on it, it appeared to be flowing in opposite directions at the same time. Considering its insignificant size, it was anything but unobtrusive.

He also found that he didn't care to look at it for more than was necessary so he averted his eyes knowing what to expect if he didn't. Here, they called it the ClearestRiver, but he was the only one in Heaven who knew it for what it was.

Happily, his eyes fell upon a group of people beckoning him to go their way.

"Shit. It's true. I'm dead." He'd known it all the time.The sight of the people in the distance forced him to confront the obvious truth. His mind had been toiling with the knowledge ever since it had happened, and it was the most typical reaction possible. However, what he didn't know was that he was exceptional in one aspect.

He'd bought something with him. No one had ever done that before.

CHAPTER 68

GOOD OLD MATH

God, *Pi* and the Devil had always envied Man's inventiveness and ingenuity: the wheel, cars, medicine. The most impressive one of all, the most pervasive, the most used and the one most deadly; was the Internet. It was vast, yet always growing. It was complete, yet always under construction. It was simple, yet absurdly complex. It was probably the most important invention Man had ever conceived and it was one particular god's most favorite creation, and that god was *Pi*.

She had chosen Earth as her home and had not regretted her decision in the least. Man, although greedy and gluttonous, had also imparted upon the World many wonders and marvels, but the Internet was a cut above them all. Not a single invention, but a conglomerate of standards, computers, and networks all in collaboration with each other designed to host the dreams and desires of individuals and entities.

No one was to know that one such entity was *Pi*, and that the Internet in its entirety was her secret lair. While Man would claim to surf the Internet from his computer, she would truly surf it like a man on a small board on a giant ocean wave. Not online, but on the line, she traversed its length and breadth depositing her waste in the form of malware and virus's. *No computer ware didn't have Pi in its midst, not one.* Like a poltergeist, she wrought havoc upon people's lives: corrupting data, creating interminable delays, causing random glitches and being a generally mean-spirited piece of code.

How could they know the root cause? They didn't know of *Pi*'s existence.

Pi cackled in delight as she toyed with people's lives deploying her probabilities to ruin lives as she played matchmaker; setting people up and dumping others. Both outcomes were equally devastating. Sometimes she believed the Internet had been built solely for her entertainment it was so amiable to her whimsical devices, *but what she didn't know was that every time she surfed the Internet's waves, an unnoticeably small fragment of her Entanglement fastened itself to it*. Individually, this wasn't even an inconsequential issue being a negligible fraction, but collectively, millions and then billions of computers each took a little out of her.

After a while, it started to add up. That wasn't the end of it either.

There was an additional feature about the Internet that was absorbing her Entanglement. Encryption. She was so ecstatic at Man's love of PI in his encryption algorithms that she failed to perceive another infinitesimal draw on her soul. A billion calculations a second syphoned off *Pi's* Entanglement. She wasn't broke, but the insatiable appetite of Man's ravenous World Wide Web had surreptitiously pilfered a hefty proportion.

Pi watched the Internet grow and proliferate ignorant of the detrimental side effect, *not knowing that it was doing to her what the* dot *in the Diamond was doing to the Devil*. Unwittingly, she had become the unknown spirit of the unnamed religion that knew no boundaries in language, materialism, sex or politics. Unknown to her, her essence was now the core of the Internet.

She was the Dot in WWW.COM.

With the dawn of the Blue Green and Checkered Sun, the World of the WWWDotCom was misbehaving, spluttering and failing. With every death of a WWWDotCOM site, and they were dying by the thousands, *Pi*'s Entanglement fled to the next closest active host.

Pi was already suffering multiple although minor symptoms, such as non-random sequences, ink of Red instead of Black and the occasional three-dimensional materializations. Nonplussed, she was so immense that she could take a few licks without concern and in the meantime, she'd hunt down the root cause and kill it. She'd kill Phil. She didn't know however, that here in the depths of Hell, Phillip had done the impossible. He'd straightened and then removed the bars of gravity that imprisoned her Dot in the Diamond.

Now a Dot of *Pi's* essence was he.

And she didn't know it.

Pi's confidence in her resilience may have been misplaced.

Her unknown and growing vulnerability in the Internet directly correlated with the destruction of the Modern World. Her exposure grew, crash by crash, 404 by 404.

Not everyone in the World was sad that the End of the World was happening.

Survivalists weren't. After false alarm after false alarm, after overdue End of the World prophesies and hundreds of irritating post-apocalypse zombie walking dead films, finally, it was happening. "THANK GOD." They were right on that point.

Dozens of survivalist communities across the States cheered when the first bombs flew, proving their self-worth and that they were right. It was a rude awaking when they realized that a couple of frozen chicken breasts wouldn't stop them breathing Mustard Gas. Now it wasn't quite so exciting, but some smarter doomsayers anticipated the total obliteration of America. They made their last stand somewhere else, on a small Pacific Island in the Philippines. They were besides themselves with glee at their cunning as they'd kept their location secret, populated by only the invited few, and that invitation was made through their own website,

"TheLastResort.com"

They watched the apocalyptic events befall the World over a single stuttering Internet connection, and shamelessly congratulated each other on their wisdom and foresight. In an obscene act of gloating, they boasted of their acumen on their blog, knowing that public transport to their remote island was impossible and hence they were safe from an invasion of those wrong sorts.The poor.Then everything started to go wrong.

The Phases of the Sun caused the generators to only work about a quarter of the time, coincidently,they determined, under the old normal Yellow Sun. The Checkered Sun momentarily breathed new life into them before they blew all their fuses and rendered them defunct.

However, survivalists knew better than to rely on a single source of power, so they turned to their backup, wind power. Then, the easterly trade wind changed direction a hundred and eighty degrees. A mad scramble ensued across the island to realign all the windmills. It was what the wind bought with it however, that underscored their folly.

"It's an ill wind that brings no good."

Nor was it by any accident that this rogue jet stream found this particular island in paradise. God and *Pi* suspected that Phillip might be brazen enough to head for the Philippines because he was its namesake. They weren't all that wrong. Phillip had indeed attempted an inquiry of the site, but events and a change of heart dissuaded further pursuit.

The wind bore radioactive material, and much worst, a disease that was sweeping over America: naturally mutated airborne Ebola.The genetically engineered Ebola the government cultivated thankfully turned out to be benign after three cycles of the Blue Green Sun. However, just as the artificial imitation petered out, three natural pathogens, took its place. Contagious Ebola, Small Pox, and infectious Flu conjoined to become a dreaded infectious disease. Those who hid in bunkers or not, still had to breathe - Ebolux wiped out those not vaporized in the nuclear holocaust.

As the ailing survivalists scoured the Internet for potential Ebolux treatments, they noticed that gradually and globally the number of WWWdotCOM sites were dwindling.

With every passing of the non-Yellow Suns, another swath of perished computers littered the wired World. With every computer death, *Pi*'s Entanglement leapt to any remaining active site, sites that were fewer and fewer to find. In a short time, *Pi*'s clandestine Entanglement was concentrated on a small number of sites.

Soon the few remaining home pages weighed heavily with *Pi*. As there wasn't a change in the total mass, *Pi* was oblivious to her acute exposure and peril. Nothing was going to stop the Sun's changing phases and with every changing phase, *Pi*'s Earthly Entanglement condensed into a shrinking number.

Soon it was down to three. Dwindling fast, it became two.

Until it was one; TheLastResort_{Dot}Com.

Finally, without much fanfare, the senior technical support manager, the teenage son of The Last Resort founder, gave up nursing the site in favor of caring for his dying parents.

He failed on both counts, but whereas the passing of his mother and father was tragic, it wasn't Universe altering, but unbeknownst to him, the death of his website was.

CHAPTER 69

WISHING HE HADN'T FIGURED IT OUT

Easily recognizing the distant group as his ancestors, John Abbott the XXVIIth started to walk towards them when he violently shuddered. Until that moment, he hadn't remembered how he'd died, but now it suddenly flooded back to him.

Phillip had killed him.

However, like all people in Heaven, his assailant was automatically forgiven. Heaven gave a feeling of warmth security and wellbeing, so Phillip actually did him a favor. It wasn't the fact that Phillip was the one responsible for his arrival in Heaven however that stopped John in his tracks.

It was what he said when he killed him.

It wasn't until now that he realized he'd said anything at all.

And what he did say didn't make any sense. And he'd spoken so little.

Just two words. Whispered actually.

He said to him, even as he was burying the knife deep into his heart, John recalled it as clear as a bell; he said "KILL HER."

"WHAT?" said John Abbott the XXVIIth to himself, "What did he say?

What did Phillip say? Kill her? Kill who? Who?

He'd just killed me, by accident. Right? Didn't he?

He spun around on his heels, and then hesitated, and then he killed me.

I think. I think he killed me.

You know what? I think he meant it. I don't think he killed me anymore, *I think he murdered me.*

I don't get it. You know, I must be paranoid, but I think Phillip did murder me.

Seriously?

NO. HE DID?

And he did say 'Kill Her.' 'KILL HER'.

"ᴋɪʟʟ ʜᴇʀ."

Meaning 'kill God or the other thing.' Right?

'Kill one of them' that's what he meant. Then he 'accidently' killed me.

WTF? I don't know. Christ. Hey, I've got the dagger thing. How did I get that?

Weird."

When John discovered he had the murder weapon in his hands. He turned his back to his family so they wouldn't see it. Why? He didn't know, just that he should.

Crouched over it, he gave it a further once over. "Look, wow, it's beautiful." He studied the point that moments before had pierced his heart. There wasn't a trace of his red blood on it. How? What? What's that?" Holding it close to his eyes, he scrutinized it with suspicion.

"There.

There's a drop of water on it; it's there right on the very tip. I didn't know a drop of water could be that small.

So how did it get there? It's nothing to do with me.

Certainly, it ain't *MY* blood.

You'd think it'll be covered with it. But it's not.

Then it's Phillip's.

I think I saw him scratch his face with it. I think he did murder me.

I'm positive of it now.

I think he wanted me to have it.

I think he does want me to kill her. 'KILL HER.' I think so.

I really think that's what he wants.

Yet God and that thing are down there in Hell. Unless he wants me to kill someone else.

A her.

He means a woman. But who?

In Heaven?

Just then a woman called his name, "J o h n." "Coming." responded John.

They were all smiles and John Abbott the XXVIIth, the Last, easily returned one of his own. Happily, he joined his ancestors and reciprocated the numerous handshakes and kisses, especially for his dad whom he wholeheartedly hugged.

"Wow." thought John, "This is Heaven."

They all had tears welling up in their eyes, including his estranged mother who stood next to this father, patiently waiting for their embrace to end so that she could begin one of her own. It took some time working down the long lineage, but eventually John faced his Greatest Grandfather, the First. The one who started it all.

John faced John. John the Last stood before the First.

"Hi John" said the First.

"Hi." responded John the Last who then thought,"Dumb.'Hi'. Couldn't I have said something more, more...better? God, now I'm holding my hand out."

The First gladly took the extended hand and shook it generously. Then he turned and introduced his wife, the Greatest Grandmother.

"John Abbott the XXVIIth, this is your great, many times over, grandmother." There was some laughing and then clapping as they embraced. It was the longest hug he'd given anyone, ever.

Because he knew it was, she.

His beloved Grandest Grandmother. Dottie.

As he faced her,Phillip's request became clear. It overwhelmed him. He knew now, what Phillip had asked.*And who he was supposed to kill.*

Phillip had given John the murder weapon, poisoned with his own blood. It was the only weapon in the Universe capable of being smuggled into Heaven. The *only* one able to kill Dottie. Phillip wanted *him* to kill *Dottie*.

John had never even harmed an animal. He felt absurd to be here in *Heaven* and asked by a man he hardly knew, to kill his *Greatest Grandmother*.

Should he consider it?

"I'm crazy. Of course I can't kill her.She's my distant Grandmom, my Grandmom. And she's a good person too, I mean she has to be, she's in Heaven.

Right? But why, why then does Phillip want her dead? Why should I trust him?

But then... then he was the one on the stage with me at Salem. He was the one handcuffed to me, and the Devil went through him into me.Then the Devil disappeared and the Black Queen of Spades grabbed me. Then I called for Ruebella. Then we were imprisoned inside Boleyn.

God. What a story. Because then Phillip freed us from Boleyn. In Hell of all places. Phillip gave us our lives back. Now he's the one under attack from God and the Queen of Spades: who's now Red.

But even… But even if I knew why, I don't know if I can. Whatever I do, I've gotta make my mind up fast."

His lower lip quivered with indecision. In the next few seconds, he would have finished greeting the grandest couple, and he'd have to make his mind up then and there. If he didn't do it then, he didn't know if he'd ever see them again. The time was now - or never.

"Dottie." said John the Last. "Yes John?" she said.

"Sorry."and he lunged forward and drove the dagger deep and hard into her abdomen. He killed her. That's what the Tear of God does.

John Abbott the Last's lethal strike wasn't the first murder in Heaven, as Basher and Smasher had that dishonor. However, this one had no similarity to theirs. Their quarry didn't carry the secret that John's victim did.

Dottie embodied a Dot of *Pi*.

Dottie had given herself freely as the reward for John Abbott the First's defiance against the Devil. She was perfect for the mouse like man who had challenged the Devil in a wager and won.

People had wondered how a mere mortal could have taken the Devil so cleverly. None, however, knew of the entity lurking in the *cow drink*, none knew of *Pi*. Nor did they know that *Pi* had given John her favor. This gave him better than short odds that he could pull off the impossible.

Pi's reward to the smallest man with the bravest heart was Dottie, for although John bore *Pi*'s colors, it was still his endeavor: to attempt, succeed or fail.

Dottie became John Abbott the First's wife. Like him, she was mortal. Like him, she didn't know she shouldered another of *Pi*'s schemes.

Pi, with the unwitting aid of John Abbott, had dispatched the Devil into a Jail on Earth, the Shoe. Under house arrest, he wouldn't be able to observe the next of *Pi*'s steps, to infiltrate Heaven.

And Dottie was the keystone. Born on the banks of the ClearStream river and freely named by her parents, how could they know the significance of that name? By that name, there was no other more receptive to host *Pi* than her.

Without her consent, without any suspicion, *Pi* used Dottie's heart as cover for her own. Out from the cow drink below the ninth sleuth gate, *Pi* rose and implanted a piece of herself in Dottie, knowing that all she needed now, was to wait.

Allowed to live her life to the fullest as the wife of John Abbott, Dottie was none the wiser, *that Pi had hidden a third of herself within.*

There wasn't any doubt that when Dottie died, she would go to Heaven, and then a large segment of *Pi* would end up there too, for her secret mission.

With *Pi* in Heaven: nothing was sacrosanct. There, she could do what she'd done to the Devil's Hell. The Chamber of the Cross was primed and ready for what she envisioned. She could build a river. And fulfill her vision.

For there was nothing *Pi* liked more than a watercourse. There was nothing water couldn't ruin. Mountains. Basements. And now Eternal bastions. There was nothing *Pi* didn't want spoiled. She'd trashed Hell. Heaven was next. Upon Dottie's ascension, Heaven became as much *Pi's* as God's. And just maybe, maybe, she could steal God's entanglement.

Exactly as the Dot in the Diamond anchored the River Styx, the Dot in Dottie anchored the ClearestRiver in Heaven. And just as the river Styx was the dark foreboding river of the nether world, the transporter of bad luck. The ClearestRiver was of the purest water, and the distributor of good luck.

It was no coincidence that the ClearestRiver was millions of times smaller than its counterpart.

~~~

The ClearestRiver, just like the river Styx, had its mouth on Earth. For the Styx, it was the Dead Sea, the lowest place on Earth, and the saltiest. *Salt thrown over your left shoulder lands there*. It was where all the dead, doomed to Hell, found their ferryman.

'...one more river,
and that's the river of Jorden, one more river,
there's one more river to cross.' Only it's not the Promised Land.

The Chamber of the Cross was the ClearestRiver's moor on the earthly plane. Only Phillip had felt it's clearest of waters. It was in that tiny distance between the ceiling and the Golden Cross that all the good luck was bestowed upon the inhabitants of Earth.

It was so little, such a thin stream of water, such a short drop.

That was the way *Pi* was. There could only be one winner. There were trillions of losers.

Dottie lay dead in Heaven. The little stream that imposed itself upon the glorious landscape suddenly started to flow. Its anchor had gone. For those who noticed it, they also witnessed something else. Enduring the tiny itch, they watched the ClearestRiver drop a millimeter. Seventh Heaven and Cloud Nine had lost even more.

CHAPTER 70

PHILLIP TAKES FIRE

Under the weight of God and *Pi's* attack, Phillip had collapsed on top of the dead body of John Abbott the XXVIIth.Unmercifully kicked when he was down, their assault continued to drive deep into his being. He'd suffered attacks from them both in the past, but never from them in person in their physical form. It made all other spells seem trivial. Not unlike the difference of a live band verses a recording.

The Devil's attacks of the past were pin prinks. He'd faced and survived the demons of his stepbrother many times, but even so, the wound had never fully healed. Bill's sudden appearance in the Ninth Level had taken Phillip utterly by surprise. In true Bill fashion, he'd scored a direct hit. This one enabled Phillip's enemies to launch their attacks.

Bonus.

It just proved that Bill always won and Phil always lost, even in the depths of Hell.

However, Phillip knew this war was coming and although stunned and on the defensive, he was not dead. He fought off the dire feelings of inferiority by digging deep into his psyche and recalling everything he'd accomplished since he became Phillip. Valiantly, he resisted.

He remembered that he was… "The first human to fly.

The first human to enter the Chamber of the Cross. The first human to… to…"

God and *Pi's* attack started to overwhelm him.

"Phillip, get with it… it… you're crippled, but you're not dead… dead….

The first human to... what was it?... first human to be on the edge of the Universe.

Yes, that was it.

The first human to... Damn... what was it again?"

His thinking wandered as the combined Eternal Mortal's attacks meddled with his thoughts and memories. At first, he could overpower the white fog of God's attack and *Pi's* corrupting effluence. Relentlessly, however, their forces of numbness and confusion infiltrated deeper into his brain and his bewilderment started to outweigh his clarity.

Then he heard God and *Pi* whisper together, "Neil Armstrong. He was the first." Citing the name of the first man on the moon muddled up all his thoughts. It was such a clever strike, it merged and interfered with his attempted countermeasures rather than meeting them head on.

It took an age for Phillip to push it out it of his mind, and when he did, the void left behind was inundated with their Entanglement. It echoed back and forth throughout his head as if it was empty. With every reverberation, it fogged up his mind and further clouded his thoughts.

God's LIGHT became whiter and denser, blinding his brain wherever it went and incapacitating his ability to recall any recollection or sustain any thought. Likewise, *Pi's* numbers corrupted and cluttered his mind rendering it unable to clasp a contrary memory that could save him.

Desperately trying to remain a living and conscious human, he fought against the sanitizing attacks. He clutched onto anything that he could claim as his own and he resumed his pitiful resistance.

"First man to fly...

First man to... enter the Chamber of the Cross... First man to... err...

First man to fly...

First man to... enter... err... the Chamber of err.... the Cross... First man to...

First man... err... First... err... Neil?..."

God made her move. Her Entangled attack formed a bridge between herself and Phillip, and *she* raced over the connection with evil on her mind. Evil from Phillip's point of view that was, for her, *she* was performing an act of good. Good for her.

Song
PHILLIP
Rhom

He knew that word. He'd heard it once before.

He'd heard it the first time when the Devil was about to enter him. Even as an invisible whisper, he didn't need to be asked twice. He heeded his RhomSong's Diamond's call.

Faster than Entanglement, he dove into the cover of his *Shoes*. Was this to be his last lucid thought and action, he didn't know. God's massive psychic intrusion sent his mind reeling. Incredibly though, the pain was more preferable than what was to happen next.

Her white fog doused out the agony and a neutralizing, numbing blankness swept through his mind like a silent blizzard.

Learning from the Devil's failures, God didn't randomly rip and tear in a frenzied attack. Instead, *she* methodically searched for the soul of the man *she* called Phil, but who claimed himself as PhilLIP.

She disregarded that he once gained Entanglement, another example of the many incredible things he'd done. In reality, *she* didn't care anymore.

She conceded that the Devil had probably done everything *she* was going to do, and had failed. He'd thought he'd found the soul and incarcerated it in his impregnable Jail.

"But what if." pondered God, "What if he was looking for the wrong thing?

What if he was looking for Phil when he should have been looking for PhilLIP.

That's it." God exclaimed.

God went about her search with redoubled vigor. *She* rifled through his brain and heart, not that *she* expected to find it there. It was too obvious and of course, the Devil would have been there too, and even he should have stumbled upon it then. Nonetheless, it just had to be done.

"Just dotting the 'i's and crossing the 't's, besides, he had three. Weird."

But there wasn't time for God to consider that implication. *She* got on with the job *she* was there to do. *She* searched his groin; he was after all a man. After striking out there, *she* decided to search the *Tear of God* in his throat and *she* had a brainstorm.

"PhilLIP would hide in a certain place. His frigging LIPs.
Frig - LIP."

She sidled up on his lips using her *Tear of God* as cover.There, *she* stealthily closed in on her target, when a tapping sound permeated out of Phillip's mind and stopped her in her tracks.

"It's that stupid *Pi*. She's here too. I better get a move on and find him before it's too late."

Just then, *she* spied movement at the edge of her vision. Right where *she* predicted, in his lip.

"There!"

Immediately, God became scared that *she* wouldn't get a second chance what with *Pi* rummaging around and making a colossal din. *Pi just might startle it and send it running to who knows where, or God forbid, Pi might by chance come down there and find PhilLIP first.* Unable to stalk her prey any longer for fear of discovery, *she* struck.

"GOT IT. EUREKA." *She* tightly clasped onto his upper torso while his tail, LIP, waggled like that of a Chihuahua.

"HAH. That'll teach him for stealing one of my tears. That'll teach him for taking the other. That'll teach... DAMN HIM."

In less than a millisecond, *she* spirited over the psychic bridge back to the safety of her body. *She* couldn't help sniggering at the feeble babbling body *she* was leaving behind, and the foolish *Pi* left there forlornly searching for nothing.

As if on cue, the empty shell appeared to start to fade away. "I... I was... the first... fly...

I... I was... first... Chamber... Cross... I... I... human to... to..."

As motionless as a statue, Phillip watched from below as his consciousness evaporated away. He knew, that if he didn't stay awake, he'd be lost forever in the blinding whiteness and confusion of what would be left of his mind. Then God and *Pi* would just summarily dispatch him and all would be forgotten.

"Everything... Me... Shoes... Rhom... Song... Everythin... M...

The S...

His eyes fluttered as comforting sleep called to him.They wavered again, then quivered, and trembled.They became heavier every second, as if they weighed a ton. He was losing,and he knew if he went to sleep, even for the briefest of moments, it would be forever.

"Stay awake... Awak... A..."

Just as God had done, *Pi* also searched for both Phil and PhilLIP. In contrast to God, who'd burst into Phillip's mind like a thunderbolt before controlling herself, *Pi* had surreptitiously entered Phillip a piece at a time through each of his hearts.

She hoped, with his mind preoccupied fending off God, that this way PhilLIP wouldn't feel her intrusion. Really though, the person she was attempting to deceive was God. *Pi* wanted Phillip for herself, and if she got him first, God was going to be the last to know. Not until she had had satisfaction. Then she'd gloat.

She'd been dreaming of settling a score with "Phils or PhilLIPs or whoevers." since ClearStream.

"No ones talk to *Pi* like that." she rationalized, and should she find Phillip first, then she was going to make sure he'd live long enough to regret it.

Sneaking through Phillip and being extremely careful to avoid the Almighty's detection, *(she thought)* she looked through Phil's mind and tried not to die of boredom at what he called his life.

His first life.

She saw that the vast majority of those memories were of nothing other than meaningless drivel. The moment his brother teamed him up with Kelly, however, from that point on, his life was a 5D thriller and an enthralling love story.

"I'ms in some of them toos." *Pi* smiled warmly."Thoses are the memories he's searching for, and thoses are the ones that might save him yets."

She continued her search and noticed that for the past month, albeit unconsciously, he'd been discarding all the older ones. He was giving prominence to the fresh remarkable memories of his rebirth. These were ones of real substance and were the ones Phillip was looking for. That was exactly the reason God and *Pi* concealed them.

She tapped one of the new memories with her fingernail to discover it was as hard as rock.

"Pitys, HA HA HA Phillip. Pitys... you can't find this memory.
HA HA Has."

The only memory God and *Pi* allowed Phillip have clear access to, was his worst memory, the pivotal event in the old Phil's life. Because of its significance, it overshadowed all other hurtful recollections combined, including those of rejection and failure. And there were a ton of them.

This one however, this one of Bill spitting in his face, outweighed them all.

Due to its momentous importance, it was the hardest memory to expunge. Because of this, Phillip's endeavor to raze it also meant that he had started on it first. Under the constant bombardment of new and meaningful experiences, it had eroded dramatically.

Being nothing more than a hollow brittle shell like burnt paper in a fire place, the last recall by Bill coupled with the exertion from the Gods Entanglement attack, left it precariously fragile and delicate.

Pi knew the recent memories were solid. Now she wanted to see if this one was just as hard.

Using the same bent finger, she gave it a gentle tap. It imploded into dust.

Pi had just unwittingly destroyed the attack's anchor.

The memory that was key to the extermination of Phillip was dead. The fog lifted.

Clarity replaced confusion.

The weight, the oppression, left Phillip's psyche.

The obliterated thought left a crack in the numbing whiteness. "My... My... G.. How long?" Phillip slurred incoherently.

He willed his stinging, watery eyes open from their latest flutter.

"They had closed?" he wondered "Or just blinked for a longer than normal time? I'm alive, so..."

~~~

He knew he couldn't have been out for long as he was still living. Barely. But this was the reprieve he so desperately needed. It was a window of time he had to take advantage of, or die. He didn't know why or how, but this was his only chance, of this, he was certain.

Out of the corner of his eye, he glimpsed a lifeline.

He saw an enlarged image of the lifeless body of Kelly caused by the magnified view through one of his tears.

"M…y… my… MY beautiful Kelly. The… The… woman who once was Bill's.

T… The woman whom he spurned for his wife. F… For his wife's father's money.

The money that he'd killed for and was his. She, she had rejected him and his money. For me. She was mine.

I bettered my brother. By a mile. I WON.

If I don't survive, it will all be forgotten. FORgotten… FOUR*gotten"*

God saw that Phillip was reaching for this lifeline that he should never have had.

"That stupid fucking *Pi*, do I have to do everything? If you don't know what you're doing, it's best to do nothing. She had to go and tap the memory. Leave it to me to clean up the mess."

God was secretly happy *Dia* had screwed up.

She could use it against her in the future, a future that God was now going to secure for both of them, because *she* had a secret weapon.

"I've got this." *She* crowed to herself. And *she* did have it.

She could do it, because *she* had in her fist, PhilLIP.

She was going to crush him and end this once and for all.

But first she was going to gloat, knowing that Pi would have done the same.

She unclenched her hand. Stared at her captive.

And screamed in shock.

"WHAT?"

She hadn't bagged PhilLIP. She had caught Frank the LIP.

When Phillip crushed Frank the Lip, he only blew his bodily remains to the wind. To rid the World of his spirit, Phillip inhaled his soul. Imprisoning it in his lips seemed an appropriate place to keep it. He never considered that the two shared the same appendage in their names. Whether this was *Pi's* doing or natural fate, he didn't know. Nor did he know if this was the reason for him to believe he was Phillip rather than Phil. No one could have foreseen the events of this past month. He was an unsanctioned entity creating an unendorsed destiny. Outside God or *Pi's* authority, outside law.

Now Frank the Lip, the man who was the World's nemesis, who had done nothing other than seek his own enrichment, had become the sacrificial lamb.

Combined, the two blunders gave Phillip a new, although tenuous, grasp on life. He saw the glimmer of non-*Pi* hope and his mind grasped a single thought out of the swirling chaos of whiteness.

The Triangle Tattoo over his heart, the illicit endorsement of the Universe.

*He had not "*FOUR*gotten."*

When *Pi's* Diamond Dot accepted his RhomSong Diamond's call, it had tarred Phillip with a Triangle Tattoo. It was a sign. Just when God screamed at her frightful discovery - in that same instance, Phillip received another.

It was at that moment that John Abbott the XXVIIth murdered Dottie with the Tear of God Dagger.

Dottie wasn't to know that *Pi* had hidden a third of her Entanglement within her. Nor was she to know that the blade was a piece of Phillip's entity, and on the tip of that keenest of all blades, was a drop of his blood. As the Tear of God pierced her heart, like an electrical current, *Pi's* Entanglement became grounded, to Phillip, to his blood made of *Rissium* water.

When Phillip absorbed the dot in the Diamond, a triangle branded itself upon his third heart. Now with the death of Dottie; a second inverted triangle seared itself on top of the first. The result was the Star of David.

Phillip winced at the pain, but the pain served a purpose. It resurrected the memory of his cryptic request. Somehow, John Abbott the XXVIIth had done what no other man could have figured out.

"He was a John Abbott worthy of his name." thought Phillip. "How he figured it out, I dunno. *What an amazing man.* Could I do such a thing? Kill my greatest Grandmother on the word of a recent acquaintance.

WOW. THANK YOU, JOHN. You may have saved me." He felt the Tear of God appear in his hand.

Drenched with the blood of Dottie.

It awakened other memories; the fog was lifting.

The inhabitants of Earth were too busy trying to survive to notice the demise of a seemingly paltry website called 'TheLastResort.com.' The Universe, however, was about to be rocked to its foundation.

The waning power supply to the website's computer had channeled *Pi's* vast Internet Entanglement into the last piece of accessible memory. Its inception date-time stamp coincided with the acquisition of a used car from a dealer called 'Honest Jimmy'.

It was in an un-readable format.

BUT when decrypted, it read. "Phillip."

CHAPTER 71

RETALIATION

All of *Pi's* internet Entanglement surged along its only rightful path to the last grounding point. Phillip. The Last Computer, the Last Resort, the Last bytes of memory - to Phillip. From its remote location on Earth, across the heavens, it sought and found him, in Level IX of Hell, outside The Devil's Jail.

Pi's internet's entanglement became his.

A third triangle tattoo singed Phillip's skin, on top of the Star of David.Then, all three triangles rotated, each offsetting each other and together they formed a nine-pointed star. This was the signal that the third and final dot had become him.

Only needing a trigger, he had become his own weapon of mass destruction.

In that moment of God's horror and of Pi's faux pas. Laid his only single chance in which to retaliate.

NOW.

He attacked with his RhomSong. He knew the trigger. He hadn't FOURgotten.

FOUR was the detonator.

R S
R h o m
FOUR
S o n g
M g

Both God and Pi screamed.

Unharmed, stood Phillip - equal to them. Alive.

He had survived when atoms couldn't.

And he had endured and had taken retribution.

It was a crushing retaliation against *Pi* who was fearsome and mighty beyond Man's dreams. Although sickening in three-dimensions and Blooded Red rather than Jet Black, she was still a force of nature without compare. Yet Phillip's attack had blindsided and struck her to her heart. He had killed her with a single word and she was now mortal.

Pi was now a pair of Siamese twins - two heads on a single curvy mortal women's body. Any vestiges of being a two-dimensional entity were gone. She was exotic and stunning, looking regal in height and posture but she wasn't the Queen of Spades any longer. Her destiny as the ruler of the Elements was over. Only through her beauty did she have any power.

Phil had been a dreamer. He entertained delusions of grandeur and lived a vicarious life through anyone in close vicinity. That was until *Pi* over indulged in her probabilities and unwittingly enabled him, through misery, to find and follow an un-calculable destiny. Now Phil was Phillip, now *Pi* was Pi. Her reign was over.

"How did I end up a mortal?" She mouthed the words to Phillip. "How?" in stereo. "How have I become... human?"

The secrets she'd kept and never told: somehow someone had discovered everyone. She couldn't believe this and knew it wasn't via God. Her mind reeled as she spoke, "What about the numbers, the probabilities, my LISP? How did you know? How did you know about Dottie? And what happened to my Diamond?"

Her Diamond, not the Devil's.

"HOW?" despaired Pi. "And how... the... the... my other Entanglement... where...?"

As if regaining her balance (and not falling into the vast split in the granite rock beneath their feet cause by their harmonized shrieks), God recovered her composure and smoothed down her gown with her hands. A clever misdirection as *she* was actually checking to see if *she* was wounded: only her ego was. So then *she* looked at *Pi*.

God too was astonished, and looked on with mixed emotions at the immortal Phillip and the mortal Pi, now a person, no longer the *Pi she* once knew. God and the Devil heard Pi's plea for an explanation, and were unable to answer her.

Inexplicably, the word "FOUR" appeared to have led to her passing. They saw and heard everything, and yet they didn't understand. They had no idea how Phillip came to know. He had been a mere mortal. *Pi* and the Devil had been eternal mortals. Even so, they didn't know how Phillip had done the impossible.

He had slain *Pi* in front of their eyes. God, filled with resentment, was astonished. The Devil was just plain envious. He'd wished for *Pi's* comeuppance for some time now, but he wished it were he that had delivered it and 'not some freak.'

All they knew was that there was still some extra piece to the puzzle, but they couldn't tell what it was. God was particularly concerned, because *she* was still eternal and wished to stay that way. Phillip's attack had struck her hard, but her Entangled Soul remained whole, so if *she* could figure out Phillip's power then maybe *she'd* keep it that way. And kill him too.

Pi as the twins, were trying to figure out how Phillip knew Dottie was a piece of her soul, and although two heads, one red and one black, were better than one, she still wasn't getting anywhere. Pi seethed at Phillip's triumph while God marveled again how clever he was in conveying his wish to an innocent and good person such as John Abbott the XXVIIth.

"How, indeed, did John Abbott the XXVIIth decipher Phillip's cryptic request, and incredibly, DO IT." wallowed the Devil, happy that he wasn't the only loser."It was unbelievable. Eh God. Beyond your understanding? Well, it was fan-fucking-tastic." He astutely read God's stoic face, eager to administer any form of meanness.

"It was a feat of trust and faith you would have been proud of." he continued."In fact, I can see his conviction has embarrassed you. So many people on Earth have given their lives for you, and really, the reason why was because you'd given them their lives to live in the first place.

But John Abbott the XXVIIth - what did he owe Phillip? And to kill his great ancestral Grand Mother, all because Phillip asked him too. W o w. He puts you to shame. Oh, and if you don't get it, he also didn't use a power of command voice. Get it now?"

His words stung God, and seeing that, the Devil continued. "John Abbott the XXVIIth did indeed take the leap of faith asked of him and committed

"A Murder in Heaven."

"Make an Enemy of God."

Got to admit, eh? That it was a courageous act, not knowing why, not knowing the consequences. An act of condemnation, of rebellion, of revolt.

He must have believed it counted for something. He must have thought it was a vital act, and a deed that actually said, *I don't know what I'm doing. Or why, but I'm trusting that it's going to fuck with God or Pi or both, and I don't care what the consequences are or what the cost is, I'm going to stand up against them by standing with Phillip. Fuck You. Fuck You All.*

That's what I think he was thinking God. In the long story of man, it was the biggest blasphemy ever. HA HA HA HA HA"

And as if his contempt couldn't get any worse, he added, "Oh. Just one more thing. The Tear of God that used to act as the spyhole was the only weapon that could be smuggled into Heaven, because it used to be a part of you. Smart eh? Phillip was pretty smart. I hate him. You must too. MORE. And…"

God had had enough, with a blink, the Devil's mouth shut down on his tongue and locked. He couldn't open it to let out the scream that was stuck in this throat. *She* smiled wickedly. He was finally muted. *She'd* always wished for this and her only regret was that *she'd* waited so long.

Although God had suffered pain under Phillip's attack, *she* remained whole, immortal and charged with Entanglement. The last thing *she* needed was a mouthy mortal mocking her.

Refocusing on Phillip it was plain to see that he was transformed. He held the answer to her burning question. Screw it that Pi wanted to know too. *She* was God, and it was her right to know.

She addressed Phillip rudely to emphasize her lack of respect for him as an imposter and to conceal her fear.

"So Phil, HOW?"

"And what's with all the dots? And what's all this about the number FOUR? How can THAT possibly hurt her?"

"God." began Phillip graciously. He repeated her inquiry. "How can FOUR kill her? Well, to answer that, I have to…"

"And what's with all the dots?" interrupted God as if *she* were addressing Phil.

"Do you want to know or not?" retorted Phillip, and most un-Phil like, before continuing.

"WELL, it's a long story. It was Kelly who incarcerated me in The Devil's Jail, albeit upon my request. Not, Ego, Rank or Vin.

Kelly. Firstly - the night when Boleyn attacked me in the car, something happened, and I started to become something different
- when the *Shoe and I* combined.

Then, in ClearStream, the Devil took away all my Entanglement in his attacks, and unwittingly completed my transformation.

That's when all this started. I think that's when you all lost me.
Making a long story short, I...What the...GAVIN?"

CHAPTER 72

TYPICAL VIN

It was impossible for Vin to be angrier. Ego and Rank had sent him on this wild goose chase twice, and now Phil had done the same. Because Phillip had commanded his mouth shut, he was unable to take the vow he dearly wished he could make. And that would be 'To get Phil.'

He knew for a fact that there wasn't any freshwater in Hell, and now he'd been doomed to silently wander around Hell until he found some."It's like he's cursed me" thought Vin.

"Mmerrmmmumm."

"Fuck. I'll get his freshwater yet." promised the revenge filled Vin to himself.

Unbound by a vow, he decided to follow Phil anyway, except, unfortunately, he'd spent so much time prevaricating that he'd lost sight of him. It wasn't however, a disaster. He knew where he was heading. So Vin made his way back to the Styx and followed the road from therein.

Being a past master at ducking out of work, Vin easily evaded the roaming demons. It wasn't until he heard a distant ruckus did he deviate from his mission. He stealthily crept up upon the scene of an obvious fracas. He got there just in time to see that whatever it was, it was all over.

Apart from some child's attire left lying on the dirty ground, there was no evidence of who had been involved or over what. Still, not realizing the benefit of not being bound by a vow, he took his time and rummaged through the clothing.

"Wow. Unbelievable, I've found something." he muttered to himself. "A golden goblet. I didn't think you could bring anything down 'ere. Wow, I think that's a diamond."

He picked up a solitary crystal sitting on a clump of mud. "This must be special,'cos you can't bring shit like this into Hell.

I wonder whose it was. Who cares, its mine now." He pocketed the swag and merrily resumed his pledge.

On the road again and still avoiding demons, Vin noticed another person who seemed to be doing the same up ahead of him. He had trod this road many times as a warden's subordinate, and knew hell-mates avoided the Styx and this road like the plague, so he took due note of his man.

"It's true." thought the mute Vin, "he's just gone through the Gate, and no one ever wants to go down to a lower level of Hell unless they have a really, really bad reason.

Encouraged with his progress, it wasn't too long before he too approached the entrance. It was at this moment, that he suddenly questioned the logic of his quest. There stood the Yellow-Eyed Demon right in front of him but he couldn't talk. "Bribe it." immediately jumped into his mind. "Or take a beating." But his sub-conscious was already honoring his initial thought.

He unknowingly had retrieved the goblet from his pocket and was presenting it to the Demon as payment, because above all, Vin hated pain. It was too late to retract his offer. He'd only suffer a greater beat down if he tried, so he sheepishly continued to offer up the chalice.

He witnessed a miracle.

A tear fell out of one of the demon's yellow eyes, and fell towards the cup and Vin accidentally caught it.

He'd never been that coordinated, so this was akin to another. The door opened.

A feeling of being moronically stupid overwhelmed him. He was after all a sub-warden and free passage was his privilege. It was only after Vin felt the familiar evil red sky of Red-Hell did he realize he had just acquired something precious.

Euphorically Vin crouched and ducked from cubby hole to cubby hole. He held the cup close to his chest daring not to put its prized cargo at risk. In the far distance, he caught another sighting of the man in front.

"Don't think I can keep up with him. Still, who cares, I'm not going to drop this cup no matter what. I'll let him go. You know what?" still muttering, "That yellow-eyed demon... was the Yellow Witch. She was the Yellow Witch that escaped out of that shoe in Witchiton Falls.

She's here. Serve's her right. I wonder why was she crying?"

Before he could cogitate on his own question, the colossal gray-eyed demon barred his progress. Then like all the other Gate-demons, she granted him passage.

He was in Black-Hell now.

"I'm going to give him his freshwater, if it's the last thing I do."

Vin always exaggerated and never followed through with anything, why would this be any different?

But it was.

CHAPTER 73

THE FULFILLMENT

God looked around. The Devil was mortal by Phillip's hand and so was Pi. Now *she* was on her own.

"It's so much easier to pick a fight when you have two other guys with you. Is it too late to back out of this?" *she* wondered. "But then I'll die anyway, slowly, as my power gradually dwindles until my Entanglement is next to zero. And if I don't finish him now, I might never find him again.

Wow. What a... a... piece of... luck?"

A scrawny man had just walked past her. His head was bowed so much that it must have hurt. He didn't, however, want to take the chance of accidently taking a life-threatening glimpse at God. So he hurried on by clutching something close to his chest.

A golden cup, and in it, was water. FRESHWATER.

He threw it into Phillip's face.

WHITE
WHITE LIGHTWHITE
WHITE LIGHT LIGHT WHITE
WHITE LIGHT LIGHT LIGHT WHITE
WHITE LIGHT LIGHT LIGHT WHITE
WHITE LIGHT LIGHT LIGHT LIGHT WHITE
WHITE LIGHT LIGHT LIGHT LIGHT WHITE
WHITE LIGHT LIGHT LIGHT LIGHT WHITE
WHITE LIGHT LIGHT LIGHT LIGHT LIGHT
WHITE
WHITE LIGHT LIgHT LIGhT LIGHT WHITE
WHITE LiGHT LigHT LIghT Light WHiTE
wHITE Whietgh WLIT WIGHT LIght WHITE
White LIght LIGHT LIGHT whITE
whiiTE whiTE wite light
Whitig Whiti Whie
WhGhe

CHAPTER 74

THE RESOLUTION

Ruebella's tear was indeed freshwater. The freshest freshwater possible, wept from a virgin witch-demon's eye. How much purer could water be?

Vin had thrown it into Phillip's face. Even though it was a small drop, like an arrow, it shot straight into one of his eyes. But so did something else.

Ever alert, God saw her chance. *She* had attacked again surmising the water would provide the prerequisite physical entry point. Even though Phillip's Achilles Heel was gone, *she* knew he had a new weakness.

Love.

He knew Love.

Imagine her disappointment when *she* attempted to reenter Phillip and fell flat on her face.

It had never occurred to Vin that when he took the goblet out of his pocket, the diamond he found would be scooped up with it. Diamonds are not only forever; they are also invisible in water. As with Ruebella's tear, it had flown through the air too. Fatefully, it landed in Phillip's tear duct, clogging and sealing it against God's fatal intrusion. It saved his life.

With no access to Phillip's being, God's attack found no target and sailed, just as Joan's attacks had done, right through him. He was invisible to God's Entanglement.

Psychically, God picked herself up off the floor, feeling dumb, embarrassed and dirty.

It was such a cheap shot. "Shit. Who cares? This is war." *She* thought.

"Even poor Joan didn't have that look on her face, the one you have now God." said Phillip disparagingly."All she did was just obey your orders, and she died because of it.

And you had the audacity to allow her to be condemned to Hell. What kind of God are you? Oh, and by the way, there are more errors in your attack. I don't know how, but I do know why."

"Hey, You Vin. Get over there, by the big guy, Ross. Ross?" ordered Phillip.

He ushered the despondent, thin and gangly Vin off to the side not in the least fearful that he'd do anything against him.

"Back to your question, God, as for the *how* - how 'ᶠᵒᵁᴿ' killed Pi? Oh, and not that I'm dismissing your sucker punch. But well, anyway, I don't want to stop my train of thought."

God, however, was nothing but thought.*She'd* attacked him with a nuclear bomb and nothing had happened.

"Anyway, I discovered a 'ᴅₒₜ'at the center of a most fantastic and wonderful diamond in existence." Phillip looked at Pi and the Devil again."It had existed and remained concealed there for eons, ruling Hell's River and making a mockery of the Devil's claim to be the sole master of Hell. Sorry Devil."

The Devil went to argue but he couldn't open his mouth.

"It recognized me and I answered its call with my RhomSong Diamond, something akin to the Entanglement shape that your attacks take.It became part of me and it played a vision of sorts in my mind.You know one of those dreams you have when you're trying to get to sleep, well, it was like that. Anyway, it showed me some interesting things.

The history of the Universe passed before my eyes. I saw many unknown truths, starting at the Big Bang. It continued right up to the present day.

One account in particular caught my attention, a tiny little tale in the long story of time. It was significant because it accentuated the subtly and deviousness with whom I was up against. Against *Pi*. It showed me the path to defeat her. May I continue?"

He knew God and everyone else wanted him too, but he was now Phillip not Phil, and considered it poor manners to monopolize the conversation without consent from his audience. There were nods from everyone.

"The story concerned the amazing feat of John Abbott the First. Not to belittle his achievement, as the courage in facing the Devil alone will probably never be surpassed. Unbeknown to him though, *Pi* played a part in his wager. She stacked the odds in John's favor. She sought the aid of those with exceptional valor and bravery. John was the cream of the crop.

It all clicked. John's reward was Dottie, his wife. Trojan Horse number two, only this one was destined for Heaven. I slapped my thigh at *Pi's* craftiness. Anyway God, the reason my attack killed her, was because I used her number. Just like people who are smitten with someone, usually someone who's not good for them: *they say they have their number.*

I have *Pi's.*

When people write down the value of PI, there are always four Dots. Three point, a Dot, one four two Dot Dot Dot. What, God? What…" He addressed her directly again but without gloating or boasting. "What if my attack removed her ability to generate anymore probabilities? It wasn't only you feeling ill with corrupted Entanglement. She too, was sick. In truth though, at first, her sickness was not much more than a sniffle. I might add that she also used a sly trick in her surprise attack. She used Boleyn as bait, in the knowledge that I would try to save her from drowning. John. Dottie. Joan. Boleyn. Vin… eh God? Mortals doing immortals dirty work.

Anyway, the number 'FOUR' started to give *Pi's* sequences some issues. Like a cough or a sneeze for a human.

That made me think.

Was the number 'FOUR' special to her? If so, why?

There are ten numbers, zero, one, two, three, four, five, six, seven, eight and nine.

So why four?

What's so special about four?

Well, it's actually a very special number.

It is the only number that has the same result whether halved or square rooted.

Two plus two equals FOUR. Two times two equals FOUR.

Then it's the only number that has the same number of letters in its name.

One has three. Two has three. Three has five. Only FOUR has four.

Next, it's ALSO the fourth character in PI. WHEN YOU COUNT THE dot IN 3.1FOUR2

One.

Two.

Three.

FOUR.

And now the most important reason of all.

There are FOUR dot's in PI (*PI*).

The dot between the numbers: 3dot142

The dots at its end: 3.142 dot dot dot.

So: 3dot142 dot dot dot.

That's FOUR.

Four is the last number anyone would think of to be important to *Pi*. There's nothing circular about FOUR. It's the first square number and the squarest number there is. For *Pi*, it was the sting in the tail of a scorpion. Her nature. She couldn't help being secretive. She couldn't help hiding in the shadows. She couldn't help spoiling and skulking.

That was the number FOUR.

It was the smallest number in the Universe. And the most deadly.

No coincidence the Chinese believe its bad luck. No coincidence there are Four Vatican keys.

Two for the plane of Earth. Two for the ethereal plane."

"So, back to the dots. As I said, the dot in the Diamond became mine.

That was dot number one, and it gave me a triangle tattoo over my third heart.

When John Abbott the First killed dottie in Heaven, that dot became mine too.

That was number two, and the second triangle tattoo. The third dot came from WWWdotCOM.

The name makes the lines of the third and final triangle tattoo, "TheLastResort.com".

Yet I said the word FOUR. There are FOUR Dots in PI.

When PI is written down; it ends with ellipses. The three dots (3.142...) (3.14159...)

No matter who writes PI, the end is always the same,

"..." "on and on"

PI is an infinite, irrational number.

So we use the three dots to denote that it continues and continues.

But there's the FOURth dot

The dot between the numbers.

Everyone talks about all the numbers after the decimal point and the three before it, but this Dot never receives its due. No one talks about this Dot in its own right. It was always the transition between the whole and the fractions, never a mystery to be unearthed or explored.

But what if... What if the three Dots didn't signal the continuation, but instead were all NULL.

What then?

What if the Dot between the numbers was also NULL. What if all the Dots are NULL?

What if the FOUR Dots of PI (*Pi*) are all NULLified? What then? What? What if?

Because that is now what they are, they are now nullified. I took the three Dots as my own.

The Diamond Dot

The Dottie Dot

The WWWDotCOM Dot

So what now. Then what?

I did what no one else could do.

There is no Mathematics that can do it. No scholar. No Philosopher. No God. But I did.

I needed complete and utter silence.

A total vacuum. Deeper than that of space. Not even the fabric of space and time.

Absolute zero everything. Absolute zero nothing.

The Devil's Jail was the only possible place to obtain that. A place where your influence God, was so miniscule, that I could eradicate your last photon of love and achieve:

True absolute zero love. True absolute zero.

A place *Pi's* probabilities couldn't find. To achieve:

True absolute random luck.

Ironically, this place was devoid of anything of the Devil's. His vibrations were already Null in that place. In the Devil's Jail - I could do it.

I created NULL.

I became NULL.

I had obtained NULL.

Now I had the power. Now I could beat *Pi.*

I could NULLify the Dots, *once all the* Dots *were mine.*

The moment the last Dot died, when "TheLastResort.com" died.

How could I tell *Pi* in my RhomSong attack that all her Dots are NULL?

What could that word be?

She had already told me about the errors in her sequences. That word was FOUR.

I claimed the fourth Dot as my own when I named it FOUR.

Spelt with the fourth letter of the alphabet, *when you* FOUR*get the vowels.*

a, *B*, *C*, *D*, e, *F(*OUR).

FOUR would turn the first "." to NULL.

FOUR would turn the "..." to NULL.

FOUR would turn 3.142... into 3142

FOUR would turn 3.14159... into 314159

What would it mean?

God? What would it mean?"

God whispered it.

"YOU
RESOLVED
Pi"

In an equally hushed whisper,

Phillip confirmed God's reticent comprehension,

"Yes God. I resolved *Pi*.

I resvolved Pi.

How could she live?"

"Yes God, that's how it was done. The special number, the squarest square number there is, is the number of Dots in *Pi*. No matter how long *Pi* is calculated to, the only fixed number of ANYTHING in Pi is the number of Dots. Whatever number of digits is used to portray PI, it always has the decimal point, a single dot '.'and always ends with '...'and once I nullified them.

THEN... PI is resolved.

Pi is resolved.

And made mortal because now she is finite not infinite.

Pi is dead.

I will continue... How about the Devil, how did he die?

And me. My name used to be Phil. It is now Phillip. How? Let me elaborate...

It all started, God, with me acquiring Entanglement when men can't. A mystery to all and yet it was so natural to me that I didn't know I had it.

It all goes back to my birth.

I experienced such lack of affection, receiving only indifference during my infancy and childhood, that I repressed all self-awareness and individuality. I dared nothing other than complete obedience, conformity and self-sacrifice.

I was defenseless against the unrelenting apathy of my parents and a never-ending barrage of insults from my brother Bill. My essence was so unworthy, that my soul started to detach from my body. Then came Bill's attack. His spit, didn't just humiliate me; it also served as a bridge. My soul started to travel up it, and into him. Only a single breath stopped Bill from killing me.That single breath was my survival. It stopped my soul's complete exodus, *by a single solitary thread.* I was still alive. But by the skin of my teeth.

It was little wonder people found me so boring. In contrast, his theft made him so intriguing and magnetic. So when the exhausted Hecate attacked me, her Entanglement almost passed right through me. It looked for my soul in all the usual spots: the Heart and the Seven Chakras.

But what little soul I had wasn't actually in me at the time. It was in my business card.

The business card wasn't just my calling card for that moment in time, it was me. I slipped it under Deloris's front door in the hope that she'd call me, a heartfelt plea, as I was so downtrodden from my time with Kelly. But as twisted as this story goes, Hecate found it when she killed her. She then used it with her Location Spell to track me down. When she attacked me, she didn't know that if she'd burnt my business card, she would have killed me, like pricking some voodoo doll.

Instead, her already weak incantation, sapped further from fruitless searching though my body lost its meaning and purpose. It wondered why it was cast at all if there was no soul to kill. Bewildered, it assumed it was her Absorption Spell instead.

It was at this time my soul returned to my body from the business card.

Its close proximity to my body enabled it to find its way home not knowing my body was under an Entanglement attack.

Hecate's attack, now an Absorption Spell, had no thread connecting it back to its supposed issuer, Hecate. So when my soul reentered my body, it absorbed me back into myself, with the addition of her Entanglement. I was in a way, a product of Hecate, a twin or a child. That's why Godiva recognized me so easily.

For the only time in my life, my weakness became my defense. Ironically, had I been a stronger man, I would have died. Her attack would have just plainly killed me.

What twists of fate Bill is responsible for? How he affected our lives. Here, today, I see him standing there, laughing like a hyena inside despite being an occupant of Hell. He thinks I can't see his secret, but I can. He's concealing a key.

The key that belongs to the Devil's Jail.

The missing Ethereal Vatican key.

On the floor behind me, floating in the mercury is the Earthly Plane Vatican key. There's one pair, the Earthly Plane keys on the front of the Vatican crest. But look on the backside of that emblem, and you'll see the shadowy inverse of the stitching, and two ghostly keys.

The Ethereal Vatican keys.

What did you do Bill? Steal the key from the Silver Demon?"

"No, she gave it to m…" Bill attempted to explain, not lie, but
Phil had heard it all before and didn't care to hear either.

"Stop, don't answer. Then you swapped the key in the door with Joan's… right?"

A smirk escaped Bill's lips confirming it was all true.

"Well, in your attempt to incarcerate me forever, you actually aided me. The door was bound to kill anyone who attempted to open it with the wrong key." said Phillip.

"THANK YOU, BILL." he said harshly with prejudice.

Since the Devil was human now, it wasn't beyond him to kill Bill. *It's what humans do.* And knowing the true reason for his demise, he was ready to do it. And he would have too, had not Phillip continued his story and effectively stolen the moment.

"It couldn't have worked out better for me. Because of you Bill, I have the Devil's Entanglement. *Because of you Bill*, I have this amazing halo. THANK YOU."

Bill's smarter than thou leer vanished from his face. He also moved himself diametrically opposite to the Devil after noticing his murderous look.

"Not finished yet." started up Phillip again, "Anyway I am a non-sanctioned destiny. Not a grand designed fate.

Of God's. Of *Pi's*.

Of anyone's.

I am a ridiculously long odds piece of natural luck, the kind of extreme luck that bore our glorious Universe into existence. I am like the luck that supports technology and even supports magic.

This amazing, colorful, wondrous Universe that you and *Pi* thwarted and corrupted. For your own gain.

I am like that luck, that one, that Universe.

That's not to say our own Universe at present isn't magnificent, but its pale compared to what it could have been, to what it will return to be.

Pi took the *atoms*.

You took *space and light*.

Combined, the two of you have forced the Universe to expand and it would have expanded forever. Its ultimate conclusion would be one of fading away into an impossibly gigantic and cold, lifeless eternity. You God would have won. *Pi's* atoms would have been torn apart by space itself.

Isn't that right God?"

There was no reply. Pi's faces soured seeing the truth on God's face.

"Now, sorry God, the Universe will return to its natural cycle, whatever that is. As I said, I know all this God, because *Pi's* dot incarnate showed me the history of our Universe. From the Big Bang onwards, to now, not the future, that is no one's to know. As a footnote, unfortunately for you God, it showed me that Eternal Mortals were not the Universe's author. You were just born into it like everything and everyone else.

Now for the bad news. You are not God. If there is a single God, then I don't know it. Maybe Evolution? If there is survival of the weakest, then there are no Universes. Only the laws that survive are present, laws such as super gravity and non-quantum atoms died upon inception, destroyed by their unsustainable architecture."

Phillip stopped to deliberate. No one moved or even breathed as Phillip stood still, contemplating. It was as if the whole Universe had stopped, waiting, wondering. Was there more?

A hush like that of a great assembly, where a hollow cough would draw unwanted attention, stilled the planes of existence.

Hell had ground to a stand still.

Hell-mates and the demons had stopped leaping into the torrent of the Styx.

They suspended their escape to witness history. So too had the occupants of Heaven.

They stopped being mindlessly joyful and gazed down upon Hell. As they paused, they began to question their existence.

How could they be happy when others were condemned for an eternity of torture?

How could God?

On Earth, the souls of the dying hovered, suspended in their ascension or descent. Some considered returning to Earth for reincarnation. Others tried only to discover it was all a myth. Not one body could sustain a used soul. Not even the animals. So they looked in the direction of the Ninth Level of Hell and waited for the newest person to proclaim himself a God to act. Phillip gazed around too, cognizant that he was holding things up, and not caring. All around him was the smell of conclusion and termination. Kelly lay dead on the ground, the Siamese twin of Pi appeared lost, and the mortal Devil looked like a circus ringmaster out of a job.

Time across the Universe suddenly bumped into life as Phillip spoke.

"God." And God shuddered. He spoke her name, but it was unlike that from before. As he called her name, a certain charm warmed her. *She* suddenly wished he'd say it again. And he did.

"God, all my life, I have looked... looked for love. I am just a middle-aged man, but you God, you are a hair's breath away from being as old as this Universe. Have you looked for anything? Not just anything. Have you... have you ever looked for... love?"

She didn't answer, and Phillip didn't insult her by expecting one.
He continued.

> "Oo'o o oooo oooo. (It's a long time.)
> Oooo ooo ooo oooooo ooo? (What are you looking for?)
> Oo oooo oooo. (In your body.)
> Oooo oo oo. (Look at me.)
> O ooo, ooo O oooo. (A man, but I know.)
> Ooo ooo, oo ooo? (But you, do you?)
> Oo ooo oooo oo o ooooo. (In the body of a woman.)
> O oooooooo, oooooooo ooooo. (A dazzling, gorgeous woman.)
> Oooo oo oo ooo oooo? (What is it you want?)
> Oooo *oo* oo ooo oooo? (What *is* it you want?)
> Ooo? (God?)
> Oooo?" (What?)

God shook. Phillip's voice wasn't anything like that of any other, being the first male to speak in her native tongue. "Is this what a man's voice in my language sounds like?" *she* wondered, because it wasn't in a tone ever heard before, in the Universe, in time. His words echoed with new notes, in-between flats and sharps, in-between tenor and bass. Lyrics of color and of sensual touch, a siren of promise? He spoke of things, of wants and of needs.

She awakened. "The words are talking to me, stirring me. Exciting me?" *she* thought. Her thighs involuntarily squeezed.

As if reading her mind, Phillip continued in her tongue. "I only ask one thing of you, God. You are beautiful beyond compare, and I, a God, am of equal standing with you. You are a super woman. I am a super man. There are no other equals with us, wouldn't you agree?"

Many things went through her mind and some were most un-God like. Now *she* couldn't help but see what Kelly saw in him. How could a mortal see these things so easily, when *she*, God, was only seeing them now?

Seeing *him* now.

A God, a male God. A male sexual God.

Pushing these sudden unwanted, strange urges aside, God struggled to regain some rational, God-like thoughts. *She* wanted to objectively question Phillip's sudden turn in demeanor and reestablish him as her *public enemy number one.* A necessary endeavor, because his words had removed himself from that list. Sadly, even as she elevated him back to pole position, he slid back down as *she* thought.

"No one had ever said such things to me."

He had said so much. And yet so little. She would never admit it, but she wanted him to carry on. She wanted to hear more. She needed to hear more.

"Snap out of it God. You are God. Forget this 'evolution' God, it has no embodiment. You rule the Universe. More so now *Pi* and the Devil are dead. (But alone?)"

Phillip couldn't read minds. But he thought it was time to continue, so he did, perfectly on cue.

"So God, for thirteen billion years, you have lived essentially alone, and have witnessed the Glory of Man even in his briefest existence.

I ask you. Is there anything quite like him? He is. Vile. Cruel. Evil. Malevolent. Ardent.

He is. Kind. Self-sacrificing. Creative. Destructive. Passionate.

Here I stand before you. The zenith of him.

Here. You see me. You hear me.

I am Phillip. Made from Entanglement but not made of Entanglement.

God.

I ask you God. Just one thing. I think you know what I am about to ask.

Man. Woman. Super man. Immortal Woman.

W O M A N. MAN. "

Oooo ooo ooooo oo?
WILL YOU MARRY ME?

God was stunned. "His darling Kelly lay dead on the floor not more than a yard from him. And here he is proposing to Me? What a snake. What a rat. A typical human man. Man. But what a man. *WHAT A MAN*. Yes, what a man. With his plain face. With his dull chin. With his slightly nonsymmetrical cheeks. Yet he's the all-time most desirable man. He was once only Phil, now he's Phillip. Experienced beyond measure. All powerful beyond knowing.

Is Phillip my soul mate? Yes.

A fitting equal? Yes.

A fitting opposite? Yes.

A fitting match? Yes.

A perfect match. YES.

Beautiful, virile.

And mine for the wanting.

Mine for the taking.

Mine.

DO I WANT HIM?

IS THERE ANOTHER?

Is he the source of my inevitable demise? Yes.

Will he be the death of my space-time continuum? Probably.

Was he the instigator of the atomic transformation, *Pi's* domain? Yes.
But, but, but...
Is he an Almighty? Yes.
Is he handsome enough for me? Yes.
Clearly too beautiful for that mortal, ugly humanoid Kelly.

I am too, stuck, in human form.

No longer can I choose another.

But now. *WHY WOULD I?*

I feel beautiful, and, and, and... I want someone to... to... touch me.

I'm the virgin maiden.

A Maiden.

A Virgin.

Ready for the taking.

Ready.

Yes. Yes, I am ready.

What have I been waiting for?

For PHILLIP.
That's what.
Flushed and with tears in her eyes, *she* answered his proposal.
"YES."

"Great." replied Phillip cheerfully, and ignored the 'if looks could kill' glare from Ross who had mouthed the word traitor amongst a plethora of expletives.

R S
R h o m
KELLY
S o n g
M g

There was no wild jerking of her body or craning of her neck. A smooth transition occurred with the return of her spirit as if she had awakened from a nap. With eyes wide open, Kelly stood up and linked arms with her fiancé.

Even the Devil let out a gasp. The Eternal Mortals had been able to bring life back to the dead, but not when God was the assassin. Only *she* could restore her own slain. For all the miracles that lay at Phillip's feet, *she* still held on to this one as sacrosanct.

However, he now could bring people back from the dead, too.

HER DEAD.

If only *she* had known he could do this, then maybe, *she* wouldn't have been so eager to say '*YES*'.

If *she'd* known - a morsel of a doubt might have caused her to consider his motives.

But *she* hadn't known.

She hadn't done her due diligence.

Crushing as all of this was, it wasn't the crux of his attack and it wasn't that that had '*mortalized*' her.

It was the single word…"KELLY."

With that word, he told her that he knew of her loneliness and of her desire to be loved and not worshipped.

If *she* had been led down the garden path, then *she* had let him. Then it was *she*, who led herself down the garden path.

He hadn't lied to her.

She'd lied to herself, because *she* wanted to believe.

She wanted to feel like a human and have the passion and the lust that they have.

To have The Kissing
Oh God .THE ALL-CONSUMING KISSING.
The Sex
Oh God .THE ALL-CONSUMING SEX.
The Art
Oh God .THE ALL ENCOMPASSING IMAGINATION.
The Music
OH GOD. OH GOD. OH GOD.
The Dance
Oh God. THE SEXY
The Sport
Oh God. THE CHALLENGE.
The Love
Oh God .THE ALL-ENCOMPASSING CHERISHING.
AND THE LUST.
OH GOD ON HIGH OF THE HIGHEST HIGHS.
THE ALL-CONSUMING LUST.

She wanted that so much.

She saw humans had it.

She thought Phillip was offering it to her.

He'd outdone her again, without a lie.

She had allowed herself to be misled and outmaneuvered.

He wanted her to marry him: *to* KELLY.

He never said he wanted to marry her, God.

As bad as that was, it was worse because he had chosen a human over a God.

He'd taken all her desires, hopes and fears, and compressed them into a single word,

KELLY.

Just as he had done with the word "Man" for Godiva, with those three letters, he told her he was no longer an impressionable boy.

Just as he had done with the word "FOUR" for *Pi,* he'd gone one better. Four letters, not three.

Here, he'd gone one better again. "Kelly". Five letters, not FOUR.

"Am I so stupid that I'd allowed myself to be outwitted in the same manner as *Pi?* Yes, I am."

"Am I so stupid that I'd allowed myself to be outwitted by a human? Yes, I am."

"Am I so stupid to fall for a man? Yes, I am." Her rage was beyond compare.

Her teeth clamped shut, grinding against each other like two continental tectonic plates.

Behind them, pent up and waiting to spew forth in an unstoppable torrent, was her Entanglement.

Answering '*Yes*' to Phillip's request had doomed her.

Now, God knew the moment *she* opened her mouth one last time, her fate would be sealed.

She would become mortal.

Like a loaded catapult bursting in tension, her Entanglement filled her mouth.

Her throat overflowed.

She knew there were only seconds left before it breached her dam of clenched teeth.

It would engulf the Universe.

Death would replace it.

Mortality.

An extra fifty years of life would be like an extra-millisecond for her.

"So what's the difference?"

If *she* was going to die, then *she* didn't care if *she* died now.

If *she* was going to die, then *she* was going to take Phillip with her.

Not stopping there, if *she* was going to end it, why not end it all. *Everything.*

S*he* was going to end the Universe in an inferno of fury.

She was not going to open her mouth in a timid whisper.

She was going to go out in a blaze of glory and bellow out her last, dying request.

The words would be swept forth on the tidal wave of her death throe Entanglement.

Taking one last gigantic breath through her nose.

She roared out with all her might.

LET THERE BE...

Phil had been almost nothing all his life until its final chapter. As Phillip, however, he had become the most relevant man in eternity, dwarfing past titans: Einstein, Beethoven, and Jesus. Yet even as Phillip, he had had to become 'nothing' to evolve, and had done so in The Devil's Jail.

And a metamorphosis he had indeed undergone. Now, in this heartbeat of time, he knew he had to become someone else. Someone more. He was once zero. Now he needed to be one. He didn't know how he knew these things, but at least The Devil's Jail eyepiece had confirmed his course of action as he entered that abyss.

The intuition that filled him now would be his alone.

No external phenomenon would come to his rescue and endorse his actions.

He would have to be… brave.

He would have to believe in himself, wholly, solely, unilaterally.

He forced his eyes open.

He needed to breathe a single breath.

He needed one pure thought.

One thought from a clear mind.

His one mind.

It must be binary.

No fractions, nor decimals.

He must be an integer.

He must take that quantum leap from zero to one.

His RhomSong must be called.

All of it.

He needed to connect with the Universe.

He had been on its perimeter, now he needed to be on its entire circumference in a single instant.

He could do it, if he could clear his mind.

He needed to connect with all the atoms.

He had been inside of one, now he needed to be inside of every atom in a single moment.

He could do it, if he could clear his mind.

In just one instance of time, if he could have one pure thought, he could do all of this.

Not with anger though, not with malice or hate. Not with revenge or glee, and neither with pity, mercy or even as a matter of fact.

The finest of neutral emotion was required.

He needed to tread on the impossibly thin line that wound its way through the myriad of human reactions and walk on the plain placid path of reason.

Now was the time to have his one perfect thought.

He cleared his mind.

Ironically, to become one, he had to become Null again.

He exorcised thoughts of the past.

Bill. Kelly. Gone.

He ostracized invading thoughts of the future.
Failure. Death. Kelly. Gone.
He wiped himself clean of emotions, of words.

They left.

Gone. Expecting to see only a void, a string of letters refused to leave.

"*Ohcftaoihpmrepesristsness*" He read them again and again.

It made sense this time.

Four, again, four words.

"*Others happiness comes first.*"

A cancer of thought, buried so deep that not even God or *Pi* in their ransacking of his mind could find. As letters undivided into a single meaningless word, they'd avoided detection.

Until now. He dis-assembled it and read it again.

"Others happiness comes first."

It pre-existed the insane war above. It had wormed its way into his psyche at childhood. Constructed as a survival mechanism, he'd applied it with any emotionally close person.

Bill, parents, female acquaintances, Kelly.

He took a step back. This concocted and fabricated thought explained his life.

It was root.

A smoke screen. A lie.

With no thoughts left to hide behind, it stood naked.

It pleaded for mercy, but received none.

Dispassionately Phillip back spaced the words.

"Others happiness comes first."

"Others happiness comes."

"Others happiness."

"Others."

""

He had white spaced the thought, the thought that was almost and appeared noble.

Incredibly, the phrase confirmed his path.

Incredibly, the neutrality used to delete it was the emotion he needed.

Incredibly, he had received a sign.

He would have broken down on his knees and given thanks, but there were no emotions left to do so.

He *was* clean.

He *was* here.

He *was* now.

God was omnipresent, but Phillip wasn't. Even though he'd touched the edge of the Universe, it had only been in passing, now he was going to do the opposite, never to have been conceived, let alone attempted.

Using all his voice of power. Leaving nothing behind.

He went all in.

Too fast for the witnesses present, he grew into a colossus taller than any building. Only the stalactite laden ceiling impeded his growth.

His three hearts stopped, primed to pump a special droplet of blood into his brain, directly.

It would carry the Universe.

He breathed in three single Hydrogen atoms.

One for each heart.

One for each incarnation of the Sun.

One for RhomSong.

He pumped.

The entire Universe flickered. Every atom, photon, all space and all time, folded, imploded, and materialized in Phillip's brain.

For all of zero seconds, the Universe stood still, alive but dead, infinitely massive, infinitely microscopic.

HE READIED TO SPEAK.

Phillip, in his whole life, had never finished anyone else's sentence. He'd never interrupted anyone.

Until now.

~~Light~~

R
honiSong * Random

I
~~ñeineration~~ Interruption * integration

G
ravity

H
adron

T
ime

He shrank back. The Universe restored. Everything was returned to exactly its original place. Nothing had changed. Except for everything. Indistinguishable by all, yet it was refurbished, reinvigorated, reconditioned.

God's obliterating and all-consuming LIGHT would have turned the Universe into a cinder in an instant, but for one thing, Phillip's interruption.

It transformed Creation. LIGHT into RIGHT.

God wasn't the life taker. Phillip was the lifesaver.

God didn't know what had happened. The Universe, they all: still existed, and their living presence proved something had gone wrong.

She didn't know that Phillip had interrupted her. Had corrupted her.

Her living presence was a telltale sign of bad things to come. She tried to entangle to somewhere, just anywhere, but she failed.

It was Phillip's one and only interruption.

If he was going to do a rude and crass thing, he would make it count.

He saved the Universe.

That counts.

Instead of God's LIGHT vaporizing the Universe, Phillip's "RIGHT" did the very thing God wished to avoid. Up until now, the damage inflicted upon her space-time continuum was restricted to her and Phillip defiling her realm with their presence. The transformation of the Universe from the old classical simple atoms to the new multifaceted model would only take place at the speed of light. And only when God entangled herself to locations anew. Only then could she infect a locale and its environment. Knowing the Universe was vast, she knew it would take billions of years for her to corrupt its entirety and destroy her source of power. It was a reasonable tradeoff to pay if it meant having Phillip as her spouse, having happiness.

However, Phillip had spurned her, and now, just when she thought she could end it all on her own terms, he had cheated her again.

Phillip's "RIGHT," his magical manipulation and mutation of her most beloved phrase had done something fundamental and foundational.

RhomSong powered by God's own entanglement, instantly enveloped the entire Universe. With her own inadvertent aid, he had now *Righted* the Universe.

With her own inadvertent aid, he had now *RhomSonged* the Universe.

Not just to a pre-God Universe, but to a post-God enhanced Universe. Now, every star, every atom would be subject to the new complex atomic mechanisms and experience its own less predictable phases.

Now, Dark Energy's prominence, the force tearing the Universe apart in an ever-accelerating head on rush, was tempered by the new atomic order. God's Entanglement was transformed and would now exist in the form of Dark Space. It would have an unknown effect on the Universe's expansion, but an impact it would have. A fitting role for the entity that was minutes earlier on a runaway train of expansion.

Pi's Entanglement, hosted in Phillip, was transmuted and would now exist in an energy known as:

entRanglement.

ENTrANGLEMENT.

Ent*R*anglement.

Third (.142... an *R for RhomSong*, an *R for Right*) times a charm. The Law of Conservation of Energy remained unviolated, and in obedience, the Universe would strive for a new balance.

Phillip hadn't only made God mortal, but she in her rage, had un-intentionally provided the means with which he could fulfill a destiny, he had now *RhomSonged* the Universe.

Maybe now, with alternating, fluctuating Space Time and random vacillating atomic forces, the Universe would settle into a new oscillating equilibrium. Time would tell. At the same time, just as God feared, God, as God, existed no more.

She bowed her head at the shame. She now, truly understood and truly empathized.

"You God Damn HUMANS."

The scar on Phillip's arm, the sign of the woman, disappeared and reappeared as a tattoo over his second heart. It sizzled so intensely that his blood, clear, pure water turned to steam whilst quenching its fiery pain. He didn't know the lines were made out of words too small to read,

Be

    Be Smart

    Be Happy

    Be Strong.

    Be Healthy

    Be Diligent

    Be Disciplined

    Try

    Only pray for the above

He did not flinch.

He didn't need or want the attention.

But neither was he Phillip now.

He was Philippe.

Philippe, man of Pure Ent*R*anglement.

RhomSong, the force born from a confluence of chance and fate, now lived outside of the realm of Phillip.

The final tattoo only enhanced his masculinity.

Kelly's grip on his arm told him that.

He'd never been a man of few words, and now he was.

He didn't need to do anything.

He was everything.

It was in that knowledge that had ended God - when she said 'Yes'.

His quirky mannerisms had worked its magic on Kelly, Joan and Boleyn.

It had also worked on her.

As with all his women, they hadn't known they were in love with him, until it was too late.

God, saw all of this. Now.

If only she hadn't given his proposal credence. If only she hadn't wanted him.

"If I'd just said nothing, then it wouldn't have happened." she thought bitterly to herself.

More than anything, she had killed herself with that one word, 'Yes'.

It is the most dangerous word there is.

She knew this.

Yet she had said it.

It had undone her too.

Even she was not immune to its fearsome consequences.

Beautiful, but human, God, fought off the tears that were seeking freedom. The radiance that was *she*, no longer was. Now she was consigned to a life of frailty in mind, body and spirit, knowing that it would be followed by aging and death.

For the children of Earth's surviving populous, their souls and consciences became theirs alone, no longer conflicted in loyalty.

Upon death, no Heaven, Hell or reincarnation would be waiting to accept their souls. Their prayers too, wouldn't be God's to ignore.

Much to the sorrow of its current exponents, the constantly misunderstood law of 'Cause and Effect' would remain unchanged. So too, the Law of Natural Selection. Possibly the only immutable law there is.

In the battle of Man verses Nature, Man's current theories of science were all but rendered null and void with the advent of the Blue Green and Checkered Phases of the Sun.

With Ent*R*anglement.

Nonetheless, Man would still seek the nature of nature; they would be at odds forever.

With his remaining, depleted, threadbare RhomSong, Philippe magically and most divinely summoned the witches, saints and a select few passed-on mortals into attendance. He forged two wedding rings from the golden chalice and another crowned with the diamond he'd plucked out of his eye.

Their entrance and presence in Hell were only possible due to Joan's latent Entanglement when she created the Chamber of the Cross. By way of Boleyn and then Vin, they provided the raw material for Joan's gift to him.

But his defeat of God had cost him. His final and last commands exhausted him beyond many bounds of recovery. Like a dropped horseshoe, his Halo clanged to the floor. Like a dulled sword, his Tear of God lost its sheen. Now, only akin to a glossy wet pebble, the smaller Tear of God adorned Kelly's hair.

Only the tattoos remained of *Pi's* Dots.

Only his three hearts spoke of deeds unsung.

Only his Shoes remained alive.

But he cared not.

Philippe was still the only super-being, but no God.

Flying might not be possible again.

None of this mattered because of all things he'd become, the most important of them all was this:

'*He was his own man*'.

He slid the engagement ring onto Kelly's ring finger, and handed one to Ross. He handed the other ring to a beautiful maid of honor. To Hecate. The root reason they were together.

Not the Blue Green Sun, not the Checkered Sun, but the Old Yellow Sun shone. Refracted by its passage through the fissure in the granite floor, Golden Purple light poured into and lit the Ninth Plane of Hell to that of Earth.

Black-Hell, Blackest-Hell, the Ninth Level of Hell basked in sunlight for the first and only time, and right on schedule for this special occasion.

" Thank you everyone. God, please commence with the ceremony." said PhiLIPpe.

The End.

Don't Make an Enemy of God

Don't Make an Enemy of God is a breathtaking escalation of everything introduced in ***The Devil Always Answers***, deeper in philosophy, wider in scale, more daring in imagination, and far more unapologetic in its exploration of cosmic morality. If the first book laid the groundwork for a modern spiritual folklore, this second installment detonates that foundation and reveals an entire universe of divine machinery operating beneath it. Mitchell has taken what could have easily been a small, clever sequel and transformed it into a sweeping metaphysical epic, proving with absolute clarity that this series is destined to become a cornerstone of modern supernatural fiction.

What makes this novel exceptional, truly exceptional, is not just that it continues the storyline from the first book, but that it fundamentally redefines its entire mythos. It reframes philosophical events from ***The Devil Always Answers*** not as isolated curses or tricks, but as pieces of a much larger cosmic puzzle involving God, the Devil, the mathematics of fate, and the fragile architecture that holds the human soul together. This sequel is bigger, bolder, and more dangerous. It feels like the moment when a story stops being a story and becomes a legend.

From the very first chapter, the reader senses that this book will play on a much grander stage. The opening scene with Tamaco, the High Priest, a brutal, archaic ritual under the watching eyes of ancient gods, sets a tone of historic weight and mythic violence. This scene doesn't just foreshadow the book's themes; it announces them. Mitchell wants us to understand that prophecy, mathematics, destiny, and rebellion have been weaving themselves into human fate long before Phil or ClearStream ever existed. The thousand-year foretelling creates a terrifying countdown that echoes across centuries and directly ties the ancient world to the novel's modern events. It is worldbuilding at its most precise and potent.

Then the narrative shifts, and this is where the author's confidence shines. Suddenly, we are at the Vatican, walking alongside Pope Gregory, a man drowning in dread and secrecy. These chapters are written with quiet psychological mastery. Pope Gregory is not just a religious figure; he is a broken soul wrapped in ceremonial clothing. His sense of impending doom becomes a metaphor for humanity's own uneasy relationship with the divine. In these passages, Mitchell shows a refined command of tone, solemn, suffocating, intellectual, giving this sequel a gravitas that surpasses the first book.

But perhaps the most unforgettable portions of the novel unfold in Hell. If **The Devil Always Answers** introduced readers to the Devil's cunning mind and his entanglement-based limitations, **Don't Make an Enemy of God** thrusts us directly into the beating heart of his kingdom. The chapters featuring Rank, Ego, and Vin are masterworks of dark humor, existential horror, and bleak satire. The author reinvents Hell as a place not of fiery torment, but of coldness, hierarchy, fear, and bureaucratic misery. The demons are towering monsters of grotesque femininity, a brilliant twist, and the damned souls scurry like unwanted insects trying to avoid notice. These scenes are written with such visual clarity that they practically storyboard themselves. One can see them on screen: the towering cliffs, the narrow roads, the icy rivers of Styx, the monstrous Gate-Demons, the eerie shift from green skies to yellow fire to gray desolation, and finally the descent into the Ninth Level, a place so cold and lonely it feels like a vacuum in the soul.

The Ninth Level sequence alone is one of the most cinematic pieces of writing in contemporary speculative fiction. The onyx cube, the diamond altar, the lava moat, the precarious wooden causeway, the transformation of the goat and lyrebird into stone sentinels, this is visual storytelling at its finest. It is impossible not to imagine this as a dramatic film scene, complete with thunderous sound design and sweeping orchestral fear. The sense of dread is thick enough to taste.

Yet beneath the spectacle, Mitchell never abandons the intimate humanity of his characters. Rank, though foolish, is oddly sympathetic. Ego, manipulative and fear-driven, is fascinating to watch as he schemes his way through damnation. Vin, with his pathological lying and opportunistic cowardice, becomes almost comedic in how thoroughly he represents human moral weakness. Their lie to the Devil, and the desperate charade surrounding Phil's empty coffin, is one of the most brilliantly constructed sequences in recent fiction. It reads like a tragic comedy, a thriller, and a spiritual parable all at once.

But at the core of this novel is Phil, the shy, almost forgettable man from Book One, who now steps into his true mythic identity. The author's treatment of Phil is phenomenal. His evolution from a reluctant descendant to a metaphysical phenomenon, the RhomSong, feels both surprising and inevitable. His Shoes, which seemed like simple enchanted objects in the first book, now reveal themselves as conduits for a fifth life-force beyond human or divine comprehension. The fusion of quantum physics, entanglement, theology, and consciousness is executed with imagination and scientific elegance. Phil's sanctuary within the Shoes, depicted like an underwater cathedral of shimmering light, is an image of extraordinary beauty. These chapters elevate the series from supernatural folklore into intellectual speculative fiction.

Mitchell also introduces *Pi*, the cosmic entity governing chance, randomness, and statistical chaos. Her voice, fragmented, mathematical, eerie, adds a new layer of intrigue. The notion that she is weakened because Phil is alive, that negative numbers have corrupted her perception, and that fate itself is destabilizing is a brilliant addition to the story's metaphysics. This expansion of the universe makes it clear that the conflict is no longer just Devil vs. Phil; it is system vs. anomaly, destiny vs. glitch, existence vs. error.

As a sequel, this book's greatest success lies in its seamless yet dramatic expansion of themes already established in *The Devil Always Answers*. Where the first book examined belief as a cage, this one examines reality as a fragile mathematical construct that can fracture under enough pressure. The stakes are higher, the dangers more unpredictable, and the truths more uncomfortable. This is not just continuation, it is transcendence.

Of course, no review is complete without gentle, constructive notes. In rare moments, the transitions between timelines and realms can feel abrupt, particularly when switching from Hell's bleak coldness to the earthly tension of the Vatican or the mundane tenderness of Phil and Kelly. Some metaphysical explanations are intellectually rich but could benefit from a slightly slower buildup to help general readers absorb the concepts. And a small handful of characters, particularly some in the mortal world, might benefit from deeper emotional exploration to match the grandeur of the cosmic events.

Yet these critiques pale in comparison to the overwhelming strengths of the novel. The writing is cinematic, imaginative, confident, and filled with moments of astonishing originality. The pacing is bold, the imagery unforgettable, and the philosophical depth profound. Mitchell takes risks, enormous, exhilarating risks, and more impressively, he lands them with precision. His storytelling voice has grown more mature, more poetic, and more fearless since **The Devil Always Answers**, and this novel showcases that evolution beautifully.

Ultimately, **Don't Make an Enemy of God** is more than a second book. It is an ascension. It transforms the first novel's clever premise into a sweeping cosmology of faith, fate, and rebellion. It deepens the emotional stakes, enlarges the world, and emboldens the mythology. The story leaves readers breathless, contemplative, and hungry for more. It deserves to be read widely, discussed passionately, and without question, adapted for the screen. With its rich visuals, complex characters, and unparalleled imaginative scope, it is a natural candidate for a major film or series adaptation, the kind that lingers in public consciousness long after the credits roll.

This is a magnificent, unforgettable second entry in a universe that promises to become a classic of modern supernatural fiction. Mitchell has crafted something rare: a sequel that not only honors its predecessor but transcends it. A triumph, bold, haunting, brilliant, and utterly original.

www.ingramcontent.com/pod-product-compliance
Lightning Source LLC
Chambersburg PA
CBHW020645110726
47901CB00001B/55